T

Book 2

King of the Desert

(

Published in Great Britain by Open Circle Publishing in 2022

ISBN 978-1-909607-22-4

Open Circle Publishing
49-51 St Thomas's Road
Chorley
Lancashire
PR7 1JE

For Henry, Poppy, Georgia, and Charlie

1

Ant shuddered as he passed the place where he'd been hanged. The gibbets were still there. Three nooses hung motionless and inviting. It had been almost two years since he'd stood in the line of unfortunates waiting to have their lives suddenly and viciously ended by Royal decree. Even so, the effect on his physiology was palpable. His throat felt restricted and his whole body had begun to shake.

Jeremiah whispered urgently in his ear. *You'll have to hurry, the King is almost there.*

The voice in his head had become more intrusive over the past few months. He'd originally thought he was experiencing the return of Cali, the invisible presence he'd encountered while travelling in the company of Patch, but this entity felt very different. Less friendly; more brusque. Ant had taken to calling him Jeremiah and there had been no objection raised by the demon.

Ant swallowed a few times, experimented with his breath, and pulled his black hood further forward to cover his anxiety. The lines of soldiers funnelled the sparse crowd into the great chamber where they had been invited to hear the King's latest decree first-hand. It had taken all of Ant's courage, slowly and painfully recovered, to bring himself to this place and to face the King that had ordered his death. In a few short months, he would be seventeen years old. A man. He felt that it was time he began to act like a man, and this was his first attempt.

Inside the hall, there was a throng of people pushing their way forward to gain a view of the King. The place was heaving with unwashed bodies. Ant settled for a relatively clear space against the wall, furthest from where the King would be. He could rely on Jeremiah's perception to give him a close view of the man he had sworn to kill.

The doors behind him slammed shut, disconnecting Ant from the outside and denying access to latecomers. A hush swept through the crowd, the cackling and snarling were stilled, and an eerie silence fell over the place. Even the soldiers lining the walls holding their crossbows ready looked nervous at the King's imminent arrival. Ant followed Jeremiah's passage as he flew over the heads and hovered over the throne. By transferring his attention, Ant was able to watch the King's entry from this privileged viewpoint.

Surrounded by a dozen courtiers, all vying for position as close to his ear as possible, the King waddled over to his throne and sat down heavily. From a distance, there might have been some semblance of regal nature, but all Ant could see was a fat man in expensive clothes with a golden crown perched precariously on his head and a sneer on his lips.

A large soldier bellowed unnecessarily at the crowd, commanding them to be quiet and listen to the proclamation to be read by Donald, the King's head of household. A weedy man stepped forward and, after several sideways glances at the King, began to read in a high-pitched whine. 'His glorious majesty has decreed that the period of suffering is now over. By virtue of his actions, the population of Gort and all its surrounding lands are now safe from the terrible affliction that descended upon them. From this day forth, common people will have their rights restored to come and go as they please. To attend the King in his palace. To bring any grievances to his Court. Normal life is hereby resumed.'

As Donald took a breath, there was a general sigh from the crowd, as if they had no recollection of what normal life might consist of. Ant wondered if they had become so used to the arbitrary hangings of men, women, and children to consider them part of daily life.

'There will be a general recruitment drive to encourage people to join the King's army. Incentives will be put in place. Any able-bodied male over the age of fifteen years who fails to put himself forward for selection will be considered having committed treason and will be hanged. A great army will be gathered for the King's protection and the furtherance of his interests.

'War is declared against the usurpers in the North who have illegally declared independence at Laketown. Any travel along the North Road beyond Gort is forbidden and all travellers coming south will be treated as hostile from this day forth.'

Donald wiped the back of his hand against his brow and hid himself behind the throne. At first, Ant thought that the King himself might have a few words to say, but he just sat there. An uncomfortable silence descended. Ant felt awkward and embarrassed by the King's lack of grace. All these people had gathered to see him and all they were getting was a hard stare following a terse and threatening proclamation. This was the same King whose solution to any disorder in Gort was to hang children.

Ant reached out to Donald, who was feeling a combination of fear and relief. *Kill the King,* he whispered into his thoughts. *Take a knife from the soldier beside you and plunge it into his back. Do it. Go on, now's your chance. Be free from the cruelty and derision. Become your own man at last.*

Ant's suggestion was lost in the turmoil going on in Donald's mind. There was no reaction other than a step away from the throne and a further burst of self-doubt. Ant returned to his observation post within Jeremiah's accommodating consciousness. Of the dozen or so bowmen who formed a guard around the King's person, Ant observed one with his crossbow carelessly pointing towards the monarch. Using all his practice, he bent his will against the metal clip that held the bowstring taut. Ant tried his utmost to move the trigger mechanism that would release the bolt, but there was no effect beyond a bone weariness that forced him to retreat back to his own body.

Ant sat down heavily, back against the cold stone. He bowed his head and allowed his hood to completely hide his features. All he could do now was to rest and try to regain some of his powers. There was a small nugget of bitterness that cursed his weakness and blamed Malachi for not teaching him well enough. This had been his chance, long-awaited and worked for. If Malachi were here, perhaps he could have pulled the trigger and done the job properly. That hadn't been his choice, though. Killing kings was something Malachi considered counter-productive. His view was that the king who succeeded an assassinated forebear would be even more fearful than his predecessor. A fearful king was a cruel and unthinking ruler.

Ant didn't care about kings in general. It was this one in particular to whom he owed revenge. This one had put a noose around his neck.

3

Jeremiah's voice became insistent in his head, rousing him from a deep place of rest. *Everyone's left the chamber. There are only a few soldiers left and they're coming your way.*

Ant sat motionless, feeling for the presence of others. He was still tired from his exertions and far from the peak of his powers. Using what little he had left, he planted a gentle thought in the nearest soldier. *The place is empty. There's nobody left here.*

He felt the tremors of footsteps passing close by, but refrained from looking up. The movements receded. He heard the sounds of bolts being slid into place. Everything went quiet.

The sunlight through the high arched windows was fading by the time Ant raised his head. Some of the torpor remained, but he had enough energy now to stand up and look around. The great chamber was cold and silent. The massive wooden throne stood abandoned, the only seat in the room. Ant walked over and sat down in it, then lay back amongst the intricate carvings in the black wood. Faces of dragons confronted him from all sides intertwined amongst depictions of iron-clad warriors wielding prodigious weapons. These dragons looked beaten and cowed; some of them had spears and arrows piercing their necks. Ant doubted that the artist had ever encountered a real dragon. He wasn't even sure that the dragons he had seen were real. They had seemed it at the time and the fire had been searingly hot, but he now knew enough about illusion and delusion from his training to make him doubt the nature of his experience.

Sitting in this big chair, Ant's thoughts went back to the more modest version that the monks used and the joy he had felt when he'd been reunited with his friends at the monastery. He thought about Pepper and Col safely secreted underground in the northern wilderness and remembered Pepper's ambition to become a soldier as soon as he reached the age of fifteen. If he were here in Gort, he'd be forced to be a soldier, then made to invade the northern lands to reclaim them in the name of this King. Ant shuddered at the way the King was so ready to send young boys to be slaughtered on the battlefield.

Ant felt Jeremiah's presence. *What?*

The place you seek is unguarded for the moment. Do you want me to guide you there?

4

Ant climbed down from the throne. *Lead the way.*

He exited the chamber by the door the way that the King had entered, passed along a long corridor to the foot of a narrow spiral staircase made from stone.

Up here, Jeremiah urged. *But hurry, people are approaching.*

The staircase wound around to the right as he climbed, and his feet left marks in the dust that had gathered on the steps. It was cold and dark, the gloom relieved only by an occasional narrow slit window that also let in a welcome breath of fresh air. It was a long trudge to the top, and Ant's legs were threatening to give way by the time he emerged into the twilight. The high tower was deserted, as promised by Jeremiah. It looked as if nobody had been there for a long time judging by the debris that had been allowed to accumulate. Small piles of stone chippings sat untidily on the floor. The setting sun cast dark shadows beneath the parapet, but there was still enough light left in the day for Ant to do his work.

In the centre of the tower, an area of stonework had been hacked out; some of the indentations had been filled with mortar but a rough circular outline was still visible. Ant withdrew a length of rope from his pocket and tied a piece of chalk to one end. He lay down in the centre of the disturbed area and held one end of the rope firmly under one of his feet. He slowly and carefully began to draw a circle that corresponded with some of the remaining markings. Once the circle was complete, he stood up, and using the same length of rope, divided the circumference into six equal arcs. There were apexes of chiselled stone that marked most of these places, but Ant meticulously checked and rechecked the positions to make sure. Once he was satisfied, he halved the rope and repeated the exercise, producing another circle inside the first. Then he made good the lines that had once joined the positions marked on the circles. Some of these were already drawn in stone, others had been chiselled out and had to be inserted. Ant had no straight edge to assist him, but his freehand drawing skills, coupled with the existing marks as a guide, were sufficient for him to complete the process.

By the time he sat wearily with his back against the parapet wall, the tower was in darkness. He could smell wood smoke from the fires below and got the occasional whiff of something appetising to remind him that it was now several hours since he had eaten. There was also a pervading, less wholesome stench that represented the thousands of unwashed bodies that inhabited the inner city. Ant waited, conserving what little reserves of energy he had remaining. Jeremiah popped into his thoughts from time to time with reassuring reports that the inhabitants of the castle seemed uninterested in visiting them in the tower.

As the light faded, Ant could detect a faint glow from the first chalk lines he had drawn. A thin tracery of light began to flow around the circle and then the whole design flared into life, a swirling coruscation that illuminated the whole tower. Ant smiled. Feelings of pride and relief began to sink into his weary frame. He breathed deeply, enjoying the familiar light show and wondering what Malachi would offer him for supper. The prospect of a long walk home had not been a welcome one. Neither had getting out of the palace with nervous bowmen on the walls and suspicious soldiers barring the one entrance to the outer city been.

Are you coming? Ant asked.

Jeremiah responded immediately. *I'm already here inside the vedhana waiting for you.*

Ant walked into the swirling lights, felt their gentle touch on his body become more substantial, and stepped out into the house he shared with his teacher.

Malachi looked up from his book. 'Is it done, then?' he asked.

'No. I didn't have the puissance to kill the King. I tried but failed.'

'That wasn't what I was referring to.' Malachi said. 'Is the device in the tower restored?'

'Oh, yes, that. I redrew it with chalk as we agreed. Anyone could erase it quite easily.'

'I doubt anyone ever goes up there after what happened with the device in the past. Did you see any signs to the contrary?'

Ant shook his head, then went over to the kitchen area and lifted the lid on the stew pot. 'Is this ready?' he asked.

'Help yourself, I've already eaten,' Malachi said. 'So now we can pay the palace a visit any time we want to. Well done.'

'It would feel an achievement if I could have done what I intended,' Ant said. 'I had a finger on a trigger and all I had to do was make it move. After all your teachings, I'd expect to be able to do that simple thing. I must be deficient in some way.'

'You've shown remarkable ability for one so young. There are sorcerers out there who have lived long lives without achieving even a fraction of your powers. Don't be too hasty to judge yourself, Ant. Killing a king isn't going to be easy, nor is it going to help anything apart from your own sense of grievance. Think about it. There may be something deep inside you that knows this and that killing isn't what would serve you. I suggest that's the reason for what you describe as failure. You might come to consider it as a very great success instead.'

'He deserves to die for what he did to all those children. There was a six-year-old that he had hanged. Imagine that? How can you defend his right to live after all the atrocities he's visited on his people?'

'I'm not defending his actions. They are as abhorrent to me as they are to you. What you have to consider is the alternative to this King of ours. Who would take his place? What frame of mind would they be in after an assassination? Maybe worse things would follow and what would you do then? Kill another king, then another? Until you found one that you liked and approved of? What if the one you chose was too weak to defend this city and allowed hordes of savages to kill everyone here? Would that be preferable to you?'

'All I know is that this King would have had me hang.'

'But you didn't. I came along in time. There is a purpose in everything, Ant. Consider carefully if killing anyone can be considered a worthwhile goal for a life such as yours.'

'So you counsel leaving this tyrant in place and just putting up with whatever he wants to do, however barbaric?' Ant was beginning to feel a little stronger with the food inside him. He'd had this argument with Malachi a hundred times before and knew almost exactly what the man was going to say.

'I'm your teacher, Ant, not your keeper. You're free to do whatever it is you want.'

'Then I'm going north to tell them about the war that's coming. The King is raising an army of children to fight for land he's never been interested in just because someone else is making a good job of living there.'

'If you see your job as being a messenger, then go ahead. But I have a feeling that the news of the war will travel faster than even you can.'

'If I can't kill this King and prevent the conflict, then at least I can join with the northerners to oppose him.' Ant moved away from the hearth; the food and the warmth had combined to make him hotter than he felt comfortable. Beads of sweat were pricking his forehead and his clothes were becoming damp and sticky.

'You should consider what that choice might entail before you embark upon it,' Malachi said. 'How would you help? What would you be willing to do? Help them kill some soldiers? Would that show the King the error of his ways? What if your friends were amongst the ones you had to kill; would you still do it?'

'I don't have any friends,' Ant said.

'Yes, you do. What about the boys you left at the monastery? One of them, I forget his name, was always intending to join the army.'

'Pepper, you mean. He's still in the north as far as I know.'

'But what of his allegiance? Is it still with his King?'

'I don't know, but I doubt it.'

'But you can't be sure, Ant. There may be another king in all but name in the north. A different king, but one that could become equally abhorrent. What do you do then? Kill both kings to end the war?'

'I'll take one step at a time. That's all I can do,' Ant said.

'No, it's not all you can do. Neither is it the best you can do. Can't you see that this objective of killing a king is going to destroy your life if you let it?'

'I have to do it. I've sworn an oath to myself not to let pass what was done to me on his orders. Killing him is the only way I can be free of my horrible memories that haunt my every thought and destroy my dreams.'

'Then go. I've taught you nothing in that case. You have every right to be angry about what happened to you. What you fail to grasp is that you will only be creating a worse situation for yourself by allowing that anger to take control. You'll be refuelling the bad thoughts and experiences with even worse ones, these created by your own actions and not attributable to the King. Grow up, Ant. Lift your head out of your anxiety and look around you for opportunities for positive action.'

'Like you? I don't see what you're doing against the tyrant. He's still on his throne, still sending innocent people to their death. What happened to your ambitions for a better monarch that you harboured for all those years?'

'I'm still working on them, Ant. Things have quietened in Gort, peoples' lives have improved. That's what I'm talking about. Answer me one question. If there was a small child in a boat on the river heading for the great waterfall of Scion, would you bring that boat to safety if it were in your power to do so?'

'Of course I would.'

'And if there was one of the King's soldiers also in the boat, would you still save the child even though it meant saving the soldier as well?'

'Yes,' Ant said, 'I wouldn't let the child drown. I'd have no idea of the implications of saving the soldier, but good or bad, they wouldn't keep me from saving the child.'

'What if the King himself were also in the boat and saving the child would also mean saving the King who you have sworn to kill?'

Ant felt he should have anticipated this question; it was so like Malachi to twist everything to suit his own argument. 'Then I would still save the child and seek some other means of killing the King.'

'What if the child was the King's son and would inherit the crown one day? Then what would you do?'

'Look, Malachi, all this is just fanciful dreaming. None of it is real. I'm not going to be ever faced with these kinds of choices.'

'You're wrong, Ant. You're facing exactly the same decisions every day, it's just that you don't recognise them. How many children's lives would you sacrifice in order to kill the King?'

'None. I don't want to harm anyone else.'

'There you are, then. That's your answer to every question that life throws at you. I'm afraid that it will be impossible for you to kill the King if that's your honest and heartfelt belief.'

'I don't agree. It's just between me and him. I owe him death and I owe it to myself to deliver it,' Ant said.

'Think about it, that's all I ask,' Malachi replied.

'That's your way, as always,' Ant said. 'Manipulation and control. Making others do your bidding by weaving words together in a way that persuades them to do what you want them to. You're doing that with me.'

9

'All I want is for you to understand the sacrifices you will have to make and the unintended consequences that will ensue if you continue to place all your ambition in one act of killing. What would have happened had you succeeded earlier today? How many soldiers and civilians would you have been willing to have die because of your actions?'

'None. I already made that clear.'

'So, you kill the King, slip away quietly. Then what?'

'I don't know.'

'Then all hell breaks loose, Ant. The civil disorder could rival the terrible times you and I saw the time we first met. There'd be arrests, hangings, and all manner of brutality. Would that be acceptable in your eyes?'

This conversation was going the way it always had, Ant thought. Malachi had spent the last two years holding back Ant's anger and channelling it into work, creating a network of vedhanas so that Malachi could travel secretly and quickly. In return, he had been taught some of Malachi's art. The man was all about persuasion. He was a master of manipulation, adept at presenting any situation in a way that prompted the actions he wanted. This argument was no different. Malachi was out to get his way as always, expecting Ant to bow down before the inescapable logic of the arguments he was putting forward.

Ant knew there was truth in what he was being told; that's what made it so powerful. But behind the truth lay Malachi's own purpose, which Ant knew from experience was often far from benign.

'I don't want anyone to get hurt. Except the King. There has to be a way.'

'That's what we are both working towards. A strategy that achieves our aims and provides stability in the long term but without massive upheaval and loss of life.'

Ant puffed out his cheeks then let out a long, slow breath. 'Then show me what to do, Malachi. If I can't kill the King, how can I prevent him from going to war?'

'You can't. He's already declared the war and is making preparations for it. We can do something, though. If there were a vedhana in the North, we could travel quickly and secretly there and back. Assist the northerners with information, help them with strategies that allowed them to defend themselves. It's not going to stop the war, but it might save some lives.'

'There's already a vedhana in the North, at the monastery.'

'Of course there is, but I was thinking about something much closer, near the border. The wilderness is much too far and inaccessible for our purposes.'

'Then that's what I'll do. Get me a horse and I'll be on my way. As soon as I've found a good place, I'll be back and we can start to wage our own war on the King. Now that I've restored the vedhana in the tower, we could place fighting men right inside the King's stronghold.'

'Exactly,' Malachi said. 'But I don't think it will be safe to go by road even if I were to accompany you. And I have many things to do that require my presence here. Go to the monastery, warn your friends, then travel south. You might want to secrete several devices to assist the deployment of men or even allow them to retreat and hide in safety. Avoiding battle can be more powerful than engaging in it.'

'So, finally, you're willing to let me leave?'

'You've always been free, Ant. It's your desire for revenge that has kept you here. You have the power to travel anywhere at all in an instant. How do you think I could possibly keep you prisoner?'

With words, Ant thought, *the kind that influence my deepest feelings. And now you're making me do exactly what your devious mind wants me to.*

2

'What's this?' Cuthbert asked.

The wizened soldier had already turned away and was fishing about in a sack. 'It's a pike,' he replied, plonking a heavy hat made of strips of iron on Cuthbert's head. 'And this is your helmet. Now move along.'

'I don't want to be a pikeman,' Cuthbert said.

'It's all we've got left. Be thankful you've got a decent weapon, there's plenty who won't be so lucky.'

'It's hardly that,' Cuthbert said. 'It's a branch from a tree that's been sharpened at one end. That doesn't make it a pike. Where's the pointy bit of metal? Without that, it's just a piece of wood.'

'We're a bit short of metal at the moment. You'll just have to make do. Now move along.'

'Here,' Cuthbert said. 'Take it back. Give it to someone else who might appreciate it. Like I said, I don't want to be a pikeman anyway. I'd rather wait and get myself a nice crossbow.'

'Don't want to bear a pike on behalf of the King? I reckon them's treasonable words. Now be gone with you; form a nice straight line over there and try not to poke any of your mates with that pike.'

'Another thing, this helmet doesn't fit.' By way of demonstration, Cuthbert turned his head sharply to the left. The helmet remained still, its nose guard now protecting Cuthbert's ear.

The old soldier produced another version of the pained expression he seemed to have adopted as his standard reaction to life and all its problems. 'Swap it with one of your colleagues if you like. Don't blame me if your head's too small.'

'Haven't you got anything else for me?' Cuthbert asked.

'Like what?'

'What about my uniform and my coat of chain mail? Something to protect me in the event that I'm attacked.'

'Chain mail isn't necessary for pikemen. You've got your pike to keep attackers at a distance. We only give mail to swordsmen.'

'Then I'll be a swordsman. Give me a sword instead of this piece of wood. It's not going to protect me at all unless the opposition is too busy laughing at my hat. Anyway, aren't pikemen at the front so they're the first ones to get slaughtered?'

'The job of the noble pikeman is to protect his fellows from frontal assault. He is part of an impenetrable barrier of deadly spikes that will destroy anything that tries to attack. Pikes are particularly effective against horses. They are the cavalryman's worst nightmare. It's an important job; now let's get on with it, shall we?'

'I would hardly call a few bits of wood an impenetrable barrier. What happens when my pike breaks, as it is bound to do? Look, if I lean on it like this, it's starting to bend already. One sharp blow from a sword or axe and it's going to be in pieces. No thanks, I really don't think I'm cut out for wielding a pike. Even a proper one with a nice piece of sharp metal on the end. Here, you take it back. Give it to someone who might be glad of it. I'll wait until some proper equipment arrives. Thanks, anyway.' As Cuthbert replaced his pike amongst the other misshapen items leaning against the wall, he became aware that the men who had previously been equipped had broken rank and were adding their weapons to the heap, which toppled over with a crash. Two of the makeshift pikes snapped in two as they fell.

'We're not being pikemen either' seemed to sum up the general consensus.

The old soldier heaved his shoulders and let out a long sigh. 'Come on now, lads,' he said. 'It might not seem much, but it's all there is. There's nothing else coming and we'll all be heading up north at dawn tomorrow. Take them or leave them. I know they're not perfect, but at least you'll be able to lean on them when you're walking along. And it's a mighty long way to the northlands. Who knows what opportunities might arise before the fighting begins? Anyway, bright lads like you lot will probably be promoted to general by then and you can ride on big horses and keep well out of harm's way.'

Some of the straighter poles were taken back at this and once it was realised that it had become first come, first served and that the last to pick would be getting the broken ones, there was a general melee that included the men who had been patiently standing in line. Cuthbert, being nearest to the collection of pikes, managed to grab one that, despite a pronounced curve, felt more serviceable than the one he had relinquished.

The old soldier stood back and let them get on with it. When everyone had grabbed what they could and the squabbling had died down, he announced that there was food available for pikemen only in the mess tent at the far end of the parade ground. Cuthbert decided that, for dietary purposes only, he would attach himself very loosely and temporarily to the ranks of pikemen.

3

The cool half-light of the monastery greeted him with a feeling of safety. Here was a place he could rest and forget all his fanciful ideas of revenge against the King. Ant regretted not returning sooner to this sanctuary, where even the horrible visions that haunted his dreams might be stilled. He felt his breathing deepen and a sense of peace flooded through his body.

He left the chamber that contained the vedhana and walked out to where he could see the sides of the cave. The soft glow of the luminescent plants was sufficient for him to see the great edifice of the monastery in all its magnificence. Despite the knowledge that he was deep underground and that a tremendous weight of rock separated him from the sunlight, Ant felt comfortable here. He sat on a low wall dangling his feet and waited.

Sounds of gentle chanting filled the air around him, the repetitious cadences seemed to be affecting the rhythm of his own body as he sat silently. As thoughts came into his head, he acknowledged them, then allowed them to float away like clouds in a clear sky. As he breathed in the stillness, he became aware of a boy in a red robe approaching.

'Rinpoche,' Ant greeted him.

'How good to see you back amongst us, Ant.'

'What of Col? He is still here?'

'Yes, he's still here and so is young Pepper.'

Ant's heart leapt with joy at the news his friends were still safe. 'Can I see them?' he asked.

'Of course, as soon as the morning meditation is over. They'll be overjoyed to see you again. Pepper has almost completed his novitiate stage and will soon be wearing a red robe like mine. He's taken to the monastic life very well and is a valuable member of our order.'

'I don't understand; he told me he was going to join the army like his father. That was always his ambition,' Ant said.

'Experience changes us all,' Rinpoche said, looking Ant in the eye. 'I detect that much has changed from the Ant who first made his way here through the caves.'

'I've grown up a bit, that's all.'

'You also seem to have acquired a new friend.' Rinpoche smiled.

'I call him Jeremiah. He helps me sometimes, though I'm not sure he likes your monastery. He went very quiet as soon as we arrived.'

Ant was still wondering how Rinpoche had known about Jeremiah when he saw a familiar figure coming out of the building and head towards them as quickly as he could without completely losing all form of monkish serenity. Even under the flowing yellow robes, Ant could tell that Pepper had filled out considerably since they had been forcibly parted. The wide grin on his face was accentuated by the extra chin he'd acquired.

The two boys embraced, and Pepper took Rinpoche's place on the wall when he left them to their reunion.

'It's so good to see you, Ant.'

'I should have come sooner, I know, but I've been busy.'

'Too busy to come back to visit your old friends who were worried about you?'

Ant felt his stomach twist at his friend's words. 'I got caught up in something,' he said. 'I realise now how that must sound, but don't forget I was a long way from here.'

'Had you forgotten how to create a vedhana to bring you back here, then?'

Ant let the question hang in the air. His friend was making him feel very guilty about the two years he had just spent with Malachi. His thoughts turned to how his father must be feeling, and that pain and sorrow touched his heart. Ant wondered how he had been so preoccupied with his own affairs that the important things had been ignored. 'I'm sorry,' he said. 'Do you know where my father is now? I really need to let him know that I'm safe.'

'I believe he's still living by the lake on the northern road, close to the border. At least he was a few months ago when I last visited.'

'Then it's even more important that I get to see him. The King is raising an army to attack the North. If he's still where you say he is, then he'll be in grave danger. I have to go to him and warn him,' Ant said.

'There's a vedhana close to the lake; one of us could take you there if you want.'

'Yes, please. I should go as soon as possible,' Ant said.

'First let's go and speak with Col; he'll be wanting to hear your news.' Pepper slid off the wall and led Ant up the path and into the monastery.

'How is it that you're still here, Pepper? You always said that you were going to become a soldier like your father.'

'Since I've been here, I've learnt the value of compassion and tolerance, things our King is completely lacking. I wouldn't feel comfortable taking orders from one so devoid of humanity.'

They entered a room with a raised area in the centre where Col was sitting on a cushion pouring tea into three cups.

'Welcome back, Ant,' Col said. 'Come and take tea with us and tell me of your journey.'

The boys sat down together facing Col, whose red robes spilt out onto the floor beside him. Ant thought he looked even bigger and stronger than ever and that he'd retained the ability to look directly into his soul with those piercing brown eyes. He felt a rush of blood to his cheeks as he struggled to come up with a rational explanation for staying away for so long. 'I'm sorry,' he began.

'There's no need for regrets, Ant,' Col said. 'You know you have been doing your best all this time and that's all you could have done. Don't pretend that things can be any different than they are, as that can only bring sorrow. Accept the here and now, be joyful at our reunion, and take pleasure in our company. Leave all your sorrow and self-criticism behind. There's no place for it here. Or anywhere, for that matter.'

Ant took a deep breath; it was as if a veil of greyness had been lifted from him and his spirit felt lighter than it had for a very long time. 'I have been working with Malachi to develop my awareness.'

'Very commendable,' Col said. His eyes narrowed slightly as he continued. 'Has this study brought you peace and joy?'

Ant's stomach lurched as he connected with the hatred he'd been holding in his heart. 'I want to become strong enough to defeat the King. To stop him hanging people indiscriminately without any sort of trial or hearing. I can't forget how boys and girls were brutally killed while I escaped because of Malachi's intervention. I have to do something, otherwise my survival of that dreadful experience will be pointless.'

17

Pepper screwed up his face. 'But you did survive and you're here. Can't you at least find the joy in that?'

'It haunts me, Pepper. I honestly believed I was dead. They threw me on top of the other bodies, but I managed to crawl into the crowd. It was horrible. I have vowed to kill the King and end his tyranny. I grew my strength and waited for an opportunity. But when that opportunity came, I was too weak and couldn't get the job done. So, I decided to return here.' Ant sipped his tea to alleviate the awkward silence, his words ringing hollow in his ears.

A familiar voice whispered to him. *Can we leave now?*

Soon, Ant replied, *I'm feeling as uncomfortable as you are.*

'I'm sorry,' Col said. 'It must be difficult for you. I'll pray that you are delivered from your torment. Meanwhile, rest here for as long as you wish. You might find that some measure of composure returns with time.'

'Yes, do stay with us, Ant,' Pepper said. 'You can become a monk, live with me and Col. We'll all be together again.'

'No.' Ant was unable to prevent the flat denial escaping his lips. 'There's things I have to do. There's a war coming; I can't just stand aside and let it happen.'

'Rubbish,' Pepper said. 'It's not your responsibility. If there is a war, there's nothing you can do about it.'

'But there is. I've been living with Malachi and he's been teaching me his craft. I had hoped it would be enough for me to deal directly with the King, but I wasn't up to it. Some things I've mastered, but others, the actions that bring actual harm, I can't seem to get right,' Ant said.

'Really? All this time? With a man who can't be trusted? You could have fashioned a vedhana and returned to us at any time,' Pepper said.

'Don't be hard on our friend,' Col said. 'Life has a way of throwing us off balance. It's how we regain that equilibrium that matters, not what took it away in the first place. I'm sure that many of the things that Malachi taught you are very useful, Ant. Take care what you do with them, though. Be your own man and stay true to your heart, however difficult that may seem. Don't let the judgement of others sway you, either. Even if it comes from someone who loves you dearly like Pepper.'

As Ant took in Col's words, he felt his heart softening. Something shifted inside him and a new sense of optimism began to form from the dark despair he was used to. 'Thank you,' were the only words he could muster.

4

Tyrant squinted into the noonday sun at the vast army heading his way. To his half-closed eyes, the columns of men looked like an impossibly long caterpillar, the kind with long black hairs. But these weren't hairs, these bristles were hundreds of pikes raised aloft as soldiers marched their way along the North Road towards where he and three others waited to prevent their passage.

The North Road had yielded few travellers in recent weeks and Tyrant had been getting increasingly frustrated by inaction. He knew in his heart that he should have left long ago; it had been nearly two years he'd lingered here in the company of Oliver and his family. He'd grown comfortable in a way that he'd never before experienced. His gut had expanded alarmingly from regular meals and lack of exercise, but that wasn't his main concern. Something had happened to his wanderlust, the force that kept him moving from place to place. He was, even if he was loath to admit it, starting to become reliant on the company of others. This alarming thought had become his constant companion as he stood at the makeshift border control that was manned at all times. Now it was being joined by the realisation that he'd left it too late.

The North Road ran through a steep-sided gorge that lent itself perfectly to a border crossing. There were other ways through the hills that Tyrant had personal experience of, but none that would accommodate horses or wheeled vehicles. If you had anything worth stealing or were in any kind of hurry, you had to come this way. The regular traffic had made his job reasonably interesting and given him a reason for hauling himself out of his comfortable bed every morning.

There was another consideration that had delayed his departure, perhaps fatally. This was Petra. The diminutive woman still insisted on hanging around him all the time. She seemed to think there was something between them after a few shared experiences that Tyrant wished he hadn't shared. He felt certain that if he left the lakeside, she would tag along, and that wasn't something he was willing to risk.

So, he'd gone against the instincts that had provided a lifetime of self-preservation and stayed in one place far too long. He could leave now, of course. Flee into the hills, walk over the mountains, and be gone. That was the most sensible choice and the old Tyrant would have taken it without pausing for thought. Now, it seemed, he'd trapped himself in a manner that no walls or prison bars had ever managed before. He thought of the gentle population of the quiet lakeside area and the devastation that a marauding army would wreak. He thought of Oliver's young daughters and what would certainly happen to them. He felt a deep sense of indebtedness that sat uncomfortably alongside his primary need for self-preservation.

'Go quickly,' he told Jeb, the youngest and quickest of his companions. 'Find Garth; tell him the King has sent an army to kill us all. Hurry, we don't have much time. They will be upon us within the hour.'

'They may just be passing through,' Thomas said after Jeb had scampered off. 'Shouldn't we have waited to see what they want before alarming everyone?'

'Armies don't just pass through,' Tyrant said. 'They destroy everything in their path. There'll be nothing and no one left in Laketown if they get beyond this pass. Now help me move these rocks to the middle of the road; at least we can do something that might hinder their passage while we wait for them to reach here.'

The formation of a makeshift wall across the road was all Tyrant could come up with as a plan. At least it kept his two allies occupied and distracted them from the knowledge they were almost certainly going to die very soon.

It was a rather pathetic wall to face a mighty army with. It didn't even reach the whole way across the road, as they had insufficient time and materials to complete it. Nor did it reach higher than Tyrant's waist. He looked at his handiwork and thought it would be almost as easy to climb over it as to go through the gap in the middle. That's if the loose stones didn't just crumble and fall over when the first man touched them. Tyrant sat precariously on top of the wall and drank the last of his water.

The army came marching four abreast, pikes waving overhead, then came to a sudden halt about twenty paces from the wall at the sound of a strident voice. A man emerged from the ranks and walked confidently over to where Tyrant was standing.

'The King has decreed that all the lands in the north are rightfully his and that anyone resisting faces punishment by death. Put down your weapons and bow down to the rightful King.' The soldier looked around him as he spoke, as if searching for some opposition to make his long journey worthwhile. 'Just the three of you, is there?'

'No, we're guarded by spirit warriors. We humans are just here for appearance's sake, you know. Otherwise, your normal travellers might turn tail and run away. Which you ought to seriously consider as your best option. Have you ever seen the effect a dragon can have on a nice neat army like yours?'

The soldier looked around again, this time with less confidence and a trace of nervousness. 'I have over five hundred men. Nothing can withstand us. Now step aside before I order my men to trample you underfoot.'

'Call those men?' Tyrant asked. 'From where I'm standing, they look like a bunch of children carrying sticks. Admittedly, there are an awful lot of them and to give you due credit, some of the sticks are quite long ones. You've even gone to the trouble of sharpening one or two of them. Even so, they don't exactly put the fear of the King into all who behold them. Tell me, are you in charge of this motley crew?'

'I'm Captain Forrester; I command the vanguard pikemen and the first regiment of sword. My general is riding towards the rear of the column. It's a narrow road and we are so very many. Now, stand aside. He will be wondering what's causing the delay and it will be worse for you if he gets impatient, believe me.'

'Then send word back down the line. Tell him that the road is guarded by invincible spirit warriors and that he should turn back and find some other place to visit.'

'I'll do no such thing.' Forrester drew his sword and pointed it at Tyrant's chest. 'Now get out of my way.'

Tyrant watched as the pikemen took their cue from their captain and lowered their weapons so that they pointed in his direction. The point of the sword was almost touching his chest, but the captain's arm was already fully extended. In Tyrant's eyes, this meant that in order to stab him, the arm would have to be pulled back to give some force to a forward thrust. The pikemen were of no interest to him for the present, being too far away to intervene.

Tyrant took a swift step to the side, drew his sword, and swiped away the captain's weapon, which fell apart on first contact. Small bits of iron showered musically onto the stony ground. The soldier took a deep breath of surprise at exactly the same instant that Tyrant took one of relief. He hadn't drawn his sword for such a long time. It was good to find that it still worked.

Apart from slicing fruit, the only use his sword had been put to since he found it had been chopping the leg off a dragon and scaring away a soldier on the spiral staircase to the King's tower. It was definitely a good sword, just how good remained to be seen.

Tyrant's main worry concerned crossbowmen. There had to be some in this long line of armed men and he hoped they were a long way towards the back. He'd had a very bad crossbow experience, which only the long and gentle ministrations of Oliver's family had prevented from being fatal. Another reason why he'd hung around the lake for so long. Perhaps he'd been waiting for this opportunity to repay his debt.

Meanwhile, Captain Forrester was staring at the shards of sword scattered around his feet.

'Magic,' Tyrant said. 'The King knows all about the magic that protects the land in the north. That's why he gave it to us. I was there when he did. My name is Tyrant; some people, including the King, call me a spirit warrior. I am invincible. If you want further demonstration, bring up as many of your best men as you want and I'll chop them to pieces before you can draw breath.'

Forrester stepped back several paces and appeared to be weighing up his options. Tyrant hoped these didn't include getting hold of a crossbow and shooting him. That would definitely hurt and also settle any argument once and for all. His spirits rose when Forrester waved a row of pikemen forward to see what they could manage. Four pikes thrust forward at Tyrant. One slash of his sword took the sharp ends off them, while the second reduced them in length to that of a short sword. Before he could administer the third sweep, they got the message, dropped what was left on the ground, then retreated. A new row of pikes appeared and were dealt with in the same manner. Tyrant was beginning to enjoy himself, despite his gut feeling that all this posturing was likely to end suddenly and tragically.

'Enough,' Forrester called out. 'Stand back. Let the crossbows come forward.'

Tyrant watched as the soldiers began to mill about in the narrow gorge, trying to make way for the ones who were able to shoot him. He had two choices now. One of them was to run away as fast as he could.

5

'What's going on?' Pugh turned to Cuthbert, his face florid in the heat and the wart unfortunately positioned right at the end of his nose even more prominent than usual. 'Why are we going so slowly?'

Cuthbert was only slightly taller than Pugh and in just as poor a position to observe what was happening, trapped amongst the ranks of sweating bodies that competed for air in the cramped conditions.

'I can't see any more than you can,' Cuthbert answered. 'Maybe we're stopping for a rest.'

'They never let us rest,' Pugh said. 'My feet are red raw and I have never felt so hungry. As for this piece of crap they gave me to carry, look at it. It's just a branch ripped from a tree, it's not a weapon.'

It had been a long dry dusty walk up the steep hill, and now Cuthbert found himself squeezed even more uncomfortably between the stone canyon walls. They could walk three abreast at best now and there was a lot of jostling and clattering of pikestaffs as the soldiers sorted themselves out. Hours earlier, Cuthbert had to cede the front where the air was fresh for a dust-laden third rank, where he only had the backside of the man in front for a view. Now he fervently wished he'd managed to retain his position.

Progress slowed almost to a crawl. He felt tired and claustrophobic in the midst of all this press of humanity. Cuthbert's mouth was parched and his personal water skin had yielded its last drops an hour or more ago. As far as he could recall, the water was being carried on a cart right at the rear of the column, and he faced the prospect of a long wait before he had the opportunity for replenishment.

When the column suddenly halted, he was struck in the back by the butt end of a pike and nearly toppled over. An officer pushed him aside as he made his way to the front. By craning his neck, Cuthbert could see him talking to a large unkempt figure who appeared to be blocking the way. He could make out two other heads behind a low wall that closed off the road. He wondered if they were the vanguard of a vast army. He hoped not. The pike he had chosen had warped alarmingly after a shower of rain, and prodding something with it was going to involve a lot of guesswork. If there was a properly equipped army ahead of them, then there could only be one outcome, and that involved a painful death for all of them.

The captain suddenly called them into battle and a few at the front stepped hesitantly forward. The unkempt man waved his sword and, as if by magic, pikes were reduced to the firewood they were more suited for. Cuthbert noted with some relief that it had only been wood that had been chopped so far, because all his comrades were still standing with their limbs attached, none the worse for the encounter. He breathed a sigh of relief. It was his turn next and he had decided to hold his pike at the very end and offer it for chopping as meekly as possible to avoid any misunderstanding regarding intent.

Before he could move forward, there was a lot of shouting at him to make way. This was difficult with all the bodies around him and there was a general melee, which resulted in several of his fellow pikemen falling to the ground and being roughly trodden on. Cuthbert used his pike to steady himself, but even so, it was almost impossible to keep his feet. A stray elbow clouted him in the mouth. He tasted the iron in his blood, and his teeth began to ache. Stones began to clatter against his helmet, small ones at first, then larger rock began to shower down. Cuthbert was trapped; he couldn't move to avoid the rain of stones. He looked up to see the whole hillside break away and head towards him.

Pugh was felled by a heavy blow and collapsed at Cuthbert's feet. As he was shifting balance to avoid him, another man cannoned into him, knocking him off his feet. He felt the patter of earth, the clatter of stones, and the thud of boulders as his mouth filled with dust and the world went black.

6

Ant stepped out of the vedhana, and smelt the fragrance of herbs in the air. The placid lake in front of him and the view of the sky over the water were a welcome sight after the gloom of the subterranean monastery.

There was nobody to greet him – the place was completely deserted. As he made his way to the elaborate entrance, he saw cooking pots left on fires and plates of food left half consumed. Outside, a grassy meadow extended to the foothills of the hills that stretched into mountains as they became more distant. Ant stood and drank in the silence. A feeling of tranquillity seeped through his being, and he very quickly decided that he liked this place because it allowed him to breathe easily for the first time in ages.

Take a look around, he told Jeremiah, *find out where everyone is.*

Ant sat on the wooden step and drank in the view of the mountains that was food for his wounded soul. The time spent working at his craft, striving to become powerful enough to be able to kill the King, all seemed a futile waste in front of the majesty of his natural surroundings. Here, he was so far away from the King's malevolent influence that he could forget about it, at least for the time being. Perhaps long enough to begin his healing process.

The fresh air entering his lungs had an invigorating quality quite unlike the metallic stillness in the monastery or the rough odour of Gort. This place spoke of cleanliness and of hope. He was glad there had been no human greeting; it was more important that he had been left to feel the very special welcome offered by this place.

You're not going to like this. Jeremiah pulled insistently at Ant's consciousness until he relinquished his meditation and gave him his full attention.

What am I not going to like?

Everyone is either gone or preparing to flee. An army approaches and they all fear for their lives. Most of the men have gone to fight.

Ant's wellbeing evaporated in an instant. Waves of desperation welled up inside him, followed by bursts of grim anger. No sooner had he arrived in this delicate place than the King was seeking to destroy it.

Whether or not the King was aware of it, the matters between them were intensely personal. It appeared that there was nothing to be done except keep to his original plan and try to make sure that this King's evil influence was brought to an end as soon as possible. Healing would have to wait.

Ant ran across the grassland, then followed Jeremiah's prompting and clambered the mountainous slopes on the lake side of the road as it headed south. The climb was long and difficult, and he found himself breathless and scrambling for footholds before he reached the top of the escarpment. Below him, the road cut through the deep gorge as it made its way south. As much as he longed to soar away with Jeremiah and see what lay far ahead of him, Ant needed to keep all his consciousness within his body as he made his precarious way across the difficult terrain.

At last he could see people scurrying like white beetles along the road. Men in makeshift white robes carrying an assortment of weapons. The sun glinted on swords, flashed off axe heads, and sparkled amongst lances and spears.

From his bird's-eye vantage point, Ant saw the thin beginnings of the opposing forces, stretched out further than he could see. The small group of northerners were plainly too few to withstand the massed ranks that were marching towards them.

Ant reached a point on the cliff wall that overlooked the top of the pass and that marked the division between north and south. Three figures were standing in front of the King's might, one of whom he could recognise even from this distance.

This was unmistakeably Tyrant. He was standing with his sword upraised, seemingly prepared to fight them all if need be. Ant sat down heavily, took a deep breath, and then he was with Jeremiah alongside Tyrant. He watched as the first wave of troops ran forwards urged on by an officer. Tyrant chopped a dozen pikes into firewood and the surge towards him stopped.

This is futile. Ant planted the thought into the officer's mind.

'Enough,' the soldier called out. 'Stand back. Let the crossbows come forward.'

Not what I'd intended, Ant thought. From the hesitant look on Tyrant's face, it wasn't what he would have liked either.

Ant turned his attention to the men in the front ranks. *Run for your life,* he suggested. *Turn around. Go back. It's your only hope.* As he visited mind after mind, Ant planted the image of a fiery dragon swooping down on them. The effect was gratifyingly swift. The column of soldiers degenerated into a seething mass of confused bodies, most of which were trying to push themselves out of harm's way.

Ant returned to his body and stood on the cliff edge. He felt into the ground, identifying fissures that had been made by long years of water flowing through them. He encouraged the cracks to widen, pushing at them with his mind. His efforts were rewarded by a sudden shift of earth beneath his feet and he was forced to step back quickly to avoid being swept away by the avalanche he had created.

The soldiers below disappeared in a shroud of black dust.

7

Tyrant was aware of the irony of the situation. Here he was, a man who had relied on his reputation to keep him alive, and now, just when his stock had climbed to its highest level, he was faced with the prospect of taking on an army single-handedly or having it completely dismantled.

He could run away and hope to rebuild his credibility, but he knew that wouldn't happen. The scorn he would be subjected to would be too much to bear, even if it were only imagined and he never had to face the ones he had let down. The longer he kept this invading force at bay, the better chance the others had of evading capture and death. Some of the lake dwellers might even have time to organise themselves sufficiently to mount a serious opposition and keep the army bottled up here for days. If that were to happen, Tyrant would have to make the ultimate sacrifice.

He held up his sword, put on his most fearsome expression, and started to yell. The effect was instantaneous and surprisingly positive. The soldiers all turned and tried to run away. Because of the cramped conditions, this was proving to be impossible and a great churning of bodies was taking place. He thought about charging into the mass and cutting a few heads off, but hesitated on the grounds that nobody would notice in all the confusion. Tyrant was still wondering what to do when the cliff face on his left detached itself with a loud rumbling noise and began to cascade down on the writhing bodies. As the earth, stones, and rocks showered down, Tyrant's mind was made up, and he turned and scarpered down the road, trying to put as much distance between himself and the landslide as quickly as he could. He was happy to see that his companions had come to the same conclusion and were already way ahead of him.

Tyrant emerged from the dust cloud to encounter another army heading his way, this time from the north. At the head were retired cavalrymen who brandished weapons of a much higher quality than he'd been previously confronted by. These were serious items – proper spears and lances, long swords, heavy axes, and short bows of the kind favoured by horsemen. His spirits lifted. The pass might be defended even against overwhelming odds provided they could keep out of the way of arrows.

'What's going on?' Garth asked. He was an enormous man with a long scar down the middle of his face from an axe wound that had divided his nose. Tyrant had spent many an hour in his company, and, despite his off-putting appearance, had found him to be a most gracious and gentle man. Like many of his fellows, Garth had chosen a peaceful life away from the King's service and had put his violent past behind him.

'We encountered a large army,' Tyrant replied. 'We stopped them, and then the sides of the canyon caved in and buried them. Did your men start the rockfall?'

'Not us; we hurried here as soon as we got word. There's been no time for getting any men up there.'

'Then we'd better do it now,' Tyrant said. 'When the dust clears, the air will become thick with arrows. Our only defence will be to get up on high before they can manage it. Their crossbows won't be as effective as they will be if we stay on the road, though some of us will need to remain to prevent any further progress. How many men do we have?'

Garth shrugged. 'Fifty, perhaps. Not everyone has weapons, though.'

'Then we should keep a dozen of the best equipped on the road and let the others go back to where the cliffs can be climbed. Make sure there are enough shields to go round; those that remain here will be in sore need of them when the arrows start flying. Anyone without a weapon can hurl rocks from above. That will be more effective than brandishing a sword down here.'

Garth picked out ten men with shields and sent the rest of them back down the track. 'What about you?' he asked.

Tyrant flicked sweat from his brow with a grimy finger. 'I'll stay here with you and hold them back as long as possible.'

'With respect, I suggest you go up top. There you can get a good view of what's going on and be better placed to formulate a strategy.'

Tyrant stared hard at Garth's expression but could discern no sign of derision. It was the 'with respect' that had alerted him. It normally meant exactly the opposite in his experience, but this time, the words were uttered with complete seriousness. 'If it's a strategy you want, then you'd better climb up there yourself. These are your men; they take orders from you.'

'Yes, but you're our leader, Tyrant. I'll be taking orders from you. And don't worry, we're willing to lay down our lives to preserve our settlement by the lake.'

A flood of desperation swept through Tyrant's gut. Now he knew he'd stayed in one place too long. First his thickening waistline and an increasing sense of wellbeing, and now this burly ex-soldier was looking to him for leadership. The world was turning upside down. He was being faced with the kinds of choices that his devil-may-care reputation had always shielded him from. Strategy, indeed. He was about to charge the whole army single-handedly before the rockslide intervened. That's the only kind of strategy he had ever employed. 'OK,' Tyrant said, 'I don't think there'll be much action down here for a while anyway.' He sheathed his sword, gave Garth a very brief pat on the shoulder, then began the long trudge back.

He was forced to take several long breaks before completing the climb, his legs and lungs crying enough at frequent intervals. He sat next to a rivulet that danced down the side of the hill and provided a welcome slake to his raging thirst. Tyrant savoured the taste of the cool water and decided from now on he would take more exercise and keep himself in better shape. His belly was pushing uncomfortably at his belt, and the knives he had stashed under his shirt were pressing into his flesh. He smiled to himself as he observed his own resolution. There wasn't much option, he decided. The days of ease and plenty had been rudely interrupted by the arrival of the King's army.

Tyrant dragged himself to his feet and continued his lonely trek up the steep hillside. As he reached the top of the climb, he could see the backs of Garth's men as they scampered along the top of the ridge at a speed he couldn't hope to match. Picking his way painfully across the rocks, he suddenly became aware of a prone figure lying partially hidden by gorse bushes. He took out his sword and approached cautiously, the dark cloak and hood covering the man completely and bringing to mind someone Tyrant had hoped never to see again.

'Malachi?' Tyrant peered into the bushes, keeping a good grip on his sword. There was no answer; the man remained curled up with his back to him and seemingly in a deep sleep. If it were Malachi, the sorcerer who had been the husband and accomplice of the dreaded witch who had been the cause of all his previous troubles, he was minded to stab him to death while he still had the chance. The only thing that stayed his hand was a slight doubt as to his identity, though wizards in dark cloaks weren't common sights. He'd only ever encountered one before and wouldn't like to have to deal with him ever again.

Tentatively, he poked the prone figure with the toe of his boot. 'Malachi,' he said, 'it's me, Tyrant. Account for yourself.' He prodded again, this time a bit harder, and was rewarded with a weak reply.

'Tyrant?' It was a young voice.

The body moved slowly and a young face emerged from the hood. 'Ant? Is that you?' Tyrant said. The boy's features were no longer fresh and youthful; there were lines across his forehead and bags below his eyes. He looked desperately tired.

'Yes, it's me. What are you doing here?' Ant said.

Tyrant sat down beside the boy, breathing more easily now that the evil ghost of Malachi had been dispelled. 'I'm living by the lake now. Your father is also here, though he keeps himself to himself. There's also Oliver and his family who took care of me when I was wounded.'

'I remember us falling from the sky.' Ant frowned. 'We shouldn't have left you to die. Believe me, that wasn't my decision, though I should have done something about it. It was you that carried Lone out of the Great Hall. Where did you take her?'

'I stranded her in the desert,' Tyrant said as he remembered the marvellous fruit he had discovered there and wished he had some now. 'She may still be where I left her; I hope she is. I wouldn't like to have to contend with her or Malachi again. That's who I thought you were, lying there in your cloak with your hood obscuring your face. How mistaken can you be, eh?'

'Maybe you weren't as far from the mark as you think,' Ant said. 'He's been teaching me his arts and I've adopted his dress as a consequence. The cloak and hood are useful for one such as I.'

Tyrant took a breath. 'How could you possibly trust such a man?'

'He's not so bad when you get to know him. I honestly believe that he means well. Anyway, he saved me. I'd be dead if it weren't for him.'

8

Cuthbert could hear a swishing sound. A sort of liquid thump, then a swooshing noise. It was very faint; he could only hear it if he concentrated hard. It was dark and his eyes were tightly closed. The darkness was the absolute kind and Cuthbert knew that if he opened his eyes, it wouldn't help. He began to remember what had happened and the realisation that he was buried beneath the avalanche caused him to panic and breathe in sharply. No air came. His nostrils filled with muck and his distress increased. He tried to gasp for air through his mouth, but the earth intruded like a black snake trying to choke him. With a great effort of will, he steadied himself and fought back the fear. By sniffing gently, he could extract a little air from the debris surrounding him, but if he inhaled too hard, his nose blocked completely.

He lay in the blackness, trying not to panic. He could feel that he was lying face down with a terrible weight on his back that prevented him from moving at all. Even his arms and legs were pinned unmercifully; he was totally trapped.

Thud. Swish. Thud. Swish. The sound of blood pumping through his body. He listened to it, fascinated and scared at what might happen if he stopped hearing it. All he could do was to listen, breathe carefully, and wait.

His mind replayed the last few seconds before he had been buried. He recalled Pugh toppling over and being showered with rocks and debris. Before that, he'd been near the front of the column, preparing to fight the defenders behind the wall. He wondered how far back the landslide had gone, whether all the army had been buried or just a few of them. Would they come digging for him soon, or were they occupied with more important matters? Would his comrades even be able to reach him? Did they even care?

Cuthbert realised that either someone had to dig him out very soon or he was already in his grave. The tiny amounts of air down here were being rapidly depleted and being replaced by his exhalation. He could already detect the second-hand nature of what was now entering his nose and how it left him more breathless than ever. He opened his mouth to scream, but the earth closed it off.

He thought the noise of his heartbeat had stopped and felt almost relieved to be ending this nightmare with blessed oblivion. He thought of all the things he'd miss doing with his life and blamed himself for succumbing so meekly to the King's tyrannical orders. Given the choice now, he'd have taken his chances and got as far away from Gort as possible. Anything would be preferable to holding a pointed stick in the face of an enemy he'd no quarrel with. It was all foolish conjecture and wishful thinking now. He couldn't alter anything; all he could do was to sleep knowing that he'd never wake again. Better to fill his last thoughts with fond memories of family and kinship than dark regrets.

It was harder to get any sustenance from the sparse, stale air, and his mind began to drift away into sunlit fields of corn with children playing hide and seek. He felt the roughness of the stalks underneath his bare knees and the shouts of excitement as the pursuers sighted their quarry.

Clump, scrape. His heartbeat had changed alarmingly – it was louder and had become irregular. Maybe this was what happened when it was about to fail completely. Cuthbert felt sad that he had to experience it when it would have been better to have passed away gently in his sleep. Now he had to cope with the pain and suffering that death would inevitably bring.

The clumping and scraping grew louder and more insistent. He no longer had to listen carefully to hear it. There was no avoiding the noise now; it felt as if his heart was about to explode and he wished it would hurry up and get this awful ordeal over and done with.

9

Tyrant's thoughts went back to the King's tower and the view he'd had of the hangings that were taking place. His only concern then had been to avoid the noose himself. It was hard to imagine the terror that Ant must have felt with the noose around his neck.

'So what are you doing asleep on a hillside so far from Gort?'

'I came to warn you of the army heading your way, too late it seems. I tarried too long with Pepper and Col at the monastery. And I wasn't sleeping when you found me, I was elsewhere.'

'Really?' Tyrant said. 'Is this something that Malachi taught you?'

'Yes, but I also have assistance from my spirit guide. He can take me wherever I choose to go because he doesn't have the burden of a body to drag along. So I go with him and leave the physical form of Ant behind.'

'Can you find out what's happening with the army? Are they intent on attacking?'

'They're afraid and confused. I've planted the idea in their minds that witchcraft and all manner of terribly destructive forces are ranged against them. For the time being, they have been ordered to withdraw to a place where they are no longer in danger of being buried under an avalanche. They will be back. But not immediately. We have a few days to decide what to do.'

'Impressive,' Tyrant said. 'And I suppose that the avalanche was your doing as well?'

'Yes, I could see no other way to stop them.'

'In that case, you have my gratitude. I was about to end my life uselessly killing men I had no argument with. As you know, I've a thing about futile gestures.'

'Taking Lone away was no futile gesture, Tyrant. Don't underestimate the value of your life.'

Trouble is, Tyrant thought, *that sort of thinking leads to fear and before I know it, I'll be curled up in a ball screaming for mercy instead of facing things head-on.*

10

The voice in Cuthbert's head said: 'There's one of them alive. No, not there, over here. That's right.' Then the scraping noises amplified, and he felt vibrations that rattled through his prone body.

Suddenly his closed eyes could detect the first suspicion of black turning to grey, but he still didn't dare to open them. 'I've found a leg,' one voice said.

Not mine, Cuthbert thought, *but keep looking, please.*

'Uh oh, another dead 'un.' The voice lost its air of excitement.

'Down here,' came another voice, 'help me shift this rock.'

The weight on Cuthbert's back was eased; he could move one arm now and use it to pull his face out of the muck. Breathing was easier; he took in a big gasp of air without being choked. He spat dust out from his parched mouth as he felt hands grab him by the shoulders and heave him out of his tomb.

He lay on his back breathing in the wonderfully fresh and life-giving air for a long time before he felt able to open his eyes. The faces staring down at him were unfamiliar and not dressed in army uniform. His heart skipped a beat. He appeared to be in the hands of the enemy who had buried him in the first place. He knew what the King's orders were under these circumstances; anyone resisting the lawful right of the King had to forfeit their life. It was simple, if not exactly fair.

'How are you, son?'

Cuthbert looked at a man with a grotesque disfiguration that had sliced his nose in two parts. He wondered at first if this were the way that all northmen looked, but the other men he could see were reasonably normal looking and he put his rescuer's appearance down to an unfortunate accident.

'I don't know,' Cuthbert answered honestly. If he were about to be put to the sword, then his situation had hardly changed for the better and he would have to reflect that. But why go to the trouble of digging him out if they were going to kill him? The only answer had to be information. They wanted to know what he knew about the army and its disposition. There had been a talk about this in training camp that had informed them of the necessity to say absolutely nothing to the enemy, even under the most painful means of enquiry. 'I don't know anything at all, really,' he added.

'Are you in any pain? Can you move your limbs?'

'Oh, yes. They seem to be OK. Can I have some water, please?'

Cuthbert sat up and drank from the proffered skin. The water tasted sweet and his parched mouth gloried in the wetness. He began to feel invigorated, despite his forebodings. There were no weapons pointing at him, only concerned faces. 'Thanks,' he said, 'but I'm not allowed to tell you anything even if you torture me.'

The big man with the cleft nose laughed, and the other men joined in. Eventually, he recovered enough to speak. 'And what is it that you think you might know that's so important?'

'Our mission, for a start.' Cuthbert felt a little bit humiliated by the assumption that he was ignorant. 'The name of our general. Our orders. Our strategy. All that kind of thing. I'm not stupid, you know.'

'So you're the general who's leading this expedition, are you?'

Cuthbert thought for a moment, sensing a trick question but unable to see the harm in answering. After all, it must be obvious. 'No, I'm just a pikeman, recently joined.'

'And how old are you?'

'Nearly fifteen. They thought I was already fifteen, but I had no means of proving them wrong, so I had to join the army. It's the law.'

'I don't remember such a law during my time in the army.'

'You were in the army?' Cuthbert asked.

'I was Captain Garth of the King's Own Cavalry. Not only that, I was part of the last army to be ordered into these parts by the King. We were also told to find our quarry and take no prisoners. We were all blinded by fear and duty until we decided to start thinking for ourselves.'

'What about me?' Cuthbert asked. 'What are you going to do with me?'

'Nothing,' Garth said. 'You are free to go wherever you please. And welcome to remain with us if that's what you wish.'

'But I'm the enemy,' Cuthbert said. 'Aren't I a threat to you?'

'I'll let you be the judge of that. It's up to you what you are and how you act. If you feel an allegiance to the King, then go back to his army. It

38

may be that you end up killing me in battle.' Garth's eyes narrowed. 'But I'm willing to take that risk.'

Cuthbert thought for a while, sipping the cool water as he did. Garth seemed much nicer than anyone he'd met in the army, but there was always the threat of hanging if he was caught as a deserter. The best solution would have been capture and imprisonment until the war was over. Then he'd know who'd won and which side to join. Imprisonment wasn't being offered and if he thought about it properly, it might not have been very pleasant even if it were. He couldn't imagine prisoners of war getting priority when it came to food and shelter at a time of conflict.

If he went back to the army, he'd be given a pike and sent into battle and probably killed. If he stayed in the north, he'd either have to fight on the other side or run away on his own. He didn't think he'd last very long either way. He was used to having food brought to him, even if it was a bit samey and unpleasant. At least it sustained him. Out there in the countryside, foraging for things to eat wouldn't be something he'd feel confident about. He'd probably eat the wrong mushroom in desperation and die of stomach ache.

It came down to which side was most likely to win, he supposed, and it was impossible for him to be sure. As he sat contemplating his decision, two men came down the road from the north. One was the big guy with the sword who had made firewood from his comrades' pikes. The other was smaller and clad from head to toe in a dark cloak. They began conferring with Garth, and Cuthbert was a little concerned that he could hear every word they were saying.

'They've withdrawn to the other side of the pass,' the big man said. 'The landslide has blocked the whole road.'

'Will they be back?' Garth asked.

'I'm sure they will try at least, though from what I can see, the road is completely impassable. Negotiating that loose collection of earth and rocks won't be easy. It's very steep, very high, and very unstable. Getting an army across will be a long and difficult process; they'll have to dig their way through.'

'So they might go back to Gort?'

'Unlikely. The King won't be receptive to excuses.' The small man in the cloak spoke for the first time.

'Ant's right,' the big man said. 'When the King sends out an army, he expects results. You should know that better than most, Garth.'

'Do or die, that's his majesty's motto, at least in respect of his subjects.' Garth laughed. 'So, what can we do other than wait?'

'There's another way across the mountains. I've travelled it myself. It's long and arduous, but can be done. I think they'll try that way. Not the whole army, but I expect they'll send some skirmishers to get behind us and make an attack from the rear.'

Cuthbert felt panic gripping his throat, and he leapt to his feet. 'Stop. I can hear everything you're saying. Don't you realise I'm here? I could go back and tell the general everything. In fact, it's my duty to the King to do so. Please don't make me party to all your plans, it's more than my life's worth.' The men turned towards him and he could feel the eyes of the hooded man staring from the darkness.

'This is the man we found in the rubble,' Garth said. 'He won't tell me his name, says it's a secret he's forced to keep by his oath to the King.'

'Hello, Cuthbert, I'm Ant and this is Tyrant.' The hooded man spoke gently to him as if they were old friends. Cuthbert was startled at the sound of his name, but didn't feel threatened by it. Perhaps this man knew him from Gort, maybe he was an acquaintance of his family. Whatever it was, he knew his name and might even turn out to be a friend.

'Garth says I'm free to go and not to be harmed,' Cuthbert said.

'I'm sorry about all your comrades,' Ant said. 'You were the only one left alive and it was difficult enough to find you under all that earth. You must have been very frightened.'

'I was.' Cuthbert thought of the deathly blackness and the feelings of absolute desperation came back into his body as if he were back under the ground. Tears welled up in his eyes and he couldn't prevent the sobs that began issuing from his mouth. He felt comforting arms enfold him and the floodgates of fear and grief opened. When he'd recovered enough to realise he had darkened the man's cloak with his tears, he stood back, feeling sheepish and unmanly. 'Sorry,' he spluttered, 'I don't know what came over me. I'm not normally prone to blubbering.'

'Sometimes it's better to let things out. You've had a hard time, Cuthbert,' Ant said. 'If you want to go back to your army, we're not going to prevent that. Even if you tell them everything you've heard, it won't make any difference one way or the other.'

'But perhaps we should become more circumspect in fairness to the lad,' Tyrant said. 'There are matters that might help our enemy and we would be better advised to refrain from speaking plainly in front of Cuthbert until he's decided where his allegiance lies.'

'What caused the landslip?' Cuthbert asked.

Ant and Tyrant looked at each other and smiled. 'First you ask us to stop giving you information, now you're trying to get it from us,' Ant said. 'Do you want the version we would like your general to know or the one that might help you make up your mind whether to stay or go?'

Cuthbert wished he'd not asked the question, though it was fundamental to his thoughts. If these people really did have a god on their side, then the King's cause was surely lost and all his army could perish in a single act. 'Sorry,' he said, 'I wasn't fishing for information, just trying to understand what my choices were. I'd certainly stay here and help you if I thought you were protected by a god.'

'Then your decision has been made,' Ant said. 'You are now officially protected by our god.'

Cuthbert saw the look on Garth's face and wondered if it were puzzlement or disquiet. Either way, it soon cleared back to his normal avuncular state. He breathed in deeply and felt the truth of Ant's words and the relief that they brought. All doubt was dispelled. The King could go hang himself; he wasn't working for him anymore. 'OK, I'm happy to stay and join you. Just tell me what you want me to do.'

'We want you to go back,' Ant said.

11

Tyrant watched as Garth led Cuthbert away. 'I don't get it,' he said.

'He'll be more useful to us if we send him back to his own army. He can keep an eye on developments and let us know what's going on. Information is the key to success, Tyrant. The more we have, the better.'

'But he's not going to be of any use to us as a spy, he's just a kid,' Tyrant said.

'I'm hardly less of a kid myself, yet managed to bury that army under an avalanche,' Ant said.

'It's not a matter of age, more of experience. You've been through an awful lot. Cuthbert wouldn't know how to gather the information we need; neither would I for that matter. All that creeping about and intrigue stuff. It's not right in any case, people should be honest.'

'They're not honest, though,' Ant replied. 'Especially those who are closest to the King. They have to do his bidding, whatever atrocities he demands. Better that we know in advance than suffer them first-hand.'

'But Cuthbert? What can he do apart from getting caught and hanged?'

'He will have my help, don't worry about him. Anyway, the truth of the matter is that he was dug out of the landslide, then we let him go. That's all there is to it,' Ant said.

'So he picks up a pike again and the next time I see him he's trying to stick it in my eye?'

'He can become our eyes and ears. He may provide the difference between success and failure. Protecting everyone by the lake or allowing them to be killed by an angry King.'

'It makes no sense at all.' Tyrant felt unconcerned about the prospect of letting Cuthbert go back to his army. There were hundreds of Cuthberts already there clutching their pointy sticks with sweaty hands and one more would make little difference. He had a bad feeling about all this spying nonsense, though. It felt unnatural and reminded him of the things that Malachi and his witchy wife Lone used to get up to. 'How are you going to get the information from him even if he manages to hear anything useful? Generals don't usually confer with common soldiers regarding their intentions.'

'As I said,' Ant replied, 'he'll have my help and that of Jeremiah, my spirit guide.'

Tyrant's heart felt heavy at the boy's reminder that he was dabbling in the black arts. 'That's not right either,' Tyrant said. 'You'll turn out just like your master if you persevere in that kind of thing. Spirits are difficult and dangerous things; you would do well to let it go and hope it doesn't bear a grudge.'

'You're thinking of Patch, aren't you?' Ant said. 'That one was different in so many ways. Jeremiah is my friend and he helps me out of choice. Lone had Patch bound to her by a powerful magic and it had to be coerced to do her bidding. Nevertheless, it saved her life. These soldiers who now live as monks by the lake are the product of Patch's benign interference. They were sent to kill us and were going about their duty until Patch helped me persuade them otherwise. Then there was the way Patch dealt with the demon at the monastery. So, you see that spirits and demons have a natural place in our world and can act for good as well as ill.'

'I'm not convinced,' Tyrant said. 'So is your boy Jeremiah like Patch? Can he transform into a dragon? If so, get him on the job without further ado and let's see an end to the King and his noxious plans.'

'Patch was and is very special. I'd describe it more as a god than a demon. There aren't many entities out there that can compare to it. No, Jeremiah is small potatoes in comparison. He can help us stay in touch with Cuthbert though.'

Tyrant looked south along the road at the enormous pile of debris that was now blocking it. 'Even if he wanted to, he couldn't negotiate that pile of rubble. It would swallow him up again if he tried.'

'There's a path across the mountains isn't there?'

'Yes, I've been that way myself, but it's difficult and dangerous. You can easily lose your way even if you have a map. I did.' Tyrant thought of the wind and cold on those exposed peaks and shivered with the memory.

'Then that's what we do,' Ant said. 'You take him over the mountains and deliver him safely back to the King's army. I'll come along as well, I have work to do on the other side.'

'It seems a lot of trouble, especially for me,' Tyrant said. 'Are you sure it's worth it? After all, there's not just the journey over the mountains, I have to make the arduous trip back.'

'Not necessarily,' Ant said. 'I want to find a suitable place to install a vedhana. If I do, then we can come back in an instant. We will also be able to transport our forces behind enemy lines.'

Tyrant's chest tightened as he remembered the feeling of being whisked from one place to another by the arcane device. If Ant was capable of creating such things, it was no wonder that Malachi had been so keen to have him as his pupil. 'We haven't enough men to defeat that army even if we do get behind them and have the benefit of surprise.'

'That may be true,' Ant said, 'but it would be good to have the option. Anyway, when the time is right, I want us to attack the King directly. I've restored the vedhana in his tower and we can get to his inner sanctum any time we choose.'

Tyrant sighed. He'd been in that tower before and it did not hold pleasant memories for him. It also bothered him that Ant seemed to have everything worked out in advance. The boy appeared to be working to some master plan of his own devising that might put all of them in jeopardy.

12

Along this path, through the trees. Not far now. He's asleep inside the house. There, up ahead, where all the lights are. Ant was barely registering Jeremiah's instructions as he hurried towards his father's home. A double-edged anticipation filled him with alternate excitement and doubt. This was an encounter he'd avoided for too long, and he had to remedy that before he went away. It was true that his father had abandoned him and possibly deserved to suffer for that. Yet he couldn't help feeling guilty that he had left it so long to seek him out and should have saved years of grieving on both their parts with a simple act of kindness. As he arrived unannounced, as hard as he searched his heart, he could find only sorrow at his neglect.

Ambrose looked older, a straggly beard greying at the fringes adorned his face and the wrinkles around his eyes were accentuated in the half-light. Even in repose, the man looked haggard and weary. Ant knew he was observing the effects of his own inaction.

'Father.' Ant tried to rouse him gently, but at his first touch Ambrose shot upright with a look of panic on his face. 'It's me, Ant.'

The wide, staring eyes narrowed as if he was trying to focus his thoughts as well as his sight. 'Really? Ant? Is that you?' Ant felt himself being enveloped by those familiar arms and he was suddenly five years old again. Tears came unannounced and uncalled for, and he found himself sobbing into his father's shoulder. Everything he'd planned, all the words he'd prepared, dissolved into the flood.

When he became capable of speech again, all Ant could say was 'Sorry.' Then the tears began again in earnest; he was crying for himself now. The familiar terror of the hanging welled up and overflowed. Ant found himself hanging on to his father in fear of being overwhelmed by grief. 'I'm sorry, I should have made time to visit you before now.' Ant finally stepped back and faced his father. He felt lighter and more expansive than he'd done for a very long time.

'You're here now and that's all that matters,' Ambrose said. 'Let me have a good look at you. My, you've grown up to be a fine man, my boy. Come inside, I have things I want to show you.'

Inside the small house, Ant was astonished to see dozens of small vedhanas all glowing with an ethereal light that swirled and cascaded around the place. It was as if the room was being lit by an array of ghostly candles.

'What do you think?' Ambrose asked.

'You're using the devices for lighting?' Ant asked.

'No.' Ambrose let out one of those familiar chuckles that Ant was used to hearing whenever his father was explaining something he found obvious, but wasn't anything of the sort. 'I've been experimenting with the patterns we use to make the devices; that's the reason for all the little ones in here. I've made some larger versions outside as well. There's something about them that I can't quite figure out, but I do know that they're much more than a device for travelling from one place to another. There's also the manner in which we direct the travel, Ant. Thoughts are too vague to be credible; at least I believe them to be so. We may think that's what's guiding us, but I know it's much more complex than that. I've learned how to send inanimate objects from one place to another, for example. Watch.'

Ant stood attentively as his father picked up a knife and lowered it into a tiny glowing device on the tabletop. It was as if it were disappearing into a well of water that extended far below the horizontal surface the device was sitting on. Ambrose pulled the knife back out and put it into Ant's hands. 'Close your eyes, tell me what you can feel.'

Ant concentrated hard, his childhood fear of disapproval tightening up his muscles in an effort to make his father proud.

'Relax, hold it gently.'

Any obeyed and felt a gentle tingling in his fingers that grew more evident as he grew used to the sensation. 'It feels alive,' Ant said.

'Yes, it does, but why do you think that is?'

'Because it's been inside the vedhana, I suppose.'

'That's the reason, but what is the cause, Ant? What is the manner of this new energy that the knife didn't possess before? Where has the energy come from?'

'I don't know,' Ant said. 'Tell me.'

'I don't know either, but I do know something happens every time an object is placed into one of these devices, even for a few seconds. A knife like this one often comes out sharper and with an edge that does not get dull with use. There's something going on in there and I'm going to find out exactly what it means to us.'

'What about Col and the monks? Do they have any ideas?'

'I've made several trips to the monastery and spent many hours talking to them about their experiences with the devices. They're aware that something's going on, but being monks, they ascribe it to divine intervention of some kind. I don't care whether it's the work of some god or not, I want to be able to understand it and so be able to use it to our advantage.' Ambrose's eyes were aglow with passion and the reflections of the many devices.

Ant breathed a deep sigh of relief. Whatever grief his father had felt at temporarily losing his son had seemingly been offset by the intensity of his desire to find out the secrets of the vedhana, the device he had unearthed on his archaeological travels and installed with such devastating effect in the King's tower. Ant felt as if he'd been relieved of a great responsibility, but at the same time, experienced a twinge of disappointment that his father could be so easily distracted. There had been no enquiry regarding his wellbeing; Ambrose was preoccupied with his research and was only intent on engaging his son's assistance.

'Wonderful,' Ant said. 'I'll help all I can, of course I will, but I have to go away again.'

'But you've only just arrived. Can't you spend at least a week or two with me? There's so much that I want you to see and experience.'

'I have important work to do, Father. The King's army is upon us and desperate measures must be taken.'

Ambrose's eyes narrowed. 'Nothing is more important than this work, Ant. It could be the key to our survival. Let someone else take care of the army.'

'Nobody here at the lake will survive the arrival of the army. Unless I intervene, that will be the most likely result. When I've finished what I have to do, I'll gladly assist in your research. Until then, I'm sorry but I have to go.'

'Stay.' Ambrose put his hand on Ant's shoulder. 'I'm telling you to obey your father and do your duty.'

Ant pulled himself away, Jeremiah's voice in his mind. *He's on his own by the lake.*

'Goodbye, Father,' Ant said. He watched the anger rise in his father's expression, then slowly die away again. As he walked out of the house, his feeling of joy at the reunion had been swept away by anxiety about his being unable to meet his father's expectations.

Good, now find those girls for me.

13

The moon had risen high into the clear night sky by the time Cuthbert was left to sit in peace near a cheerful fire and given a sizeable chunk of flatbread to gnaw on. His mind remained firmly buried under tons of rock and he found himself forgetting to breathe.

Two girls came and sat beside him in the semi-darkness. 'I'm Marigold,' said one.

'I'm Camomile,' said the other.

'Pleased to meet you,' Cuthbert said. The two girls broke into hysterical laughter. Cuthbert wondered what was so funny and worried that it might be him.

'I'm Daisy,' the smaller girl spoke again.

'I thought you were called Marigold,' Cuthbert said.

'I was. Now I'm called Daisy. What's your name?'

'Cuthbert.'

The girls began to howl with laughter, holding their sides and rolling around on the floor. Cuthbert began to feel embarrassed. Either there was something hilarious about the way he looked or spoke, or these girls were mentally deranged.

'I'm not really Daisy and she's not really Camomile,' the little one said. 'We were tricking you. I hope you don't mind.'

'Not at all,' Cuthbert said.

'Are you married?'

'No, I'm not. Are you?'

The girls found this just as funny as whatever he'd said before. When they'd calmed down a little, the small girl introduced herself again. 'I'm really Bee and this is my sister Cassie. She's not married and you can have her if you want.'

This remark prompted Cassie to leap onto Bee and start wrestling with her; all the time the girls were screaming with laughter.

Cassie sat up. 'Take no notice of her. She's never going to find a husband that would put up with her.'

'Yes, I will,' Bee said. 'I already have, anyway. We're practically engaged.'

'Who is this unfortunate man?' Cassie said.

'I'm not telling.'

'That's because you've made him up.'

'No, I haven't.'

'Then spit it out, tell us who he is.'

'Tyrant,' Bee said.

'Rubbish.' Cassie laughed and pushed Bee over. 'He's never going to marry you. He's already got Petra.'

'He doesn't like Petra. He told me,' Bee said.

'That's not what Petra thinks, and that's what matters. Anyway, he's far too old for you. He'll be dead soon, he's so ancient. You wouldn't want a dead husband, would you?'

'What happened to you?' Cassie turned her attention to Cuthbert, who was reluctant to speak again in case it prompted more laughter.

'I was buried under a landslide.' Cuthbert waited for the mirth, but the girls were now sitting watching him with serious faces. 'I nearly died; it was horrible.'

'Oh, you poor man,' Cassie said without even a suspicion of a smirk.

'You've got muck all over you,' Bee said. 'You look awful, like you've been working down a mine.'

'You need a bath,' Cassie said. 'Come with us, we'll show you where to go.'

'We promise not to look,' Bee said. 'You can trust us.'

Cuthbert followed the girls to the lake, where the water was glinting invitingly in the light of the full moon. The prospect of cleaning away all the earth he'd accumulated was irresistible, and he began to take off his clothes. The girls stood and watched him until he stood in his patched and holey undergarments. 'You better leave me to it now,' he said. 'I can manage on my own now. Thanks for showing me the place.'

'Don't worry,' Bee said, 'we've both seen one before.'

'One what?'

As the girls dissolved into mirth again, Cuthbert was left in no doubt what they were referring to. 'I'd rather be alone,' he said.

'We'll look away until you get into the water,' Cassie said.

'We promise,' Bee said, turning her back on him and facing a tree.

50

When he was sure that the girls were being true to their word, Cuthbert whipped off his pants and ran quickly into the lake. The cold shock of the water was invigorating, and he felt a new energy coursing through his body. He swam with big splashing strokes to get himself warm again, then stopped to luxuriate in the cleansing properties of the lake. He could feel himself healing as he bathed; the terrible happenings of the day were being washed away and replaced by a new optimism. He breathed deeply and closed his eyes.

14

Oliver's sleep had been fitful, disturbed by visions of soldiers pouring through the pass and down to the lake. He reached out for comfort from his wife, but encountered only the hard outline of his crossbow. Sitting up, he remembered how he had opted to keep watch at the roadside rather than continue home after the landslide had stopped the King's army from any further progress.

Garth had seemed perfectly content that there was no longer any prospect of an attack, but Oliver hadn't felt as convinced. He imagined there would be troops slowly clambering their way across the shifting piles of earth and rock, and that they could arrive and attack him at any time.

'Good morning, hope you enjoyed your sleep.' A friendly voice came from one of Garth's monkish soldiers who was using a bush as both hiding place and reclining chair.

Oliver felt guilty and embarrassed at his dereliction of duty. 'I'm sorry, I must have dozed off,' he said.

'Nevertheless, you provided me with essential assistance and I thank you for it. Your snores kept me alert all through the long night, as well as providing me with companionship. They may even have kept marauding animals at bay and they certainly frightened off the King's army for they haven't had the nerve to show their faces either.'

As he trudged back to his home on the lakeside, Oliver tried to fathom the true meaning of his colleague's words. Were they sarcasm or truly meant? He concluded that they were gentle banter and that the monk had probably woken up shortly before he had.

His wife, Freya, was busying herself making bread and boiling porridge.

'The girls should be up and helping you with breakfast,' Oliver said. 'I'm sick and tired of telling them and I'm worried that you're doing too much. You should be taking more rest in your condition.'

Freya looked at him and smiled. 'You make it sound like I'm ill. I'm just carrying a child and it's happy to be carried whether I lie down or move about. I've done it twice before, don't forget, and I don't remember you being so concerned about my welfare then. You still expected a meal on your plate whenever you bothered to come home from your soldiering.'

'But you're older now, Freya. Things are different.'

'Not too old for nature to take its course. If you had doubts about my ability to bear another child, I didn't notice any when you were providing your enthusiastic assistance to the process.'

'I didn't say you were too old, I only want you to take care of yourself. The girls are old enough to make breakfast; it's something they should be doing regardless of your pregnancy. Where are they, anyway?'

'I don't know; I thought they'd gone to find you last night and were helping you with your guard duty.'

'So they're not in their beds?' Oliver felt a flush of alarm. The lakeside was generally a benign place and in their two years living here, only an occasional bear had disturbed the peace. Even so, the idea of his daughters being out all night concerned him despite them having shown ample evidence of being able to look after themselves. After all, they'd made the hazardous journey across the mountains with Tyrant and been none the worse.

Oliver found the girls sleeping beside the lake, Cassie in the arms of a man and Bee a little distance away. His heart filled with anguish at the thought of his little one being intimate, but his anger was stayed by the gentle smile on her face as she slept. The man was little more than a boy, hardly older than Cassie. Oliver took a few deep breaths to steady himself before calling the girls from their slumbers.

'Wake up,' he said, 'you need to be home and helping your mother with the breakfast.'

Cassie sat up sleepily, disengaging herself from the prone figure beside her. Bee jumped up and ran to Oliver, her face ablaze with excitement. 'Cassie's got herself a husband, Dad. Look. His name is Cuthbert and he's very sweet. They're going to get married and have lots of babies. Tell him, Cassie.'

'It's true.' Cassie smiled. 'Say hello to my father, Cuthbert.'

A frightened face peered over Cassie's shoulder. 'Hello,' he said.

'This isn't the way to go about things, Cassie. You should have brought the young man home, let your mother know what your intentions were. She'd have been able to tell you things you need to know about this kind of thing.'

'He's a soldier,' Bee said. 'He's only just arrived. He came with the King's army to attack us, but he's not going to do that anymore because he's in love with Cassie.'

Oliver's face grew hot and his breathing became fast and shallow. How many more were there? Had he missed the army breaking through? Was the war already lost and the north under occupation?

'Garth dug me out of the rockslide, otherwise I'd be dead.' Cuthbert got to his feet and offered a tentative hand.

Oliver took it and shook it briefly before realising that his gesture might be construed as approval. Cassie stood next to him and allowed herself to be enveloped by his arm.

'So you're one of us now, are you?' Oliver said.

Cuthbert looked down and shuffled his feet. 'I've told Cassie that I have to go back to the King's army. It'll only be for a while, though. Then I'll come back here and take care of her.'

Oliver couldn't believe what he was hearing. Of all the boys Cassie could have chosen, she ended up with one of the enemy. He took Cassie by the arm and dragged her away. 'If I ever see you anywhere near my daughter again, I'll put an arrow through your head.' Cassie began to cry and Oliver bundled her along the track back home.

Bee followed, protesting loudly.

15

Tyrant was explaining for the tenth time how he was perfectly capable of finding his way over the mountains. Petra was having none of it. She'd already packed a few 'essentials' into a bag, which Tyrant had difficulty lifting. He untied the string and examined the contents of the sack she'd given him.

'There's a rock in here. You're expecting me to carry a rock over the mountains? Look up there, can't you see that there are plenty of rocks to be gathered on the way? The whole mountain is made of rock, what makes you think we might need another one?'

'It's my cooking stone,' Petra said. 'I use it to make flatbread; you expect to eat on the journey, don't you? You'll be complaining soon enough if you don't get fresh bread for breakfast, I'll bet.'

Tyrant shook his head. He remembered times when he'd not had fresh bread from one year to the next and when a crumbly old crust dipped in rainwater seemed like a feast. His belly may have been full these days, but he knew that his spirit had diminished. The trek over the mountains had been the opportunity to get back to the life he'd once been perfectly happy with. When he'd been constantly on the move with only a knife in his belt, the clothes he stood up in, and his wits to sustain him. He should have left two years ago, before the rot of complacency set in. Now he'd spent too much time in the company of this diminutive woman and she'd laid solid claim to his life. It was as if he'd bound himself in rope, then handed the end of it to her.

'See what I mean,' Tyrant said. 'There's no place for cooking stones on a military expedition. We'll have to move quickly, be prepared to fight our way out of trouble. We can't be lumbered with kitchen equipment. Or women, for that matter.' As soon as he had said the words, he regretted them. Now there was nothing that would stop Petra tagging along. He knew her well enough to be aware of this, but his mouth had run away on its own without any pause for consideration of the effect it would have. Her face clouded, and the tight brown skin gathered into deep lines that radiated from the corners of her eyes. At first, Tyrant was sure she was going to attack him, but all she did was take the bag, carefully remove the cooking stone, and drop it on his foot.

'There you are, take it or not, it's your choice.' She tied up the bag again and began to walk towards the mountains, her tiny legs scurrying like a demented beetle.

Tyrant ran to catch her up. 'We have to wait for Ant and Cuthbert.'

'Don't mind me,' she said. 'I'll just show you the way. After all, you'll never find it on your own. You'll just get lost again and find yourself a tavern to waste your time in while we're left to fight off the King's army. That might be fine for you, but the other two might be sensible enough to want to avoid that total waste of everyone's life. If it's important work you're doing, you'll not get it done without me and you know it.'

Tyrant stopped in his tracks, and let her stride off ahead. Cuthbert emerged from some bushes and looked around him as if he were expecting trouble.

'Don't worry, lad,' Tyrant said. 'Petra's gone on ahead, you're safe from her sharp tongue, at least for the time being.'

Cuthbert's face changed from worried to puzzled and then reverted to sad. 'Do we really have to go today?'

'The sooner we set off, the sooner we get there and get on with the job.'

'Yes, but I think I want to stay here. No, I do really want to stay here and join your army. I don't want to go back to my own, it wouldn't be right. I can't be made to fight against you again; I'm on your side now.'

'Exactly right.' Ant arrived and stood facing the boy, hood drawn back to reveal his youthful features. 'You are a trusted member of our army now; that's what you've chosen and that's perfectly right and proper. But your job lies back with your previous employer gathering information that will save lives on both sides.'

'I still rather stay here; I've met someone and need a few days to make things right with her father.'

Tyrant laughed. 'You're a quick worker, son. Hardly been here five minutes and you're on the job already. Who's the unlucky recipient of your less than obvious charms?'

'We're in love and I want to marry her, but her father told me never to see her again when he found out I belonged to the King's army. I need to explain things properly.'

'What have you told this girl and her father?' Ant asked.

'Only where I came from and the fact that I'm going back.'

'Did you say why you're going back?'

'No, I didn't get the chance to explain. He got very angry and took his daughters away.'

'Two of them, eh?' Tyrant chuckled. 'You're a bit of a dark horse, if you ask me. No wonder the father was a bit upset.'

'At least let me find Cassie and tell her what I'm doing. That I'm going to be spying for you and that I'll come back here for her.'

'Cassie?' Tyrant felt a rush of blood roaring in his ears. 'You've bedded Cassie, you little wretch?' He grabbed Cuthbert by the throat and watched as his eyes began to protrude in fear and pain.

'Enough,' Ant said, prising Tyrant's fingers away from Cuthbert's neck with surprising force. 'Leave him alone, he's got important work to do. Did you tell anyone at all of your intentions?'

'No.' Cuthbert rubbed his neck and looked warily at Tyrant. 'I didn't tell Cassie and there was no chance to tell her father.'

'Then that's just as well. The less people there are that know your true role in all of this, the better.'

'But Cassie and her family think I'm their enemy, I can't bear the thought of that. I love her and want to be with her. That's why I can't leave now.'

'Listen,' Tyrant said, 'if you break that girl's heart or even upset her in the slightest, you'll have me to answer to. It's only the small possibility that Cassie actually likes you herself that stays my hand from killing you on the spot, spy or no spy.'

'Think about it,' Ant said. 'If you really care for the girl, you'll leave things as they are. Imagine the anguish she'd experience if she knew what you were engaged in. Better that you do your job, end the war, and come back to her as a hero.'

'But she might find somebody else,' Cuthbert said.

'And so might you for that matter,' Tyrant said.

'These things have a way of working out for the best,' Ant said. 'Stop worrying about her and keep your mind focussed on what you have to do to save her life. If you don't succeed, there's every likelihood that she'll be roughly used by dozens of your comrades in arms, then killed as an insurgent by orders of the King. You wouldn't want that to happen, would you? If you want to prevent it, you will have to be brave and determined. You will also have to listen carefully and do everything I say without hesitation. Do you understand the importance of what I'm saying, Cuthbert? It's in your hands to save Cassie and you can't do that by remaining here.'

Cuthbert nodded meekly at Ant, who continued to gaze at him intently. Tyrant began to feel uneasy about what was going on here. What Ant was doing made him uncomfortable because it reminded him not so much of Malachi, but his wife Lone. Tyrant couldn't help wondering how much of this had been Ant's careful manipulation of matters towards his own ends. After all, it was he who had buried the poor lad in the first place, then directed the rescue through his demon, Jeremiah. Had he contrived to put Cassie and Cuthbert together as well?

Tyrant found himself looking at Ant in a different way. This was no longer the simple youth he'd first encountered; this was a young man who had been under Malachi's influence for two long years. For that matter, where was Malachi in all this? Was Ant being controlled in exactly the same manner as he was controlling Cuthbert? Tyrant shook his head in confusion. He'd thought he'd left this kind of intrigue behind when he'd marooned Lone in the desert. At least there was no sign of her; as far as Tyrant was concerned, she was worse news than a dozen Malachis.

16

Lone was conscious that regrets were the poison that soured even the sweetest fruit. Had they been absent, she might even have liked this hot, abundant place where she had lived in reasonable comfort for what had seemed an age. As it was, every moment that passed brought her new recognition of ways her life could have been different. Should have been different, in fact.

She shouldn't have allowed herself to be marooned here. All it would have taken was one step into the vedhana as Tyrant made his escape, but she had hesitated and he took the damned device with him.

She should have recognised the true power of the spirit she had summoned. The two years she had spent researching and performing the rituals to enable her to do that had proved a spectacular success. But she had remained unaware of its true nature until it was too late.

She should have been the ruler of the world by now.

She should have been more careful in her use of the captive spirit.

She should have recognised its imperfect manifestations as wilfulness rather than lack of ability.

She should have got to know her demon better.

She should have been more sympathetic to her husband.

Lone broke off her self-critical litany as an ungainly figure made its way unsteadily down the sand dune and stood in front of her.

'Patch,' she said.

'Lone,' it replied.

'Have you come to gloat?'

'Not necessarily, though I can't promise anything. Circumstances have changed. I might let you go.'

'Forgiveness isn't a quality I would associate with a demon,' she replied, her blood racing in her ears at the prospect of her life being returned.

'Quite right. It's not my decision and it involves no forgiveness at all, you'll be comforted to hear. The world hasn't suddenly turned upside down.'

'So get me out of here.'

'Don't you want to know why you're being released?'

'Does it matter? As long as you take me out of this awful situation, I don't care why.'

'But you should,' Patch said with a chuckle. 'Though knowing might make you want to stay here forever.'

'In that case, I expect you're going to tell me anyway and make me suffer.'

'Perhaps. Perhaps not. Knowing there's something awful that you should know but don't is worse than knowing. So, all I'll say is that I've been overruled and that something much worse than me has decided you have a purpose.'

'What purpose?' Lone shuddered at the thought of an entity worse than Patch suddenly taking an interest in her.

'That would be telling.' Patch showed his huge square teeth.

'So when do I get back to what I laughingly consider civilisation?'

'Patience.'

'I haven't got time for that. Take me away from here now, that's what you're supposed to do.'

'Not quite, my instructions were merely to keep you here out of harm's way. Now, I'm giving you the freedom to do whatever you want. So, you have become master of your own destiny once again. Or as much master as any of you humans are. You're all the same, always wanting instant answers to everything.' Patch flickered out of existence and left Lone with her angry protests unsaid. All she could do was to fling herself onto the sand and beat her fists against the ground.

17

The strap on Petra's bag was cutting a painful groove in Tyrant's shoulder as he trudged breathlessly up the steep slope. The pain it caused was nothing, though, compared to the constant sound of her voice.

'I told you the stone was essential, but you wouldn't listen, would you?' she said. 'That bread you ate so much of wouldn't be half as good done any other way.'

'I'm carrying your stone, what more do you want of me?'

'I want you to learn to respect other people's opinions. I want you to listen to what you're being told. It's for your own good. You can't go through life thinking that you're the only person in the world and that nobody else matters.'

Yes I can, thought Tyrant, *it's served me well to this point.*

'Anyway,' Petra continued, her tiny legs working hard to keep pace with Tyrant, 'you've never properly told me about where we're going and why.'

'That's because I don't know myself. All I have to do is to show Ant the way across the mountains so that he can get round the army with Cuthbert. The rest is up to him.'

'What if we meet the army coming this way? Have you thought of that?'

'I suppose that's a possibility we'll have to deal with if it happens.' Tyrant wished he'd discussed this very real prospect with Ant. It should have been obvious to both of them that a scouting party, at the very least, would almost certainly be sent and, more probably, a sizeable contingent of the King's finest warriors.

'How?' Petra asked. 'Ant and Cuthbert are just children, they won't be up to much in a fight. It'll be you and me, Tyrant, and the two of us can't fight off an army.'

'I know we can't.' Tyrant, already short of breath from the climb, found himself panting even harder. 'We'll have to keep a weather eye out and take cover if we see anyone approaching.'

'Brilliant,' Petra said. 'We're climbing a mountain, if you hadn't noticed. Until we get to the top, there's not much of a view. There could be any number of hostiles hiding up there waiting to pounce for all we know. Look around you. They could come marching over the brow of that hill any time they pleased and we'd be none the wiser.'

'Jeremiah is up ahead, scouting. Don't worry. We'll get plenty of warning if anyone approaches.'

'Who's Jeremiah?' Petra asked.

Tyrant winced and looked back to make sure that Ant and Cuthbert were still lagging way behind. He hadn't meant to tell Petra about Jeremiah; it was Ant's secret and he didn't want his spirit guide to become general knowledge. He quickly considered making Jeremiah a fictitious fifth human member of the party, but had the feeling that she'd not let it rest until she'd laid eyes on him. She'd also be pestering the others for information about their mysterious companion and then Cuthbert would no doubt start wondering as well. 'He's a secret. Nobody has to know about Jeremiah; he belongs to Ant and he's invisible. He's a spirit.'

'A demon?' Petra asked. 'Like that dragon we saw at the monastery? The one that originally looked like a comical horse? That's wonderful! Now I understand why you're not bothered if we encounter any enemy soldiers.'

'He's not that sort of demon. I believe he only acts as a lookout for Ant; I don't think he can actually do anything physical.'

'Yes, but can you be sure?' Petra's face was aglow with excitement. 'We thought that horse was pathetic until it transformed into a dragon. This one might very well be the same, keeping its true powers hidden. After all, that's what they do isn't it?'

'All I know is you have to keep quiet about him. Cuthbert isn't allowed to know; he's going back to his army and he might let something slip if he knows about it.'

'I didn't know he was going back. Nobody tells me anything. Why would he want to go back when he seems such a nice boy and we dug him out of an early grave after all?'

'Shush,' Tyrant said. 'Don't say any more, please. These matters are all very secret and I'm not allowed to tell anyone, not even you.'

'He's going to be a spy, isn't he?' Petra said.

'Yes, but keep it quiet. Don't even mention it in front of Ant, he gets very anxious if he thinks his plan might be public knowledge. And I'm certain that Cuthbert won't be happy if he finds out that anyone besides Ant knows about him.'

'You can rely on me,' Petra said. 'I'm the soul of discretion, I am. It's you and your blabbermouth that everyone has to worry about.'

Tyrant opened his mouth to speak but decided that enough damage had been done for the day. He sat down on the nearest rock and ignored the sharp discomfort it provided. He could still see the lake, a tiny glistening sliver far below them. A cold wind whipped around his neck. Ant, enveloped in the protection of his cloak and hood, sat beside him and motioned Cuthbert to follow Petra, who was clambering enthusiastically ahead.

'I've had to tell Petra about Jeremiah,' Tyrant whispered.

'No matter, she's your woman and I'm sure she can be trusted.'

Tyrant jumped from his perch as if it had suddenly scalded his backside. 'No, she's not,' he gasped, desperate to convince at least Ant of the true state of affairs between him and Petra. 'I don't have a woman, never have, never will. I don't believe in them. They're nothing but trouble. Take that Lone for instance, she was nearly the end of us all. If it weren't for her, I'd be a rich merchant enjoying the good life in Gort, taking my leisure on my exotic fruit plantation. Instead, she's there and good riddance to her. But I wish I'd never set eyes on her.'

Ant laughed. 'How did you two get together in the first place?'

'She bewitched me. Set up a fight, stole all my money, then approached me when I was most vulnerable. After that, it was witchcraft all the way.'

'I was talking about Petra, not Lone.'

'We met when I was undertaking the difficult and dangerous task of escorting two young girls through the perils of the forest,' Tyrant said.

'I suppose that involved a lot of fighting?' Ant smiled.

'Yes, but also bickering and a great deal of sarcastic comment. You don't know Bee and Cassie, do you? They're quite a handful, I'll tell you. I tried to leave them with Petra for safekeeping and to protect my sanity but had to return to deal with two ruffians. Then more trouble arrived and we all went to the lake, where we've remained ever since. That's it. There's nothing else between me and her. If I had to pick between her and Lone, I'd be sorely tested to decide who made the worse companion. At least Lone used to keep her opinions and thoughts to herself. With Petra there's a constant mithering that drives me potty.'

'She cares about you, that's for certain. I can't imagine you ever encountering someone as warm and loving as her.'

Ant's words burned into Tyrant's heart. He looked up at the tiny figure scrambling manfully up the scree slope and something shifted inside him. It was as if a great weight had been lifted from his shoulders and even his vision felt clearer. It wasn't nagging, it was her way of expressing her love. He knew that, but had refused to acknowledge it up to this point. Now he felt a warmth that he'd been denying himself all his life. Tyrant breathed deeply. Lone was far less dangerous.

'Show me your sword,' Ant said.

Tyrant passed it, handle first, to Ant.

'You found this in a vedhana?'

'Yes, the one in the King's tower.'

'And does it possess magical properties?'

'I don't really know,' Tyrant said. 'It's a damn good sword, chops things to bits without much of an effort on my part, but it seems to be just a sword for all that.'

Ant held the shining blade in front of his eyes and examined it closely. 'There's an inscription in the metal but it's very faint.'

Tyrant looked hard at the mark underneath the hilt that he'd not noticed before. Something about it troubled him. 'I've seen that symbol before, many years ago,' he said. 'It's the image of Ishtar. Nowadays, even speaking her name is punishable by death. Walking about with a picture of her on my sword isn't the best news I've had. Still, if I didn't notice it, perhaps nobody else will.'

Ant handed back the sword and Tyrant accepted it with a sense of foreboding. Were its remarkable properties as a result of the inscription? Did Ishtar really exist? Was she somehow watching over him? He shuddered at the thought and remembered his misgivings about Ant's demon friend. 'Your friend Jeremiah, he is reliable, isn't he? Petra's right about these hills. They're likely to be crawling with soldiers and I'd rather it wasn't a total surprise when we meet them.'

'He's useful but requires direction, Tyrant. A bit like any of us, I suppose. I sent him ahead this morning and he could see no signs of any hostile forces heading this way. But that's not to say there aren't any. We need to keep our own eyes open.'

18

Malachi watched the smug grin disappear from the High Steward's face as the response was announced. 'The King will receive you in his private chambers.' The soldiers holding tightly onto his arms relaxed their grip but didn't let go completely until they received a reluctant nod.

The King was eating. Three waiters hovered around him, fetching him items and clearing away the mess of discarded food. Malachi decided that the two years since they had last met had done nothing for the King's corpulence unless it had been to increase it to the level of obesity.

'I thought I'd see your miserable face one last time before I have you hanged.' The King wiped grease from his mouth with the back of his hand and fixed Malachi with a look of contempt.

'It was kind of your majesty to grant me this opportunity.' Malachi stood at a respectful distance, aware of the bodyguards to his right and left. Both had small ornate crossbows pointed at his head. The weapons looked ridiculous, but Malachi didn't doubt their effectiveness. 'I see that you have acquired a new tapestry; scenes of the far southern desert, if I'm not mistaken. Your influence is more far-reaching than ever.'

'Not so complete that it has taken two long years for my men to hunt you down only to find you living bold as brass right under their noses.'

'Your majesty, I should point out that I was discovered only when I presented myself at the gate to your castle. I'm here of my own free will.'

'Even so, I have decreed that your life must be forfeit for the fiasco you presided over. The abominable thing in my beautiful tower gave rise to untold trouble and inconvenience. Not least of which is that I'm deprived of its use.'

'That's what I've come to see you about,' Malachi said. 'It's about time that you were made aware of the true nature of the devices and how valuable they will be to your ambitions. I've spent this intervening time on your behalf, searching tirelessly for the secrets of their construction and use, and now I come to you armed with that knowledge.'

The King swatted away the last remaining waiter who was gallantly trying to wipe the royal face with a cloth. 'I'll have nothing to do with those things; they nearly lost me Gort.'

'It wasn't the devices, your majesty, it was a collection of evil entities who chose to arrive by that route. They would have got here anyway; the device wasn't responsible for their attack. If you remember, I told you at the time that the device wouldn't work as a portal into the underworld and I was right.'

'Nonsense, demons poured out of it. They even made disparaging remarks about me and I'll never forgive you for that.'

'The vedhanas, as they are known amongst the wise, are merely transport devices. They can take you from one place to another in an instant. They work for humans as well as spirits. I can take your majesty from here to anywhere you might wish to visit in but an instant. No travelling time involved. It's exactly what you need if you wish to remain the unassailable ruler of the known world.'

The King had lost his air of disdain and was leaning forward, intent on hearing more. A posture that accentuated the rolls of fat circling his midriff. 'And I suppose you expect me to forgive you in return for supplying me with this information?'

'No, your majesty, I expect you to reinstate me as your trusted advisor.'

Malachi watched as a fleck of foamy white spittle gathered in the recess of the King's mouth. He knew he had to be careful now, more than ever. The capriciousness of this King was legendary. To incur his displeasure in even the most minor way could be fatal.

'Trusted? After your device caused so much death and destruction? After you failed to protect your King from ridicule?'

'Your majesty will recall that it was Ambrose who installed the device and Ambrose who fled in the face of its misuse. I have always remained your loyal and faithful servant.'

'Even after I condemned you to death and put a price on your head?'

'I knew that once your great wisdom and understanding could be focussed on my individual situation, there would be an opportunity for forgiveness.'

'He duped me, you realise. Cheated me as if I were a common vagabond. I trusted Ambrose and that's what hurts most.'

'It was a dreadful betrayal and one that deserved to be punished. Have you expressed your anger and disappointment to him?'

'Alas, no. The wretch has disappeared. I'm informed that he fled to the north and is cowering there, awaiting my inevitable wrath. Circumstances have prevented his apprehension, but these are temporary delays, which will soon be overcome. I have sent an army north to quell the rebellion and bring him back to face justice.'

'How is the war progressing, sire?'

'Slowly. But that is the nature of wars. I will prevail, I always do.'

'Now that I am restored to your majesty's side, I'm sure that matters will take a much more positive turn.' Malachi could feel the King's sense of wellbeing returning in his presence. The old familiar patterns of thought were reassuringly present and making themselves more conspicuous.

The first few minutes in his majesty's company were always going to be the most perilous. Now he felt confident that he could once again play this bastard like the fat trout he was. The stirrings of energy around the palace told him that the time was now ripe.

'The army your majesty bravely despatched to deal with the insurrection in the north has been thwarted in the first instance. The road north has been blocked and no further progress can be made except through the mountains, which is a most unwise and difficult route to take. My advice is to withdraw your troops to Gort and prepare for a much more serious threat from the south. The northerners have stayed where they are for two years, they're not going to give you any trouble if you leave them alone for now.'

'Do I detect that you're siding with your friend Ambrose? Is this a ruse to throw me off his scent?' The King's face was deeply furrowed in what Malachi hoped was mock suspicion.

'On the contrary,' Malachi said, 'the recalcitrants in the north, including Ambrose, can wait to receive their punishment for abandoning their King. Meanwhile, we need to preserve our strength if we are to resist an attack from the south.'

'And what is this supposed threat from the south, eh?'

'A King has risen up in the Southern Desert and has managed to band together all the disparate factions in that vast land. They have raised a huge army and as we speak are preparing to march north.'

'How do I know what you say is true?' the King said.

'Would I bother your majesty with petty mistruths that would only lead to my swift demise? Am I not the first to impart the news of the problems on the North Road? Have you received any report that soldiers have been lost in the avalanche that cut off the road?'

There was polite but insistent knocking at the door, then a senior army officer poked his head nervously into the room. 'Come, come,' the King said. 'Tell me your news and it better be good.'

'News from the North, your majesty. Your army has engaged the enemy and dealt it a serious blow while incurring only light casualties itself.'

'What about the avalanche?' the King asked.

The soldier's face grew bright red. 'I was coming to that, sire. There has been a rockfall that prevents any further action for the time being.'

'How long until the road can be reopened?'

'I don't have that information, sire. I think it may take some time.' The soldier looked down at his boots.

'Some time? What sort of report is that? Of course it will take some time, everything takes some time doesn't it?' The King rose slowly to his feet as if to make the force of his words stronger. Malachi stood quietly, enjoying the exchange and feeling the King's obvious pleasure at being forewarned about the news. The officer's discomfiture was obvious. Malachi knew there was nothing more disconcerting or rarer than a monarch who knew what was going on.

'I meant to say some considerable time.'

'And by considerable, what do we mean? Is a day considerable? Or a week? Or a month? Or even a year? Which is it to be?' The King had approached the officer and was now shouting in his face. He was too close to the entrance to be able to back away without leaving the room completely.

'I believe that the blockage is fairly permanent, your majesty.'

'Then either you are a dunderhead or the man who sent you is. Which is it to be?'

The officer's florid face began to take on a purplish hue as he wrestled with the enormity of the question and the consequences of any answer. Malachi had experienced first-hand the way that the King reacted to any suggestion of being contradicted and it had not been a pleasant sight. The soldier was no doubt similarly aware of his predicament and was faced with either admitting his own failings or passing them up to his superior. He had to choose between the wrath of a king and the wrath of a general, a difficult choice indeed. Malachi allowed himself just the smallest of smiles.

'I will investigate the reason for the inadequacy of the information and report back, sire.'

'Then go and do that. And while you're at it, tell my Chief of Staff that his position is being reviewed because of your incompetence.'

The officer saluted and backed out of the room. The King turned to Malachi. 'Do you think they intended to inform me about the avalanche?'

'Perhaps not, sire. What the man told you had a paucity of detail that was practically insulting to one so wise as yourself. They know exactly how many men they lost but failed to say. They also know it will take many months to clear the road, and because the work will take us through the winter, it may be a whole year before the connection is remade. Add into that the consideration that the northerners may disrupt the activities, it may be even longer.'

'Do you know how many were lost in the battle?'

'Your majesty, there were no casualties caused by the battle because there was no battle. Seventy-four of our troops, mostly pikemen, were lost in the rock fall. None of the enemy was hurt. One of our men survived being buried and was dug out on the northern side. He is presently being returned to us, having been recruited by them as a spy. His name is Cuthbert.'

The King smiled. 'And do my generals know anything of this spy?'

'No, sire, only you and I are privy to that information.'

'Then perhaps I should appoint you as my new Chief of Staff, Malachi. What do you say to that?'

'I will serve in whatever capacity your highness sees fit. However, putting me in charge of your army seems to me to be a wise choice and one you won't regret.'

19

Cuthbert decided that he rather liked walking in the company of the little lady. She kept up a constant stream of engaging conversation, telling him about her history, travels, and adventures. He wished he'd done something even as remotely interesting that he could respond with. All he had to tell was mundane and ordinary.

'So Tyrant,' he said, 'tell me about him. Is he as mighty a warrior as everyone says he is?'

'Nothing of the kind, mighty warrior indeed. Don't make me laugh. If it weren't for me, he'd be in an early grave by now. As for fighting, I'm more than a match for that big clumsy fellow.'

'There's a rumour of an invulnerable spirit warrior fighting on the side of the north. That's not Tyrant, then?'

'That's not anyone, don't be daft. There's no such thing, it's all stuff and nonsense. He's just a man, that's all, and will squeal loud enough if he's struck just like any other man.'

Cuthbert looked behind him; Tyrant was trudging along twenty or thirty paces behind with Ant alongside him. 'So why are we walking into the enemy's hands, just the four of us? I can't fight, you're a bit small for battle if you don't mind me saying so, and the man in the hood is no better equipped than either of us. I've been counting all along on Tyrant. I saw him in action before the cliffs came down on top of me and have to admit being impressed.'

'I wouldn't worry if I were you,' Petra said. 'There are unseen eyes watching over us. I can say no more about it, so don't ask.'

'Are you a sorceress? I knew it. You are, aren't you?' Cuthbert's blood began banging in his ears. He should have known it the moment he set eyes on the diminutive figure. It was obvious now he came to think of it.

Petra said nothing, just scurried on ahead leading the way, leaving Cuthbert panting in her wake.

They seemed to have done most of the climbing now; they were high up following a windswept ridge between two huge peaks. Below them on both sides were precipitous slopes of broken stone, while the path ahead was too narrow to accommodate more than one at a time. The others were holding closer order now and Cuthbert was glad of it.

He thought of Cassie and a dull ache clenched his abdomen. He wondered what she was doing now, what she was thinking, and whether there was any hope at all for him. The frail softness of her body haunted him with a hollow pain in the base of his stomach.

His foot slipped on a loose stone and released a cascade of skittering rocks that almost carried him over the edge. He felt a steadying hand on his shoulder and heard Tyrant's voice close to his ear. 'You don't want to be daydreaming while you're up here. Keep your mind on your feet, feel the ground beneath your toes. We're almost over the hardest part; it will be downhill all the way soon enough without you having to dive over the edge to speed things up.'

Cuthbert took a breath to steady himself, then stepped cautiously, allowing his leading foot to achieve stability before raising his trailing leg. This slowed him down considerably and meant that Petra and Ant were getting much further ahead. After another hour of painful progress, the path began to head downwards, widen, and streaks of green could be enjoyed in the soil. When he raised his head to survey the forest below him, his companions were nowhere to be seen.

Instead, coming towards him was a line of familiar figures. Some of them were struggling to keep their heavy pikes aloft in the breeze. All of them walked awkwardly under the burden of heavy packs. Cuthbert looked around desperately for somewhere to hide, but he was perched up high with no obvious refuge and the cries from below left him in no doubt he'd been sighted. Tyrant, who had been in close order just moments before, was nowhere to be seen.

20

Lone watched a line of ants dancing in the heat haze as they crawled slowly towards her across the trackless dunes. A new buzz of excitement grew inside her as the blurred image began to resolve into a line of twenty or so camels. She was able to make out that some of them carried men swaying gently to the awkward rhythm of camel gait.

Over the five days since Patch's appearance, her initial jubilation had been replaced by frustration and anger. She had begun to believe that he'd come merely to taunt her and the talk of her release was only mockery. It hadn't felt like that at the time, but how else was she to judge when there had been no signs of any change in her circumstances. Until now.

A swarthy man with a pronounced squint, wearing an enormous curved sword with an ornate silver handle, rode at the head of the procession. When he saw her, he jumped off his mount onto the sand beside her. 'What have we got here?' he asked, reaching out to grab Lone's arm.

'I'm in need of safe passage out of this desert,' she replied, trying to keep this initial encounter as friendly as possible. After all, she expected to be travelling with these men for a considerable time. She twisted away from his grasp and took a few paces backwards.

'And I'm in need of some female company,' he said. 'In fact, we all are.' He turned to face his men who were in the process of dismounting. 'Me first,' he shouted, 'then you lot can do what you want with her.'

'Let's be clear about this,' Lone said. 'This is my oasis, my water, my fruit. If you want to drink, you will have to pay the price. That price is civility and respect. Otherwise, be on your way and find somewhere else to water your animals.'

'I am Bulgar, and I claim this place as my province and you as my conquest. If there's anyone who wants to dispute that, I'll be glad to draw swords with them and settle the matter. Now, how many more of you are there?'

'No more, I'm alone here and have been so for a very long time.' Lone watched the men assembling at Bulgar's side. They seemed a travel-weary bunch, robes stained with brown sand and tired eyes staring out through the slits in their loosely wrapped headscarves. 'Now, let's put aside this misunderstanding regarding my availability as a consort of any kind. I'm a married woman and wish only to get back to my husband.'

Bulgar lunged at her with both hands, grabbed her, and held her fast. His sour breath filled her nostrils as he spoke. 'Your husband won't mind if we borrow you for a while, and if he does, he can talk to my blade if ever we meet.'

This time there wasn't the option of disengaging and stepping back out of reach again; his grip was too strong. She also feared that her careworn clothes wouldn't be able to withstand any sort of tussle without falling to pieces and leaving her naked. Negotiations were proving difficult enough already without that added disadvantage. It would be much simpler if she could just gently persuade Bulgar to back off. His cooperation would undoubtedly make her travel plans much easier and she would be spared the awkward task of having to deal with a disparate group. The smell of his breath was, however, beginning to make her nauseous and all her good intentions were lost when he pulled her towards him and tried to kiss her on the mouth.

As she strove unsuccessfully to avoid his searching lips, Lone produced an angry spasm of energy that her hand directed into Bulgar's chest. His grip immediately slackened, he lost interest in groping her, and clasped his hands on his heart as if trying to protect it. Lone immediately regretted the strength of her response; it had been her intention to disable him temporarily, but, instead, she'd felt his heart explode and it was only a matter of a few more seconds before his body realised what had happened and shut down completely. Now she had to handle the rest of them without killing them all. Traversing the desert without any assistance wasn't a good option. She'd end up wandering around in circles until she died of thirst. These men knew the right direction to travel and, more importantly, where water could be found.

Bulgar's eyes protruded, his face went purple, then he flopped down onto the sand at her feet. Lone picked the scimitar from his corpse and held it aloft. Maybe killing him was the best thing to do. His breath did smell something awful and that would have made dealing with him, however compliant he might have become, very unpleasant. 'Bulgar is dead by my hand and now I proclaim myself your leader. If anyone wants to fight me then do it now, otherwise I command your allegiance.'

The men just stood and looked at her as if unable to believe what had just happened. Then one of them stepped forward, unwinding his scarf to reveal his face. 'A woman cannot be a leader,' he said. 'I will fight you so that we are not dishonoured.'

'What's your name?' Lone asked.

'I am Janvir,' he said.

'Tell me, Janvir, will all your comrades accept you as their leader if you defeat me?'

Janvir turned with outspread hands and there were a few shouts of 'yes' and the remainder nodded agreement. 'They will,' he said.

'Then I appoint you leader whether or not you fight me. All I ask is respect from you. Don't you agree that the slayer of Bulgar deserves respect? Or do you need me to kill more of you before you decide?'

'How did you do it? He just collapsed and fell; you used no blade on him,' Janvir said.

Lone took a deep breath. 'Witchcraft,' she said. An audible gasp came from the men and Janvir took a step back. 'I am a witch, or more accurately, a sorceress who was stranded here by an evil spirit. You would do well to think about the advantages to be gained from having me as part of your group. You might also think about the disadvantages of me treating you all as enemies.'

Janvir lowered the short sword he was clutching. 'My blade is of no value against witchcraft. If you promise not to harm us, we'll give you respect.'

'Then welcome, Janvir, and your men. I will treat you all as valued friends. My first gift is food and the best water you have ever tasted.' Lone breathed a sigh of relief at the neutral expressions that had replaced the overt animosity.

It was the first step in the right direction of getting out of her confinement, but there was so much more work to be done.

21

Tyrant lay still, head buried between two inadequate rocks, while the rest of him was relying on a tiny gorse bush as a shield. The soldiers were nearby; he could hear their voices, but he didn't feel sufficiently confident of his camouflage to risk any movement that might attract their attention.

Gradually, the voices reduced in volume and it seemed that the danger was passing. Tyrant stayed where he was, listening intently for the footfall of a less talkative type who might have taken it on himself to look around without shouting to his mates about it. Under the circumstances, Tyrant felt that keeping perfectly still was an essential prerequisite for successful concealment. He had been very concerned about the adequacy of his hiding place, but as the voices grew more distant, this was replaced by a feeling of pride. Most men would have been spotted right away.

His breathing was getting easier as he relaxed, confident that the danger had well and truly passed. There was no need to break cover yet, he decided, unless he counted the thorns that were pricking his backside and he'd pretty much grown used to them by now. When he did pull them out, he fancied he might even miss them.

He decided to count twenty more breaths before he poked his head over the rocks and spied out the land. At the count of fifteen, he felt something touch his leg. He froze, waited, then felt it again. It was either the exploratory nuzzling of an inquisitive animal or the toe of somebody's boot. In either case, his attention was going to be required, so he rolled over on his back to take a look.

Standing above him was a familiar hooded figure who was grinning from ear to ear. 'You do realise that your arse has been sticking up like a bad potato in a sack of greens?' Ant said.

Tyrant got to his feet and surveyed the hillside. 'That may be the case, but they didn't see me. That's what comes from being able to keep very still. It's a talent I have.'

'It's not much of a talent if you ask me,' Ant said. 'It's fortunate for you that they weren't inclined to search very hard.'

'And what makes you so sure of that?'

'A suggestion I was putting in their minds, that's all. They were convinced there was nobody else to see. Otherwise, they might have put an arrow into that big backside of yours just for the sport of it.'

Tyrant carefully removed the sharp pieces of gorse that were adhering to his person. If the boy wanted to think he'd kept the soldiers away using his mystical wiles, let him. His arse may have been poking out a little, but it was a motionless arse and those were the most difficult to spot.

'What happened to Cuthbert?' Tyrant asked.

'He's back with his own side. We've delivered him safely and in a way that will provoke the least suspicion.'

'That's that, then,' Tyrant said, 'we can go back to the lake.'

'Not yet. We have to keep going. I want to follow behind them in order to locate a vedhana. That way we can be sure of having access to Gort without having to get through enemy lines.'

'I thought you said you'd redrawn the device in the tower,' Tyrant said.

'I have, and we can use that if we need to. It may not be the best place to be turning up, though. Better we have an alternative that nobody else knows about. As soon as someone sees the vedhana has activated, there will at least be a guard placed on it even if they don't undo all my good work.'

Tyrant readied himself for another long hike, and his mind suddenly remembered the most difficult aspect of the journey so far. Petra. 'Where's Petra?' he asked.

'She was leading the way, with Cuthbert close behind. She'd have been the one who encountered the troops first. They took her unawares before she had time to conceal herself,' Ant said.

'I don't understand how we came to be caught cold by a bunch of soldiers. Where was that weird friend of yours while this was happening? I thought he was supposed to be keeping a lookout and that we'd get plenty of warning.'

'Jeremiah has been a bit difficult to pin down of late; he's not always as close by as I'd wish,' Ant said.

'Who's in charge between you two? I can't see the point if you can't rely on him doing his job. It's worse than not having him at all. We could have walked straight into a trap and been killed. Now we've definitely lost Cuthbert and let Petra fall into the hands of the enemy. Or worse, she may have been killed by now for all we know.' Tyrant tried to feel relieved at the prospect of no more Petra, but instead encountered a hollow feeling in his abdomen, which he hurriedly put down to hunger.

22

'What have we got here?' The cracked voice brought back only bad memories of fear and confusion involving the selection of pikes and the issue of substandard equipment. Cuthbert tried to remember the name of the wizened sergeant, but his mind had been put in such turmoil that it wasn't coming up with any suggestions that felt appropriate.

'Sergeant...' Cuthbert left the rank hanging in the air.

'Where's your pike, boy?'

'Lost it, sir.' Cuthbert winced; this wasn't the reception he'd hoped for, though at least this old soldier recognised him, even if it was for all the wrong reasons.

'And your helmet too, I see. You'll never make a soldier if you leave your equipment lying about the place. Where are the others?'

Cuthbert caught himself looking back up the slope where he could see Tyrant's backside protruding from the inadequate protection of a scraggy bush. He felt his face burning as he quickly returned his gaze to the sergeant's unsympathetic features. 'Er, there are none. Just me. I'm all alone.'

'So, everyone else is captured or dead?' The sergeant's question didn't seem to relate to Tyrant or Ant and, once he realised this, Cuthbert began to calm down. Even so, maintaining he was alone on the mountain trail with that prominent arse less than fifty paces away was not going to be a strategy that was going to last very long. All he could think to do was to prepare a surprised look for when Tyrant was spotted and hope for the best.

'Dead,' Cuthbert's voice sounded shrill in his own ears and he tried to bring it down a few octaves as he continued, 'and buried. There's only me left.'

'Captain Forrester? Was he killed?'

'Yes, everyone's dead.'

'A whole company of pikemen?' The sergeant was twisting his face as he spoke. 'Fifty men?'

Cuthbert began to understand the enormity of the event he'd been caught up in and his whole body began to shake as the memory of being buried alive snatched away his ability to breathe. 'I don't know how many,' he said, 'but there were no survivors apart from myself.'

'That can't be right. We thought we'd lost a dozen or so when the cliff walls came down, but presumed that all the rest of you were on the other side of the blockage and continuing to fight.'

'There was no fight, not really. Captain Forrester led us bravely, but we were no match for him.'

'Him? Are you telling me that our army was destroyed by just one man?'

'There were three men standing in the way of our advancing army, but only one of them stepped forward to challenge us. He disarmed Captain Forrester, then a dozen or so of the front ranks. Then he brought the whole mountain down on our heads.' Cuthbert could still smell the black earth that had clogged his nostrils and feel the breath being taken from his lungs. He'd described everything as he'd seen it but found his words difficult to swallow. Had Tyrant really done all that?

The sergeant opened his mouth to speak, but was distracted by urgent shouts. Three men emerged from the woods, dragging a small body with them. Cuthbert's heart sank at the sight of the way Petra was being carried and feared her dead. Then he realised that the noise was coming, at least in equal measure, from her. 'Put me down, you ratbags, or it'll be the worse for you. I'll slice you up and throw you out for the foxes. I'll make you wish you'd never been born, you ignorant ruffians. I'll…'

'Sergeant Grew, sir, we've apprehended a spy.' The men stood hanging on to their squirming bundle, who continued to complain loudly.

'What manner of creature is this, I wonder?' Grew asked.

'I'm a person; leave me alone. Tell your bruisers to unhand me,' Petra said.

'Let her go,' Cuthbert said. 'She's my friend, er, my guide. She's taking me over the mountains to re-join our army. Put her down, she's easily upset.'

'I thought you said you escaped alone,' Grew said, 'and that there was nobody with you.'

'I did and there is nobody else at all. I was referring to my poor unfortunate comrades in arms. Obviously, I had to have a guide, though.

Nobody would attempt to cross these mountains without one unless they were completely mad.'

'We did,' Grew said, 'and we got this far.'

'She'll help us get back if you let her go.'

'We already know the way back and she looks more like a spy to me than a guide. You know the penalty for spying.'

'Just because she's small doesn't make her a spy. She's just a normal person doing a kindness for me. I won't let you harm her.'

'I rather think you're not in any position to be making demands,' Grew said. 'And as far as we know, you could be a deserter yourself. The penalty for desertion is the same as for spying.'

'What kind of deserter would be undertaking a perilous journey back to his regiment, bearing information of the highest importance? I don't think the general will agree with you, Sergeant Grew. If you don't let her go and treat her with civility, I'll be forced to tell the general that you jeopardised my mission and refused to assist me.'

The look in Grew's eyes changed from derision to anger as the implications of Cuthbert's words seemed to sink in. 'We'll take her back with us,' he said, 'but any trouble from her and I'll treat you both as spies, general or no general.'

The soldiers placed Petra on the ground, then stepped back sharply as they released her. She grabbed hold of the slowest one and sunk her teeth into his arm. Cuthbert grabbed her arm and pulled her away. 'Leave it,' he said, 'they'll apologise in their own good time. Meanwhile, don't start any more fights.'

'I've not finished with you three, not by a long way,' Petra said.

'What about this warrior you were telling me about? Who is he and what is he capable of?' Grew asked.

Cuthbert looked into the grizzled face and took a breath. 'I think that kind of information is best told directly to the general and he can decide who else can be party to it. Military secrets aren't something to be revealed to all and sundry. With due respect, Sergeant Grew, I don't believe that you would be considered senior enough to be trusted with information that might cause widespread panic if it became common knowledge. I suggest you get me back to army headquarters and let them be the judge of that.'

'Our orders are to attack the enemy from the rear,' Grew said, 'and that's what I intend to do.'

'Then count me out. I'll take my vital information back without your help. By all means, carry on over the mountains and fight if you must. How many are you; ten?'

'Fourteen,' Grew said.

'Then you will be responsible for thirteen deaths apart from your own. You're no match for them. Even if there were a hundred of you, none of you would survive.'

Grew's face contorted again; this time Cuthbert imagined that this was an expression of the pain being caused by the thinking process. 'I suppose we'd better get you safely back; that's what the general would want. We'll turn round then.' The troop formed up behind him and turned their backs on Tyrant and his inadequately camouflaged arse. Cuthbert breathed a sigh of relief, then realised that Petra was still in a state where she could explode at any moment and get them both killed.

23

Lone watched with an animal concentration as the shabby group sat devouring her dates and nuts. She counted twelve of them and wondered if they considered thirteen to be a lucky number. In which case they should be happy to have her along as replacement for the boorish Bulgar.

Happiness was not, however, the predominant feeling she was receiving from these men. Janvir seemed the most positive, perhaps on account of having been handed the leadership without having to risk his life. The rest were a morose bunch, introspective and hardly making a sound other than slurping and smacking of lips.

'We need some more bignuts,' Janvir said.

Lone felt a wave of anger at his childish demands but, instead of telling him to get his own fruit, she channelled the energy and used it to dislodge several of them from high up in the tree closest to where the men were sitting. The nuts fell to earth with a series of ground shaking thuds, causing the diners to scatter in panic. 'Will they suffice or do you want more?' she asked. Janvir didn't reply. 'Tomorrow, we travel north. Tell your men to gather all the provisions they can carry ready for the journey.'

Janvir shook his head. 'There is nothing to the north but a vast desert. We're going south, back to where we came from.'

'But I need to go north, Janvir, and you owe me your assistance.'

Janvir took a stick and scratched a crude map in the sand. 'Here we are,' he said, poking a hole in the sand. 'Five day's travel due south will bring us to where we can sell our fruit at a good profit and live comfortably for a while.'

'And if we go north?'

'We cannot go north; it would take weeks to get through the desert. Even if we could carry enough water to do that, there would be nothing but death at the end of our journey. To the north lies a city built on the banks of the magical River Oort. Its inhabitants do not welcome strangers and they are protected by the river god. Few who venture north ever return.'

'But there will be food and water once we get out of the desert; that's the important thing. We can deal with anyone who wants to deny us passage.'

'No, our way is south to our homelands. There's nothing for us in the north.'

Lone wondered if these men were just another one of the many tribulations that had been heaped upon her by that vengeful demon Patch. She had all the necessary personnel and equipment on hand to take her back to where she needed to be, but they were tantalisingly out of reach. She realised that even her legendary powers of persuasion would be sorely pressed to make this recalcitrant bunch take her north. Another plan was needed and she had to formulate it quickly if she wasn't going to be stranded forever.

'Tell me what you know about the north and the people who live along the River Oort.'

Janvir swept back his long hair with his fingers and flakes of sand dropped onto his shoulders. His brow was studded with pearls of sweat, as if he was finding Lone's presence uncomfortable. 'I've never been there, but we have one with us who has made the trip.' He called over to the group, who were still eating as if their lives depended on the fullness of their bellies. 'Moussa, get yourself over here.'

A stocky man with a bushy black beard reluctantly dragged himself from the feasting mob, still clutching a handful of dates. 'Leave us to talk,' Lone told Janvir, who looked relieved at being dismissed. 'Now, Moussa, tell me about yourself.'

Moussa looked at her suspiciously through narrowed eyes and chewed slowly. 'What do you want to know?'

'Where do you come from?'

'Now, or originally?' He spat a pip onto the sand in front of her. Lone sighed inwardly; this man needed a lesson in cooperation, but she was reluctant to harm what was probably her only source of information regarding the route she needed to take with or without this surly bunch.

'Tell me first what function you serve in this band of nomads.'

Moussa's eyes flared up for an instant as if suddenly recognising the situation he was in. 'I'm the best camel driver you will ever find. My camel is the only one to be relied on to find water; she brought us to this place. If she had not, we would all be lying out in the sand with blackened tongues. But these men never show any gratitude. Oh no, quite the opposite. When we get back home, I'll struggle to get my fair share of what we bring.'

'What do you want, Moussa? To be leader? To command fear and respect from the others?'

'Respect would be nice, but I'm not like Bulgar. I don't have the muscle to make the men do my bidding.'

'So you're happy to follow Janvir now?' Lone said.

Moussa spat, raising a tiny eruption of sand. 'That man's no leader, whatever he might say or do.'

'Then who amongst you is?'

'Nobody, that's the truth of it. We relied on Bulgar and now he's dead we'll all be going our separate ways.'

'I'm going to travel north,' Lone said, 'tell me what I might find on the way.'

'Death, most likely.' Moussa smiled. 'If you escape the desert and reach the river, there is only one place to cross. There you will encounter savage people who have no tolerance for outsiders. They will never allow you passage.'

'But you have been there, haven't you?'

'Yes, a few years ago when I was persuaded to join a trading expedition and had no idea of what to expect.'

'Then tell me all you know.'

Moussa looked intently into Lone's eyes for a moment and she saw a flash of menace in them. 'It would be a waste of breath, both mine and yours,' he said, then stood up.

Lone got quickly to her feet and held him in her gaze. 'What do you mean by that?'

'Look over there at my comrades; what do you think they're doing?'

'They're eating and playing dice,' Lone said.

'We are men with no possessions and no money. What do you think are the stakes in the game?'

'Perhaps you all play for the sport of it,' Lone replied, feeling a sense of unease at the man's confident dismissal of her request.

'We have already drawn lots for who slits your throat as soon as you are asleep. The game is to decide in which order we violate your warm corpse. Believe me, you aren't going north, lady. You won't be going anywhere.'

Lone felt her blood grow cold in her veins as she visualised the men's intentions. Then it grew warmer with the prospect of vengeance. 'Why are you telling me this? I'll be on my guard from now on and you might find it more difficult to catch me unawares.'

Moussa shrugged. 'I'm not the one who has to wield the knife. Anyway, nobody can remain awake forever, not even a witch.'

'That may be an assumption that you live to regret. You should tell your comrades to play another game for the privilege of being the last to die in the attempt. But first, I need you to tell me your story. Come with me.'

Lone led a reluctant Moussa away from the glare of the campfire and into the trees. 'Here,' she said. 'This is my hammock, perfectly placed in the cool of the vegetation and away from the crawling things that inhabit the sand. You can sleep here if you tell me everything you know about the north.'

Moussa's white teeth glowed in the semi-darkness. 'I would be happy to share your bed, lady.'

'Don't worry about there being enough room; you'll be having it all to yourself,' Lone said, managing a smile at the man's effrontery.

'Your loss, lady,' Moussa said. 'I've had my share of wives and none of them has ever complained. You might want to reconsider.'

Lone shook her head, still smiling.

24

My goats were grazing high above the City of a Thousand Tents and I sat looking down at the enormous caravan being assembled. How I longed to be a traveller of the desert, visiting far-off places and bringing back exotic goods and special foods to feed my family. A familiar figure appeared far below my rocky perch, sending up puffs of sand as he scrabbled his way towards me.

'Demba, my friend, you looked as if there was a lion chasing you,' I said to the boy when he arrived, gasping and sweating.

'You have to go down there right now,' he replied. 'They need another camel driver and they're setting off very soon.'

'They won't take me; I have no camel. Even my biggest goat won't pass muster. Believe me, I've thought about it so many times. I've dreamed of having a goat so big that it could carry me, but it has never happened. Every time one gets to a decent size, someone slaughters it and eats it.'

'I told them you were the best driver in the city and all you needed was the camel. They have the camel, Moussa. The driver just toppled from it and fell dead. Just like that, no warning. I saw it myself. One moment he was up there barking out his orders, then his face went black and he fell dead. If you come now, they say you can have his camel. But hurry, there are others vying for the position.'

My heart filled with the joy of a thousand stars, the arrival of a long-lost friend and the prospect of a long and prosperous life. My goatherding days were in any case drawing to a close, as I could no longer stay up in the hills now that I was twenty years old. I should have been down in the city to make enough money for a dowry before it became too late and no self-respecting family would allow a goatherd to court their daughter. Needless to say, I ran as if the hounds of hell were scorching my tail and arrived breathless at the end of the caravan where a large female camel stood looking down her nose at me.

The supervisor poked me with the end of his whip and sneered into my face. He had the breath of a very sick goat and it almost emptied my stomach, what with all the excitement and the running as well. 'I'll show you,' I said. 'I'm the best camel driver you'll ever see.'

The camel looked at me and I at her. She opened her mouth slightly and pursed her lips as if she were going to whistle. Then she spat in my face. It was like being struck by a warm pat of dung; a feeling we goatherds were used to, as it was the standard method of rousing a boy who was sleeping on duty. I stood my ground, feeling the foul liquid dribbling off my chin. 'There,' I said, 'she likes me already. I told you I had a way with camels.'

She spat at me again, but this time I was ready and raised my hand to catch the snot. As I did so, she bared her teeth and sank them into my forearm. I can tell you it hurt like a thousand insect bites all at once; like the jaws of a lion would feel as it began to devour you. But I held my ground despite the excruciating pain, as I couldn't afford to let the supervisor see my agony. I put my mouth to the ear of the beast and whispered to her. 'I will honour you above all others,' I promised. 'I will treat you as a member of my family. I will give you precedence in all things as if you were a princess and I were your slave. I'll not sleep before I know you are comfortable and I'll not ride you until you allow me to. I'll not burden you with weight that you can't easily bear and I'll always love and cherish you as long as we both shall live.'

As I spoke, the pressure on my arm eased. She was an old camel and a wise one. I could tell she was thinking things over. I looked directly into her left eye and she gazed back at me with the look that penetrated my heart and allowed her to know that I meant what I said. She let go my arm and made farting sounds with her lips. 'There, now we are friends,' I said for the benefit of the supervisor.

'Very touching, indeed,' said the man, 'but it looks to me as if you got drowned in spit, then suffered a very nasty bite. Either you get on her back right now and show me some control or I'll get someone who can do it.'

There was a chorus of shouts from the crowd that had gathered; there were at least ten men clamouring for their chance. I later learned that this supervisor was a cousin of my friend Demba and that's who I owed even this fleeting opportunity to.

'Now,' I said to the camel, 'I have to ask you to take me up on your back. Please, I beg of you.' I tapped the camel lightly on her nose and watched the flare of annoyance in her eyes gradually fade. She then went down on her knees to allow me to alight and as she regained her feet, I sat proudly aloft, looking down at the supervisor and feeling like the greatest king in the world must feel when he sits on his throne. I leant forward and whispered my thanks, repeating all the promises I had made to her and adding a few more for good measure.

'You're hired,' the man said, 'though I would have bet good money that the camel would kill you before allowing you to ride her. She's got a bad reputation; that's why you got your chance. Now, there are four other camels for you to tend as well, but don't go getting any ideas. Everything those beasts carry back from the expedition is the property of the deceased owner's family. You're just the driver, understand?'

'Yes,' I answered, 'glad to be of service. I'll take good care of these beautiful camels and bring them back safe and well festooned with valuables and all I'll take for myself is what I can fit into the tiny pockets of my pantaloons.' That's what I said, but in my heart was my real intention. To sell everything I could before I returned to the City of a Thousand Tents and keep the proceeds for myself. As far as I was concerned, these were my animals from here on in. It was only fair, and fate had decreed that the owner was now forfeit, first of his life, and then of his beasts.

Men came bearing skins of water, which they tied to the drooping backs of my camels. I took all but one off Genna, for that's what I decided to call my old camel, and redistributed the weight onto the other beasts. They looked at Genna for a lead, asking for permission to bite and kick, but she took care of me in the knowledge that I was already being true to my word.

My family joined the cheering crowd that saw off the largest cavalcade ever assembled in the city. It was only as we entered the barren desert with the sun to my left that I realised I'd never even asked where we were going and for what purpose. The other camel drivers naturally despised me and would beat me with their whips if I tried to make conversation. I was left at the very end of the line, a position that meant that if I faltered or fell, there would be nobody to see or help me. I resolved to take good care of myself and I knew that they would be coming to me last, when all other food and water had been consumed. Only then would they remember Moussa and be grateful for his work.

The caravan was so long that it would have taken me hours to ride to the front, even if it halted completely. All the important people were at the front, leading the way and deciding where to stop. When they slept in green oases and cooled themselves with cool water, poor Moussa was left lying in the sand with only Genna and her sisters for company.

The weeks turned into months and still there was no sign of our destination. There was an old driver who seemed to have grown tired of animosity and beatings who told me that we were bound for the edge of the world where no man had ever been before and where untold riches were there for the taking. I offered the observation that if no one had ever been there, it was no surprise that the riches were untold, but he wrinkled his brow and flicked me with his whip. I resolved to hold my tongue even when confronted by arrant nonsense in the future.

One by one, my camels were taken forward, bearing their water skins and then returned unburdened. I was left with one half-empty skin of my own and very little in the way of food. My comrades further up the line seemed to have been stripped of everything, for they started to beg a swallow of water here and a bite of fig there. I had to sit up at night holding my knife at the ready in case they stole the rest of my water. It was only Genna's vigilance when I fell asleep that kept it safe. More than one of my erstwhile tormentors was sent packing with a bleeding limb.

We were months into our journey when the whole caravan was out of food and water and still the sun fried our skin and there was no sign of our destination. I had imagined that the old driver's words were fanciful, but now realised that the folly of which he spoke could be true. They took the first of my now unburdened camels from me so that they could feed its blood to the Grand Vizier and his son at the head of the caravan. It was only a matter of time before they took all of them and left me to bleach my bones in the sand.

I remembered my promise to Genna, as I am a man of my word, and resolved to do something before it became too late. I still had a small amount of water secreted under Genna's saddle where it was safeguarded by her reputation for violence. None of the other drivers would even approach her, let alone take the risk of interfering with her equipment. I would use this water surreptitiously to moisten her parched lips; she knew its vital importance and would have defended it with her life.

I halted my little posse of camels at the foot of a dune and watched as the rearward part of the caravan disappeared from sight. I took a little water, gave a few drops to Genna, and waited. After an hour, there was still no sign of interest in my disappearance. I reasoned that they had little incentive to turn around and search for a man and a few camels when their own lives depended on finding water up ahead. 'Genna,' I said, 'it's you and me now. We have to find our own way or risk being butchered to provide a rich man something to drink.' She had been sitting in the sand giving me welcome shade, but my words made her stand up then invite me to alight upon her back. She turned aside from the path that the caravan had taken and we travelled for the rest of the day with the sun at our backs. I never gave her any instructions or direction, content to leave my fate to the camel beneath me.

It was long past twilight and she continued to bear me under a million stars. She kept on plodding through the sand, stopping only when one of the other camels collapsed and lay prone in the sand. I moistened Genna's lips then fed the remaining water to the stricken beast, but even this failed to revive the poor thing and it rolled back its eyes and expired despite my ministrations.

The sweaty warmth of the night was replaced by the dry furnace of the day and still Genna kept on going. I was barely able to hang on to her saddle by the time she came to a final halt and fell down heavily onto her knees. I thought that this was the end of my paltry and difficult life, and I spent some time bemoaning all the things I'd been denied and every opportunity that I'd missed to do something worthwhile. I prayed on my knees to the star gods in the sky to allow me one more chance at this human existence before abandoning me. As I prayed, Genna began to make that awful camel sound that curdles your insides. 'Can't you see I'm praying?' I said. 'It's not polite to disturb a man at his prayers and I suggest that you make whatever peace you can with whichever deity presides over camels like you.'

She seemed to take exception to my response and, before I could ascertain her intentions, I was flying through the air, propelled by a mighty blow from her neck and head. I landed face down in the sand next to a rock, which would have surely spilled my brains had I landed on it. As I was spitting out the sand, I discovered a small leather bucket that was lying by the rock. When I picked it up, I found that it had a long rope attached that had been buried in the sand. The end of the rope went beneath the rock I'd almost been killed by.

The rock slid aside easily and beneath it was a deep hole about the width of my forearm. From this came the cool, delicious smell of water. It was a well. Genna had found it amongst this endless tract of featureless desert and I had been saved from certain death by my beloved, but recalcitrant, camel.

***

Moussa paused from his telling and looked down at the sleeping Lone. The moonlight outlined the softness of her throat and a million stars reflected in the blade of his knife.

25

The soldiers have taken the little woman into the forest.

Ant registered Jeremiah's first words for a long time with some annoyance. 'Where have you been? I needed you here.'

Sorry, master, I've been unavoidably detained. I got back to you as soon as I could.

'Master? You've never called me master before. I don't like it.'

Sorry, master, I mean, Ant, sorry again.

'What do you mean by detained? Who detained you and why?'

Er, nobody really, it's just that I was so far away trying to find things out for you.

'Where exactly?'

Gort, master, I went all the way there to see what was happening. Oh, sorry, I mean Ant.

Ant felt uncomfortable with Jeremiah's words, and the lightness seemed to have disappeared from their relationship. Jeremiah was acting like a servant, which Ant had never considered him to be. He had always assumed that Jeremiah could decide to go his own way at any point and was grateful for what assistance he could bring while he remained. Now, there was a difference to the relationship that he couldn't fathom. Still, Ant was glad to have him back. He needed to be able to follow the soldiers at a discreet distance and know what they were doing. Jeremiah was essential for that. He would also be the only means of safely keeping an eye on Cuthbert and communicating with the boy once he had been received back into the army.

Tyrant was still sitting on a ridiculously inadequate rock and looked like a hen squatting on an oversized egg. His face was set in a solid frown. Ant could feel the energy brewing inside him and knew that his next action was going to be to charge down the hill, waving that sword of his. If that happened, the outcome could only be bad. He'd be forced to assist Tyrant in his attempt at slaughtering everyone and he wasn't certain he was up to the task. In the heat of battle, things would move too quickly for subtle persuasion. Even if they somehow prevailed, the situation would be messy in both physical and tactical terms. As things were,

Cuthbert was successfully inserted back where he wanted him to be, and the only complication was Petra, who should never have been involved in the first place. Why Tyrant had insisted on bringing her along was quite beyond him.

'Stay here, I'll see what's happening down there and what's in the minds of the soldiers,' Ant said.

'I'll come with you,' Tyrant replied.

'You can't, not unless you can leave your body behind. I'll not be taking mine.'

'So, your unreliable friend has shown up at last, has he? Tell him it's his fault that they have Petra, and if anything happens to her, he'll have me to answer to,' Tyrant said, shifting uncomfortably on his perch but at least showing fewer signs of preparing to rush headlong into battle.

As Ant connected with Jeremiah, he felt a momentary jolt of unfamiliarity as if it was the first time he'd tried this and Jeremiah was reluctant to accept him. Then he was swooping free through the trees, following a gaggle of dirty, tired men as they trudged back the way they'd come.

Petra was being held in the middle of the group, her hands bound behind her and her mouth threatening all manner of punishment for her captors. She stumbled and fell, and unable to break her fall with her hands, she hit the earth hard with her face and lay completely still. As rough hands dragged her to her feet and pushed her forwards, her torrent of abuse temporarily stemmed.

Treat her kindly; she's a special friend of the Colonel.

'Stop!' The sergeant's voice froze everyone in their tracks. 'Untie that woman's hands.'

She's only tiny; she couldn't possibly pose a threat.

'Allow her to walk freely, just keep an eye on her, that's all. No more rough treatment. We have to deliver her safely to the Colonel for questioning. If she's hurt, we'll be on latrine duty for months.'

Cuthbert went over and put a protective arm around Petra who, thankfully, was remaining quiet, at least for the time being.

That Cuthbert is a brave lad, maybe even a hero. He'll be warmly welcomed back at camp and his testimony will be invaluable in the fight against the North.

94

'Come on, lads,' Grew shouted, 'we've done well. When he sees what we've brought back, I'll bet the general lets us all go back to Gort for a rest.'

Ant moved his attention to Petra. *We're close by. Be patient.* He felt her shock of recognition at his words, then the flood of energy that accompanied it. She stopped, looked around, and took a deep breath before smiling uncharacteristically at her captors and continuing with more of a spring in her step.

'Well?' Tyrant asked as soon as Ant opened his eyes and sat up.

'They're both unharmed and being treated well. There's no need to act hastily; we can afford to wait for an opportunity to rescue Petra without compromising Cuthbert. I've no doubt that if we attack, he'll side with her and that wouldn't be good.'

'I've been meaning to ask you about that,' Tyrant said. 'What's so important about getting Cuthbert back to the army? You've got Jeremiah to do as much snooping with as you might wish. Why put the lad at mortal risk?'

Ant felt the doubt behind Tyrant's words and this disturbed him. Of all the people involved in this plan, Tyrant was the one who most needed to be kept onside. If he lost faith, the whole situation might easily be lost. 'Cuthbert can be relied on to physically assist us, Tyrant. That will prove crucial at some stage. Eavesdropping and whispering in people's ears is all very well up to a point. If we are to prevent widespread bloodshed, Cuthbert will prove invaluable.'

'I still don't see how,' Tyrant said, 'but if you say so, then I'll go along with it. I suppose your powers aren't limitless, so I can't expect you to do everything on your own.'

'Thank you,' Ant said, but he could still feel the uncertainty in the reply and wondered what he might have to do in order to resolve the problem.

26

Lone opened her eyes to the sound of cloth tearing. Above her, Moussa's ample backside appeared as the rip opened. Then the whole of him fell through the hammock and was deposited on the sand beneath. Lone didn't know whether to laugh at his discomfort or cry at the demise of her beloved hammock that had taken her weeks to make. The bewildered look on his face made up her mind for her, and she let out a chuckle.

Moussa rubbed his sore back and looked across at her, his face changing to a look of horror. She followed his gaze to the prone figure lying face down in the sand. 'I suppose that's the one who drew the short straw and had to try to kill me.'

Moussa nodded. 'What happened? How did you do that?'

'I don't like to be disturbed when I'm resting. There are certain precautions that I take that your friends should be aware of. One of these seems to have killed your comrade.'

'You fell fast asleep during my story,' Moussa said. 'I thought that nothing could rouse you, not even my exciting tale.'

'I didn't find your story either exciting or useful.'

'But I was just getting to the good bit where I encountered the dwellers of the River Oort. But if you don't want to hear it, I'll leave you to your hammock.'

Lone looked at the tattered wisps of cloth blowing in the gentle breeze. 'You've destroyed my precious hammock; the least you can do now is fetch us some breakfast and finish the story. It had better be good, though, otherwise I might take my sorrow at losing my hammock out on you. And while you're at it, get your men to retrieve their comrade's body.'

As Moussa shuffled off, still rubbing his back, Lone looked at the black tidemark of once-wriggling insects that had formed an outline around where she slept. It never ceased to amaze her how many creepy crawlers lay invisible in the sand, just waiting for an opportunity to bite her while asleep. It had been much easier to control them up there in her hammock.

She thought about the situation she had been placed in and had to admit that it could have been much better. As things stood, if she remained with these men, she faced the prospect of a new corpse every night. That wouldn't assist her to persuade these men to help her get back to the North. Every failed assassination attempt had to increase the animosity they felt towards her. Unless something changed, she faced the prospect of a diminishing potential workforce and the chance that one of them would succeed where his fellows had failed.

She should get rid of the lot of them, she supposed, but then what would she be left with? The camels and horses could carry food and water for her journey but they would need tending and she doubted her patience would last long if she had a bunch of uncooperative beasts to contend with. A couple of horses might be fine, but she doubted that they could carry enough water for her to have a decent chance of survival. Those camels looked as if they were a law unto themselves, as Moussa's interminable tale was testament.

Once out there in the desert, she'd be at a disadvantage because she had never tried to survive in such a wilderness before. These men were the repository of survival instincts built up over years of desert travel and would know instinctively what to do under almost every circumstance. She watched Moussa return laden with food and resolved to hear the rest of his story before she decided what to do.

He sat down opposite her and began to eat silently. Two men appeared and dragged their fallen comrade away, then Lone and Moussa were left undisturbed.

Moussa continued his tale.

27

So, my lady, you will recall that I had been saved by my camel who had brought me to a secret well in the middle of that vast trackless desert. Now I had water, I began to feel the hunger that had built up inside me. I had more than a careful look at the smallest camel, but had no illusions about my fate should I try to use one of Genna's sisters to sustain me. No, lady, we were all in this together.

When the skins were all filled and the moon was bright enough to continue safely, Genna carried me once again and I let her choose the direction. She chose wisely, for after only a few hours, I saw the red glow of a campfire up ahead and the first signs of vegetation. Genna and the other camels stopped and began to devour the first scrawny bush they encountered, but I urged her to continue towards the more succulent grasses that must lie ahead.

There were six men sat around the fire. I was greeted cheerfully and admitted to their group. There was no animosity or suspicion directed my way. They accepted me as a fellow traveller and treated me well, sharing their food and drink. Genna was happy that I had been true to my word and brought her to some decent fodder.

Yes, my lady. I know you think that the details of camel driving are not the stuff of which interesting stories are made, but bear with me for a few more moments, for I had encountered the first inhabitants of the north and it is these people that you expressed a wish to hear about.

No, my lady, I could not have just jumped to this episode without telling you of the circumstances leading up to it. That would have been most unsatisfactory and made for a very dull telling indeed.

Yes, my lady, I am getting on with it.

They asked me where I was from and where I was going, but I gave them the impression of a man too long in the desert whose brains had been fried by the sun and his faculties dulled by too long without water. They only smiled and allowed me to follow when they set off in the morning. There were three more nights to spend with these kindly men, and I still think of them as that, even though they did try to steal my camels during our journey together. They can be forgiven for that, lady, for men have to obey their instincts and it is not unreasonable to try to liberate some poor camels from the care of a simpleton who might not be able to look after them properly. Genna bit one of them quite badly and I showed my knife to another's throat before they decided that the animals weren't, after all, worth such trouble.

They led me to a city, the magnificence of which you cannot imagine. This place was astride the river and there was a bridge so long that it went completely to the other side and so wide that it could accommodate ten camels side by side. Not only was it long and wide, but it was made entirely of stone. I can tell you that it took my breath away, or rather it would have if I had any left from looking at so many walls and houses.

The whole city was surrounded by a stone wall so high that you could have stood three men on each other's shoulders and they still wouldn't reach the ramparts. Inside was an awesome array of bazaars that sold everything I ever saw or heard of and a million things I never did. There were stalls with sweet things of every colour, entire streets of them. Then there were the cooking fires, a whole area filled with vendors of the most aromatic and succulent hot food. My stomach leaps with anticipation even now as I recall the sights and smells.

Genna's wrath was a small price to pay for access to all this opulence. I sold her sisters one by one and feasted daily in a manner that even the richest man in the City of a Thousand Tents could not dream of.

It was several days after my arrival that I heard a great commotion and witnessed crowds running to line the walls of the city. I joined the throng and managed to get myself a view of what was going on.

It was the caravan I had left that had finally arrived. I have to say that, although somewhat depleted in numbers, it nevertheless provided an impressive spectacle. They must have found food and water aplenty for the men looked fierce and strong again, riding proud and upright under the gaze of the city's inhabitants. The Grand Vizier and his son were dressed in their ceremonial finery and the sun flashed off the precious stones that adorned their necks and chests. Their voices bellowed out in greeting. 'We come in peace, brothers of the north. Admit us to your fair city so that we may be friends and share in the bounty of this wonderful realm of ours.'

They rode slowly towards the gate, but their passage was blocked by a diminutive figure. This was a tiny man, half or less of normal size, so that he looked more like a child. He was dressed in a golden turban and wore a jacket with no sleeves and baggy pants that were the colour of the sky.

'Stand aside,' the Grand Vizier shouted down at the little man. The crowd pressing my sides seemed to take a sudden inward breath all together, as if in alarm. As for myself, I found nothing so threatening in the voice to warrant any sort of reaction, but several people around me even felt it prudent to flee the walls altogether.

'Go home, don't come back. We don't want your kind here.' I could only just make out the little man's words; they were spoken in such a high-pitched voice that I felt like laughing. Nobody around me was even smiling; it was as if they were bracing themselves for something terrible.

The Grand Vizier nodded to his son, who drew a long, curved sword from its scabbard, then trotted his horse towards the little man. My crowd gasped as if it were a single person, then one or two voices were raised in anguish. I felt sorry for the little man, but if he chose to stand in the way of someone as important and short-tempered as the Grand Vizier, he should have known that his head would be chopped off as a lesson in manners.

Behind the Grand Vizier rode a huge army of our finest fighters; by now they were brandishing their weapons and ready for battle. From where I stood, I could see no defensive force to counter them. Unless I counted the little man in the golden turban, which I, of course, didn't. I felt like the people around me were helpless in the face of this invincible force and that the Grand Vizier and his men would take over the city without opposition.

The sword flashed in the sun as it attempted to sever the little man's head. It made no contact at all. Its intended victim disappeared completely and the Grand Vizier's son was almost unseated in his surprise. Then I saw an amazing thing; the little man reappeared on the walls only a short distance from where I was standing.

Had I wished, I could have taken three strides and then touched him. Those nearest to him had the opposite idea, though, and I was forced backwards in the rush to get away. Soon, there was only me on the walls to witness what happened next.

The little man raised his arms and, as if in response, a column of sand rose out of the ground in front of the Grand Vizier and his men. The sand twisted into a whirlwind that grew in size and intensity. I had to cling to the walls for dear life, unable to see what was happening down below. For what seemed an age, the wind blew sharp sand into my face and threatened to dislodge me. My arms grew tired, and I feared I would have to let go and fly off the walls to be smashed to pieces below. Then, mercifully, the hurricane finally eased and died down completely. I struggled to my feet to find the little man had gone from the walls and the people were streaming out of the gate as if anxious to aid my stricken comrades, who had been flattened by the whirlwind and now lay still under a thin covering of sand.

As I watched, the full horror of my mistake revealed itself. These people weren't dashing out to offer help, they were robbing the corpses of anything valuable or useful, even to the clothes that they wore. It was a terrible sight. Not a single man or animal, it seemed, had escaped instant death at the hands of that weird midget in a golden turban. I saw men fighting over the Grand Vizier's jewels and I realised that the crowd had anticipated what was going to happen and had left the walls to be in a better position for looting.

Which means, my lady, and my heart sank almost to the ground at the realisation, that this was not the first time such a massacre had taken place. It seemed that this was how visitors to the city were customarily treated, and it saddened me to behold.

When I asked about the man in the turban, I was faced mainly with frightened silence. People were reluctant to talk openly about him, but I did find out that he was a cruel master who frequently preyed on the inhabitants. People would disappear suddenly and without trace. Any major wrongdoing was summarily punished by death. But the worst thing of all, lady, made my blood turn as cold as a mountain stream.

It was the river itself. I thought of it as the benign giver of life when I first beheld it, but it turned out to be the exact opposite. Oh, yes, you could drink its life-giving waters, of course you could. But bathing was only for the foolhardy, demented souls who had been driven mad by the constant heat of the sun. Many of them never returned to the shore. The denizens of the river were numerous, rapid, and deadly.

That's why, lady, the city had grown so powerful. The bridge provided the only safe passage across the treacherous waters and the city controlled the bridge. The little man with the turban, who they called Zaire, had the ability to destroy any who might attempt the crossing without permission.

I stayed there for almost half a year, working in the bazaars and enjoying an easy life. I fell in love on numerous occasions, but without family or means, I had no chance of ever getting myself a wife. If I had, I'd still be there, believe me. So, I left the city and the story of my return to my homelands is one of a long and difficult journey, during which many obstacles were faced and overcome by the sheer willpower of a brave man and the graciousness of the gods.

But I can see from your face that you are weary now and that the telling might be best left for another time.

28

The air was cool and pleasant in the forest and the damp grass felt soothing as it brushed against Tyrant's calves. It was the kind of day and the kind of place that he would have been very happy to savour in the times when he had nowhere in particular to go and nothing pressing to achieve. Instead, Tyrant sighed with regret as he trudged slowly through the forest in the wake of Petra's captors. He regretted ever getting involved in all this nonsense. The fight between the North and the King was none of his business and something that others had managed to contrive. If he died trying to put a stop to it, they would undoubtedly think of other ways to provoke conflict. People are like that when they attach themselves to a place or a person or even a thought, then defend it with other people's lives.

Tyrant thought of Petra and how he'd somehow managed to attach something of himself to her. Admittedly, it was mostly her doing, but he had given way to the woman's constant assault on his sensitivities. The fact that they had spent a lot of time and shared some unique experiences didn't help. Now, she was in the hands of the enemy and he only had this boy's word that she was being treated well. That bothered him.

Ant was also beginning to worry him. He couldn't recall ever having agreed to either this journey or the plan it was based on. Yet, here he was, blundering through the woods, getting ever closer to an enemy who would welcome the chance to kill him. And all on the flimsy word of a boy who fancied himself as a magician and had a dubious relationship with an elusive and unreliable demon who might not have their best interests at heart. It would be uncharacteristic of a demon if he had.

As he walked behind Ant, picking his way cautiously over fallen trees and skirting the most generously thorned bushes, Tyrant couldn't help but think about how angry he'd get if any harm came to Petra. The first wave enveloped the men who had taken her, then extended to the whole of the King's army. He visualised killing as many as he could of them before they overwhelmed him. The imaginary action made him feel even more angry. Even if he succeeded in killing ten or even a hundred, it wouldn't make a difference to anyone but him. All those dead boys like

Cuthbert would be of no concern to a King who could call on replacements aplenty.

He let out a loud snort, which made Ant turn towards him in alarm. 'Are you unwell, Tyrant?' he asked.

'I can't do this,' Tyrant replied, his breath coming in great whoops as he tried to control himself. 'It makes no sense to put Petra and Cuthbert in danger. Why have you allowed it?'

'Petra is fine, believe me. And Cuthbert is exactly where we want him.'

'He's where you want him, Ant, but I don't think it's in the lad's best interest.'

'Why do you care what happens to Cuthbert, especially after what he did to Cassie?'

'Knowing Cassie, I'm sure that nothing happened between them that wasn't her idea from the start. She's a strong girl and gets what she wants; in this case, it was Cuthbert. The boy wouldn't have stood a chance so I can't blame him for anything. He certainly deserves some consideration. Not least because Cassie will be upset if he never returns to her. You don't need a spy, Ant, you have that Jeremiah to do your creeping about for you.'

'We already discussed this and what I said then is still true. Cuthbert can help us prevent a full-scale war and protect the northerners from the King. You'll have to take my word for it.'

Tyrant felt a gust of calm sweeping through his body. The boy was right. He knew what he was doing. All he had to do was go along with whatever he said and everything would work out for the best. Petra would be returned unscathed and the army would retreat to Gort and stay there. He could relax.

A sudden vision of Lone came into his mind. He remembered the way he had felt in her presence, how she could make him think and do almost anything. It was only after she had been rendered unconscious that he had been able to strand her in the desert. Ant was having the same effect; his words were just as compelling. Tyrant felt uneasy at the thought that Ant might be just a younger version of Lone. If that were the case, there was only one thing he could do about it.

29

Lone was only half listening to Moussa's long account of his journey through the desert. She felt like stopping him and giving him a good shake, but she reasoned that there might be things she might learn about the journey she would almost certainly have to take.

Her predicament was obvious when she thought about it. How much of it was still being manipulated by Patch was hard to tell, but she doubted that the vindictive demon had finished with her completely. What saddened her most was the obvious power that Patch wielded, and how she could have used that while he was in thrall to her. It was an opportunity that would never come her way again.

Moussa finally arrived at the City on the River, and her interest was piqued by the way it sounded even larger and more opulent than Gort. The small figure in the golden turban was even more interesting and made her determined to see this place for herself. But how?

'Thank you, Moussa, for your captivating tale. I would prefer it if you stopped at this point and allowed me to ask you some questions. Would that be agreeable?'

Moussa pulled a face that indicated disappointment, but fell dutifully silent.

'Was the man in the golden turban the ruler of the city?' she asked.

'No, there was a King who lived in his palace on the north side of the river. It was a magnificent sight, lady, with tall minarets at each corner and thousands of bedrooms to house his many wives.'

'Did you actually see this King in the flesh?'

'Not, I, dear lady, but I have spoken to those who have. They say that, although he is thought to be very old indeed, his appearance remains that of a young warrior.'

'This King, does he have a name?'

'They call him Khan, lady, and bow solemnly at every mention of his name. He has a mighty army, they say, and is ruler of the whole world.'

Lone smiled. 'The whole world apart from the parts that you and I inhabit. Still, it seems to me that there are powerful forces at work in Oort City and there is all the more reason for me to go. Take me there, Moussa, and I will make you a very rich man with a thousand camels and twenty wives.'

Moussa smiled at the thought. Whether it was the prospect of the camels or the wives, Lone couldn't be certain other than he was tempted by her offer. 'Tell me who and what you need for the journey. How many camels, which men, and how much water we will have to carry?'

'It's not so simple, lady. There are the other men to consider, not least of which is our new leader. He has decreed that we return south laden with fruit to sell in the city bazaars.'

'How many men, Moussa?'

'Two is all it will take to drive the camels; myself and another. But we will need at least ten camels; Janvir will be left with only five. They would barely carry the water the others will need to get home safely. There will be no capacity for any goods to sell when they get there. He will never agree to let us have his camels in any case.'

'Who besides you is the best camel driver?' Lone looked into the man's eyes, which were wide and receptive at last.

'Janvir is almost my equal. His camels are soft and responsive, never any trouble. The others have wilder and more unruly beasts in the main.'

'Then it will be the three of us; you, me, and Janvir. Pick your camels carefully, but don't tell the others what we're planning.'

'But I haven't agreed to any of this even if it were possible, which it isn't.'

'If you don't want to live the rest of your life in luxury, the envy of everyone you meet, then I'll find someone amongst your colleagues who does.'

'It will be hard and dangerous, lady.'

'The rewards will be immense.'

'What about Zaire, the terrible man in the golden turban? Nobody can withstand his magic, not even you.'

'That's probably true and I don't intend to let it come to that. Imagine if Zaire were to be working at our command? Then how would our prospects appear?'

'Can you do that? Bring him under your control?'

'I have succeeded with far more powerful beings than Zaire,' Lone said, feeling the truth of her statement and letting it seep into Moussa's hardened heart. She could see on his face that he was starting to believe that becoming rich was a real possibility. Now she had to decide what to do with the others, the ones she didn't need. The ones who were trying to kill her.

30

The King waved Malachi into one of the ornate but excruciatingly uncomfortable chairs that flanked the throne. The several others already in the room were not offered such dubious consideration and remained standing. Malachi recognised Vargas, the King's explorer and trusted confidant. He knew exactly what to expect from the tall, deeply tanned man who looked down his nose at Malachi as if examining an unwelcome insect that was crawling under his boot.

It was obligatory to wait until the King spoke and there was a brief and uncomfortable silence in which barely disguised looks of hatred were directed Malachi's way. 'Vargas has recently returned from the southernmost part of the world and I would like you to hear his report, Malachi, as it differs greatly from that which you wish me to believe. One of you is wrong and I need to decide which one of you it is. Much depends on my being able to trust the counsel I am offered, don't you agree?'

Malachi found himself nodding in unison with Vargas.

'Good, so you must see that false information, however genuinely offered, is something that a king cannot countenance. This may be the result of misunderstanding or misinterpretation, but nevertheless has to be regarded as detrimental to the crown and needs to be eradicated. Wild speculation does not serve anybody and I regard it as a treasonable offence.

'So, I need to choose my source of information wisely. Vargas, tell Malachi what you have found in the south of my kingdom and why you believe that what he has told me is false.'

Vargas stepped forward and faced the King, a slight smirk on his face. 'Your majesty, I have been your loyal servant and trusted advisor for many years and can proudly state that the information I have provided to you has always been accurate. There is nobody in this world that has studied its geography more assiduously than I have and I can safely say that my knowledge is unsurpassed. It was with a great deal of puzzlement and no small degree of alarm that I heard Malachi's assertions. I have been to the most southernmost reaches and can categorically state that there is nothing there but miles of inhospitable desert. The idea that an army of any sort could suddenly emerge from that arid wilderness is not only absurd but, in my humble opinion, reckless in the extreme. Where such a notion comes from is quite beyond my comprehension.'

Malachi waited until Vargas had finished polishing his self-importance on the King's garments, though he was sorely tempted to afflict the pompous idiot with a coughing fit or even some more permanent constriction in his windpipe. He held his silence and waited.

'So, Malachi, what do you say to a man who has been there and knows it all? Do you want to retract your advice in the face of the facts?'

'Your majesty, I would beg you to permit me to ask a few questions of my learned friend in order to clarify matters and understand more of where our knowledge might be different and why,' Malachi said.

'By all means, but I hope you realise how much depends on your answers. If I think you have been misleading me, whether deliberately or not, I am inclined to take a dim view.' The King settled back in his throne with a fat smile on his face.

'Vargas,' Malachi said, 'I would like to understand more about your mapping explorations. What exactly do you think lies to the south of this kingdom?'

'The whole world is one kingdom, ruled by one King, our King.'

'Very well, if you insist, I'll rephrase the question. What lies at the southernmost part of our glorious monarch's kingdom? And if you say more of his kingdom, I'll come over there and strangle you.'

'There, there, no need to get shirty,' the King said with obvious enjoyment. 'Vargas is correct in his assertion that everywhere is part of my kingdom.'

'Yes, your majesty, it is,' Vargas said.

'Including all the places that you haven't been and all the cities that you're unaware of? I understand the principle, your majesty, but in practical terms, what Vargas is agreeing to is absurdity in its extreme.'

'Are you questioning the validity and extent of my realm?' The King's face puckered as he spoke; any sign of amusement had disappeared.

Malachi knew he had to tread a fine line between showing Vargas to be a fool without including the King in that description. 'Your majesty can only rule over a land that has been identified and explored. It's unreasonable to pretend that even as august a monarch as yourself could possibly do otherwise. The extent of your kingdom has therefore been defined by Vargas and his colleagues. If he hasn't managed to visit some part of the world, then that must lie outside your realm. You are unaware of its existence and its people are equally unaware of yours.'

'Arrant nonsense,' Vargas spluttered into life as Malachi's words struck home. 'I have travelled the length and breadth of the world and can assure your majesty that his reign is secure in every part.'

'Tell me then,' Malachi said, 'what lies to the south? It's a simple question.'

'And an easy answer,' Vargas said, 'for I have travelled recently to our southernmost outpost and beyond. All that lies to the south is an arid desert where fierce heat prevents there being any life at all. There are no subjects there for our King to rule.'

'How far into this desert have you ventured?' Malachi asked.

'Several days' journey, until our horses were too hot and thirsty to continue. There is nothing out there, I can vouch for that.'

'Then you have not gone far enough to find the place I have told the King about. Where there is a city as large as Gort and an ambitious King.'

'Impossible,' Vargas said, 'and even if it what you say is true, nobody could make a longer journey through the desert than I did.'

'What if there was water in the desert? Would that change your view?'

'There is no water, how could there be?'

'There are deep wells, their locations known only to the local inhabitants. You can be forgiven for your error; it's an easy one to make. I hope that the King will forgive you in the knowledge that your omission was made in ignorance rather than malice.' Malachi was watching the King's face, which had relaxed into its normal expression of slight boredom.

'I don't accept your wild fantasies about water in a desert,' Vargas said. 'Everything you say is pure conjecture, whereas I have seen the place with my own eyes.'

'How about the north? What do you say about that?'

'The northernmost part of the kingdom is a wilderness as cold and bleak as the southern desert is arid and featureless. Neither place is inhabitable and therefore of little concern to the King.'

'Then perhaps we should journey together so that I can show you just how badly mistaken you've been,' Malachi said.

'Such a journey, even if it were possible, would take months, years even. The King would grow old awaiting our return. What possible service could that be to him?'

'None, I agree, if the trip were to take that long. With the King's permission, though, I can take you there and back within one day.'

The King's eyebrows raised. 'Now that's an interesting proposition if ever I heard one. What do you say, Vargas? Are you willing to accompany Malachi?'

Vargas stood open-mouthed and nodded.

31

The straps of his pack had chafed the tops of Tyrant's shoulders until no matter how he adjusted the load, it caused him discomfort. As he walked, he wished for the days he had been able to travel light, bearing only what he could stuff in his pockets. In those days, his arms could swing free and so could his mind.

Ant kept slowing down the pace, stopping from time to time, forcing him to wait impatiently for a few seconds and disrupting the steady rhythm he liked to maintain. Because of this stop/start regime, there was less opportunity for a proper rest break, where he could discard the pack and stretch out his weary body on the soft carpet of forest vegetation. The same vegetation that clung to his legs and tried to trip him at every step while he was walking.

The unexpected sight of a man tending his garden in front of a substantial house was a welcome distraction. The man, an old wiry figure dressed in what Tyrant could only describe as rags, pulled a long fat carrot out of the ground, then straightened up to smile at them.

Tyrant stopped and smiled back, more at the delicious-looking carrot than the man.

'We need to keep moving,' Ant said.

'I need a rest and some lunch,' Tyrant replied.

'You've only just had breakfast,' Ant said and carried on walking.

'Have you any food to spare for two weary travellers who have been walking for many days and living on scraps?' Tyrant asked.

'You're welcome to share what I have,' the man replied, still with a grin on his face that was beginning to look a little bit forced by now.

'Thank you kindly,' Tyrant said, heading towards the house and the distinctive smell of cooking. His stomach rumbled in anticipation and it was in no mood to take notice of any entreaties from Ant. 'We can catch up easily, it will avoid us having to keep pausing. I hate all that stopping and starting, I like a proper walk where once I get going, I can keep on going. It's better for my legs.'

Tyrant picked up a few carrots from beside the man's feet and began to chew on one. It tasted sweet and earthy and could have done with a wash, but he finished it quickly and started on another. 'Shall I take these inside for you?' Tyrant asked.

'If you like, though I doubt there will be any left for the pot by the time you get there,' the old man said.

Tyrant munched his way to the doorway and peered inside. There was a small pot warming by the fire, the size of which concerned him. Whatever its contents, they could hardly be sufficient for his own ravenous appetite and he had the old man and Ant to consider. Ant ate very little, as far as Tyrant could tell. He just nibbled at bits of vegetation as he went along, like a goat might. As for the old guy, he had a house and garden that provided an almost limitless opportunity for food. Tyrant began to spoon the broth into his mouth. Although some of the meat was very chewy, it tasted remarkably delicious and he could feel its nourishing effect coursing through his body. The sense of wellbeing that he felt as he ate this wholesome food set him to thinking that he probably needed this to keep himself alive and that it was vital for his survival. By the time the old man came in, followed by Ant, there was very little left in the pot. They both looked at him for a long while without speaking.

'I was hungry,' Tyrant said.

'I can see that,' the old man replied. 'You've polished off some offal I'd been boiling up to make stock for my soup. If you'd waited, I could have provided you with something much more edible.'

Tyrant chewed on a carrot, then handed the empty pot to the old man. 'It tasted good enough to me, but if you have something else to offer, I'm still a bit hungry.'

'We don't have time,' Ant said, 'we need to be pressing on.'

'We're following some soldiers that have captured two friends of ours,' Tyrant addressed the old man. 'Can you tell us how far ahead of us they are?'

The old man shook his head. 'I've seen nobody at all for three days apart from you two.'

'They must have taken another path,' Tyrant said, 'otherwise they would have come here for food just as we did.' As he spoke, he heard a commotion coming from outside the house. A swift look through the open door confirmed it to be caused by a troop of soldiers approaching the house and he could make out the distinctive figure of Petra amongst them.

As Tyrant's eyes searched the tiny dwelling for an escape route or hiding place, his stomach started to make gurgling noises. 'What exactly was in that pot?' he asked.

'Lots of different items; intestines, lungs, that sort of thing,' the old man replied.

Tyrant felt his guts starting to heave and a severe gripping pain began gnawing at his abdomen. 'What animal?' he gasped.

'Mostly squirrel; that's all I can catch around here.'

As the nausea reached its inevitable crescendo, Tyrant dashed outside and emptied the contents of his stomach at the feet of the leading soldier. The retching continued long after there was nothing more to expel, and Tyrant remained helpless, bent double over a patch of bespattered cabbages. He was aware that the troop had stopped to watch him suffer. Petra broke ranks and ran over to comfort him, holding his head with one hand and rubbing his belly with the other. Her two guards stood, swords drawn, to either side.

No sooner had the vomiting subsided, though, Tyrant found himself with no less of a priority than throwing up had been. Grasping the tops of his trousers to afford himself the quickest and most efficient way of dropping them, he sprinted into the woods and deterred any potential followers by calling out 'I need to shit!' as he ran. Nobody, not even Petra, decided to follow him.

The evacuation process was long and arduous, but eventually he felt well enough to stand and pull up his trousers. When he arrived back at the house, the soldiers were still there and being addressed by Ant.

'You are welcome to remain as long as you need and to share what little food we have,' Ant said. The old man was nowhere to be seen.

The leading soldier looked meaningfully at Tyrant as he emerged from the shelter of the trees. 'I think we'll be sticking to our own food and we have to be on our way. How long have you two been living out here in the forest?'

'Two years,' Ant replied, 'since the madness that consumed Gort drove us from the city.'

'Is that your father?' The soldier pointed to Tyrant.

'No,' said Tyrant.

'Yes,' said Ant.

'Make up your minds,' the soldier said. 'In any case, you'll both have to come with me. You have to join the army, it's the law nowadays. The way it is, you could be thought of as deserters and, strictly speaking, should be hanged on the spot, but you might be able to convince my superiors to be lenient if they accept your story of being out here all that time.' He turned to Tyrant. 'Give me your sword.'

Tyrant weighed up the situation as his hand moved slowly down to his sword hilt. Twelve men – three of them were close enough to engage, but there were several holding crossbows out of his range and showing intense interest in what he was going to do. Then there was Petra, Ant, and Cuthbert to consider. If anything kicked off, they'd be caught up in the fighting. There was little prospect of being able to protect himself, let alone the others. Anyway, the squirrel-induced sickness and diarrhoea had left him so weak he could hardly stand, never mind wield a sword in any meaningful way.

Mustering as much cheerfulness as his ravaged guts would allow, he pulled the scabbard from his belt and handed the sword to the soldier. 'I've always fancied being in the army,' he said, smiling at Petra and the white-faced Cuthbert, whose mouth was hanging open as if he wanted to say something but couldn't quite decide what it might be.

'What about your son?' the soldier said.

'What son? I don't have a son,' Tyrant replied.

'Well, whoever he is, he has to come along as well. Where's he gone?'

Tyrant supposed that Ant had ducked back inside the house but, if he had, three soldiers failed to find him when they went inside to search. They did return with the old man, who complained loudly about being manhandled.

'Leave him, he's too old. I doubt he'd last the journey in any event.'

Without any further mention of Ant, the soldiers continued their journey, with Tyrant and Petra in their midst.

32

Lone thought about the major problems she had to overcome before her plans could stand a chance of success. The journey north would be long and arduous, with no guarantee of survival. Even if she did reach the fabled City of Oort, there was the river crossing to negotiate and a powerful sorcerer to deal with. Even if she were successful, there would be another desert to cross before she reached the southernmost part of the kingdom she knew.

First, though, she had to convince this recalcitrant band of ruffians to give up their precious camels and at least two of them to steer her safely through the desert. It felt as though Moussa was almost convinced, though that was when he was directly under her influence. Her experience had taught her that might not hold in the face of his argumentative brethren. At least he was a start, even if only a small one.

She needed to make a grand gesture, some demonstration of her powers that would persuade these men once and for all that she wasn't to be opposed. Shaking a few bignuts from a tree or even stopping their leader's heart hadn't done the trick. It needed to be much more blatant, more showy. She thought of Malachi and wondered what he'd decide under the same circumstances. Not for the first time, she wished he were with her, despite some of his obvious failings. Whatever he came up with, she imagined it would be bloody and gruesome.

There was no Malachi, but she knew she needed help. Her previous attempts to conjure up a demon and bind it to her will had failed. She had spent days in meditation, recited spells for hours and all to no avail. At the time, she had suspected that Patch had caused this isolation as part of the punishment he seemed to think she deserved. That may have changed; after all, he had allowed her to be found by humans, so perhaps that applied to spirits as well now.

Lone removed herself as far from the men as she could without abandoning the shade of the vegetation completely. She sat in the sand, closed her eyes, and began to chant the words of the summoning spell she had developed from years of trial and error. Almost immediately, she felt a response; it was as if she had dangled a ghostly fishing line into the spiritual ocean and it was being tossed around by ripples of attention. She waited, repeating the invitation over and over again.

She could feel a strong presence and several other weaker ones. She concentrated her thoughts on welcoming the spirit and offering a way into the physical world through her. The presence receded and her breath stopped in disappointment at the chance lost. Then she felt it return, stronger this time. *Come and join me,* she said, *in the land of the living.*

The reply was too faint for her to decipher, but it was at least a response and she sat patiently, uttering a spell of attachment to try to strengthen the bond that was forming between herself and whatever it was that she had contacted.

The pull was two-way. Lone could feel her essence being gently submerged in emptiness. It felt soft and welcoming, and she had to resist a strong urge to relax and surrender. It was an effort, but she had practised the technique of tethering herself to her physical body for long hours, and it was that which saved her from the void.

Hello, Lone.

This time the voice was clear in her head, and the use of her name took her by surprise. She knew the importance of names in the spirit world and how they could be used to exert power over others.

How do you know my name?

Everyone knows your name, you're famous.

Famous for what?

The reply was the tinkle of unreal laughter. Lone began to feel uneasy; she needed to be the controlling mind in this situation. Whatever it was that she had snared, it seemed to be establishing the upper hand. It might even be teasing her.

She thought of Patch, wondered if he might have returned in another guise to taunt her further, but dismissed the thought. He had said and done what he wanted to. This encounter didn't have the Patch hallmark of serious disdain. There was a lighter, more frivolous taste to proceedings, which Lone found disturbing. It was as if the agenda was being set for her instead of by her.

Why have you come? Lone asked.

Because you called me. Also, I've not exactly come from anywhere, I've been here all the time. It just seemed appropriate that I announced my presence at this particular time.

So you know what's been going on?

If you mean your hilarious attempts to deal with the entity that you call Patch, then yes. Rather you than me.

So you know of Patch?

Yes, and it still cracks me up to refer to him as that.

If there's a more appropriate name for him, then tell me what it is.

There are many more names you could give him, but his real one is something he'll have to tell you himself. I wouldn't like to spoil his fun in any way.

So Patch sent you? Lone was beginning to become less uneasy and more exasperated. She needed help and commitment; she had to be able to place her trust in any ally, otherwise she would be putting herself in grave danger.

Originally, yes. He asked me to keep an eye on you and keep him posted. Now he's gone, I'm hanging around out of curiosity. I want to see how things turn out for you.

If all you're going to do is watch, then I'd rather you got out of the way and let me find a demon that's willing to help.

I can help. What do you want me to do?

What are you and how can you help? Lone felt the first stirrings of hope since she'd started the conversation.

I'm Cali; I can tell you things. Useful things.

What about something to sort out these men and get me my camels for the journey?

I can tell you that they all want to see you dead, including your friend Moussa, he of the long pointless stories. If you wanted to know about Zaire and the City of Oort, you could have saved yourself the risk of being bored to death by asking me.

Then I will ask you, but first I have to get my camels and some men to drive them.

Lone was feeling a good deal better about Cali now that she had professed to know about the city and what might lie ahead. The basis of their relationship still needed to be established, but at least she was being

118

offered assistance without any need for coercion. That might be necessary at some point, and she had one or two things that might surprise Cali, especially if she thought she knew everything she needed to know about Lone. But that was for later.

Tricky. These men are treacherous beyond belief. Their downfall may be that their treachery extends to each other. You might want to consider that.

Or I could kill all of them bar two or three, then make the remaining ones my slaves.

Lone felt Cali's response as a tickle in her chest before the laughter reached her mind.

33

'Sorry, got to run,' Tyrant apologised to Sergeant Grew then fled into the woods. He sat with his backside hanging over a fallen log and groaned loudly. His guts felt as if there were a shoal of sticklebacks swimming around inside them and his not infrequent belches had the taste and smell of rotten eggs. It was not surprising that the procedure involving strict supervision to prevent a possible escape had been quickly discontinued. Tyrant had the feeling that his disappearance would come as some relief to Grew. Progress had been drastically slowed by having to wait around for Tyrant to recover sufficiently to continue.

This time, when the nausea had abated, he hardly had strength to pull up his trousers before collapsing into a relatively unspotted area of greenery and curling up into a weary ball.

It was Petra who found him and began pulling at his shoulder. 'They're fed up of hanging about. If you don't come now, they're going to leave you behind.'

'I can't walk another step,' Tyrant said. 'Tell them they'll either have to wait or carry me.' He watched with half-closed eyes as Petra began pulling up some plants. 'Are those for me, to make me feel better?'

'No, they're for me,' Petra replied.

'Why? Are you sick as well?'

Petra made no reply as she nibbled away at a root, then she was gone.

Tyrant sank back into an uneasy sleep, disturbed by visions of snakes gnawing their way out of his stomach.

He was awakened by the sound of retching and took a moment to check that it wasn't his own. Petra was bent double against a tree, her tiny frame convulsed by frequent spasms. Tyrant dragged himself to his feet.

'Leave me alone,' Petra said, 'I'll be alright in a few minutes.'

'Where is everyone?'

'Gone.' Petra heaved twice then continued, 'When I started throwing up, Grew was convinced that whatever you had was contagious and they couldn't take the risk of all getting it. So, they told me to go away and left you where you were. It's been an hour or so now, the effects of the root should be wearing off soon.'

'What about Cuthbert?'

'He's gone with them; wasn't he supposed to? I thought that was the plan. Get Cuthbert back to his own army.' Petra stood up straight, her leathery face pale but her eyes bright.

'That was Ant's plan. I'm not so sure it's a good one anymore. I'd feel better if Cuthbert came back to the lake with us.'

'I still think the plan is a good one,' Ant said, appearing suddenly from behind a bush.

'I pretended to be sick, Ant, just like Tyrant. They let me go because of it,' Petra said.

'I know, I was watching all along. It was a good ruse but it needed me to plant the idea in their minds. I had them in fear of their lives by the time they decided to abandon you,' Ant said. 'Now we need to carry on following them, but this time be more careful. They still have Tyrant's sword; we need to get that back.'

'No, we don't.' Tyrant had settled back down onto the ground now and felt ready for another sleep. 'They can have it for all I care. I never did reckon much for swords; too visible for my liking and scant protection against a well-aimed crossbow bolt. A sword raises expectations, especially that particular one. Without it, I can go back to being the Tyrant that isn't worth bothering with because he's got nothing and isn't interested in what anyone else has. Having that sword made me pretend to be something I'm not and I'm well rid of it.'

Tyrant felt a swell of resentment, but it wasn't strong enough for him to engage further with Ant. He fell asleep wondering how Ant had managed to delude himself so completely and resolved to ask him that when he had enough energy to listen to the reply.

34

Malachi stepped out of the vedhana and into a room lit only by the ghostly light of the device. From outside came the sounds of a bustling marketplace, vendors calling out their wares, and other voices raised in protest or query. He turned to Vargas, and even in this dim light, could see that he was still shaken from the sudden transfer from the King's tower.

'This is the City of Oort, named after the river,' Malachi said. 'If you are fortunate and knowledgeable, you can get here overland in little more than two weeks from our southernmost border. Which means, as I have advised the King, that they could be at the walls of Gort inside a month. It would be a shame if your denial that this place even exists were to put our monarch's life at risk, don't you agree?'

'What is this thing? Some kind of magical illusion to trick me into agreeing with you?'

Malachi drew back the substantial iron bolts that barred the entrance. 'It's actually a convenience placed here by some monks so that they can do their shopping. As you can see, they keep it nice and secure, closing the door from the inside as they leave. These transportation devices are very powerful weapons that have to be guarded carefully, so I would suggest that you make as little commotion as possible when we venture outside. If the wrong people knew that this vedhana existed, they could be inside the King's palace in an instant and cause no end of trouble. It is, as you might say, a double-edged sword.'

The door swung open, letting in bright sunshine and stifling heat. Malachi stepped quickly through the doorway, pulling Vargas with him, then swiftly closed the door behind them. The crowds milling about in the marketplace seemed oblivious to their sudden entrance. 'We shouldn't take too long about our business here; the longer we stay, the more chances there are of complications. I only want to show you the river and demonstrate that this place is no more an illusion than Gort itself.'

'It's not necessary,' Vargas said. 'I'm convinced of what you say and apologise for doubting you. I hope you'll explain to the King that I was only acting in what I thought were his best interests. Now, let's return to Gort before someone discovers that device and our return is blocked.'

Malachi breathed deeply; the air was fragrant with spices and blossom. 'Look at this place, Vargas, it's magnificent. There must be ten times the number of inhabitants we have in Gort, yet you were in complete ignorance of it and tried to impose that ignorance on the rest of us. Follow me, I want to show you the river.'

'I've admitted my mistake, please take me home. People are giving me strange looks and that makes me nervous.'

Malachi strode on with Vargas complaining in his wake. As he cleared the marketplace, the vista opened up to reveal the wide expanse of the river and the bridge rising gracefully from the bank. 'There, what do you think of that? Do you think that anyone in our kingdom would be capable of such a magnificent feat of engineering?'

'No,' Vargas replied, 'it's truly remarkable and I'll tell the King that. Just take me home.'

'Your spirit of adventure appears to have deserted you and I always thought of you as this intrepid explorer who was afraid of nothing. What has happened to that man, eh, Vargas?'

Malachi followed the stream of camels and handcarts onto the bridge that was wide enough to accommodate twenty people walking abreast in both directions. At the highest point of the middle span, he stopped to lean on the parapet and look down into the river. He was aware of Vargas arriving to stand beside him before a third person joined them.

Malachi took his eyes off the mesmeric swirling of the deep waters to look down at the figure standing next to him, who barely reached up to his waist. He was wearing a sky-blue shirt, loose white trousers that billowed in the breeze, and a magnificent golden turban.

35

Moussa approached her with his characteristic crouching shuffle, hands clasped in front of him and head slightly bowed. Lone found it both amusing and irritating that even his walk made his devious intentions transparent. She felt like striking him dead on the spot to teach him a lesson.

'I have spoken long into the night with my comrades and they have difficulty in giving up any of their camels unless you can guarantee them adequate recompense. Our beasts are our livelihood, lady. Without them, we will starve,' Moussa said.

'I don't need all their camels, only a few of them. There will be payment for the ones who accompany me, they can make reparation for the extra camels on their return.'

'Yes, lady, I explained all that, but they are a suspicious lot and doubt your word.'

Lone laughed. 'They are probably more concerned with the chances of you returning with their money. I suspect they find it hard to believe that such honesty is possible in this world. Come on, Moussa, tell me what arrangement you have been able to make rather than the difficulties you faced in reaching it.'

'My comrades have developed a strong liking for you, lady, and wish to help you in any reasonable way they can. For myself, I am willing to guide you to the City on the River and have a close friend, Demba, who will also help with the camels.'

'The goatherd from your story?'

'Yes, lady, Demba, my good and old friend who was instrumental in creating the opportunity for me to get started in the camel driving business. Naturally, being the man that I am, I returned the favour as soon as it was possible for me to do so. And may I say that your attentiveness to my tale makes me feel very proud to be keeping the interest of such a fine and educated lady as yourself.'

Lone felt a mixture of excitement and amusement as she watched this man clasping and unclasping his hands in front of her. The words he was speaking did not tally with what she knew. They were all intent on killing her, including Moussa, and it was just a matter of how effective their new plan would turn out to be. Creeping up to her sleeping figure in the night had been tried without success, and she wondered how inventive they might have become in identifying her weaknesses. 'So you gave some of your camels to Demba to help him out?' she asked.

'In a manner of speaking, yes.'

'How exactly did you return the favour, then?'

'On my return to the City of the Thousand Tents, I discovered that my friend had prospered in my absence and was able to afford the measly sum necessary to purchase those fine beasts from me. He's never looked back since and every day he thanks me profusely for the good fortune I have brought him.' Moussa looked up at her without raising his head from its position of supplication, his teeth bared in a smile that Lone imagined would do equally well on a lion about to bite.

'What about Genna, your faithful camel who saved you from death? Do you still have her?'

'No, sadly she died many years ago. There'll never be another to compare with her; she was a princess amongst camels.'

'What happened to her?' Lone asked.

'She was getting old and even more cantankerous than ever. She even took to attacking me at every opportunity. What else could I do? I practically gave her away to someone who I thought would take care of her in the dignity of her final years but, alas, I had been mistaken and the lying rogue who robbed me of her killed her in a fit of rage when she bit him. It's something that I will regret to my dying day, but there are circumstances beyond our control in this harsh world and we just have to get on with life as we find it.'

'Your kindness and generosity overwhelm me, Moussa,' Lone said, receiving a vigorous nod in response. 'I want to make haste to begin our journey. How many camels do we have?'

'Seven, lady, including a gentle and kind beast for you to ride in comfort. Demba and I will attend the camels, which will bear enough food and water to get us all through the desert, provided that we find a well or two on the way.'

'I need you to get three more camels and load them with bignuts,' Lone said.

'That's neither wise nor possible. Those things are too big and heavy to carry and provide little in the way of nourishment. Better to keep to water in skins and small fruit. You don't need the bignuts, lady.'

'But I do need them and I insist that we take them. Perhaps three camels won't be able to carry the amount I need. Let's try and see, shall we? Then we can decide if we need more camels. I don't want the poor camels to be overloaded; better to take a few spare ones, do you think?'

Moussa's head was shaking from side to side as if he was trying to dislodge a swarm of bees. 'You don't understand, lady. If we take more camels, we need more food and water. Then we need more drovers, which means more camels to carry the food and water for them. It's not possible to do what you say.'

'If seven camels can carry enough provisions for three people and themselves, then it makes no sense why five more, three carrying bignuts, won't be sufficient.'

'It's not that, you'll not be leaving enough camels for the remaining men to get home.'

'Then tell them to stay here. It's comfortable enough; there's enough food and water and they can await your return laden with riches and glory.'

'If anything should happen to us, though, they would be stranded here for ever. They can't take that risk.' Moussa stood with his arms wide apart.

'Moussa, I have grown weary of your excuses. Get your friends in order and begin loading the camels. If they have any problems with that tell them to speak to me directly.'

Moussa allowed his arms to drop to his sides, shrugged his shoulders, then turned away.

Lone waited for the inevitable attack.

36

The cold wetness seeping up from the ground and soaking into his clothes became more uncomfortable than the prospect of waking up, so Tyrant reluctantly raised himself to a sitting position and began to rub his eyes. The stomach cramps had been replaced by a ravenous hunger, though he found the thought of squirrel was enough to bring back waves of nausea.

Petra was asleep beside him, curled up in a tiny ball like a frightened kitten. Tyrant breathed a long audible sigh, then a shorter but louder one. When this failed to stir the sleeping figure, he made a coughing noise, then blew his nose into his sleeve.

'Wake up,' he said, 'we need to get some breakfast.'

'Oh, you're finally back with us, are you?' Petra replied. 'You've slept almost the entire day as well as all night. You can have some of this bread if you want.'

'As long as there's been no squirrels near it. Where's Ant?'

'He went off to retrieve your sword.'

'I told him I didn't want it back.'

'He said something about him needing the sword, even if you didn't. That it was important in ways that you didn't understand.'

'Then he's welcome to it. Come on, let's go,' Tyrant said.

'If we hurry, we might be able to catch the soldiers before they reach the main army,' Petra said.

'That's not what I had in mind; we need to get as far away from soldiers and armies as possible.'

'So you want to turn round and head back to the lake?'

'No, it's just as bad there and they have high expectations of me. I'd be better off with Cuthbert; at least his army doesn't rely on me to act the invincible warrior. Can you find your old house from here? I thought that might be worth a look before I decide what to do.'

'We should try to find Ant at least and ask him what he wants,' Petra said.

'Why?' Tyrant replied. 'Ant may be a boy, but he's got all the ideas and ambitions of a man. I don't want to be involved in them anymore. I can't even remember why I agreed to come this far with him in the first place. It must have been an attempt to get as far away from the lake as quickly as possible after the way I faced up the army in that stupid manner. I don't know what came over me. Instead of running away as anyone with any sense would have done, I decided to end it all by attacking them. If it hadn't been for the landslide, I'd be dead for certain by now, sword or no sword. It may even have been some crazy notion from having the sword that puddled my mind. No more, Petra. I'm off on my own from now on, no disrespect to you, and it's about time I did. First, though, I'll see if I can't get your house back, leave things more or less as they were when we first met.'

'I doubt that it's still standing,' Petra said. 'Anyway, I don't need it anymore. I prefer to travel around with you. We're a good team.'

'If I wanted to be part of a team, I'd have you in it. Problem is, I'm not a team player. I like to make mistakes that affect only me. Responsibility for others wears me down. The people at the lake think I can lead their army and protect them from the King. Well, I can't, and it's not fair of them to lay that on me. I never asked them to do it. I never pretended to be anything I'm not. And I'm certainly not some mighty warrior who can make a difference.'

'You're just saying that because you're tired and hungry. I believe in you, Tyrant, I've seen what you can do,' Petra said.

'How far is your house from here?' Tyrant said.

'Not far. Up through those trees, then along a bit. No more than half a day, maybe less.'

'Then we'd better save our breath for walking,' Tyrant said. 'Not that you listen to anything I tell you.' He hoisted the heavy pack back onto his sore shoulders and tramped after Petra. His mood had not been improved by the conversation. He might as well have been talking to himself. No matter how many times he told that woman she wasn't wanted, she ignored him and carried on as if they were joined at the hip.

The journey was shorter than anticipated and there was plenty of daylight left when they reached the house that Petra had abandoned in the face of the overwhelming savagery that had descended after the horrors of Gort had spread this far north. He knew that she blamed him for it all and felt aggrieved that she had persisted in that notion despite all the careful explaining he'd done. If it weren't for him, she'd most likely be dead by now, but she didn't appear to realise it.

There was an unusual smell about the house that Tyrant couldn't place. It had a sweet, rotten taste to it, but was more complex than just vegetation that had been left too long. There was smoke coming from the chimney, but whatever was cooking smelt mighty peculiar.

'Someone's here,' Petra said, 'and they've planted up my garden. I've never seen it so productive.'

'Of course someone's here,' Tyrant said, 'and we need to tread a bit carefully. Don't go charging inside shouting the odds and demanding your house back. We need to act a bit more subtly than that.'

Before Petra could reply, two men emerged from the house, both carrying loaded crossbows. Tyrant decided that this was possibly the worst reception he could have wished for, then realised that any number of crossbows in excess of two would have been more awful and that his original thought was both inaccurate and completely pointless. He put it down to weakness and hunger.

'Hello.' Tyrant raised both hands to show that they were empty and display his weaponless belt. 'We're just passing through and we wondered if you had any food you might want to share with us.' He smiled as sweetly as his dental state would allow.

'What's in that bag?' The short, mean-looking man nearest to Tyrant walked towards him, keeping the crossbow levelled at his chest. His red-haired companion sidled to the right, so that Tyrant had to turn his head to keep him in view. One in front, one to the side, a difficult situation to deal with without being shot.

'Nothing much,' Tyrant said, stepping closer to the man in front of him. 'It's actually a rather heavy stone that my companion here has me carry around for her in case she might want to make some flatbread. You're welcome to take a look.' He unslung the bag from his shoulder and swung it hard and fast at the short man, who took one hand off his weapon to catch the bag, but the weight of it took him by surprise. It hit him in the chest, then knocked the crossbow out of his hand.

Tyrant held onto the strap, accelerating the bag by turning in a circle, then releasing it towards the red-haired man who had two choices. Either he could shoot Tyrant in the split second it took the bag to arrive and then get flattened by it, or he could drop his bow and catch it with two hands. He opted for the latter approach and Tyrant thought that this was both expedient and sensible. The red-haired man rocked on his heels as the bag struck him, then was thrown heavily onto his back by the almost simultaneous arrival of a fast-moving Tyrant.

'Tell your friend to stay away from his crossbow and nobody needs to get hurt,' Tyrant said.

The red-haired man opened his mouth to speak, but no words came out. Tyrant looked back at his companion, worried that a crossbow bolt might already be on its way. Petra had the man's hair in one hand and was drawing a blade across his throat. The red-haired man complained loudly at the sight of his companion's death. Tyrant tried to explain that the whole situation had been caused by a misunderstanding, that no harm had been meant to either of them, and it was just that Petra was having a bad day.

Tyrant released the man's right hand as he turned around to see what Petra was doing. This turned out to be a mistake. Instead of watching in horror what was going on, the red-haired man produced a knife as if from nowhere and tried to stab Tyrant through the heart with it. All Tyrant had time to do was to turn away from the thrust and be stabbed in the shoulder. He reached beneath his shirt for his own knife in order to retaliate, but couldn't find it. While he was rummaging in his underclothes, looking for his knife, he had to fend off another slashing blow at the cost of a cut on his forearm. His shoulder began to hurt very badly and there was a worrying amount of blood flowing down the left side of his body.

Tyrant managed to grab hold of the wrist holding the knife and held it away from his body while he once again considered reasoning with the red-haired man. One look into his eyes convinced him that there was too much fury and bloodlust in there for a quiet word to suffice in bringing the situation under control. After a momentary hesitation, he smashed his forehead into the man's face, catching him just above the bridge of the nose. Now it was the red-haired man's turn to bleed, and the blow loosened his grip on the knife enough to allow Tyrant to wrest it from his hand.

A fist crashed into Tyrant's head as if in confirmation that the fight had not been entirely knocked out of his opponent. Tyrant's response was an automatic stab to the throat that ended any further interest in proceedings for the red-haired man. 'Why did you have to do that?' Tyrant said, clutching his shoulder, which was still pouring blood at an alarming rate.

'He was going to shoot you, what did you expect me to do?' Petra replied.

'I had everything under control; we could have reached an amicable arrangement here, but instead we have two corpses. Can't you understand that it's better to make friends with people or at least scare them enough to keep away?'

'You've hurt your arm and shoulder,' Petra said.

'No, I haven't. I've been stabbed by this man after he saw what you did to his friend. If you hadn't been so hasty, it wouldn't have happened.'

'There'd have been no need to stab you, as you'd be lying dead with a crossbow bolt through your head,' Petra said. 'You'd better come inside the house and I'll see what I can do to stop the bleeding.'

Tyrant ducked inside the doorway and was greeted by an intensification of the strange smell and the sight of a large metal canister sitting on the fire. From the top of the canister protruded a metal tube that was bent to one side, then ran in a gentle slope down to an earthenware receptacle. The tube was festooned with rags and there was a bucket suspended from the ceiling that was dribbling water onto the steaming cloth. Tyrant picked up the jar and sniffed the clear liquid it had been collecting. Then he tasted it gingerly. As he swallowed a small amount, the back of his throat felt as if it were on fire and the conflagration continued down through his chest and into his stomach. His eyesight began to blur and his brain stopped thinking altogether.

He took another, larger sip and the process repeated itself. Three more mouthfuls, and his legs felt as if they belonged to another person altogether and he sat down heavily, still clutching the jar.

'This is good stuff,' he said, then felt a weariness descend over him that couldn't be resisted, so he finished the remaining liquid in one swift gulp before allowing himself to collapse into welcome unconsciousness.

37

A cool mist was rising from the river, obscuring the surrounding banks and the rest of the city on either side. Almost as soon as Malachi had become aware of the little man's appearance, the hordes of passers-by seemed to evaporate as quickly as the mist had descended. The three of them were alone and hidden from view, despite being in the centre of a highly populated area that a few minutes ago had been very crowded.

Malachi smiled, then he raised his hands, palms together, placed the tips of his fingers on his forehead, and made a low bow towards the little man with the golden turban.

The little man looked up and nodded in response. 'Who's this then, Malachi?'

'This is Vargas, a trusted servant of my King. He's been getting a geography lesson from me.' Malachi turned to Vargas, who was looking even more nervous than before. 'This is Zaire. I suggest you are polite to him as he's the avatar of the Spirit of the River and wields most of the power in these parts.'

'I don't understand,' Vargas said. 'What's an avatar?'

'I like to think of it as a physical representation of something that isn't normally in physical form, though I'm open to correction by anyone who knows better. Are you happy with that description of you, Zaire?'

'It will suffice, though I like to think of myself as the representative of all natural energies, not only those associated with the river. The whole life force of the city and its surroundings is embodied in me. It's a good place to be.'

'Why are you so small, then?' Vargas asked. Malachi gave an inward groan and hoped that Zaire was in one of his more accommodating moods.

'What you see is small, but my being is vast,' Zaire said.

'That's all very well, but don't you think that something a bit more impressive would be better. At least someone of normal height, perhaps,' Vargas said. Malachi breathed a sigh of disappointment that anticipated Zaire's reaction to the comment about his physical appearance. It was a subject that he was particularly touchy about, though Malachi knew he could easily fly into an awful rage, even about the most trivial of remarks. It didn't look as if Vargas was going to survive long enough to tell the King what he'd witnessed and this whole trip would be a waste of time.

'He means no slight, Zaire,' Malachi said, 'he's just taken aback by the whole concept of how mighty you are and how gentle and pleasing your appearance is. He doesn't understand what fear and terror you could strike into the hearts of anyone who beheld you should you change your physical body to more fully reflect the magnificence of your being.'

Zaire laughed, a deep booming noise that belied the size of his chest cavity. 'Don't fear for your companion, Malachi, I'm in an expansive mood today. The first chill waters of the distant snow melt are coursing through my tepid waters, bringing a new sense of invigoration and optimism. Your words are as eloquent as ever, but remember that I can see behind them. You need this man to survive this encounter and to corroborate your story to his King. I can only surmise what significance that might have in the great scheme of things that you are contriving to bring about.'

'Thank you for your forbearance,' Malachi said. 'I take it that our arrangement can be made official then, at least in terms of communicating it to our King.'

'If what you say is true, then yes. My concern lies wholly with the river and the land that surrounds it. You're welcome to anything and everything else,' Zaire replied.

'So you will assist my King in extending his province to include your city?'

'Assist is a strong word. I will not prevent it unless I judge it to be detrimental to the health of the river and you have promised that the new regime will divert the streams of waste matter that constantly pour into my waters, causing me distress,' Zaire said.

'And so we will, you have my word on it. In Gort, we have created drains that carry the effluvium to the plains outside the city where they are valuable in promoting the growth of all kinds of crops. It will be doubly effective here where the desert is so barren. We will grow food in places where there was only sand before. Everyone will benefit.'

'I like the sound of that, Malachi, but you know that I do. Take care that what you tell me is true and not some manipulation to achieve your own ends. I can be a powerful friend to you, but you wouldn't be wise to abuse that situation.'

'I will have the best interests of the river at heart at all times, Zaire. I will need your assistance though, and not merely your passive acceptance of any regime change. The passage through the northern desert is a long and difficult one. You can ensure that we can find the water we need for the journey, can't you?'

'The water under the desert is connected to the river and I can make it more accessible if needs be. That isn't an arduous task and I'll do that willingly. What I won't do is to interfere in any negotiations or fighting.'

'That's all I ask, Zaire. Get us across the desert and our army will do the rest. We'll clean the river and make the desert blossom.'

'Take care with your promises, Malachi. I don't like to be disappointed and I'm not sure that the words you speak are ones within your power to deliver.'

Malachi felt the touch of malevolence that accompanied Zaire's response and, deep inside, part of his being trembled. He took a deep breath. 'You are both wise and perceptive, oh great one. My words are hollow and borne on a wind of hope rather than conviction. It is my King who pledges this to you, I only can speak on his behalf and offer you his most solemn promise.'

'Then it is your King that will answer to me if the promise is broken.'

38

As he squeezed his tiny frame into the wooden box, Tyrant tried unsuccessfully to restrain himself from giggling. This would be the one hiding place where his brother wouldn't think to look. It was almost impossible to hide from a twin brother who knew everything about you and could anticipate your every move. Seth was always one step ahead of him and had an uncanny knack of knowing exactly where he was at all times.

Until now. He'd never think to look for him in a fish box.

The joke was a glorious one, but it wouldn't work if he betrayed himself by laughing. Tyrant stilled his glee by concentrating on his fear and hatred of fish. He brought back to mind the grotesque fish head with its cold staring eyes that Seth had chased him with until he'd had to run screaming to his mother for protection. Even after her intercession on his behalf, the fish head would poke its foul face out of Seth's pocket from time to time and give him a nasty look that made him squeal.

Now, he was in a box that had only recently been vacated by dead fish. Big ones, probably, because little ones might be able to wriggle out from between the slats that allowed him a restricted view of their house so he could watch for Seth's approach and stay particularly quiet.

He wondered if he should stay hidden like a little mouse or take the opportunity to scare Seth by leaping out and making a big noise. It was a bit too cramped in the box for him to make a quick exit. There would have to be a lot of telltale wriggling before he could emerge, and that would give the game away and spoil the surprise. A perfect hideaway like this one was something to be savoured, and he settled in for the long term, trying not to let the smell get into his stomach and make him throw up.

He squeezed his eyes tight shut to combat the smell, but instead, the fishy face appeared and looked at him. It disappeared when he opened his eyes, which was a big relief. He'd checked the box carefully before he'd got in, but you never know with fish; they're slippery customers and you never can tell where they might be hiding.

While he watched and waited, Tyrant thought of the latest telling off they had received from mother. She'd found them sitting on the bridge, legs dangling over the water and dropping pebbles onto the crocodiles' heads. That was Seth's best fun idea ever and they'd both laughed so hard they'd nearly fallen in. Mother had been distraught and even carried on admonishing them days later. Tyrant and Seth had been banned from the bridge and had to content themselves with throwing stones from the bank, where it was almost impossible to hit a croc.

Tyrant caught his breath. Seth was coming out of the house, his eyes casting around. *You'll never find me here,* Tyrant thought, then wondered if the very act of thinking might give him away. Seth looked directly at the box, but then something else attracted his attention.

Seth's face crinkled in alarm and he shouted loudly for his mother to come. Tyrant couldn't see what was causing his distress because of the restricted view from his fish box and he was reluctant to move in case it gave the game away.

His mother's eyes were wide with fear and she scooped up the wailing Seth and clasped him to her chest. A man came into view; Tyrant was impressed by his brown leather boots that had a golden buckle on the side. It wasn't the boots that were important, though, it was the bright thin sword that poked out towards his mother. She was screaming now and Tyrant tried to get out of his box and run to help her, but his whole body had been paralysed by fear. He couldn't move; he couldn't breathe. All he could do was watch as the sliver of metal advanced until the point of the sword was touching Seth's back. It didn't stop there. It carried on. It pierced his brother's skin and went deep inside him. His sobs turned to screams, then stopped completely. Only his mother's pleading continued, then her screams turned to pain.

The sword splashed crimson as it emerged from his mother's back. Her voice changed from screams to an anguished sigh, then her legs crumpled and she fell to the floor, still clutching Seth. As she fell, she looked into Tyrant's eyes, her loving kindness shining for one last moment before it was extinguished forever.

Tyrant woke up screaming, his shoulder split apart and in terrible pain. His mind was filled with the face of the man with the sword who had killed his mother and brother. It was a memory he'd succeeded in erasing for all these years, and now he knew he could never forget it again.

That face. It was his own.

39

I need Tyrant's sword.

It's in Grew's pack.

Get it while he's asleep.

The tiny voice in Cuthbert's head had been wittering away all day. Most of the time he could ignore it, but as evening closed in, it had increased in volume and persistence. Now it was so loud that he worried that others might hear it. Problem was, he had no idea how to reply other than to talk to himself, and that didn't seem a very good idea with the other soldiers close at hand.

He headed off into the thick forest with a shout of 'I need to shit' and without a backward glance. Once safely out of earshot, he tried to converse with the voice in his head. 'Where are you?'

Close by.

'Can't you get the sword yourself?'

Too risky.

'If I can get it, what do you want me to do with it?'

Leave it somewhere I can see it. Propped up against a tree next to the path would be good.

'What if I'm caught?'

You'll think of something.

'Why do you want Tyrant's sword? Is it because it's magic?'

You have no idea how much energy this takes, I can't go into details. Just get the sword. Tonight.

Cuthbert suddenly felt his mind clear and it was as if he had just stepped out of a fog and into the sunlight. He felt part of his surroundings again now that the distraction of Ant's voice had gone. He heard rustling in the undergrowth and quickly dropped his trousers. As he squatted, two smiling faces peered over a bush.

'Grew sent us to check you'd not run off, young lad.'

'I'll give you the pieces of shit to take back to him if you think he needs a progress report.'

The heads disappeared. 'Get on with it, we'll wait here for you.'

'No need, your appearance has put me off entirely,' Cuthbert said. 'I might as well come back now and try again later.'

'Listen up, lads,' Grew was saying as Cuthbert re-joined the group, 'there's one more night out here before we get back to the main camp where soft beds and plenty of food await us. I want you to all smarten up in the morning, make yourselves look as much like soldiers as you can. I know that's difficult for some of you, but I want us all to look like a tidy unit as we march back in. Altogether, in ranks and in step, if that's not too much to ask. Now, get your heads down, we're going to get an early start in the morning. I want to be entering camp before midday and we still have a lot of marching to do.'

Cuthbert smiled at his recollection of the few attempts Grew had made to teach the raw recruits the art of synchronised marching. The concept of being in step was something that, even after countless demonstrations and practices, had eluded most of them. At best, there had been times when half the troop were in step and the other half not. Problem was that it was then impossible to work out which one was which and Grew just had to bellow at them all. Cuthbert's marching step generally consisted of left, right, then a little skip so that he could lead with his right again because the man next to him was. He sincerely hoped for Grew's sake that there would be nobody to observe their return.

As he lay huddled up on the hard ground surrounded by farting and snoring, Cuthbert remembered Ant's ghostly voice and the instructions he'd received. Grew was on the opposite side of the fire, the light flickering across his open mouth and sparkling from the trail of drool that dribbled down his chin.

Cuthbert stood up, holding his stomach as demonstration of his need to defecate. A couple of men stirred as he walked over their prone bodies, but nobody challenged him. He could disappear into the forest and never return for all they cared. He thought of Cassie and his heart thudded in his chest. A flood of emotional energy swept through his solar plexus and down into his guts. The churning down there was so strong that his pretence was turned into an urgent necessity and he had to run to get a decent distance from his sleeping comrades before squatting.

Grew was making intermittent pig noises, which were occasionally embellished by a high-pitched whistle. His head was lolled back on top of his pack and Cuthbert could see the haft of Tyrant's sword poking out. He reached down to try to ease it out from underneath the bag and met Grew's eyes that were staring right into his. It was only then he noticed that the snoring had stopped.

His heart was beating so hard it felt as if it might burst from his chest. His first instinct was to run away, but he quickly realised that would be futile. However long it might take, Grew would have the forest searched until he was found. Then he'd really be in trouble; a double deserter. Maybe they'd hang him twice.

'Quick!' Cuthbert hissed. 'Wake up!' He gave Grew's shoulder an unnecessary shake. 'There's someone out there in the forest.'

Grew raised his recumbent form onto one elbow and shook his head. 'What are you on about, lad?'

'I had to relieve myself, and while I was doing it, there was a rustling noise. I'm sure that there's someone hiding there. Maybe they intend to kill us all in our beds.'

'Don't be stupid, we're soldiers. It's our job to attack people, not the other way round. Even if there was someone out there, which I doubt, they wouldn't dare come near us. Go back to bed. More importantly, leave me in peace.'

'But shouldn't you go and check?' Cuthbert said.

'If you're so bothered about it, go and check yourself. If you don't come back or we find your mutilated body in the morning, I'll know you were right and that I should have been worried.' Grew closed his eyes and settled back down.

'I'll go, just to make sure,' Cuthbert said. 'Lend me your sword. If I do meet someone in the woods, I'll need a weapon.'

'You can't have my sword, it's a good one. If you want, you can take the one that big fellow gave me before he got sick. It's tied to my backpack.'

'Got it,' Cuthbert said, then scampered off into the forest.

He found that he was breathing in big gasps after his ordeal, then a sense of accomplishment took over and a feeling of euphoria swept through his body. He'd done it. He'd successfully obtained Tyrant's sword exactly as Ant had requested. Maybe he was better at this spying business than he'd given himself credit for.

He stumbled around in the darkness, looking for a suitable tree to place the sword against. It needed to be where Ant could find it, but not so obvious that one of the soldiers might see it in the morning. In the dark, it was impossible to choose. The last thing he wanted was to lose the sword entirely; to leave it where it was never found again. There had to be some subtle mark he could leave to guide Ant.

After considerable thought, Cuthbert decided to return to camp with the sword and to place it in position when the light was good enough for him to make the right choice. He'd also have a better idea of the direction of march and there'd be less chance of the troop finding it when they moved off. There was the other problem he'd have to face sooner or later. Grew would ask him for the sword and, as he could think of no reasonable answer, he decided that he'd keep the sword until he'd come up with something more plausible than 'I dropped it in the dark forest and couldn't find it again.'

He could see the comforting glow of the fire and hear the animal noises being produced by sleeping soldiers when his blood froze as he felt a hand on his shoulder.

'Give me the sword,' Ant said.

'Ah!' Cuthbert let out a yell loud enough to wake the dead in the next valley. 'You can't do this to me. They'll find us together and then I'll be in trouble.'

'Then don't be so noisy. Give me the sword.'

'I borrowed the sword from Grew. What do I say about it when he asks me for it?'

'You'll think of something.'

'But I can't think of anything, that's the problem. I'm not cut out for all this spying business.'

'You managed to get Tyrant's sword. That was the hard part. I'd say you were doing just fine.'

Cuthbert's hand was shaking as he passed over the sword. 'What if they catch me or find out that I'm helping you?'

Ant made no reply before he slipped away into the darkness. Cuthbert waited until his jangling nerves had calmed down a little before creeping back into the camp and lying down amongst the soldiers. His dreams were about spectres chasing him through the darkness. His legs were moving fast, but he couldn't make any progress.

***

Grew loomed over him like a dark cloud on a rainy day. 'The sword?'

Cuthbert wondered if that was the answer, that he should use the magic sword on the ghosts that were pursuing him. Maybe that was a good idea. 'Thank you, I will,' he murmured.

'Where is it?' Rough hands began to shake him, pulling him into a sitting position where he came face to face with the real Grew and not the one from the dream who had been much more kindly.

Cuthbert thought fast. He'd known this question would be asked and that his life might depend on the answer he gave. It needed to be inventive, plausible, and convincing. "I dropped it in the dark forest and couldn't find it again.'

'Stupid boy,' Grew said, 'there's no time to be looking for it now, we've got to get going. On your feet. Quick march.'

Grew seemed anxious to reach the main camp in good time; he kept pressing them on until the grumbles about sore feet and missed lunch became an audible protest. 'It's all downhill from here on,' he shouted. 'You'll be able to put your feet up when you get there.'

Cuthbert had been a soldier for a very short time, and in none of the various stages of his career, had putting his feet up been an option. In one respect, though, Grew was true to his word. It was all downhill, some of it very steep indeed and involved painful sliding and a sore backside.

Cuthbert busied his mind working out what to say when he was questioned. The part right up to the landslide was straightforward enough, except he doubted he should identify Tyrant as the lone assailant who had held the entire army at bay and was in the act of charging right at them when they were submerged under the rock and earth. Cuthbert's chest constricted as he remembered the horrible ordeal of being buried alive. He decided to leave out all mention of Tyrant.

He could truthfully recount that he had been well treated after his rescue and allowed to go free, but that might not go down well with the Colonel. He thought of Cassie and his chest erupted in pain, his guts constricted, and a deep longing suffused his whole body. He should never have left the lake, he thought. His place was with Cassie and he'd be better spending his time proving his worth to Cassie's father than embarking on this unsatisfactory expedition. He'd tell them that he escaped and that Petra was a wild woman of the hills that befriended him. Even to him, it all sounded a bit weak, but he resolved to deny knowledge of anything else they might ask.

It was long after a missed lunch that the camp came into view. Grew had them all smarten themselves up as best they could, particularly as everyone had mud smeared up their backs. He approached Cuthbert with a short length of rope in his hands. 'It's just for appearance's sake, boy,' he said. 'I need to make it look as if I've taken good care of you.'

'But it's as if I'm a prisoner. I never tried to run away. It's giving the wrong impression,' Cuthbert said as his hands were tied behind his back.

He remained in the company of two disgruntled soldiers who were denied the chance to grab a late lunch in order to guard him while Grew was making his report. Mercifully, the process was a brief one and Grew emerged from the commander's tent looking as miserable as ever.

'Do they want to talk to me now?' Cuthbert asked.

'No, they don't. They seem to know all about you and everything else without me having to tell them. Strange really. Anyway, they've lost interest in the north. We're all going south to the desert, they say. There's a huge army being raised from all the southern cities and we're to join up with them,' Grew said.

Cuthbert felt panic rising in his stomach. If he went south, he might never see Cassie again. Then he thought of the positive side of things; that the northerners would be spared any onslaught and that Cassie would be safe and far away from any war. This made him feel a little better, but regret even more that he hadn't stayed by the lake. If only he'd made a break for it on the night he'd retrieved the sword and gone back with Ant.

At least they weren't going to question him. That was a blessing. 'I don't want to go south,' Cuthbert said. 'Can't I be one of those staying behind to guard the King or something?'

Grew's face became even more morose than usual. 'I'm very sorry it's come to this, boy, and you have to accept that it's nothing personal.'

'What?'

'I'm afraid they've got it into their heads that you're some sort of traitor and were sent to spy on us all.'

'That's ridiculous,' Cuthbert said. 'Who told them that?'

'Seems the order came from up high, the King himself. You're not coming south with us.'

Cuthbert swallowed, unable to make any further protest despite his heart knowing what was coming next.

'You're to be hanged before we break camp and move south,' Grew continued.

'When's that?' Cuthbert asked.

'First light in the morning we leave, but you're to be hanged right away. I've sent for the rope and there's a handy tree over there that should do. At least you won't be fretting about it all night, eh?'

40

Tyrant was trying to remember who had hit him hard enough to make his head hurt so badly. His memory wasn't working very well; he could recall being slashed with a knife, which explained the tearing pain if he moved his arm, but he had no idea of what form of bludgeoning had been visited on his poor head. If he moved it at all, the throbbing turned to sharp agony. His eyes hurt when he opened them to see Petra lying uncomfortably close to him.

'You're awake at last,' she said. 'If it hadn't been for the noise you were making, I'd have taken you for dead. At least you kept nice and still while I stitched up your wounds.'

Tyrant noticed the earthenware jars lined up against the far wall and the apparatus that was still in operation, dribbling liquid and belching steam. A sweet astringent odour started his stomach churning.

'My head hurts,' Tyrant said.

'No wonder. You drank almost a whole jar of that stuff. It's a miracle you survived with all the blood you lost. A sore head is the least you could have expected.'

'What is it?' Tyrant asked.

'That thing on my fire is a still. Haven't you seen one before? I took you for a hard-drinking type that would know his stuff.'

'How does it work?'

'These pots over here have the mash in them that bubbles away until it's ready for the still. Then you pour the liquid portion into the still so that it boils away. The pipe collects the steam and the water on the pipe cools it down so that it drips into the other pot,' Petra said. 'My dad had one; not as sophisticated, but it did the same job.'

'Yes, but what does it make?'

'Taterlicker; that's what you've been drinking. The most powerful drink in the world. A small sip of taterlicker has been known to send men off their heads, start fights, even give them romantic notions.'

The look that came into Petra's eyes as she spoke the final part of her sentence made Tyrant forget his headache for a moment and worry about more dangerous things.

'And you drank nearly a whole jar,' she concluded. 'That's why you've been asleep for a whole day and night.'

'You're making some more?' Tyrant asked.

'Yes, there's plenty of mash, and once the process is started, it's quite simple. Anyway, I used most of what you didn't drink for washing your wounds.'

'You wasted it on cleaning?' Tyrant said.

'It might stop your cuts festering; would you rather that than me use a bit of taterlicker on them?'

'It was just that I was wondering if I might have a little taste of it to take away this headache.'

'It's what gave you the headache, you lummock. You'll leave it alone if you know what's good for you. Here,' she said, offering him a plate with some spherical white objects rolling around on it, 'eat something, you need to get your strength back so you can heal.'

'What are these?' Tyrant asked, chewing his way through the bland, stodgy food.

'Taters, the garden's full of them. Our friends, who were lying dead outside until I spent a whole morning dragging them away and burying them without any help from you, planted the whole area with them. It seems they were in the taterlicker business in a serious way.'

Tyrant breathed in the heady smell, felt his head protest painfully, and realised that the throbbing had subsided enough for his thoughts to be formed properly. 'Then we should take it over. We could make a good living from all this.'

'We?' Petra's eyes held a bright twinkle and Tyrant realised the import of his proposal.

'Well, it's your house, seems only fair.'

'And you want to live here with me?' Petra's twinkle had turned full beam.

'You'll need someone to protect you and the licker,' Tyrant said, knowing exactly where this conversation was leading, realising that it might have even already arrived there, and that there was no going back now. Headlong flight might save him, but he felt too weak to try that, even in the desperate plight in which he'd placed himself.

It had all started long ago when he and Petra had been marooned in the desert for a while. Looking back, that was the best time he'd had in his whole life. No threats, no duties, nowhere to go, just good food and clean water in plentiful supply. And Petra's company, which he had told himself at the time, was a burden to be shouldered in order to enjoy the rest of it.

Now he looked at the diminutive woman, her face dark tanned and creased like old leather, and remembered how he had felt in the instant that he had believed she'd been killed by the soldiers in the forest. Then, he'd shrouded it with anger to prevent the sadness coming through. Now, he knew that, despite her sharp tongue and constant use of it, he would miss her company more than anything else.

Worse still, when he thought about returning to his previous way of life, a solitary nomadic attempt to survive in a harsh world, his stomach developed a hollow feeling. The sense of freedom that had once been euphoric had been lost somewhere along the way. If he thought of life without Petra, his guts churned as if they contained a dozen rotting squirrels.

His devil-take-me attitude and carefully fostered reputation for having nothing and needing even less seemed to have vanished. He'd become too attached to people. He cringed at the thought of himself stupidly charging single-handedly to battle a whole army. That had been an action born out of duty to people like Oliver and his family and his inability to abandon them, even though he couldn't have made any significant difference.

Now, lying here in Petra's bed with his head throbbing and his arm feeling like it was in danger of detaching itself once and for all, he wondered what all the effort he'd put into that flawed reputation had achieved. He felt weary and in need of a long rest. If that meant staying here with Petra, well, he'd made worse choices in the past.

'Anyway,' Tyrant continued, 'you always said we were a team, and a good one at that.'

Petra's only response was to lie a little more snugly by his side.

41

The attack she'd been anticipating wasn't long in arriving. Lone felt Cali's breathless whisper.

They are heading this way with murderous intent.

'Then let them come; I need to move on and if this is the only way, then it has to be taken.'

Six are heading this way with swords and knives, three have hidden themselves in those trees. They have bows.

'Then it's the ones with arrows that have to be taken care of first. You go and do that, Cali, while I wait for the others. But hurry back, I might need you here as well. Six is rather too many for me to cope with all at once.'

That's not something I can help you with, Lone.

'Look, Cali, I need you to step up here. The arrows will be flying in my direction soon enough if you don't. Just strike them dead any way you like; no need for subtlety.' Lone felt a shiver of frustration at Cali's reluctance to assist her. She considered casting a binding spell and using it as a form of compulsion, but decided the whole process would take far too long and she'd be bristling with arrows by the time it had been completed. 'I could make you do it, Cali, but I rather you did it of your own volition.'

You've mistakenly taken my lack of ability as a sign of unwillingness. I'm a sprite, an inanimate breath of consciousness. I can't manifest anything physical. All I'm capable of is watching and listening. I can't even reach into human minds and influence them like many of my kind can. I'm sorry, Lone, but you're on your own as far as this fight is concerned.

Lone took a deep breath as she realised the implications of what Cali was saying. There was always the chance she was lying. Lone knew all too well how unreliable demons could be, but that made no practical difference if she wasn't prepared to help. Problem was, she'd assumed that Cali would have similar powers to Patch and wouldn't have picked such an obvious fight if she'd thought it would have to be faced without the assistance of overwhelming force. One or two of them weren't a problem, but all ten, some of them with arrows to shoot her with, was another matter altogether.

At the back of her mind, she'd been fairly sure that Cali was just Patch turning up to have a bit more fun with her and, if that were the case, she'd reasoned that he wouldn't let her be killed as that would spoil whatever plans he'd laid for her. It might still be the case that if she did nothing, Patch would turn up and intervene on her behalf. The prospect of relying on that made her nervous.

'What can you do, Cali?'

I can watch and report back to you. The three archers are within range now; they have strung their bows and notched their arrows. They're underneath the bignut tree almost directly behind you.

The other men were now in plain sight, advancing down the slope of the sand dune and making no attempt to hide either their weapons or their intentions. Six men, including Janvir, Moussa, and his big friend Demba. Even if Patch turned up as a dragon and incinerated the lot of them, it would mean that her chances of making the journey north through the desert would be severely reduced.

She stood her ground as the men stopped a dozen paces in front of her. This, she knew, was to keep a safe distance from her when the arrows began to fly. Cali had said the archers were directly behind her, and this wasn't the ideal situation for Janvir and his companions as they stood a good chance of being hit by any arrows that missed her.

As if realising this, or perhaps catching sight of the archers getting ready to fire, they started to move sideways. Lone moved with them, keeping her back to the bowmen and trying to avoid being outflanked.

'What is this, Janvir? Have you grown tired of living?'

'You intend to take our camels, lady. We cannot permit this. In the desert, our camels are more precious than our lives.'

Lone's hair bristled on the nape of her neck as she felt the energy of the men's resolve. She might persuade some of them to give up and run away, but not all of them.

And she also had the problem of the archers.

It seemed that the die had been cast and this time she'd chosen the wrong game.

42

Being lost in these woods hadn't been in Ant's plan. Getting the sword from Cuthbert had gone smoothly enough, but he decided too late that trying to make his way back to Tyrant and Petra in the dark had been a mistake. He'd reasoned that the steep slope would keep him on track. The forest stood astride a ridge running north–south; it appeared a simple task to head north by keeping the same altitude as best he could. To go higher would take him east and lower, west.

What he'd failed to take into account, was the local variations in topography. Knowing the general lie of the land wasn't much help in the dark while he was clambering around in a thickly forested hillside. There were too many twists and curls, too many unexpected drops to fall down, and climbs to make where there really shouldn't have been any.

Jeremiah's absence didn't help matters. He had done one of his disappearing acts shortly after the sword had been retrieved and was out of reach. Ant wondered where he took himself off to at times like this. He presumed there was a constant pull back into the spirit world and that one day he'd stay there and never return. Whatever the reason, Jeremiah's absence was inconvenient and disconcerting.

The morning glow rising from the bristling hills gave Ant the comfort of at least being able to get his bearings. Now that he could determine east from west, he needed to find out where he was in relation to the main army camp and also where he'd left Tyrant and Petra.

He sat down on a fallen log and began to concentrate on exploring his surroundings with his mind. At first, he established a deep sense of presence, feeling the earth beneath his feet and the wood he was sitting on. The earth energy came flooding up from his legs and he encouraged it to rise all the way through his body until it exited at the crown of his head. The flow increased in power and intensity as he breathed fully and deeply, drawing the energy in, then expelling it with the out-breath.

Ant followed the upward flow of energy with his consciousness. As he rose, his mind's eye surveyed the landscape. There was a promising indentation in the hillside that might provide sufficient protection for a vedhana. A warm glow at the top of the ridge identified a small house where Tyrant and Petra were sleeping. It was very close, a few hundred paces, that's all. If he'd successfully retraced his steps, he'd be far away from it by now. Getting lost had been a positive thing after all.

Before he had a chance to return his awareness to his body, Ant felt a strong pull upwards and into the infinite void. At first, he resisted, fearing that he might not be able to return and that his physical form would be abandoned to die. Then he became aware of Jeremiah. For a brief instant, Ant could see and feel what his spirit guide was seeing. A great river flowed under a bridge that connected two halves of a great city. It was beautiful, a magnificent place that made Gort a provincial town in comparison. Ant called to Jeremiah, *What are you doing there?*

Ant was shocked by the reaction his question produced. Jeremiah screamed a ghostly scream that felt more like fear than surprise. Then he disappeared altogether, leaving Ant with feelings of confusion and alarm. He called and called, but Jeremiah did not return, and no matter how much Ant tried, he could find no trace of him.

Slowly and carefully, Ant reconnected with his body, funnelling his thoughts down the energy tube and back into his head. The worry about Jeremiah persisted; he had a feeling that he'd seen something and somewhere he wasn't supposed to see and that Jeremiah had been shocked by him turning up in his thoughts like that.

The sheltered spot that he'd identified was as good as he could have hoped to find. Once he pushed his way through the thick bushes, he stood in a clearing surrounded on three sides by precipitous slopes, themselves heavily overgrown. Ant busied himself constructing the device assisted by the coil of thin rope he carried in his pack.

The sun had arced overhead and was on its way down before the vedhana was complete. Ant sat exhausted on the mossy ground and watched as the tendrils of light began to swirl above the intricate pattern he'd made. He was satisfied that, even at night, the steep sides and copious vegetation would screen the ghostly flickering so that it was visible only if you pushed your way through the dense foliage and entered the blind ravine. Unless someone knew where to look, the vedhana would be safe. Ant was more concerned that he might not be able to find it again.

Now he could travel anywhere he wanted to that had a similar device to receive him. He could return to the lake, visit the monks, or spy on the

King. He could even return to Malachi and the house they had shared for two years. When Ant's thoughts turned to the next part of his plan, he wondered if Malachi was making similar progress.

Ant felt happy that he'd now achieved two of the three tasks he'd set out to perform. He'd placed his spy in the enemy camp and he'd created a portal so that he could keep tabs on the army as it strove to advance north. His third requirement involved Tyrant, which is why he'd had to retrieve the sword so carelessly given away. Tyrant, without his sword, was of little use. Even with his sword, he might turn out to be more of a liability than an asset.

Tyrant was fast asleep on the bed when Ant entered the house. His snores sounded like the howls of a wounded wolf interspersed by a noise that might have been made by a confused pig. The porcine theme was echoed by the state of the room, though the prevailing smell was more suggestive of a low-class drinking establishment.

'Wake up,' Ant said, prodding Tyrant's chest.

One eye opened. 'Go away,' Tyrant said. The eye closed.

'It's me, Ant.'

Tyrant let out a long sigh. 'I can see who it is. Now go away, Ant.'

'I need you to help me. Look, I've managed to retrieve your sword for you.'

'Don't need your help, don't need anything.'

'Please, Tyrant. Wake up and talk to me.'

'Don't want to talk.' Tyrant's eyes opened and stared slightly to Ant's left, as if he was having difficulty focussing. 'See if you can find another full jug like this one.' He tried to toss an earthenware pot towards Ant, but it slipped from his fingers and landed on his chest.

Ant cast a look around the untidy room, but every pot he examined was empty. 'There's no more of it in here,' he said. 'Shall I look outside?'

Tyrant sat up slowly, holding his swaddled shoulder protectively. 'She's hidden it all, says I drink too much. I need more of it to help with the pain. I've had my arm nearly cut off; I'm injured. I need more medicine.'

'Well, I can't help you. I presume you're referring to Petra; where is she?'

152

'Dunno, hiding my licker maybe or making some more mash. She's made loads of it. A bit for my pain isn't too much to ask, is it? You tell her when you see her.'

'I'm sorry about your shoulder; maybe if I take a look at it, I might be able to help.'

Tyrant settled back down on the bed and closed his eyes. The snoring returned and gradually increased in volume.

'Leave him alone.'

Ant turned to see the diminutive figure staggering under the weight of an earthenware pot almost as large as she was.

'He's injured, he needs his rest. Some bugger nearly chopped his arm clean off. I've sewn it back on best I can, but I doubt he'll ever be the same again. His fighting days are over,' Petra said.

Ant watched as she placed the pot on top of a stack of logs in the fireplace, then struggled to fix an elaborate lid with a long tube attached. Finally, she got everything in place and turned around to face him. 'I've brought his sword,' Ant said.

'Better you keep it because he'll not be needing it. He's stopping right here with me from now on.'

Ant looked from the small woman to the big, sonorous lump on the bed. Of course; it's what she'd been wanting all along. That's why she'd been keeping close to Tyrant all this time. Injured or not, though, he needed Tyrant for the next stage of his plan and this turn of events was proving awkward. He'd have been wiser to have heeded Tyrant's plea to leave Petra behind at the outset.

'There's many that might want to take this place away from you, especially now you're making licker here. He'll need his strength and his sword if you're to survive,' Ant said. Her face set even firmer at his words.

'I can look after myself, don't you worry. Anyone who wants to lay claim to all this will have me to contend with. They won't know what hit them.'

'I'm sure you can, Petra. But don't you think Tyrant will want to move on as soon as he's well enough? That's his way, isn't it?'

'That's in the past. He's spent the last two years with me by the lake and never wandered off. It's only the army's coming that's changed that. Now we are both better here, safely hidden from all the trouble.'

'He'll want to get back to the lake and protect his friends there,' Ant said.

'I doubt it. Anyway, he knows that he can't make a difference and he'd only be getting himself killed if he tried.'

'That hasn't stopped him in the past. Anyway, he's needed in the fight against the King. It's important to everyone that he uses his strength and his special sword on their behalf. It's their only hope.'

'You take the sword, Ant, if it's so special. Use it yourself or give it to Garth. You don't need Tyrant.'

'The sword doesn't seem to work like that. Nobody else who's handled it has found it to be anything special. Grew handed it over to Cuthbert without a second thought. He wouldn't have done that if he'd felt the power that it has. It's the same with me; it's dull and lifeless in anyone's hands apart from Tyrant's.' Ant drew the blade from its scabbard and held it aloft. The blade was grey and dull. He went over to the bed and carefully laid the blade next to the recumbent Tyrant. A transformation occurred. The unremarkable weapon took on a whole new appearance. The metal changed before their eyes and began to reflect the light as if it were a highly polished mirror. The haft, which had seemed a rough wooden handle, now had intricate carvings on it.

Tyrant stirred, snorted, and his hand shifted so that it was touching the sword. A long sigh interrupted his snoring. His breathing became more even and mercifully quieter. The colour was returning to Tyrant's cheeks.

'Look,' Ant whispered, 'the sword is healing him.'

'That's good,' Petra replied as she scraped a knife on a flintstone, sending showers of sparks onto the kindling under the logs. Wisps of smoke heralded a few reluctant flames; she bent close and blew gently on these until they developed into a healthy blaze. 'Maybe he'll not need any more licker and we can sell this new batch instead of him drinking it all.'

Ant laughed as much in relief as anything else. Tyrant had looked as if he might never get out of that bed. 'Who's going to buy that stuff? It smells dreadful and anyway there's nobody lives around here. If you're counting on passing trade, then you're going to be disappointed.'

Petra gave him a glare that might have ignited the fire without her having to go to the trouble of using a flint. 'This is the finest taterlicker in the land. We're going to sell it in Gort; they'll pay top price for this, mark my words.'

'How are you going to get it all the way to Gort?'

Petra looked over at Tyrant. 'When he's recovered his strength, we'll carry the licker ourselves. Won't take more than three days if we don't dilly-dally.'

'There's an entire army positioned between here and Gort. You won't get past them easily; they're going to be looking out for anyone coming from the north.'

'Then we'll wait until they're gone or maybe sell the licker to them. Soldiers like a drink, they may turn out to be our best customers,' Petra said.

'I'm not sure your plan will do anything other than get you arrested and your licker confiscated.'

'We'll wait until the army's gone. There's no rush, we've got everything we need here.' Petra smiled.

'You might think that, but how long will it be before Tyrant gets itchy feet and decides to take a look at what's going on? You know him better than I, but my wager will be on him chancing his arm as soon as it's healed.'

Petra's smile disappeared. Ant knew that his observation had a truth in it that she couldn't ignore. 'What if I offered you a way to sell your licker in Gort without fear of being intercepted by the army, or anyone else for that matter?'

'That would be nice, thank you very much,' Tyrant said as he opened his eyes and sat up. 'I'd appreciate a sip of the good stuff, Petra, just to ease the pain a little.'

Petra offered him a small cup. 'Here, drink this.'

Tyrant put it to his lips and gulped it down. 'Yuck,' he said, 'what was that?'

'Rainwater.'

'I need a drop of licker.'

155

'You'll be having water from now on; look at you. Practically healed already. It's that magic sword that Ant brought, that's all you need. I'll not be having you drinking all the stock like you have been. If you want to do this seriously as a business, you'll promise me not to touch another drop, or I'm going to stop making it.'

'What's the point of it if we can't enjoy a little of it ourselves from time to time?' Tyrant's face wrinkled like a scolded child.

'What's the point of it if I make it and you drink it all, then lie there incapable of anything but a loud noise and a bad smell?'

'She's right,' Ant said, trying not to make his amusement too obvious. 'If it's to be a business, then you have to leave the stuff alone. You'll drink yourself to death in short order if you don't.'

Tyrant let out a long sigh and put his hand to his injured arm. 'It feels much easier; that licker has done it a power of good. I reckon I'm only a couple of jars away from a full recovery, then I'll give up the stuff for good. High days and holidays excluded, of course, and whenever there's a need for a good celebration. But otherwise, I'll stick to rainwater and the occasional flagon of good ale.'

'It's that sword, not the licker. If anything, the licker was making you worse,' Petra said.

'What's this plan of yours, Ant? Are you joining us in the licker business?'

'I've installed another vedhana not fifty paces from where we are sitting. You can use it to travel to Gort with your licker and bring back the goods you barter for it. Nothing could be simpler.'

'That won't work,' Tyrant said. 'There's no point carrying our wares into the King's tower; we'd be arrested and hanged for sure. That place is a nightmare; I hope I never see it again. The device in the tower is one that I wouldn't want to use again under any circumstances.'

'The vedhana in the tower isn't the only one in Gort,' Ant said. 'Don't you remember the one I made in the cave?'

'I do,' Petra said. 'It took me into the desert.'

'It's in a cave where the entrance is too narrow for an adult to get in or out of. I can't see what use it can possibly be to anyone,' Tyrant said. 'I'm hungry, is there anything to eat?'

'I'll do you some taters,' Petra said. 'What about you, Ant. Are you hungry too?'

Ant suddenly felt ravenous as he reconnected with his body and felt into it. He'd been keeping his attention elsewhere, thinking and feeling his way through the conundrum he was faced with. Now, he felt close to collapse and his stomach churned and gurgled in anticipation of some long-awaited nourishment.

'Don't be using up all those taters on food. Can't we eat something we don't make licker from?' Tyrant said.

'There's lots of taters growing out there, enough for a whole lake full of licker. There's precious little else bar a few weeds and a handful of herbs,' Petra said.

'Poor lad looks starved,' Tyrant said. 'Give him the last bit of cheese as a biting on.'

Petra handed Ant a fist-sized lump that smelt like strong horse piss.

'Avoid the black bits,' Tyrant advised, 'there's something not quite right about those. The green part is fine, if you don't breathe through your nose while you're eating it.'

Ant bit into the cheese; the taste was sharp and salty but less of a problem than the odour. He couldn't help but wolf down the whole piece, black bits and all. The strong smell that returned whenever he breathed out seemed a small price to pay for the feeling of satisfaction his body was enjoying. In sharp contrast, the taters turned out to be a hot pile of white mush that tasted of nothing at all. He devoured them quickly, aware of the look that Tyrant gave every mouthful.

'I don't see how using the vedhana helps,' Petra said.

'It saves us carrying,' Tyrant replied. 'We can take our licker to the cave close to Gort, then we can sell a bit at a time. Much better than having to carry the whole consignment through the forest and along the road. I didn't much fancy our chances of getting it safely to our customers without a lot of hassle. Now Ant has brought us the solution.'

'So we walk to Gort, sell the licker, buy things we need, and transport them back here. Makes sense. That way we stay together,' Petra said.

'And only Petra is small enough to get in and out of the cave, so whatever you put in there will be safe,' Ant said.

'Apart from children,' Tyrant said.

'I doubt there'll be any bother from them. In all the years me and Pepper and Col used the cave, nobody else disturbed us.'

'Fair enough,' Tyrant said. 'If you show us your new vedhana, then we can get our business under way.'

'Hold on,' Petra said, 'you're a sick man; you need to eat up your taters then get a good rest. Plenty of time for that when you're healed.'

Ant took a deep breath; his eyes felt heavy and his legs weak as tiredness overwhelmed him. As he lay down on the floor, he heard Tyrant's voice gradually fade into nothing.

43

'Look.' Vargas pointed to the men dressed in dark red robes who were in the process of opening the door to where the vedhana was hidden. 'They'll find the device. We'll not be able to get home now.'

Malachi smiled as he watched the men, laden with baskets of fruit, disappear into the darkness and close the door behind them. 'Give them a few minutes to be on their way before we follow. Take the opportunity to sample the wares available at this magnificent marketplace. Take some exotic titbits home for your family. You do have a family, don't you?'

'Yes, I have a beautiful two-year-old daughter called Dana. She gets so excited every time I walk into the house. If I could take her something nice to eat that would be good. But what about those men?'

'Fear not, Vargas, it's their device. We're only able to use it following its discovery by my clever assistant. Those men are monks on a shopping expedition and of no concern to us. Look at these, have you ever seen the like?' Malachi brandished a large brown fruit with green fronds growing from its top.

Vargas took hold of it and sniffed suspiciously. 'Smells good, I wonder if that can be relied on as a measure of the taste.'

Malachi nodded to the stallholder who deftly brandished a knife and sliced a chunk out of the fruit. Vargas chewed on it, his eyes grew wide, and he let out a long breath. 'Amazing,' he said. 'I've never tasted anything so good. How much are they? How many can I buy?'

Malachi took a small piece of gold from his pocket and gave it to the stallholder. 'As many as you can carry. Now we should be getting back to our King; you have much to report to him, I think.'

***

The King received them in his private chambers and was obviously in a hurry to hear all about their trip as he only kept them hanging around outside for a couple of hours.

'Your majesty,' Vargas said, 'Malachi has taken me to see the wonders that he has spoken of and I can confirm that what he tells you is

159

true. There is a city standing on both banks of a great river that rivals even Gort in its size and magnificence.'

Malachi listened to Vargas telling the King exactly what he needed him to and felt satisfied that the trip had been successful. Vargas's testimony would be crucial if he was to persuade the King to move his whole army south.

The King's face puckered and those tiny eyes glared back at the two men. Malachi judged that the King was in no mood for gentle small talk; something had upset him and he was likely to vent his feelings on the nearest person. Malachi took a mental step backwards and kept quiet, resisting the urge to embellish the story that Vargas was telling and letting him keep the King's full attention.

'So, you admit to being wrong?' the King said.

'I admit that my knowledge was lacking, your majesty,' Vargas said.

'You surely know the penalty for misleading your King?'

Malachi watched as Vargas's face began to redden as he caught the King's mood.

'I advised your majesty to the best of my knowledge and ability. This city is so far away as to bear no threat to your glorious kingdom. Now that Malachi has revealed its existence, though, it brings new opportunities that were previously merely hidden.'

'You were wrong before and that means you could be wrong now. How am I ever to trust your word ever again?' The King's face had taken on a blotchy appearance that Malachi put down to repressed anger. Something had seriously pissed him off and Vargas was about to receive the fallout.

'I am but a loyal and faithful servant, your majesty, and have always served you honestly,' Vargas spluttered.

'Honesty is of no use without accuracy, and accuracy is fundamental when the safety of my kingdom is concerned. What's the point of sending you off on all those expensive jaunts to far-off places if you can't see what's under your nose? I've had enough of your excuses; from now on I'll have others advise me on what's out there in the far-flung reaches of my lands. This city of yours should know who its true king is and could already have had that important lesson had it not been for your assurances that it didn't exist. Well, I think you should be taught the difference

160

between something that exists and something that doesn't. Take a few deep breaths, Vargas. That's existence. Try to bear it in mind right up to the moment it ceases.' The King turned to the soldier nearest to him. 'Take him down to the courtyard and hang him. Now. Right away. Immediately. And be quick about it; I might have another customer for you shortly.' The King's gaze rested on Malachi now.

As Vargas was dragged screaming and struggling out of the room, Malachi considered making a plea for mercy. As things stood, the man was no longer a threat to his authority. By showing him the City on the River, Malachi knew he had put Vargas completely in awe of his knowledge and power. This was something that might have been useful had Vargas remained close to the King. 'Your majesty,' Malachi said, 'I am humbled by your instant grasp of the situation and the decisive manner in which you act.' He gave a deep formal bow and began to back slowly towards the door.

'You're not going to plead for the life of your colleague, then? Some might find that a touch uncaring,' the King said.

'It's neither my place nor my intent to question the actions of my King. If you feel that Vargas has let you down and is of no further value to your cause, then you are left with no other choice than the one you have made.'

'So you agree with my decision to have the wretch hanged?' The look on the King's face was that of a snake ready to strike. Malachi knew that any answer he made was likely to antagonise the already extremely tetchy King further. To disagree with the King was, of course, an act of treason and for this, he might very well end up swinging by Vargas's side. On the other hand, a flat agreement could be construed as evasion. If the King decided he wasn't being open and honest, that could lead to accusations of untrustworthiness. He might save his skin for the moment, but be storing up difficulties for the future. There were going to be more delicate conversations to be had with the King in an even worse frame of mind. If he couldn't manage this one, it would not bode well for his plans.

'Vargas was guilty of arrogance and misleading you because of it. He should pay for his error, but if he does so with his life, there will be no opportunity for him to make amends. That's my only observation, your majesty.'

The King's cheeks reddened as the half-smile dropped off his pudgy face. 'That sounds to me like a criticism, Malachi. Am I to conclude that you disapprove of my actions?'

'It is not in my remit to offer either approval or disapproval, your majesty. I am not the king, you are.'

'If you were king, though, then what would you do? Answer me that.'

'I fear I would make a very poor king, for I lack the wit and imagination to perform as a king should. That's what we all lack in comparison to you. Imagination could be characterised as being Vargas's major failing. He couldn't bring himself to believe there was more to this world than he could see and touch.'

'You think I have imagination, then?'

'In abundance, your majesty, that's one of the reasons you are such a successful king. All I can do is to try to present you with the best information I have and leave the rest to you.' Malachi felt the atmosphere in the room begin to lighten. It was possible that the King's mood was becoming a little more amenable, but he couldn't be sure if it. Care was still needed if he was to escape unscathed.

'Are you trying to flatter me? If you are, then you are making a grave mistake. Kings are not susceptible to that kind of thing; we hear it every day of the week and it goes in one ear and out the other. Sometimes it irritates us and we have to deal severely with it. It's a form of deceit and insincerity, don't you know?'

'I offer only the truth as I perceive it,' Malachi said.

'You haven't answered my question,' the King said.

'The question concerned what my actions would be if I were you. To that, I answer honestly that I would do exactly the same as you are doing.'

'No, that's not what I meant. I want you to tell me what you would do with Vargas if you, Malachi, were king. Come on, now don't be afraid to speak your mind.'

'Then I would try to use my imagination to decide if I could foresee circumstances where Vargas might be of use to me in the future. If there were none, then I would make sure that he didn't ever let me down again.'

The King's face twisted as he digested the words. Malachi became a little more nervous as the silence grew longer. He might have been too clever for his own good here; the King's lack of patience was legendary and had been particularly absent so far. There was every chance he would grow weary of the exchange and send Malachi off to join the hapless Vargas.

'I have been sorely tested by Vargas's wrongdoing, but you are right in one thing, my imagination is a special quality that has served me well. We are about to send the army south, are we not?'

Malachi breathed deeply; the crisis seemed to have been averted for the moment at least. 'Indeed we are,' he said.

'And your friend Vargas has more knowledge and experience of those parts of my kingdom than anyone else, hasn't he?'

Malachi nodded.

'So, I think we should send him with the army to act as guide. When this is over and we have secured the City on the River, then I might have him hanged. Until then, he can be your responsibility and I don't want to ever see his face again. Now get out and prepare for the long march.'

Malachi backed out of the room as quickly as decorum would allow, then made his way as quickly down the stone staircase that led from the King's chambers down to the main courtyard.

44

Tyrant watched the boy sleep, with Petra fussing around the place tidying up what was a hopeless mess and better left to the more natural solution that time and decay would provide. The whole house stank of something eyewateringly foul, which he suspected might be his own body odour, in which case it would follow him wherever he went, regardless of Petra's efforts.

He had to admit that, since he'd got his sword back, he felt much better. The savage headaches had dissipated, possibly due to his drastically reduced intake of licker that had been enforced by Petra, and his wounds were no longer smarting every time he moved his arm. He picked up the blade, looked at his reflection in the shiny metal, then carefully returned it to its scabbard. When he rose to his feet, his head was clear and his legs no longer refused to support him. The thought occurred that he might be best advised to stay off the licker and keep hold of the sword, just until he was properly healed at least.

Outside, his theory about the smell was only partially justified. His own smell had receded to a faint whiff, demonstrating that there must be something even more vile rotting away inside the house. He hoped that Petra didn't manage to find it in case she expected him to deal with whatever it was that had decided to hide itself and then decompose. Better not to risk the chance of it being someone he knew.

The garden was a testament to the single-mindedness of the men who had set up the licker still. As far as he could see was the dark green foliage of tater plants. His worry that they might run out if they kept eating taters was obviously ill-founded. By the time they'd used up half this crop, the next one would have grown. That's the thing with taters, once you get a few, they keep on going, even if you don't particularly want them to.

The fresh air was invigorating enough for Tyrant to feel like a wander around. He had half a mind to try to find where Ant had made the vedhana, but he assumed it would be well hidden and he might not see it even if he passed a few paces from it. Undeterred, he ploughed his way through the thick woodland, enjoying the feel of the earth beneath his feet, and even the frequent thorn pricks felt they were only reminding him he was still alive.

There were worse places to end up, if he was going to end his days here. That's obviously what Petra wanted, and some of the stubbornness that would have made him run away seemed to have left him. Whatever he'd been running from was deep inside him and, like his smell, would go wherever he went. Not that he ever wanted to confront that feeling that surfaced every now and then to remind him that pain was all there could be in life. Better to keep busy and keep moving.

Petra was tending an open fire in the garden. When she looked up and saw him, Tyrant could see that there were tears in her eyes. 'Making more licker?' he asked.

'I thought you'd gone; you had that look in your eye when you left the house,' she replied.

'We have an agreement,' Tyrant said, 'that we're going into business together. Though I can't deny I didn't get that feeling. The one that tells me to keep on moving and never look back.'

Petra stood up and walked over to him, her hands down by her side and her face still lined with sadness. 'Go if you want to. There's no need for you to stay on my account; I can manage perfectly well by myself.'

'And a little bit better with me around, I hope,' Tyrant said. 'Show me how you make the licker so I can help.'

Petra just stood there, her tears drying on her cheeks and her face still showing signs of doubt. Tyrant leaned down and took her right hand in his. As he held it, something loosened inside him and he felt his own tears beginning to force their way through his reluctant eyes. A great sadness descended that burnt his chest and left him without any breath at all. A faltering vision of his mother's face danced into his consciousness and devastating feelings surfaced with it. He went down on one knee and the two of them managed a clumsy embrace, despite the disparity of size.

Petra was the first to break off, smoothing her hands down her thighs and turning back to the healthy blaze that was licking around a large pot. 'This is the mash,' she said. 'You have to boil the taters for a long time, then throw away the water to get it.'

Tyrant peered inside the pot and prodded the thick white sludge with a stick. 'Doesn't look like licker yet,' he said.

'It has to be fermented first,' Petra said, waving her hands to indicate the rows of smaller pots arrayed along the side of the house. 'The secret is to get the sediment from a finished batch to start off the new one. It's a continuous thing and easy if you already have the process started.'

The tops of the pots were lifting slightly to allow gas to escape, making a faint clattering sound as they fell back into place.

'After they've stopped bubbling, I strain off the water and put it in the still. Some of the mash is used for the next batch, and so on.'

'Looks easy enough,' Tyrant said. 'It's a wonder that more people don't do it.'

'You have to have the stuff to make it ferment, and I've no idea where you might get that. There's another thing; Ant has told me to throw away the first few cupfuls that come through the still. He says it's poison and was responsible for your bad headaches.'

Tyrant brightened at this news. 'So, it's not such a harmful drink as we might have thought, then?'

'No, but that's something to be happy about for our customers. I'll not be having you drinking it; this is business, remember?'

'Maybe the odd sample to check for quality, maybe?'

Petra laughed. 'There's no arguing with you, is there? A spoonful now and again shouldn't harm. It's drinking regular that I'm worried about.'

Tyrant felt more worried about not drinking regular, but decided to keep his thoughts to himself. It had been embarrassing enough being overwhelmed by unwelcome emotions, and he didn't want to get into an argument where his weakness might be exposed again.

They left the mash to cook and returned inside the house where Ant was still sleeping. 'He looks so young,' Petra said.

'That's because he is young,' Tyrant replied. 'He hides inside that thick cloak of his and wears a sombre expression, but that doesn't stop him from being a frightened child. He's trying to change the world, but I fear all he's going to achieve is a change in himself that he might not like.'

Ant stirred, yawned, and slowly raised himself to a sitting position. If he'd heard what Tyrant was saying, he made no indication of it. 'I'm still a little bit hungry,' was all he said.

Petra busied herself putting together a plate of food for him while Tyrant sat down beside him. 'I took a look out there for your vedhana and either I was looking in the wrong places, or it's very well hidden,' Tyrant said.

'I'll show you when I've had my food,' Ant said.

'I'm not sure I want to use that thing for transporting licker. It's a powerful device and not entirely predictable. I might end up somewhere I don't want to be or stuck inside that cave with no means of escape. I think I prefer to walk.' Tyrant could see the weariness in Ant was more than exhaustion and hunger. There was something gnawing away at the lad, that seemed plain. Same as me, trying to keep his feelings separate from his thoughts.

'Who taught you about the first runnings of the licker being bad? Was that Malachi?'

Ant gave a shudder as if a cold wind had suddenly reminded him to be cold. 'No, not him. It was my father who told me. He's studied ancient ways for a long time and making licker seems to have been a common obsession. He told me that it's something called wood spirit that is produced first and if you keep drinking it, you'll go blind if it doesn't kill you first.'

'That's quite a handy bit of knowledge for someone in the licker business,' Tyrant said. 'Don't want to be losing good customers or getting a bad reputation.'

'The other thing I remember is that it's important not to let the pot get too hot. If it boils, the licker gets swamped with water and ends up as weak as ale,' Ant said.

'Maybe we should invite your dad to visit us and show us what he knows. Are you going back to the lake to see him now?'

'No,' Ant answered quickly. 'He's wrapped up in his research and doesn't want me bothering him. I have things to do in any case.'

'Like what?' Tyrant asked.

Ant stared hard at the floor next to Tyrant's feet. 'I'm concerned about Cuthbert. I think I made a big mistake in letting him go back to the army.'

'Then tell him to slip away as soon as he has the chance and head back to the lake. I know someone who'll be overjoyed to see him, even if her father might not be so happy.'

'That's not so easy for me to do at the moment. I had expected to be able to tell him what to do, but I've lost contact. I have to be very close now before I can speak to him,' Ant said.

'Like as close as we are now?' Tyrant couldn't help himself from grinning. 'That's not much of a trick.'

'While Jeremiah was helping, it wasn't a problem. I could have accessed Cuthbert from here if I needed to. Without help, I would have to get much closer, and even then, it's a big effort.'

'What's happened to your pal Jeremiah? Has he gone missing again?'

Ant spread his hands out wide. 'I fear it's worse than that. He may have left me for ever. Anyway, I have to carry on as if I'll not be getting any more assistance, and that means my plans for Cuthbert aren't possible anymore. He could be in danger and I don't want to be responsible for his death now that I have no means of protecting him.'

Tyrant rose to his feet and took a long breath. 'Cassie would never forgive me if I let her beloved come to harm. I can't think what persuaded me this spy business was a good idea in the first place and now it seems quite the worst thing we could have chosen for the boy.'

'Hold your horses.' Petra looked around from the cooking pot she was tending. 'You've promised to stay here with me, Tyrant. Or has the licker addled your brain so badly that you forget everything you say the moment you say it?'

'I'm not leaving you, just helping Ant to right a wrong and save Cuthbert from harm. I'll be back before you know it.' Tyrant picked up a plate of taters and began to eat them.

'You're damn right you're not leaving me; I'm coming with you, whatever you're intending,' Petra said.

'How far is the army from here?' Tyrant asked.

'Three hours, two if we hurry,' Ant said.

'There you are,' Tyrant said. 'There and back before nightfall, pop Cuthbert and Ant into the vedhana, and off to the lake with them. We'll be here nice and cosy, ready to do business. But you'll have to stay and mind the still. We can't leave it to its own devices, nor do we want any passers-by deciding it's been abandoned and drinking all the stock.' He could see by the frown on Petra's face that she wasn't happy. 'I've told you my wandering days are over; I can't say it more plainly than that. But if Ant's going to rescue the boy, he's going to need a bit of help and I'm the one to give it.'

'I need Tyrant to guard me while I contact Cuthbert,' Ant said. 'While I'm doing that, I have to leave my body and I'd feel better if it were guarded. Tyrant's right, we'll be back before nightfall.'

'Then woe betide the pair of you if you're not. I'll not be putting up with any excuses from either of you. And I'll hold you personally responsible if anything happens to Tyrant. We've a chance of some long-awaited happiness and I'll not have you spoil that.'

'The sooner we leave,' Tyrant said, 'the sooner I'm home.' That last word gave him a warm feeling in his chest, and he watched Petra's eyes sparkle in response.

Tyrant ploughed rapidly through the forest, with Ant struggling to keep up. The wounds in his arm had eased to the point that he rarely felt them, even while using his sword to hack a way through thick undergrowth. When he burst through into a vast clearing strewn with abandoned tents and littered with discarded food, he realised with a jolt that they were too late and the whole army had upped and gone. Petra wasn't going to be best pleased.

45

Cuthbert struggled awake with a feeling of disappointment that he'd managed to sleep away the last few hours of his life. Even with his hands and feet bound, there had to have been something better to do all night than sleep. He tried to bring Cassie's face into his mind, but her features kept slipping out of focus. Did she really exist? Had that wonderful night been merely a trick of his imagination? The feelings flooded back, and a small taste of the warmth and excitement teased him into desperate regret. These were experiences he would not be allowed to repeat and the thought that at least he'd had his night of love did nothing to assuage them. Better, far better, to die without the knowledge of what he was going to be denied.

Grew was telling him something, but all Cuthbert could do was to stare at the coil of rope he was carrying. 'So, your feet will be untied so that you can walk; there'll be no easy ride to where you're going,' Grew was saying.

Cuthbert said nothing, his eyes fixed on the rope. He remembered the feeling of hardly being able to breathe that he'd experienced under the landslide. The way that the air refused to flow freely into his nostrils and the terrible panic that had built up inside him. He wondered what it would feel like when he was hoisted aloft with the noose around his neck. Would he die through slow strangulation, desperately trying to suck in air through his distended windpipe, or would the sudden jolt snap his neck and end his life in an instant? He'd never watched a hanging, but he'd heard that the dead man always soiled his trousers as he died, and this made him feel very sad. Cuthbert didn't want his last act on this earth to be shitting his pants; it wasn't fair to have to die that way.

'Oh, this,' Grew said and looked down at the rope he was carrying, 'isn't for you. It's too thin for a hanging; it would slice off your head completely and that's not what we're after. Beheading is supposed to be done with a sharp axe, though it seems to have gone right out of favour since this King came to the throne. He prefers his miscreants to dangle. This is to tie down the gear we've piled on that old cart over there. We're supposed to have been prepared to leave long before now, but nothing seems to be ready.'

Cuthbert met Grew's gaze and wondered what this information might possibly mean to him.

'You've not been listening, have you?' Grew said.

Cuthbert could only manage to nod, though whether it was in agreement or denial, he was unsure.

'It's the shock of bad news, I imagine,' Grew said.

Cuthbert tried valiantly to imagine what news could be worse than the situation he was already in. Surely any change in circumstances had to be for the better?

'In case you missed it, you're to be taken to Gort. Someone there wants to interrogate you properly. I'm sorry it had to come to this, but it's out of my hands,' Grew said.

Cuthbert's whole body began to shake with relief. 'So, I'm not going to be hanged, then?'

'Don't look so happy; by the time they've finished with you, hanging will seem like a blessed relief.'

'Yes, but surely anything's better than being dead. Where there's life, there's hope, that's what they say.'

'More like where there's life, there's terrible suffering. I don't want to worry you, but you have no idea what they're going to do to you, have you?' Grew said.

'Ask me questions?'

'From what I've heard, they start by breaking your fingers and toes one by one. Then they might ask you a question or two. If they like the answers, they might just chop a few of them off before they ask some more. If they don't, they'll just sever your hands and feet as a means of encouragement. Then there's crushing of the testicles, gouging of the eyes, and general prodding with sharp instruments. Not pleasant and might take days if you're particularly unlucky. Either way, it's a lot worse than a nice quick hanging. Pity about that,' Grew said.

Cuthbert couldn't imagine anyone being so vindictive as to torture him in the way Grew had described. He'd tell them the truth and hope that they forgave him, that's what he'd do. 'I don't believe you,' Cuthbert said, but the conviction in Grew's voice had him worried.

171

The journey began inauspiciously with Grew insisting on tethering him to the back of the cart with a rope around his neck. With his hands pinioned behind his back, Cuthbert was frightened that if he fell over, he'd be unable to get back up and dragged along until he died of strangulation. A more pressing problem soon presented itself, however. They were hardly out of the campsite before Cuthbert's nose began to itch. The way his hands were tied made it impossible even to rub it on his shoulder. He tried using the side of the cart to scratch it, but the lurching motion only succeeded in giving him a splinter which, once the initial pain subsided, did nothing to assuage his itch.

Grew was sitting, legs dangling, at the back of the cart. One of his hands was employed trying to steady the unstable heap of paraphernalia and the other clung on to the side to prevent himself being thrown off. Cuthbert realised that one of the cart wheels wasn't entirely circular, and this provided the lurching motion that threatened to eject the load on every revolution. It was as if the cart itself had grown weary of its labour and was trying to lighten its load.

The quivering pile that Grew was striving to hang on to consisted of items that appeared either dysfunctional or useless. There was a roughly hewn table that must have been knocked together by someone bereft of carpentry skills that had too much time on his hands. It probably weighed as much as three or four men. The solitary horse struggled to make progress, straining against the cloying mud, the tangle of vegetation, and the inappropriate geometry of the cart wheel.

'Why do I have to be tied around my neck?' Cuthbert asked. 'It's dangerous; I might fall and be choked to death. If I must be attached to the cart, can't you put the rope around my waist at least?'

'It's standard procedure; can't be changed even if I wanted,' Grew said.

'But it's unnecessary and dangerous.'

'There's a reason for it, just as there's a reason for everything that the army does. It's experience, you see. Long years of transporting prisoners and making all the mistakes available has led to this procedure being adopted,' Grew said.

'I can't for the life of me understand why I should be dragged along like this. Surely the whole point is to get me safely to Gort?'

172

'First of all, the rope around your neck is to make sure that you walk along quietly without dragging your feet. Your hands are tied behind your back to prevent you undoing the rope around your neck. Simple but effective, eh?' Grew said.

'There'd be more sense to it if the rope was around my waist.'

'Ah, but then you could let yourself be dragged along, thus increasing the burden on the poor overworked horse,' Grew said.

'If you're worried about the horse, why don't you just get rid of all that junk on the cart?'

'This?' Grew looked shocked at Cuthbert's suggestion. 'I'll have you know that this is valuable army property and to be safeguarded at all costs. It's way higher on the priority list than your worthless hide.'

'It looks like rubbish to me. I'd have left it behind.'

'And let it fall into the hands of the enemy? They might take advantage of it and use it against us,' Grew said.

'What enemy? Do you think there's an army of northerners on our heels looking to capture items of shoddy workmanship? What do you think they'd do with that awful table? Sit around it plotting against us? It would be a better military option to leave it and let them drag it along if they were stupid enough.'

Grew gave one of his strangled laughs. 'You're looking for sense where there is none, lad. Better to do like me and accept things as they are without worrying too much about the whys and wherefores.'

'That's alright for you, you're not being slowly strangled on your way to torture and execution. Do you really think they'll do nasty things to me? Perhaps they've changed their minds and don't want me hanged after all.'

'You can think that if it helps, but I can tell you that you've been officially convicted as a spy and sentenced to death. So, you'll hang as a matter of course, there's no going back on that. As for the interrogation, my guess is that you'll get a trainee who needs the practice,' Grew said.

'Is that good?'

'No, that's bad. He'll be more interested in technique than the effects of what he's doing. He might even be under examination, trying to impress his teacher. I'd prefer someone who's already trained and might have lost a bit of enthusiasm myself. Though it's a grim prospect you face in any event,' Grew said.

'You wouldn't consider letting me go, would you?'

'If it were up to me, I'd let you go like a shot. Trouble is, it's not my call, and if I turn up without you, it'll be me that gets the trainee torturer and I'm sure you wouldn't want to wish that on me. No, you've had it, I'm afraid. Unless you're expecting a gang of your northern pals to suddenly turn up and rescue you,' Grew said.

A small group of soldiers overtook the cart without bothering to help with its obviously difficult passage. As far as he could work out, they were now at the very back of the column of troops and losing ground all the time. Cuthbert thought about Tyrant and wondered if it was possible he might be saved. Probably not, he concluded. The whole plan had been to return him to the army and Tyrant was probably well on his way home by now. As for Ant, he'd had no contact since he'd returned Tyrant's sword and seemed to have abandoned him. A cold realisation that he was on his own seeped through his guts and he sucked in air to try to quell the panic. Grew was right, there was no hope at all and it would be better to try to end it as quickly as he could.

46

Moussa clutched the knife tightly but kept it down by his side. He tried not to look beyond Lone to the archers behind her in case she caught his glance and guessed their secret. He had no doubt that she could strike any one of them dead, maybe all of them at once. They'd all agreed that arrows were their best chance. They doubted that even she could deflect several well-aimed missiles at the same time.

Still, best to hang back a little.

He looked nervously to his side. Amongst his accomplices, there were three who he knew would be reluctant to fight if it came to that. That left Janvir, who might attack out of bravado and a mistaken sense of leadership, and Demba, the big idiot who refused to believe that Lone was dangerous at all and that everything that had happened so far was ill fortune. As for himself, he had resolved to turn tail and run at the first sign of trouble.

Lone was slowly moving sideways to the left of the group, forcing them to turn and face her, even though this made it more difficult for the archers to avoid hitting them as well as Lone. The thought came to Moussa that she was manoeuvring her position because she was aware of the bowmen and this made his blood run cold. He tried to dismiss his fear as impossible. They had spent hours making a large circle in the desert to get behind her without being observed. It couldn't be true that she'd seen them.

Moussa watched Lone's face; it was calm and impassive. She looked as if she had everything under control and this worried him even more than the thought about the archers. She'd killed Bulgar merely by placing her hand on his chest and stopping his heart. Moussa wondered if she could do that to all of them, even without any physical contact. His throat felt dry and constricted and his brow had begun to spring droplets of perspiration that were stinging his eyes. Were these symptoms the first sign of her attack?

He recalled the way that Lone had listened intently to his tale and the way her face had looked then. It had been relaxed, softer, as if betraying a weakness deep inside her that she normally kept well hidden. Maybe

Demba was right, that they were overestimating her powers and that she was only a frightened woman who desperately longed for a man to hold and protect her. Not that he'd designs on that particular role. He wasn't equipped for it, not after that unfortunate episode when he'd been discovered with one of a rich man's many wives. He'd been helping him out, he'd explained. A man with so many wives couldn't possibly keep every one of them happy without causing himself potentially damaging fatigue. Moussa winced as he remembered how he had narrowly avoided losing his head, but at the expense of his testicles. He'd grown used to not having the same carnal desires as other men and he was able to ride a camel for long distances without the discomfort and swelling that was commonplace in others.

Janvir might have fitted the bill, though. He was young and energetic. Maybe he should have tried to woo her before committing to a frontal assault.

Moussa let the others shuffle across to try to keep Lone sideways to the archers; this gave him the chance to keep further away from her and therefore less likely to be pierced by an arrow. They should have been shooting by now; the arrangement was that they would distract her as soon as the archers were ready. Moussa glanced quickly to his right and caught sight of the men's heads in the shade of a big tree. Now, he thought, before she makes us all suffer. He was finding it hard to breathe and there was a painful pressure in his chest. Was his heart about to explode?

Lone stopped moving, her eyes closed, and she raised her hands level with her hips. Moussa felt a distinct tremble in the ground beneath his feet, then Demba raised his sword and ran forward towards the defenceless woman. At the last second, she opened her eyes and stepped quickly aside to dodge the blade aimed at her head. The sword hissed past her left ear, she raised her hands and pushed the sword arm so that it continued its progress, and Demba staggered off balance. As he leant to his left, Lone's right foot hit his standing leg and he crashed to the ground, looking more embarrassed than hurt.

The rumbling sensation stopped as quickly as it had begun. There were still no arrows flying. Perhaps they were afraid of hitting Demba, in which case they should have remembered what was agreed and taken the risk. Moussa felt like screaming out instructions to them, but was finding it harder and harder to draw breath. A quick glance over at the big tree failed to detect any archers.

Demba clambered to his feet. Lone stood over him, watching carefully. This was the opportunity they needed. If they all attacked at once, the woman was doomed.

47

Lone watched the faces of the men who confronted her. Apart from the big man at the front, their expressions showed a lack of stomach for a fight and a dread of what might be done to them. She looked at Moussa, who was hanging back nervously and seemed ready to run away at the first belligerent act. He was looking everywhere except directly at her; his eyes kept flicking over to his right and towards the big tree where the archers were concealed.

Janvir stood impassive with the blank-eyed Demba to his right. They were all waiting for the arrows to fly.

'Do something, Cali, I'm about to be killed.'

I would if I could, but it's not possible for me to change the physical world.

'Then scare them, mess with their minds, distract them. Anything at all.' Lone took a deep breath and mustered all the strength she had left. 'At least tell me where the archers are now,' she asked.

Under the tree.

Lone felt into the earth beneath her feet, connected with its deep power and followed a line of energy that flowed into the roots of the huge bignut tree that overhung the archers. She channelled every bit of her remaining power into that connection and sent a pulse of energy up into the canopy. She hoped it would be enough.

The effort left her exhausted, and it was a struggle to open her eyes again and regain contact with the physical world. She was just in time to take evasive action as Demba swiped his sword at her head. She stepped backwards and swayed to allow the blade to pass harmlessly, then instinctively pushed Demba's sword arm and helped it on its way. This made Demba twist off balance, his weight transferred completely to his left leg, and she took the opportunity to kick him hard on the knee joint. She felt a satisfying crunch as bone and ligament parted and the big man collapsed to the ground.

'Come on, Cali, at least you can keep me informed of what's going on.'

The men are reluctant to attack you. Janvir is the only one you have to worry about.

'Yes, I know all that. I've got my own eyes to tell me what's going on in front of me. The archers, are they still ready to shoot me?'

No, two are dead, their heads crushed by falling nuts. The other is incapacitated; his arm has been broken.

'Now, go and bury your dead comrades,' Lone said, pointing to where the archers had been hidden.

Janvir's face twisted with alarm. 'What do you mean?' he asked.

'Did you think you could surprise me with your little tricks? I knew about your archers all along. Now two are dead and one injured. I hope you're satisfied that you're no match for me, or do you want me to kill you all just to make the point properly?'

'Is this true?' Janvir said.

'If it weren't, why is it taking them so long to shoot me?'

Janvir peered over towards the tree, narrowing his eyes against the setting sun. Demba tried to get to his feet, but his injured leg gave way and he collapsed in a heap, still several feet from the sword he'd dropped. Lone thought about kicking him in the head for good measure, but decided that might hurt her more than it did him.

She was breathing more easily now that her confidence was being restored. These men appeared to be a spent force, which was just as well, for she had no energy left and all she wanted to do was to lie down and sleep. 'Make preparations for our departure,' she said. 'You, Janvir, will accompany me with Moussa. We will take eight camels and a horse, food on one camel and water on three in addition to what we might load on the ones we ride.'

'That makes only seven camels,' Janvir said.

'Oh, yes, I want you to load the remaining camel with bignuts. Now get on with it.'

'We'd be better taking smaller fruit,' Janvir said. 'The bignuts are too heavy and contain only a small amount of nourishment in comparison.'

'The bignuts aren't for eating. I need them for when I get where I'm going,' Lone replied.

'But there's no market for the things; it's not worth the effort to get them there,' Janvir said.

'I have my own reasons for requiring them, that's all you need to know. It has nothing to do with efficiency or with commerce. Just do as you are told.'

'What about the others?' Janvir asked.

Lone's head began to swim, and her eyes were finding it difficult to focus. If she didn't lie down soon, she'd be in danger of collapsing, and then the men's courage might return when they saw her helpless. 'Tell them to take what beasts are left and go home. I've no intention of doing them harm, though that might change if you hang about here talking instead of doing.'

Janvir turned and marched off over the sand dune with the remaining men following, two of them struggling to help Demba limp along. Moussa alone remained.

'I hope my lady realises that none of this was my doing and that I would not have harmed a hair on your head,' he said.

'Of course you wouldn't.' Lone suppressed her amusement at the man's effrontery. He seemed to conveniently forget that he'd been brandishing a knife at her moments ago. 'Now, go and assist Janvir; keep an eye on him on my behalf.'

Moussa seemed reassured by her words and scampered off in the wake of the others. Lone staggered on shaky legs back to her leafy sanctuary and lay down in the shade.

'Keep watch, Cali, wake me if there's any sign of trouble.'

48

The more she saw of camels, the less Lone liked them. They were recalcitrant and wilful animals, prone to biting and spitting. Sitting perched on top of that unseemly hump being swayed around for hour after hour made her nauseous. It was as if she were being buffeted in an angry sea.

They had selected a ragged beast with bald patches and a crooked jaw that pointed away from the direction of travel. Her only consolation, and this was a small one, was that at least she wasn't being forced to travel with that misshapen travesty of a horse that had taunted her for so long. She recalled every detail of her dealings with the demon she knew as Patch and winced at her lack of appreciation of what she'd managed to snare and bow to her will. Had she known then what she knew now, she'd be sitting in the palace and enjoying the kind of life she felt entitled to.

It seemed that Patch had deceived her at every point. While she'd been convinced that the peculiar horse was all his limited talent could manifest, his power would have had her prevail over anyone who stood against her.

She wiped sweat from her brow with the tail of her headscarf and tore her eyes from the mesmeric backside of Moussa's camel. He was leading the way, with Janvir and Demba behind her. Demba, despite his pronounced limp, had announced himself fit to travel and, after looking into his eyes, she'd acquiesced. She could see no vestige of animosity in the man now, despite him being the only one to raise a blade against her. It appeared that he'd learned his lesson and was almost certainly a better recipient of her trust than any of the others.

The days were unbearably hot and the nights uncomfortably cold. There seemed to be no compromise out here in the sandy wastelands and, if she were feeling the fatigue from the journey, her poor camel was beginning to suffer terribly. Its gait had slowed to a determined plod, whereas the camels accompanying them seemed to glide effortlessly along. Lone wondered how much longer either of them could bear to continue.

'How much further?' she called out to Moussa, who was striding off ahead, seemingly oblivious to the discomfort she and her mount were experiencing.

She shouted three more times before getting his attention. He slowed his string of camels and waited until she closed down the distance between them. 'Not far, maybe two days' ride before we get to the City on the River,' he replied.

'You said that two days ago,' she said.

'Ah, yes, but I was referring to the distances a camel might normally be expected to travel. Unfortunately, we have laden them with superfluous items, which have made progress much slower. It was your choice to bring them, my lady. I advised against it, if you recall.'

Lone remembered no such advice, nor had she been made aware of the extension in journey time that her decision involved. Had she known, she would certainly have rethought her choice, if only for the sake of the poor camels.

She took a long drink of water, feeling the warm liquid seeping into her parched body. She knew it would have but a brief stay; the heat would bring it to her surface as sweat almost as soon as she'd taken it in. Moussa gave her a long, careful look before he urged his camels forward again. Something about it unsettled Lone and she felt a sudden shock of fear.

'Cali?'

Yes, Lone.

'Can you travel to the City on the River?'

Of course.

'Tell me what you see.'

Give me a moment. OK, I'm back. It's a big city on either side of a river. I think you'll like it. There are interesting things for you there.

'Like what?' Lone felt slightly alarmed at Cali's description. Interesting might mean challenging or even dangerous.

There's a presence that derives its power from the river. I've spoken to him and he seems amenable to you, providing he doesn't feel there's a threat to his river. I think he's grown a bit stale and complacent. There's not much going on that interests him at the moment.

'So, he won't prevent me from entering the city?'

No, why should he?

182

'It's just that Moussa described a small man in a golden turban that destroyed a whole army of men.'

That sounds like him. I'm sure that you have nothing to fear, there are visitors passing in and out of the city all the time.

'What else can you tell me, Cali? Can you travel even further afield and bring me news of my husband, Malachi?'

The last time I looked, he was in Gort and advising the King.

'Could you give him a message? Tell him of my situation and that I'm trying to travel north.'

That's not something I can do. I'm sorry, Lone.

'But you can talk to me, why not him?'

I should explain my nature a little more clearly to you, then. I suppose you might think of me as smoke from a fire. I can drift where I like and some people might even be able to detect my presence; those with a strong sense of smell, let's imagine. You, on the other hand, are solid and fixed in comparison, because your spirit is inextricably bound to your body. It may leave from time to time, like when you sleep, but it has to stay relatively close or risk never being able to return.

'That doesn't explain why you can't speak to Malachi.' Lone thought about her husband and wondered if he'd made any effort at all to find her.

I was coming to that.

'OK, I'm listening, there's nothing else for me to do apart from moan about my sore backside.'

As I was saying, I'm a diffuse being. That's good for watching and listening, but not so useful for influencing or doing. Other beings have different characteristics, just as you humans are quite different from each other. I have to be careful I don't antagonise others like me who might not take kindly to what they would see as interference. Just as smoke can be dispersed by a wind, they could render me ineffective or even worse.

'But what has this got to do with Malachi?'

He's already being influenced by a being much stronger than I am. Someone who I wouldn't wish to antagonise. If I make my presence known, it might be harmful to me. In any case, it would be inappropriate to risk not being able to function, even for a while.

'Is it Patch you're talking about? Is he the one who's making Malachi do whatever he's doing?'

183

No, certainly not. The being you know as Patch is much too important to be directly involved in human affairs.

'He's been interfering in mine, though.'

Ah, yes, that's because it amuses him. You definitely irritated the hell out of him with your binding spell and the things you made him do. He's just having a bit of a laugh at your expense, that's all.

'I'm not finding it funny.'

You're not supposed to, Lone.

'Has Malachi been searching for me at all, or was he glad to see the back of me?'

I don't know the answer for sure, but I would guess that's where this other entity came in. It may be that he was recruited to look for you. Whether he found you or not is another matter. Though I think it's unlikely that Patch would allow that while he still thought there was fun to be had.

'How far is the city? I'm getting weary of this journey and fear that my camel may drop dead at any moment.'

Based on your slow rate of travel, I'd say you were still at least two days away.

'So, Moussa's telling the truth about that, then.'

Not exactly.

'What do you mean?'

The city is two days away if you were travelling in the right direction. You're not.

49

Tyrant stood in the middle of the empty space between the trees that was littered with the detritus of an army. He breathed in deeply and considered his next move. 'Right,' he said, 'let's get moving. The quicker we run, the faster we'll catch up with them.'

'It's no use,' Ant said, 'they're too far ahead of us. They'll have left at dawn, so they have more than half a day's start. Even if we run, it will take days for us to catch them.'

'I don't see how that can be,' Tyrant said. 'We'll be faster than them.'

'But not fast enough, Tyrant. Even if we were twice as fast, which we're not, it would still take us days to catch up.'

'I don't get it,' Tyrant said. He knew he could run much quicker than an army could move with all the paraphernalia it carried with it. A slow walk would be all that was possible for them in his experience.

'Well, why don't we work it out? It looks like they're headed south towards Gort. Once they reach the road, it will be easy going for their horses and carts, and we might not have as much advantage as we do in the forest here. How far to the road do you think?'

Tyrant looked around at the lie of the land. 'The road is downhill from here, probably less than half a day for the army to reach it,' he said.

'In which case they will already be on it and probably travelling faster than we can through the woods.' Ant poked in the ashes of a fire with his finger as he spoke. 'So, if we run all day, we'll still be just as far behind. Then we'll struggle to move much faster than they can. How far to Gort, if that's where they're headed?'

'Less than two days, I'd say, once they hit the road.'

'So, we'll not catch up with them until they get there. Maybe they'll let Cuthbert go home if the army isn't intent on invading the north any longer.'

'I don't understand why they're retreating,' Tyrant said. 'I thought the whole point was to drive northwards and attack the people at the lake. If that's no longer the plan, there's nothing for us to worry about. We can leave them to it. I just wish we'd not made Cuthbert go back; he's not going to be able to return to the lake now. I don't think I'll be very popular with Cassie when she finds out what I've done.'

'How do you think Petra's going to feel if you set off on a long, fruitless quest that will only end up with you wandering the streets of Gort?'

'She'll understand,' Tyrant replied without any feeling of conviction at all. She'd assume he'd gone off on his own again despite all the fine promises he'd made to her. His homecoming, whenever it might be, would not be a pleasant prospect under those circumstances.

'I doubt it,' Ant said. 'I have a better plan. One that will keep the peace between you and Petra and has a better chance of getting Cuthbert back than running in the wake of the army. We can go back to Petra and then use the vedhana I built to travel to Gort.'

'Hold on,' Tyrant said, 'you'll not get me back in that tower again. I'd rather take my chances on the open road than be delivered directly into the King's stronghold, where they have a tendency to look unkindly on intruders.'

'There's another device we can travel to; we don't have to go to the tower,' Ant said.

'The one in the cave is equally useless. I don't think you would be able to get out of it now that you've grown a bit. No, if we're going to Gort, then we'll have to use our legs and the sooner we start, the better.'

'There is a third vedhana close to Gort,' Ant said. 'One that I am reluctant to use, but it has much less risk to us than the one in the tower.'

'It seems that Gort is positively bristling with devices these days. Where might this latest one be?'

'Malachi's house, on the hills overlooking Gort,' Ant replied.

'And won't Malachi be just a little upset if we step out into his living room unannounced? The last time I saw him, I'd just returned from dumping his wife in the desert, where she's probably just a jumble of bleached bones by now. I doubt he'd be overjoyed to see me.'

'Then we're going to have to hope that he's not in when we arrive,' Ant said.

***

The red glow of the fire guided them as they scrambled through the forest in the fading light. Petra was sat stirring a bubbling pot as sparks danced in the air above her head. The crackling of the healthy blaze was augmented by the clinking of numerous lids as they allowed gases to escape from the array of smaller vessels arranged on the ground beside her. She looked up at Tyrant, smiled, then her brow furrowed. 'Where's Cuthbert?' she asked.

'The army had decamped,' Tyrant replied. 'We were too late.'

'So, you just gave up on the poor lad? It was you who got him in there, don't you think you should show a bit more effort in helping him get out?'

'We could have chased them all the way to Gort and still not caught up with them,' Tyrant said.

'You could have at least tried.' Petra took the wooden spoon from the pot and waved it in Tyrant's direction. 'You could have done a bit of running, or are you too old and tired for that now?'

'Tyrant wanted to do just that,' Ant said, 'but I told him it would be pointless. In any event, he was worried that you would wonder where he was and think he'd deserted you.'

'If that's true, then he's a bigger fool than I imagined,' Petra said. 'I knew exactly what he was doing; saving Cuthbert from a bad experience in the army, that's what.'

'We said we'd be back before nightfall,' Ant said. 'It would have been days or even weeks if we'd set off in pursuit.'

'So you gave up on account of me, is that what you're telling me?' Petra said.

'No, it was based on practicalities,' Ant replied.

'I was asking Tyrant, not you, Ant. Well?'

'Practicalities,' Tyrant said, feeling he'd better keep a common front with Ant or both of them would be in for a tongue lashing. Typical woman – *I'm damned if I do and damned if I don't. There's no pleasing them.*

'So, you're just going to hang around here getting under my feet and trying to drink your way through the licker I've worked so hard to produce?'

'No, not at all. I'm off to Gort to get Cuthbert and help him return to the lake. Ant's going to take me through the device so we don't have to do all that running, that's all.'

'You can't get out of the cave and neither can Ant, I wager. Surely you're not contemplating going back to the King's tower? You'll never get out of the palace alive, and how's that going to help Cuthbert? No, you should have run after him.'

'There's another vedhana close to Gort,' Ant said. 'It's at Malachi's house. That's where we're going.'

'And how's Malachi going to feel about you just turning up?'

'I don't think he'll be there,' Ant said.

'But you're not sure?' Petra replied.

Tyrant felt relieved that her questions were now being aimed at Ant. He knew that any answers he had to give would be inadequate. It was better that Ant bore the brunt of the questioning; it was his idea after all, though listening to Petra was making him think that it was a pretty bad one at that.

'While I lived there, he was rarely at home, always busying himself elsewhere. I hardly saw him from one month to the next,' Ant said.

'We'll set off first thing in the morning,' Tyrant said. 'If there's licker made, I might as well take it to sell in Gort. With any luck, I'll be able to exchange it for a cask of ale. That would be nice, wouldn't it?'

Petra's face wrinkled into an expression that could have been amusement or derision, Tyrant couldn't make up his mind which.

'Beer? You'd sacrifice all this hard work for some beer? There's more pressing needs than beer, I'll have you know. Before we even think about beer, we need some chickens, some pigs, wood to make animal pens, and corn to feed the hens. Then there's flour to feed ourselves, cloth to mend and make with, and proper sheets for our bed. We need tiles to mend the roof, stones to fix the holes in the walls. Even more important, we need seeds to plant so we can eat through the winter. If you want to make more licker, we could do with many more pots; this big one already has a crack in it and needs to be replaced. We could do with an axe to chop firewood, a hammer and nails to build fences and—'

'Fine, I get it,' Tyrant said, 'there are a few things we need as well as beer. It's just that beer cheers me up when I'm unhappy and you've always set great store by my state of mind. What's the point of having everything if we're miserable?'

'What's the point of sitting around getting drunk when you can be doing something useful that will make you feel much better in the long run. You drink to forget yourself, Tyrant. Isn't it about time that you realised you can't get away from yourself and you'd be better off learning to live in the real world rather than hiding away in self-administered oblivion?'

Tyrant could think of no answer other than 'yes' and something inside him was making it impossible for him to express agreement with such a round condemnation of the way he'd conducted his entire adult life.

'Anyway,' Petra continued, 'if you're going to Gort, I'm coming too.'

Tyrant opened his mouth to protest, but no words came out. He looked over to Ant, who was shrugging his shoulders in silent acceptance. Tyrant said nothing. It was pointless trying to dissuade her and, surprisingly, he felt a warm comfort when he thought about her staying by his side rather than being abandoned in this remote place where anyone could happen along and turn nasty towards her.

50

Lone stretched her arms above her head and luxuriated in the gentle coolness. The sun was beginning to show signs of rising, but was still not powerful enough to obliterate the stars from overhead. These moments between the frigidity of the night time and the searing heat of the day were precious to her beyond measure. She thought of her homelands in the north and the way that the dampness could linger all day there. When she returned, she would better appreciate the exquisite pleasure of a cloudy day.

Moussa was watching Demba as he struggled to heap provisions on the backs of camels. His eyes widened as he became aware of her presence beside him.

'Which one of those is the North Star?' Lone asked, pointing upwards to where she could see the unmistakeable constellation of the handcart.

Moussa's eyes flitted everywhere, as if frightened by the prospect of finding the correct star. He thrust out an arm and indicated a few bright stars to the east. 'There, my lady, do you see it?'

'I thought it was over there,' Lone said, pointing due north.

'*Ah*,' Moussa shook his head, 'a common mistake. We call that star Makkar, the deceiver. Because it's so bright, unwary travellers follow it as if it were the North Star, but it moves around the heavens. Were we to follow that, my lady, we would be going around in circles forever.'

'Really?' Lone stifled a grin. 'We wouldn't want to be doing that, would we?'

Moussa narrowed his eyes as if trying to decide whether he'd been believed or not. Lone remembered a description once applied to her husband, Malachi, by an unkind observer. *You can tell when he's lying because his lips are moving.* While not entirely appropriate for Malachi, who was prone to promoting his version of the truth, it seemed totally apt in Moussa's case, whose prevarications had become more outrageous than ever since they set off on this journey.

According to Cali, going around in a big circle was exactly what Moussa was doing. Lone had a good idea of what he hoped to achieve by this. She looked over to her camel, who was munching unenthusiastically at the desiccated shrub she was tethered to. She wondered how much longer she would be able to carry her. The way she looked this morning, she might not last the day. Maybe that was why Moussa felt he could lie so obviously.

'I'll take your camel today, Moussa. Mine is in need of a rest,' Lone said.

Moussa's expression flicked from shocked horror back to disdain. 'But you wouldn't like my camel, my lady. Yours is much better for you. Don't worry, it's stronger than it looks. It's good for many days yet.'

'I have to learn to master any camel if I'm to travel back to my homeland. When we get to the City on the River there's still another desert to cross. I'll take your camel, you ride one of your pack animals, and mine can take a day off.'

Moussa's mouth opened, but nothing came out for a while except short breaths. 'My camel likes only me to ride her,' he said eventually.

'A great camel drover such as yourself can easily persuade her to take me, surely? Or have you no control over your beasts?'

'Of course I have,' he said, 'but she has her preferences.'

'And so do I have preferences, Moussa,' Lone said. The look on his face confirmed her deduction that they had been leading her around the desert, waiting for her camel to give up the ghost. Then they would have ridden away and left her stranded. Maybe they were going to be even more subtle and gradually increase the pace until she was left too far behind to do anything about it. Whichever way they chose, the result would have been the same. The reason for the circular route was so that they didn't get any further away from where they'd left their comrades than they had to.

Moussa's camel showed no signs of unwelcome as it bent its front legs so that she could alight. In contrast to hers, which needed cajoling to maintain even a steady plod, Moussa's camel, even after days of hard travelling, felt as if it needed to be restrained to stop it from breaking out into a canter. She breathed a sigh of relief and turned her mount towards the fading point of light that was the North Star.

Moussa and the others followed without comment. Lone had Cali to guide her now, and she was infinitely more reliable than Moussa. A decision needed to be taken about how to repay Moussa's duplicity, but that was something she could take her time over. She enjoyed thinking about the possibilities. It provided a welcome distraction from the heat.

The walls of the city appeared as a diffuse apparition on the horizon that Lone at first put down to an optical illusion. It persisted, though, becoming gradually more substantial until she could see the gaps between the stones and the substantial portal that guarded the main entrance.

'Are we going to be opposed when we try to enter?'

There was a pause before Cali replied. *No, the presence of travellers is commonplace.*

'What about the little man in the golden turban, won't he be interested in newcomers?'

Lone felt a vibration in her head as if a tiny bell had been chimed. She realised that this must be Cali's version of laughter when she replied, *None such as you; he has more important things to occupy his attention.*

Lone wasn't sure whether to feel relieved or aggrieved at the slight. 'Maybe you should introduce me to the little man,' she said.

I'm not sure that would be wise; he has a reputation for having a fearsome temper and a short attention span. Unless you have something he's interested in, I'd give him a miss.

'The first thing I want to do is bathe in the river. It's been far too long since I last had access to a decent amount of water.'

Not advisable, Cali said, *there are things in the river that are very dangerous. The people who live in the city are afraid to go near the water and with good cause.*

'I'll take my chances,' Lone replied. 'This isn't some kind of luxury I'm talking about; it's a necessity if I'm going to keep from going crazy in all this heat. The sand has invaded every part of my body and I'm desperate to wash it away.'

Don't say I didn't warn you.

Lone lead her entourage through the gate and down crowded streets until she came to the river. It was wide and fast flowing; the power of all that water was something she could feel in her body and this made her all the more determined to bathe.

At the great stone bridge, women were busy washing clothes close to where the parapet entered the water. They splashed around in the shallows, raising wet items above their heads and whirling them around so that droplets of water cascaded onto the heads of the women closest. Lone could see that nobody had ventured more than ankle deep, even though the day was mercilessly hot. She longed to walk out until she was entirely submerged and let the water carry away the accumulation of too long in the desert.

'Wait here,' she told Moussa, 'I need to bathe before we do anything else. Let the animals drink their fill.'

She urged her mount down to the waterside, then tapped her camel twice on the snout with her stick. The front legs bent compliantly into a kneeling position and she hopped off, rubbing her sore backside to try to restore some circulation. Instead of diving for the water, as she had expected, the camel hung back, reared up, and then turned away.

'They are afraid to drink, my lady. These waters are cursed,' Moussa said.

'Don't be ridiculous.' Lone threw her headdress to the ground, hitched up her clothing so that it didn't trip her up, and ran into the river. She wished in that moment that she could have thrown off every stitch and plunged naked and free into the river, but she resisted the urge and went in fully clothed.

The water was deliciously cool and invigorating. She felt the detritus of years swilling out of her hair as she submerged completely. When she surfaced, she could feel rather than hear, the collective gasps from the people lining the bridge parapet watching her. She felt her robe tangle in her legs as she lay on her back in the blessed coolness. Fools to deny this wonderful pleasure because of mindless superstition.

She could see the faces of the multitude through her water-filled eyes. Their expressions were a mixture of wonder and excitement. She exulted at her own no-nonsense attitude and her demonstration to one and all that this river was just that. A river, nothing more.

The current was carrying her underneath the bridge, but she felt comfortable to allow it and relaxed in the gentle movement. Her voluminous clothing retained enough air to allow her plenty of buoyancy, so she could just lie still and let the river take her where it wanted.

I think you should seriously consider getting out of the water now. Cali's voice held an unusual urgency.

'But I'm enjoying myself.' As she spoke, something brushed past her legs.

Don't say I didn't warn you.

As she considered Cali's words, she was grabbed around her middle and plunged into the depths.

51

As he emerged into the harsh sunlight, Malachi remembered Ant's hanging. Just as Ant had in the past, Vargas had a noose around his neck and a distressed look on his face. The three soldiers who were attending him were engaged in a discussion regarding whose turn it was to pull on the rope and hoist Vargas aloft.

'Let him go,' Malachi said, a little more breathlessly than he would have liked. It would have been more helpful to exhibit a state of unhurried calm, but had he taken more time on the stairs, the situation would have been beyond retrieval in any case.

'He's to be hanged right away; direct orders of the King. You were there, you heard him,' Gerant said. He was the overbearing, over-fussy head of the King's personal bodyguard and Malachi had the impression that he was the one who wanted to pull on the rope, despite it not being his turn.

'He's to be released if you don't want to be the next one for the rope, Gerant,' Malachi said.

'Can't go against the King's orders, I'm afraid. More than my life's worth, you understand.'

'The King has changed his orders and asked me to convey them to you. I've done my part, now it's up to you. If you do decide to hang him against the King's wishes, please do bear in mind that I'll make sure that all three of you are executed together, so you might as well have a talk about who's going to go first for that as well.'

Gerant narrowed his eyes and clenched his fists. The soldier next to him dropped the rope so that Vargas was no longer having to stand on tiptoe to avoid being throttled. 'If you're wrong...' Gerant said.

'If I'm misleading you, then the King will know soon enough and deal with me accordingly. Now get back to your duties; there could be a crowd of would-be assassins hammering at the King's door while you stand around debating.'

The soldiers left the scaffold as if it had suddenly transformed into a nest of vipers, leaving Malachi alone with Vargas.

'Am I reprieved?' Vargas said. 'Has the King had a change of heart?'

'No, the King's heart is as stony as ever. I've persuaded him to stay your execution while you can be of service to me, that's all. Now, let's get you down from there and find you a change of pants. You've got work to do.'

Malachi stood in the vast courtyard and watched as Vargas walked awkwardly up the steps and back into the palace. He shuddered with the remembrance of awestruck crowds watching their fellows being hanged, and wondered what it would feel like if it became his turn to swing on the end of a rope. He had no doubt that would be inevitable if he continued to play the King in the way that he was.

The stench of human excrement dissipated with Vargas's exit and Malachi breathed in the moist, still air that hung limply in anticipation of the release of a thunderstorm. He wondered if he was getting too old for all these machinations, particularly now that Lone wasn't with him to urge him forward towards greater ambition. It made him sad to think that she'd been lost. Despite his best efforts, he'd been unable to detect even a trace of her. It was as if she'd been erased from this world completely.

He put that down to that demon they had known as Patch. He shuddered in recollection of the way Lone had treated him while in ignorance of how powerful he really was. Not only powerful, but capricious and vindictive. It now appeared that just about everything that happened had been in some way manipulated to suit the demon's requirements.

The fact that he'd repeatedly warned Lone and advised her to release Patch before it was too late was little comfort. And here he was, acting exactly as if Lone were still here and calling the play. The risk was high and unnecessary, but he felt compelled to continue. It was as if he needed to prove to himself that lofty ambition wasn't her sole preserve and that he could change the course of history in exactly the same way that she had originally planned.

Having left an appropriate distance between them, Malachi followed Vargas into the building and walked slowly along the corridor of prison cells, most of which were open and empty. As he passed into the main palace building, he heard the sound of raucous laughter coming from one of the dining rooms. Inside, he encountered several high-ranking soldiers brandishing foaming tankards and howling with laughter at something the

196

man at the head of the table had said. Malachi recognised him as General Conningsby, the man who led the army that attacked the North.

Conningsby's face crinkled in distaste as he looked up at Malachi.

'I see you've returned from your campaign in the North, General,' Malachi said.

'Indeed, just landed, so to speak. It's been a long hard march and I'm glad to be back.'

'I wouldn't get too comfortable; your presence is required in the south as a matter of urgency.'

'We'll see about that nonsense; the army's place is here in Gort where it can best protect our King. That's what I'll be telling him when I see him,' Conningsby said, his face adopting a smirk that Malachi presumed was meant to demonstrate some kind of superiority.

'Then I'd avoid the use of the word "nonsense" in relation to the wishes of the King if I were you. Where is your army, anyway?'

Conningsby waved his arms. 'Following on, they'll be here in a day or two.'

'So, you decided to ride on ahead and leave the rest of them to wander back at their leisure?'

Malachi's words provoked him into banging his tankard on the table and his face took on a reddish hue. 'I'll not be questioned by the likes of you, Malachi,' he said.

'But you will, because you answer to me now, General. The King has appointed me to be the head of the army, so it's my duty to ask questions and it's yours to answer them. What if the North decided to mount an attack on your retreating men?'

'They're in no position to attack us, rest assured. The road was blocked by an unfortunate landslide, so that there's no possibility of them attacking us, or us them for that matter. That's why we returned to Gort.'

One of the officers pushed back his chair and clomped his way over to the corner of the room where a barrel squatted on a wooden trestle. He thrust his tankard under the tap and twisted it. A few dollops of brown sludge were deposited in his receptacle. He smacked the top of the barrel, then tried rocking it from side to side. 'We've run out of beer,' he reported, his face betraying such sadness that he could more appropriately be reporting the loss of a thousand men in battle.

General Conningsby returned his gaze to Malachi. 'You may be the titular head of the army, but you should realise that when it comes down to a choice, the King will listen to me and ignore you. I'm the one with military experience and I've never let him down and he knows it. So, leave me to deal with the King and be thankful that I'm minded to tolerate you for the time being. When that changes, I'll pull the rope myself and then you'll see who holds the reins of powers around here.'

'When you report to the King, bear in mind that he has other means of knowing what went on in the North,' Malachi said.

Conningsby's eyes widened. 'Including you, I suppose?'

'Yes. The previous report was delivered by your erstwhile superior who is, sadly, no longer with us. His testimony conflicted with the facts and the King took a dim view. I wouldn't want you to suffer the same fate. You say that the King trusts you, but remember that situation can change the instant you are caught in a lie.'

Conningsby frowned, and he stared at the table in silence for a long moment. 'Leave us,' he said, waving his arms to dismiss the men around the table.

'Wait,' Malachi said, 'there's a spy that's been arrested who I need to question. You might use your time more usefully by finding him and bringing him to me.'

'There'll not be much left of him by the time our inquisitors have done their work. Have no fear, they'll find out everything he knows without you having to get involved. We've got a few very enthusiastic juniors who are itching to learn the trade; you can rely on them being very thorough,' Conningsby said.

'I would prefer it if I could speak to him first and I think that would be in both our interests. The information he might have about the loss of a substantial number of good men might be best kept between us, General, and not disseminated more widely.'

'As long as you allow the questioners their practice eventually, I don't have a problem with that. I'll order that his tongue is cut out as a precaution before they start gouging his eyes out and that sort of thing,' Conningsby said.

'Where is he now?' Malachi asked.

The soldiers, who were all standing uncertainly by the door, looked at one another. One by one, they shook their heads. 'Well?' Conningsby bellowed.

'We're not sure where he is. Probably under armed guard and possibly still in transit,' the soldier nearest Malachi said.

'Then go and find him; ride out to the back of the column if you have to,' Conningsby said. The soldiers filed out, leaving Malachi alone with the general.

'You are, of course, going to tell me what the King already knows?' Conningsby asked.

'Of course I am,' Malachi answered. 'I only need your reassurance that I can rely on you to take care of the action when it comes and allow me to form the strategy.'

'And what might your strategy be?' Conningsby asked.

'There's a city in the south, as yet undiscovered. It holds immense riches and will massively expand our King's influence. I've advised the King to commit the army to that end and to abandon any attack on the North. There's much richer pickings to be had in the south.'

'And you want me to go along with that? Wage war in the south far away from here leaving the King all but defenceless?' Conningsby said.

'My intention is that the King accompany you on the campaign. He will be safe in your care and will want to lead the cavalcade as it enters the newly conquered city. A long and difficult march followed by lots of fighting and bloodshed. I presume that's the sort of thing that appeals to you.'

Conningsby smiled. 'You're right; it's the reason I joined the army. I can't wait to get started. Now, what was it I ought to know before I see the King?'

52

Tyrant handed over the small jar of licker and watched as the tavern owner sniffed at it suspiciously. Tyrant doubted the man was able to detect any smell other than his own violent body odour, but held his peace. The man's nose wrinkled; his eyes shot a glance at Tyrant that he interpreted as pleasant surprise, but could equally have been nausea.

'It's the highest quality, made for a very discerning clientele,' Tyrant said. As he looked around at the human detritus strewn around the dismal place that called itself the Four King Inn, Tyrant regretted his choice of the word discerning.

As if reassured, the man put the jar to his lips and took a large swig. As soon as he'd swallowed, he was overcome by a violent coughing fit, his eyes threatened to pop out of their sockets, and tears began to dribble down his bright red cheeks. As if this might help, the tavern owner began banging himself on the chest with his fist. Gradually, the paroxysms reduced and the man was able to croak out some words.

'That's good stuff,' the man gasped. 'How much can you let me have?'

'That depends on how much you're willing to pay,' Tyrant said.

'Times are hard,' he replied. 'Customers are few and far between and those we get are generally penniless. It's more like a charity than a money-making enterprise.'

'You seem to have a good turnout of penniless strays this evening,' Tyrant said. 'You'd be hard pressed to fit any more in here.'

'That's not normal, believe me. It's because the army has returned. They've been arriving in dribs and drabs for a couple of days now, and the second thing they desperately need is a good drink. The thing they need most is in very short supply these days. Most of the ladies willing to give comfort to a returning soldier were hanged a couple of years ago when they were thought to be possessed by evil spirits because they were so friendly. Once the army moves away again, this place will be empty.'

'Pity,' Tyrant said, 'I'd better take my licker somewhere else, then.'

'I didn't say that, did I?' The tavern owner put his hand on Tyrant's shoulder, a move that might have got his nose broken had Tyrant not been intent on conducting a delicate negotiation. Petra wouldn't be impressed if he reported that he'd not sold any licker because he'd smashed the owner's face in. She'd expressed the opinion that he was incapable of getting a good price and he wanted things to go well to prove her wrong.

'Then put your money on the table. Two crowns a jar. How many jars do you want?' Tyrant said.

This time, the tears that appeared in the man's eyes had not been chemically induced. He took a sharp intake of breath before answering in a voice that had become high-pitched and girlish. 'Two crowns a jar?'

'They're big jars.' Tyrant indicated the size with his hands.

'Even so, two crowns is much too steep. Anyway, I'm not interested in a jar at a time; I'll need a constant supply once my clients get a taste for it. No point teasing them with a promise, then being unable to deliver.'

'You can have ten jars a week,' Tyrant said. 'We have other customers to look after as well.'

The man's face screwed up as if in pain. 'I'd rather be the only one selling it. Better for you as well if there's less competition. If the tavern next door starts selling it cheap, you'll not get as good a price from me as you might otherwise.'

'That makes sense,' Tyrant said. 'You can have our entire production and exclusivity in the whole of Gort, but it'll cost you three crowns a jar. That way you'll be able to sell it for whatever price you want.' Tyrant wondered if Petra could make ten jars a week, then there was the problem of getting it delivered. Still, best to aim high when it comes to business.

'I couldn't sell liquid gold for three crowns a jar,' he replied. 'I'll give you half a crown a jar and that's my best and final offer.'

Tyrant's heart almost burst with excitement and he struggled to try to keep a cool exterior. Petra had suggested that they try to sell the licker for one crown per five jars. That, she'd said, would be a very good price and enable them both to live like kings with all the best food and finest clothes. Now this man was offering him five crowns for ten jars instead of two. He wanted to shake the man's hand and rush outside to give her the news, but managed to hold himself in check. He had a nagging feeling that if he took this offer and reported the negotiation to Petra, she would decide that they could have had more and that he'd not wrung the best out of the situation. He crinkled up his face in what he hoped would look like disappointment and picked up his sample jar from the table. For good measure, he gave his head a very slow shake in the way that Petra did when she was especially displeased with something he'd done.

'Wait,' the tavern owner said, 'if you can assure me that the strength won't be diluted, I might be able to factor in letting the stuff down myself and thereby improving my margins. It's too strong to drink as it is, after all. Shall we agree on six crowns for ten jars?'

'Seven would get you the exclusive deal,' Tyrant said, 'otherwise we'll sell it where we can, for the best price we can get on a week-to-week basis.'

'Seven crowns for ten jars is agreed, but they must be big jars and the licker must be strong. Otherwise, I won't pay.' The man thrust out his hand and Tyrant squeezed it hard in an attempt to disguise how badly his was trembling.

Outside, the air was cooler and the claustrophobic gloom of the tavern was replaced by a brightness that hurt Tyrant's eyes. Petra and Ant looked at him expectantly. Tyrant took a breath so that he could savour the moment.

'Well?' Petra said. 'Did you sell any licker or were you too busy enjoying yourself to bother?'

'Ten jars,' Tyrant paused for dramatic effect, 'ten jars a week. Seven crowns for ten jars. How's that for negotiation?' He smiled a smile that included the whole world, but most especially himself for being so clever.

'What about the jars?' Petra asked.

'I didn't understand your question,' Tyrant replied. He'd been expecting something more along the lines of *well done* and felt a little bit confused.

'Ten jars a week; that's a lot of jars. Surely you told him he'd have to supply his own jars? We can't have him accumulating hundreds of them at our expense.'

'No, I sort of implied that we'd sort all that out. I wanted to get the best price I could without giving him an excuse for chipping me down.'

'So we have to make the stuff, and ten jars a week is an awful lot to make, put it in our own jars, and I don't know where we're going to get them from, and transport it all the way to Gort? And all that absolutely free of charge?' Petra folded her arms over her chest and stuck out her chin.

'Seven crowns is a good price, even if it does include transport and packaging,' Tyrant said. He looked at Ant in an effort to get some support, but the boy quickly looked away, his face contorted in barely concealed mirth.

'Well, you can go back in there and tell your man he has to provide the jars. And another thing, how much money did he give you? I hope you explained that we require the first payment upfront as a sign of good faith.'

Tyrant felt deflated. His moment of triumph had somehow evaporated. Petra seemed consumed by the detail of the transaction rather than impressed by his shrewd negotiating. With a shrug of his shoulders, he ducked inside the doorway and was once again welcomed by the Four King gloom.

'Jars,' Tyrant said. He had to raise his voice so that he could be heard over the general hubbub, which had grown louder because of the fight that was taking place.

'I told you they had to be big jars and you said that they would,' the tavern owner shouted back, one eye on the distress his rudimentary furniture was receiving from the wrestling bodies.

'Yes, but I need you to supply them,' Tyrant said.

'Where would I get all those jars from?'

'That's my point; jars cost money and they'll be ending up here and in your possession. It seems only fair that you should buy them in the first place,' Tyrant said. He quite liked the way he'd expressed himself and thought it sounded very businesslike and persuasive. He doubted Petra or anyone else could have said it better.

'So, you bring it in jars and pour it out into a big barrel. Then you can take your jars home with you. After all, they do belong to you,' the publican leered back in his face.

Tyrant wondered if this arrangement would impress Petra and suspected that it wouldn't. It did seem to be the best he was going to get, though. 'I need you to give me seven crowns for the first batch of licker, then,' Tyrant said.

'You'll get your money when I get the licker and it's the right strength,' the man said. 'Who ever heard of paying for something before you get it?'

'It's a gesture of good faith,' Tyrant said, feeling the limpness of his response and wondering what Petra's reaction was going to be.

The tavern owner let out what sounded like a genuine laugh. Tyrant's words kept him amused for quite a while, then he clapped him on the shoulders. 'If you want a gesture of good faith, then I'll give you one,' he said.

Tyrant adopted a defensive stance and decided, business or not, he'd not refrain from retaliation if this man started trying to slap him around.

'Be my guest, enjoy the famous Four King hospitality. Drinks on the house. Now that's a gesture of goodwill if ever I saw one, don't you agree?'

Tyrant did agree. He agreed wholeheartedly. He couldn't think of anything more generous or appropriate. Problem was, he didn't think that Petra would agree. He looked at the sea of soldiers swimming in beer and good humour and longed to join them. 'I have my business partners outside; are they included?' he asked.

'How many?' The man's face clouded.

'Two,' Tyrant replied.

'Two more like you?'

'No, not like me. A boy and, er, a lady.'

'Ah, it's a family business. Well, the Four King Inn is a family friendly establishment. Invite them in; I'll find a clean table for you.' Tyrant watched as he started dragging protesting men two at a time across the floor and propping them up against a wall. He looked well-practised in the technique and Tyrant felt a twinge of respect for a man who had perfected his craft.

Ant and Petra allowed themselves to be led into the gloom and be guided to where three tankards of ale had been placed after the owner had thoughtfully tipped the table slightly to allow some of the brown fluid that had pooled on the tabletop to run onto the floor. Tyrant had never been so royally treated in any establishment before and was suitably impressed.

'What are we doing in here?' Petra asked. 'It's horrible. It's full of drunken soldiers and they're all staring at me.'

'It's because you're a woman,' Tyrant said. 'They don't see many women in places like this and they're just admiring your beauty, that's all.' Tyrant said the words with as much sincerity as he could muster, but he had a bad feeling that Petra's presence would inevitably require him to do some serious fighting. He decided that any direct comment, even a positive one, would have to be met with ultimate force to prevent the situation from getting out of hand.

'I don't see why I have to be dragged in here and paraded like a prize cow,' Petra said.

'It's all part of doing business; it would be impolite to decline the owner's hospitality. We need to build up a good relationship and refusing his invitation would set us off on the wrong foot. Don't worry,' Tyrant said, picking up the tankard in front of Ant, 'he's providing all our drinks on the house.'

'Tyrant's done well, Petra,' Ant said. 'After all, our main purpose is to find Cuthbert, and he's managed to get us in amongst all these soldiers and looking as if we belong. It's a very good strategy.'

'There you are,' Tyrant said. 'I'm surprised you didn't realise what I was doing, Petra.'

'That might be because you didn't know it yourself until Ant conveniently explained it to you. From where I'm sitting, it looks like an excuse to sit in a tavern and get drunk,' Petra said, picking up her ale and taking a tentative sip. Her face crinkled up as she tasted the beer.

'I'll go and ask around,' Ant said.

'I'll come with you,' Tyrant said, then sat down again with a thump when he saw the glare in Petra's eyes. He smiled an apology for his discourtesy, and Petra looked back at him with some warmth in her eyes. He raised his tankard to her.

'Here's to business and good beginnings,' he said.

Ant returned with two men who sat at the table and looked expectantly at Tyrant's ale. The owner came over with two more beers and slapped them down in a manner that suggested his largesse was being sorely tested and that the limit of his hospitality had been reached.

'These two fine soldiers are pikemen,' Ant said.

'Elite pikemen,' one of the soldiers corrected.

'Oh, really?' Tyrant asked. 'What's an elite pikeman, then? How does he differ from an ordinary pikeman?

'We have proper pikes with shiny metal bits and everything. Most of the others just have sticks. We're more for ceremonial than fighting, so we keep ourselves at the back.' The soldier looked around as if worried about being overheard. 'To tell the truth, we've been forbidden the use of our pikes for fighting in case we damage them or get them dirty. It's our job to protect them at all costs, even to the extent of running away and hiding from any trouble. Of course, the enemy don't know this, and just the sight of all our glitter would probably make them retreat anyway.'

Tyrant suppressed a laugh. His opinion, borne out by experience, was that pikes were more of a hindrance than a useful weapon. It amused him greatly that this seemed to have been confirmed by the upper echelons of the army. 'Our friend Cuthbert's a pikeman,' he said.

'Yes, we know,' the soldier looked at Ant. 'They were right at the front when the landslide came and were mostly buried. We're not allowed to talk about it, but we could see a little of what was going on at the front. The North had a big man who brought the sides of the hills down on us when he attacked.'

'We heard that this Cuthbert survived because he was a northern spy and knew what was going to happen. They sent a raiding party over the mountains and when they attacked the northerners, they captured the spy and brought him back for hanging,' the other soldier said.

Tyrant began to feel queasy; it was either the beer or the conversation, so he took another large swig of ale to try to settle the matter. 'How do you know that Cuthbert's a spy? Couldn't he have been a prisoner captured by the North?'

'All I know is that he was sentenced to hang by a military court. I expect he's dead by now, they usually carry out the sentence right away.'

'No hanging about in the army,' the other soldier said with a laugh that nobody else took up.

The news put Tyrant off his ale to the extent that he finished what was in front of him, then allowed himself to be taken back outside without testing the resolve of the tavern owner by requesting further hospitality.

'What do we do now?' Petra asked. 'If the poor boy's dead, there's no point in continuing to look for him.'

'It sounds bad; I feel awful,' Ant said. 'It was all my idea and now it seems I've only succeeded in getting the poor lad killed.'

'There's a chance they've brought him back to hang, in which case they'd take him up to the palace,' Tyrant said.

'We could ask at the gate, see if a prisoner has been brought back,' Petra said.

'Maybe I should do it? You two might make them wonder why you're not in the army yourselves.'

Tyrant watched from a safe distance as Petra addressed a soldier guarding the gate. Then she moved to another, who shook his head and pointed inside the palace grounds. She walked through the stone arch and disappeared.

Tyrant looked at Ant, who had just been standing mournfully by his side all this time. 'The sun's going down, it'll be dark soon. We need to find out what's happened to Petra. It doesn't look like she's coming back.'

'I'll go,' Ant said and walked off slowly. Tyrant wrestled with the decision whether to risk accompanying the boy, but by the time he made up his mind, Ant had made his way through the gate unchallenged.

53

Lone was unable to prevent herself from being dragged into the depths of the river. She could feel strong jaws gripping her midriff and she was being rolled around and around as she was carried deeper into the water. It was all she could manage to hold her breath in the knowledge that as soon as she began to inhale water, she was finished.

Whatever it was that held her fast, it had a tiny mind that worked on instinct alone. Even had she been able to communicate with it in some way, there was no prospect of dissuading actions that were purely automatic. In the dizzying swirl of her passage, she had no means of determining what she was dealing with, nor had she the strength remaining to fight. Even if she'd been able to detect its heartbeat, she had insufficient puissance to affect it.

She concentrated on not breathing and conserving what little life she had left. As she relaxed, thoughts came streaming through her mind as if it were reviewing her life prior to letting it go.

She thought of Tyrant and how she'd manipulated him into helping her travel to Gort. She'd thought to control him like a puppet, but in the end, he was the one who put paid to all her plans and dumped her in the desert with no means of escape.

Then there was Patch, that weird manifestation of a horse, who proved to be infinitely more powerful than she had imagined. Rather than being compelled to do her bidding, he had played her as a fool and only revealed his true nature when it was too late for her to take advantage of it. A sudden hopeful idea rose from this memory. Perhaps Patch wasn't finished with her quite yet; after all, he had implied there was a purpose to her release and that suggested that higher powers retained an interest in her wellbeing. If she died now, she'd be no use to anyone. Maybe Patch would rescue her.

Her mind began to swirl with fog; cloudy tendrils of thought drifted past without the substance necessary for her to cling on to and decipher. There was a burning in her chest and her lungs were screaming for relief. Her head struck the river bed and the swirling stopped. For a moment, it seemed that the jaws had released her and she gave a feeble kick at the sand to try to propel herself upwards towards the surface. Then the great mouth fastened on to her again, she felt teeth tearing into her back, and the rolling motion began again.

Malachi's face swam into view, and she wondered if he'd bothered to look for her after Tyrant had banished her to the desert. Even if he had made the effort, she doubted that he would have been able to find her as long as Patch wanted her hidden. *He'll be too wrapped up in his ambitious schemes to worry about me,* she thought.

She had no more strength or will to control the overwhelming impulse to open her mouth and breathe. She knew that as soon as she filled her lungs with water, death would follow closely behind.

Her eyes were tightly shut in an effort to concentrate all her awareness on overriding her body's insistence on breathing, even though there was no air to breathe. Water rushed past her head, her body suddenly felt lighter, and she wondered if this was the prelude to her dying process. Her will no longer held sway over her instinct and she opened her mouth and took a deep gasping breath.

A coughing fit convulsed her as water found its way into her lungs. As she tried to expel it, she realised that most of what she was breathing must be air and that only a tiny amount of water was getting in. Her mind became clear again, even while her body was convulsing. Through a veil of liquid, she could see the bridge receding as she was being swept along in the current. There were figures on the shore and her water-filled ears could detect shouting from their direction. After breathing carefully for a while and taking stock of her situation, she began to strike out for the shore. With every kick of her legs, she expected the beast to return to finish the grisly job it had started, but they remained unencumbered and she began to make good progress.

By the time she reached the shore to be grabbed by several pairs of hands, some of her normal composure had returned. 'Let go of me,' she said. 'One of you get me a blanket and the rest of you can stop looking at me.'

'You were underwater so long that we thought you were dead,' Moussa said. 'One moment you were swimming on the surface, then you went down. I never thought it possible that anyone could hold their breath for that length of time.'

'You should know that you underestimate me at your peril,' she replied. Whatever it was that had grabbed her had been invisible to the onlookers standing on the shore. She wondered if the people on the bridge had a better view of what had happened.

It's not advisable to swim in the river.

'Cali?'

I tried to warn you, but it was too late.

'What happened to me?'

You were taken by one of the giant beasts that live in this stretch of the river. They are used to eating humans because it is traditional here to throw the dead off the bridge instead of burying or burning them.

'Why did it let me go?'

It didn't let you go; you were rescued and carried up to the surface.

'Who was responsible for that?'

I suppose you might say that I was, Lone.

'But you told me you could have no effect on the physical world; how could you save me?'

I interceded on your behalf.

'Thank you.'

He wasn't interested in you at first, that's why it took so long. Then he asked me about Malachi and I told him you were his wife. He seems to know your husband and has some regard for him.

'Has Malachi been here?'

Yes.

'Looking for me?'

Perhaps, but I detected there may be another purpose to his visit, something that the river spirit is party to.

'Can I talk to the river spirit myself? Can you arrange that?'

I don't know if he'll want to speak to you; he gives the impression that he's preoccupied with other matters and it was a big effort for him to do what he did for you.

'Then ask him when he last saw my husband. I need to know that, at least.'

Lone wrapped the blanket tightly around her torso. She didn't need it for warmth, the heat was more than sufficient to comfortably dry off her clothes while she wore them. She needed the blanket because she had quickly realised that her wet clothes were almost completely transparent, a factor she'd neglected to anticipate in her anxiety to feel the cool waters around her body.

Cali came back almost immediately with an answer. *He hasn't got time to talk to you; there are things happening that need all his attention. As for your husband, he last spoke to him three days ago while he was standing on the bridge.*

Then he must still be close by. Lone's spirits rose at the thought that Malachi was not only searching diligently for her, but had almost found her. Now that there was the prospect of having someone to share the burden with, the toll of having to survive alone in this inhospitable environment began to weigh even more heavily on her. 'Find him, please Cali.'

I can locate him, that's not a problem, but I don't dare communicate with him, it's too dangerous for me.

'Where is he?'

Gort, in the King's palace.

'That can't be right if he was here three days ago. Either the river spirit was lying or you're mistaken.'

I'm not wrong and the spirit of the river was not mistaken.

Lone sat down by the river and watched it flow steadily past as if it were taking away all her hopes with it. Malachi had been here and she'd been so close to salvation. Now she faced weeks of hard slog across the unforgiving desert. She didn't think she would survive the rigours of another desert crossing.

54

Ant pulled up his hood to shroud his face and ordered his thoughts as he passed under the stone archway that led to the King's palace. Two soldiers bearing what he now recognised as ceremonial pikes, not to be used in case they became scratched or dirty, stood quickly aside.

Ant also had to press himself protectively against the wall as two officers came through the gate on horseback, hooves striking bright sparks in the gathering gloom. They had the air of men who were reluctantly engaged in a matter that they wanted to quickly resolve. The spare mount they dragged behind them had a similar demeanour, sliding in their wake, creating its own incandescent shower.

You know me, Ant suggested. *There's nothing to concern you.*

One of the soldiers raised a hand in an uncertain wave, which Ant responded to with a nod as he trudged slowly up the slight incline and across the deserted courtyard. Ahead, light blazed from almost every window and doorway in demonstration of the activity going on inside. He could see no sign of Petra, though he knew that she could make her tiny figure very difficult to find if she wanted to hide.

With a deep breath, he approached the place where the gibbet stood with its three nooses ready for immediate use. It seemed he was destined to keep coming back to this place; perhaps he needed a reminder of how brutal life could be. On the other hand, the old wounds that it brought to the surface were so painful as to render him almost incapable of coherent thought. He recognised that his breathing had stopped only when the lack of air forced him to inhale deeply and stand gasping for a few moments. A deep sense of dread descended on him, and he looked around nervously, anticipating sudden capture. His neck hurt where the noose had tightened and he felt as if he was back on the scaffold.

He decided to get out of this dreadful place as soon as he could and turned back towards the gate. A small movement in the very corner of his vision caught his attention. Someone was standing in the doorway that led to the prison cells. Ant's breath caught again. He couldn't bring himself to look directly at the figure. Instead, he turned his back, quickened his step, and hunched his shoulders.

'Ant.'

The voice sent chills through his body, even though it was instantly recognisable. He stopped and waited.

'Ant.'

Barely able to control his shivering, Ant turned around slowly to see that the figure had detached from the building and was nearly upon him. 'Malachi,' Ant said, 'you gave me a fright.'

'You'd better come inside, this place has bad connotations for both of us,' Malachi said. 'It's good to see you again; I'm glad to have you back. There are things going on that you need to be aware of.'

Ant's head immediately filled with a dozen questions that Malachi might be able to answer. The main one concerned the whereabouts of Cuthbert, but there were others involving Jeremiah that were almost as pressing. He nodded and followed Malachi into the corridor sparsely lit by candles placed in each window arch. They proceeded through several doors and eventually he was shown into a room with a polished table surrounded by ornate chairs.

'We won't be disturbed in here,' Malachi said. 'It's the King's private dining room and nobody comes here unless the King decides he wants to entertain. I left him eating in his chambers, so he's not going to need his dining room tonight.'

'You've been talking to the King?' Ant asked.

'Since you left, I've become very close to the King. He relies on me for counsel these days. Why do you think the army has been withdrawn from the North?'

'That was you?' Ant asked.

'Yes, that was my advice to the King. But the attack was stopped by other means, as you well know. What I need you to tell me is exactly what happened when the army arrived in the North and was confronted by your friends.'

'Why do you refer to them as "my friends"?'

'Because they are your friends; or are you going to tell me that I'm mistaken and everything you've done is on behalf of the King?'

'You know what my feelings are concerning the King,' Ant said.

'There's a very old saying: "my enemy's enemy is my friend". Does it apply in your case?'

'I suppose it does, though the people in the North want no trouble. I merely sought to prevent them from being needlessly slaughtered,' Ant said.

'Very commendable; I'm sure you appreciate that between us we've done a good job in that regard. I hear that the only lives lost were those of the King's soldiers and I'm interested to know how that happened. What exactly did you do, Ant?'

'I wanted to stop the fighting,' Ant replied, 'so I sort of wished the walls of the canyon down on their heads. I sent energy down the cracks that were already there and it loosened the rock enough for it to fall.'

'Interesting, that's something my wife used to be able to do on occasion, though I doubt she ever succeeded on such a scale as you have. Are you sure there were no outside influences? Did it feel like you were getting assistance from anywhere? Maybe there were others involved that amplified your efforts?'

'I don't think so, there was nobody else around. Apart from Jeremiah, of course. I don't know what happened to him; he deserted me when I most needed him.' Ant studied Malachi's face but, as usual, apart from the odd twitch of that large nose, it remained impassive. He knew that he was being interrogated, but hadn't been able to decide to what purpose. Was Malachi really trying to find out what happened? He already seemed aware of what Ant had been doing.

'That's demons for you, wholly unreliable and likely to be more hindrance than help. Still, you had a good deal of his attention and that must have been useful while it lasted.'

'I surprised him,' Ant said, 'and since then he's kept well away from me.'

'Really? How did you manage to do that?'

'I was looking for something and I projected my spirit out of my body to get a better view. Suddenly, I had a glimpse of something through Jeremiah's vision and felt that he was shocked to find me there. He might even have been afraid, it was that intense. Then he was gone almost as soon as he detected me,' Ant said.

'Can you remember where he was?'

'It was the city in the desert where the monks gather their food,' Ant said. As he spoke, he saw a flicker of something dance across Malachi's face. It could have been surprise, but there seemed to be an element of concern involved. It was gone in an instant and the face went back to its normal repose.

'What did you do after the army's passage was blocked?'

'I had Jeremiah search for survivors. Unfortunately, we were only able to save one person, a soldier named Cuthbert. That's why I'm here, to look for him,' Ant said.

'Why would you need to do that?'

'I persuaded him to re-join the King's army, but I fear I made a mistake in doing that. I've a feeling that his life may be in danger and I want to protect him. Without Jeremiah to help, I've been asking around Gort, but been unable to find out anything other than he has been sentenced to hang,' Ant said.

'Forget him,' Malachi said, 'he's no concern of yours any more. You've done what you can for him and it's very commendable. You need to think of yourself and what part you intend to play in the forthcoming events.' His voice dropped to a whisper. 'You need to decide if your overriding ambition remains that of getting rid of our monarch. Well?'

Ant wondered if his answer would determine his fate and decided that, one way or another, it would. If he answered truthfully, would he be confessing his treason and be returned to the gallows as a result? 'I don't see why this King should be allowed to get away with the things he's done. He was having children hanged; what worse outrage could there be? How can anyone justify killing a young girl and throwing her body into a heap of corpses?' Ant shuddered at the recollection of her eyes staring at him in dead accusation as he was piled on top of her after they hanged him.

Loud footsteps clattered along the stone outside, making him nervous. He winced inwardly as he imagined the soldiers arriving to take him away after Malachi had successfully lured him in here to await their arrival. How far could he trust the man who had saved him from the same fate as that unfortunate girl? 'Will you help me find Cuthbert and save him from the gallows?'

Malachi looked back at Ant as if trying to fathom his deepest secrets. 'I can't do that without compromising a position I've spent an enormous amount of hard work and sharp risk to attain. You have to realise that

215

there are many people who have the ear of the King and countless others who desire it. Almost all of these individuals are inimical to me and would be happy to assist my downfall in any way they could. They search for any signs of weakness in order to use it to their advantage. If I were to find your friend and intercede on his behalf, it might have serious repercussions for me. There's the possibility that, if portrayed to the King in a certain way, he could decide I had been acting against his interests. At the very least, there would be explaining to do and a certain loss of confidence.'

'We're talking about my friend's life; it's far more important than you keeping face with that capricious monarch of yours who could quite easily have the whole royal household killed if he gets out of his bed on the wrong side,' Ant said.

Malachi sighed, his eyes flashed briefly, and Ant felt a sudden burst of positivity to contrast with all the downbeat words he'd been hearing. 'There's something important that I need you to help me with. If you agree to do that, I'll try to save your friend.'

'If you save him, I'll help you, provided it doesn't involve sacrificing anyone else's life.' Ant said. 'I'd like to know more of your intentions to help me decide how I feel about it.'

'All in good time,' Malachi replied. 'There are things that can only be revealed at the appropriate time in case the very act of saying or thinking them might make their achievement more difficult. There are, as you are all too aware, beings other than humans who inhabit our world. Even our thoughts can be privy to their probing and their allegiances may be directly opposed to our intentions. Take Jeremiah, for instance. Can you be sure that he has only your best interests at heart? You've been very close to that one for a long time, but even so, there seems to have been room for misjudgement. If he's not your sole preserve, who else might he have been in touch with? How many of your secrets did you share with him? Are you certain that he hasn't passed them on to others?'

Ant felt himself getting hotter. The room had felt cool and airy at first, but now there were drops of perspiration forming on his forehead. 'I did wonder how much of what I was doing got reported back to you,' Ant said.

'Some, to be sure. But I always found your Jeremiah very guarded and difficult to contact. There were glimpses afforded to me of the action in the North, but little of what I saw came from Jeremiah. If it had, there would be no reason for me to seek this information from you now.'

'What do you want me to do, Malachi?'

'A little more of what you're particularly good at. I have need of a more comprehensive communications network, which you can help provide. There's also the job of ferrying people about and making sure they pop up in the right place at the right time. To the uninitiated, these portals can be quite unpredictable.'

'Nothing more than that?'

'For the moment, that's all I can think of. There will be other tasks, I'm sure, but that's the gist of it for the present.' Malachi gave him a thin smile that did nothing to soothe Ant's suspicions that he was being told only what Malachi knew he wanted to hear.

More clattering of feet on hard floors made Ant start. This time, it sounded as if there were dozens of men stomping their way towards them. Malachi's face became even sterner. 'I think we may have company and it's not someone you'll be glad to see again. When you get your chance to leave, get out of the palace as quickly as you can and find a man called Vargas. He lives in the big house close to your father's. Tell him I sent you and he'll look after you. In the meantime, you'd best be ready to meet your King.'

55

The King swept into the room, followed by a torrent of followers. His eyebrows arched when he saw Malachi. 'I've got people scouring the palace for you, yet here you are waiting for me. How do you do it, Malachi? Can you anticipate my every move?'

Malachi decided that the King's words held more approval than menace and bowed low. 'Your majesty finds me unprepared for our meeting; I am still engaged in giving instructions to my assistant.'

'Assistant?' The King squeezed himself into the seat at the head of the table. 'The great Malachi needs assistance, does he?'

'With the exception of the truly great such as yourself, we all need as much help as we can muster.' Malachi turned to Ant. 'You may go now,' he said, 'and remember your instructions.'

As Ant left, Malachi watched as Conningsby took the seat at the King's right hand, giving Malachi a smug look as he did so. The chairs close to the King filled rapidly with senior advisors and Conningsby's generals. All told, there were more than a dozen of them. Malachi took the seat at the opposite end of the table to the King. His half of the table remained unoccupied and he drew puzzled glances from the others as if they were uncertain whether or not to spread themselves out.

Servants brought platters laden with food, which were placed within reach of the King who started to eat as soon as the first one arrived. While there were some hungry stares at the sumptuous display, nobody else had the temerity to take any and the King seemed content with that situation.

'We've been discussing your advice regarding the city in the south,' the King said. 'My generals all agree that an expedition to conquer it would be arduous and likely to fail. They are concerned that I would be left here in Gort relatively unprotected in the event that the northerners gathered a force to attack. Do you agree with them, Malachi? Or has it been your purpose all along to engineer a situation that leaves me vulnerable?'

Malachi watched a thin smile form on Conningsby's face as the King spoke. 'I agree with the guidance to this extent; the campaign will be long, the trek through the desert will be difficult and we will need as many troops as we can muster if we are to succeed. Where I disagree concerns the matter of whether it will be in your majesty's best interests or not. There is an opportunity to more than double the size of the kingdom, to rule over a magnificent city twice the size of Gort, and to obtain access to a great deal of wealth. What has to be done to achieve this is admittedly not easy, but nor is it impossible. Quite the contrary, all we have to do is to turn up outside the city in sufficient force for them to capitulate. There'll be a long journey but a magnificent prize at the end of it.'

'There you are,' the King said as he turned to Conningsby. 'I told you Malachi would explain the political imperative in words that even you military types can understand. Are you telling me you can't manage to get your men across a desert?'

'No, your majesty.' Conningsby's cheeks had reddened and the smirk had disappeared from his face. 'If you so command, it will be done, as always. There may, however, be losses due to the harsh environment.'

'Let me get this straight,' the King said. 'The army is reluctant to embark on a campaign that will provide me with immense benefits because it might be a bit hot and the men won't like it?'

Conningsby looked as if he'd swallowed something too big for his gullet. Malachi sat quietly, trying not to enjoy the man's discomfiture too much. He knew it would be his turn to face the King's enquiries soon enough.

'Your majesty,' Conningsby spluttered, 'there are other, more compelling reasons than the discomfiture of my troops.'

'Then why start with that one, eh? Perhaps you need time to make up a better reason to deny me my rightful place as monarch of the whole world?'

'It's too risky,' Conningsby said. 'Your majesty might be placed in peril. The army of the North may descend on Gort while we are engaged in the south.'

The King moved his attention to Malachi. 'What do you say to that?'

'The risk of an attack from the North is negligible, your majesty. They have no army and no desire to venture south. Perhaps the general has forgotten that the road is blocked to the extent that our own troops had to be withdrawn because there was no prospect of engaging the enemy. Unless someone spends a year or two rebuilding the road, Gort would be safe even if there were a hostile army coming from the North.'

'You can't be certain of that,' Conningsby interjected. 'The King will still be left unprotected.'

'But that's where you're wrong,' Malachi said, 'because the King will be in your care all along. His majesty will travel with the army so that he can make a triumphal entry to the city.'

It was the King's turn to look flabbergasted. 'Are you telling me I have to endure months of hardship, Malachi? A trek through an uncharted desert? Surely I'll be safer in Gort, and much more comfortable?'

'Safer, perhaps, but personal safety isn't your main concern when the opportunity to conquer new lands presents itself. That I know from our discussions. Also, your new subjects will need to see their King in person, not have his greatness extolled in absentia. They aren't going to become loyal subjects of a King who is only a rumour to them. Once they've experienced you in all your glory, you will have a long and peaceful reign ahead of you,' Malachi said.

The King sat with his hands to his temples as if his head had become too heavy for his neck to hold up. 'How long will it take?' he said.

'I estimate it will take one month to reach the furthest boundary of your existing kingdom, then two weeks' travel across the desert,' Malachi answered.

'Six weeks in transit,' the King said. 'I've experienced lengthier journeys and been away from Gort much longer in the past. I am concerned about the desert, though.'

'I have arranged the very best guide and obtained the assistance of a local river spirit who will ensure a supply of water,' Malachi said.

'Can you trust this entity?' the King asked.

'He's willing to assist us because he feels that having you as King will be in his best interest.'

'That's very perceptive of him. I only hope he keeps that point of view until we no longer have to rely on it. I need to consider all the implications, Malachi. There are hardships to face, but I have never shirked my share of hardship if it had to be endured on behalf of my subjects. But this brings new difficulties that have to be overcome. I need to be satisfied that adequate preparations can be made to prevent my undue suffering. For example, the effect of the desert heat on my best wine has to be considered. I can't be expected to drink vinegar with my meals – that would be too much. Unless the wine and certain other essentials for royal travel can be protected, I can't see myself agreeing to this at all.'

'I'm sure that Donald can make the necessary arrangements for your majesty's comfort, and we all appreciate the outstanding qualities of leadership that will be needed if the campaign is to meet with success,' Malachi said.

'It all seems a bit rushed,' Conningsby said. 'No sooner do we return from the North than we're off again. Can't we allow our troops a good rest and give ourselves time to consider the matter?'

'Let me summarise the matter in hand so that you can give the King the benefit of your military advice,' Malachi said. 'We have discovered a city in the far south which is bigger and potentially more powerful than Gort. As things stand, they are ignorant of us and our intentions. Because they have desert all around them, they have grown accustomed to isolation. Furthermore, the river spirit who has protected them in the past has sided with us and will no longer keep them safe. They are ill-prepared and unsuspecting. This situation will not last forever. If they decided to raise an army and march North, we would have difficulty in resisting them. They could be hammering on the gates of Gort within a few weeks.'

'Gort can be defended,' Conningsby said. 'Nobody has succeeded in breaching our inner wall.'

'While we are cooped up in our stronghold, they would be free to do as they wanted with the rest of the kingdom. We've never faced an enemy with the resources that they have. More people live in the City on the River than in the rest of the world. The army they could raise would be beyond anything we might imagine. At present, though, they have few soldiers used to handling only internal matters. Their city is protected only by the desert to the north. Tell me, General, from a military standpoint, do you believe that time is not an issue and that we should wait for them to come to us?'

Conningsby shook his head. 'If it is as you describe, then we should attack as soon as we are able, but I doubt that things are as simple as you make out. There are important military principles that need to be adhered to. For example, we need to send a scouting party to determine the exact size and disposition of their forces and the nature of their defences.'

'Then come with me,' Malachi said. 'I've already taken Vargas to the city and he's seen everything I describe. You and your generals are welcome to accompany me.'

Conningsby shook his head even harder. 'You'll not get me in one of your devilish devices, Malachi. I'm as likely to end up in the far reaches of hell as where you intend me to go. Neither can I risk losing any of my generals. A scouting party is the answer, traditional ways are always the best.'

'Isn't the element of surprise an important aspect of military strategy?' Malachi said. 'And won't that be lost when our scouting party, as you describe it, arrives there? Won't the response be to ready a massive army against attack as soon as they get wind of what we're up to?'

'Our scouts are very competent; they're trained to sneak up on the enemy, observe, then sneak away undetected.'

'I doubt sneaking across desert has been one of the skills they've acquired,' Malachi said.

'Enough,' the King interjected. 'You two can squabble all you like, but I don't want to have to listen to it. General, I take it that, apart from one or two details, you are in agreement with Malachi that the military advantage is with us for the moment but may be lost if we wait.'

Conningsby opened his mouth, but no words emerged.

'Well?' the King asked. 'Are you advising me to attack this city now or do you urge caution? What is the military imperative?'

'Attack.' Conningsby sounded as if he was having difficulty clearing his throat.

'When?' the King asked.

'Now, as soon as possible. But…'

'No buts required. I have your answer. Now work out the details between you; I have to confer with Donald regarding the safe transportation of essentials through an inhospitable landscape.' The King allowed himself to be helped to his feet by a couple of courtiers, then waddled out of the room without a backward glance.

Malachi claimed the seat that the King had vacated next to Conningsby. 'We need to talk,' he said. 'In private.'

The general waved away his staff and stopped the servants from removing what remained of the King's supper before they followed them out. 'I know what you're up to, Malachi, and you're not going to get away with it,' Conningsby said.

'Then you had better tell me what it is that I won't be allowed to do so that I can avoid wasting my time in the attempt.'

'You want the King and the army out of Gort so that you can take over. I wouldn't put it past you to be in league with the southerners. You plan for us all to perish in the desert and for you to take the crown for your own,' Conningsby hissed.

Malachi laughed out loud; he felt genuinely amused at the old general's accusation. It was exactly the plan he had formulated in the first place but then rejected as being too onerous and unworkable. Usurping a king was a relatively easy matter compared with the management of the after-effects. Chaos made him uncomfortable and the outcomes were far too unpredictable. 'Very good, General, I applaud your imagination and am gratified by your estimation of my abilities. However, that is not my plan, nor do I think for a moment that it is yours. You and I need to reach agreement about our mutual interest, otherwise one of us will have to go. I can't have all this bickering into the King's ear at every juncture. I won't have you arguing against me in front of the King. Our disagreements will have to be kept to ourselves while we concentrate on the items we can agree.'

'You can't threaten me, Malachi. I can have you butchered where you sit any time I desire.'

'That may be true, but there're many who've tried just that and I'm still here. Don't underestimate your own danger were I to be inclined to act against you. I propose that we put all this aside now and speak plainly about matters. If, after we've been honest with each other, you can see no advantage in cooperation, then there may be the necessity for one of us to remove the other.'

Conningsby yawned, then reached out to drag a large piece of meat from the King's partially demolished feast. As he chewed, he filled a goblet with the King's wine and sloshed it into his mouth. When the meat had been reduced to pieces small enough to swallow, Malachi was able to make out some of what he was saying again. '...threaten me, I'm the one that issues threats and carries them through. I've a whole army of threats.'

'I'm not threatening you, only suggesting an alliance based on mutual advantage to replace the hostile suspicion we reveal every time we speak. Answer me this question, what's your ambition? Do you want to be king? Do you want a bigger army? What drives you on if it's not the imperative of self-preservation?'

'I certainly have no wish to be king,' Conningsby said, 'though the prospect of a better army is one that appeals. It's not so much the numbers as the equipment. I barely get enough to provision the troops and the purchase of proper weapons is getting to be impossible. The King provides me with lots of recruits, but that's not the basis of a good army. I need seasoned men with good equipment. Are you telling me that you can help me get this?'

'That and much more. The city in the south is such a major prize that our King will provide you with anything that you demand. When the campaign is successfully concluded, you'll have another enormous city and huge area of kingdom to defend. Not only that, there'll be a vast population from which to draw recruits. Believe me, the world we know is but a fraction of that which exists as evidenced by the City on the River. There will be more campaigns to mount, wars to fight, and invasions to perform. Is all that in your best interests, or am I mistaken?'

'Yes, I like what you're saying, of course I do,' Conningsby answered, this time bothering to pour a second cup of wine and push it towards Malachi. 'The problem is that I don't trust you. What do you get out of all this? Are you vying to be king yourself?'

Malachi smiled and took a sip of the wine. It was very good wine and testament to the haste with which the King had departed. 'I'll leave the ruling to our King and the army to you. My plans are much more mundane. When the City on the River has been incorporated into the kingdom, I'll provide, through my devices, the only viable method of transporting goods between there and Gort. Produce would rot before it reached here by conventional pack animals. I'll be able to exact a fair price for the service, but one that will make me very wealthy indeed. That's the basis for our mutual interest, General. I need you to be successful.'

Conningsby narrowed his eyes to slits and remained silent for a long time. He poured more wine, then raised his cup. 'It all sounds mighty plausible to me, Malachi, but then everything you say seems to have a ring of truth about it. Problem is what you leave unsaid, but let's put our differences and doubts to one side and see how we go. Can you intercede with the King to have the royal armouries opened up and my soldiers given decent weapons?'

'I can do better than that; I can give the order myself. The King is already in agreement with me on this matter.'

'That's a good start then. I'm a great believer in quid pro quo as we go along. Apart from my thanks, is there anything I can do for you, Malachi?'

'Yes, there is one thing, call it a gesture of good faith if you like. I want the prisoner, Cuthbert, delivered to me unharmed. All his faculties intact, you understand, without having been subject to even the mildest interrogation.'

Conningsby's face grew stern. 'I don't like your implication that I have to give you a gesture of good faith; is my word not enough?'

Malachi smiled. 'The gesture of good faith is entirely mine; I need Cuthbert to convince someone to assist us. His cooperation might be key to the whole affair and he has made the release of your prisoner his condition.'

Conningsby visibly relaxed again. 'Very well, I'll have him wrapped in soft feather down and delivered to you as soon as we've located him.'

56

It was dark. Cuthbert was tied to a wagon that lurched alarmingly as it made a slow passage down the forest track. Grew had abandoned his uncomfortable perch on the cart and was at the front now trying to coax some effort out of the horse. Everyone else was engaged in pushing or pulling and there was a lot of puffing and panting involved. Between puffs and pants, the men were begging Grew for a rest, some water, something to eat, and an explanation as to why the cart shouldn't just be left where it stood.

Cuthbert had a very bad feeling about it all. The rope around his neck didn't help his peace of mind; one slip and he'd be dragged behind the cart and as good as hanged. Although Grew had not painted a rosy picture about what lay ahead of him in Gort, he still felt that dying on the way wasn't his preferred option. His thoughts distracted him from concentrating on where he was putting his feet, and he fell headlong into the mud. There was a sharp yank on the rope, then it slackened. He lay there with his hands bound behind his back and wondered if he should shout out to Grew to come and help him.

He heard the arrival of men on horseback; there were angry shouts, some of which sounded as if his name was being called. The new arrivals seemed belligerent, and that determined Cuthbert's course of action. He did nothing, just lay in the mud and kept still. In truth, there were few alternative options. He couldn't even get to his feet if he wanted to.

The shouting died down, the horses rode off out of earshot, and the creaking of the cart became a distant memory. Cuthbert breathed out his relief at being free again, then his chest tightened at the realisation that he was in a pretty parlous state. His hands were bound tightly behind him so that he couldn't use them to help himself stand. Every time he tried, he fell over sideways. He rolled out of the mud and his progress was halted by the trunk of a sturdy tree. Squirming brought the back of his head against the trunk and he pushed with his legs so that his back began to slide upwards, supported by the tree. He had almost regained his feet when a slight imbalance made him slide off to one side and he found himself deposited in the mud once again.

Panting with exertion, Cuthbert used the recovery time to think about his next move. Even if he managed to stand up, he would be not much better off. Blundering through the forest would be perilous without hands to feel his way and to break his inevitable fall. He arched his back and manoeuvred his hands until they were underneath his buttocks. They didn't want to go any further, and his arms felt as if they were being dragged out of their sockets as he tried to get them past his backside. He wished for a slacker rope, longer arms, and a thinner bottom, but realised that he had to make do with what he had been given. With a great effort, he forced his arms past the widest part of his arse and found himself rocking helplessly on his back like an upturned turtle.

For a long time, Cuthbert thought that he had become stuck in that position, bound hands stuck against the back of his thighs, and was condemned to lie there until he died of thirst or was eaten by some passing carnivore. He began to think of what might lurk in these dark woods. There were bears and wolves, no doubt, but it was the other, unseen, denizens that had him most worried. He could feel something on his leg moving slowly down from his knee towards his crotch. It felt like some dreadful serpent intent on burrowing its way into his insides. On the other hand, it might possibly be a trickle of water from his wet trousers.

The back of his neck was being eaten by a hundred carnivorous beetles. Either that or he'd encountered some stinging nettles.

He rocked himself harder, partly to dislodge any animals of evil intent, and managed to move his hands over his thighs until they were caught behind his knees. Now he felt almost folded in two, but there seemed a little more wiggle room than before. By straightening his legs and tipping himself back so that he rested on his head, he managed to move his bindings down to his calves, then one last painful heave extricated his legs and they were free.

Now he had the luxury of being able to pull down his pants and take a pee. Although all of his clothing was pretty much sodden, Cuthbert had been reluctant to pee in his pants, despite the discomfort. It just didn't seem dignified. The relief, combined with the massive improvement of having his hands in front of him, brightened his mood. There didn't seem to be anyone intent on pursuing him, which was good. All he had to do now was retrace his steps over the mountains and he'd be back at the lake, where Cassie was waiting.

A little further consideration of his situation brought him to the conclusion that his prospects of managing that were remote. His hands were still tied. He had no food or warm clothing. He had only a vague idea of which direction he had to travel. The only thing he had to assist him was a length of rope around his neck tied to a rotten piece of timber. Part of him longed for the simplicity of being dragged along behind the cart.

He carefully removed the rope from around his neck, then untied the substantial piece of wood that had once formed part of the cart. It didn't feel right for him to throw the items away, so he wrapped the rope around his middle and stuck the wood into his makeshift belt. This made him feel better, though he couldn't decide why this should be. The likeliest explanation was that, should he ever encounter him again, Grew would demand their return. He could easily imagine Grew's first words being 'What have you done with the back of my cart?' At least now he could offer the timber as a peace offering to try to reduce the irritation Grew would be feeling at his escape. Cuthbert didn't feel as if he'd escaped. It was more of a sense of having been abandoned in this inimical woodland.

Now that his hands were in front, he could use them for groping his way in the dark and they were ready to break his frequent falls and stumbles. Progress was slow and painful; the forest grabbed at his ankles with prickly tendrils and barked his shins with carelessly fallen trees. Worse, though, was the knowledge that he wasn't alone and the fear that accompanied it. He stopped for a breather and discovered that the rustling sounds that he thought were the result of his passage continued all around him. Were these circling wolves? Or maybe a great lion or two preparing to pounce? He'd once seen a lion in Gort, a tired specimen that gazed mournfully at him with sad eyes from a substantial cage. Out here in its natural habitat, a giant cat like that would consider him easy prey. His only defence would be to proffer his rotten piece of wood and hope that the beast choked on it.

A series of terrifying shrieks froze him where he stood. His breathing stopped while he waited to see what had made them. Nothing appeared, and the shrieks weren't repeated, but Cuthbert knew that he had to get out of this forest. These weren't the cries of any animal he could imagine; they had to be the sound of a tortured soul bemoaning its loss of physical form. He thought of the crushed bodies of his comrades beneath the rockfall and wondered whether their ghosts would recognise him. This wasn't something he wanted to put to the test as he knew that such an encounter would probably frighten him to death, even if no physical harm was intended. Compared with this, the threat from fleshy animals, even a lion, was minor.

His stumbling brought him crashing out of a thick patch of clinging bushes and into an area clear of trees. The moon was bright enough here for him to realise that he'd managed to arrive at the North Road. To his right lay Gort, to his left, the blockage that would prevent his passage to the lake. His other choice was to turn around and go back through the dark woods. Cuthbert thought of the pass across the mountain, the windswept peaks, the cold, and the perils of falling to his death. He remembered his family in Gort, sitting around a homely fire and longing for his safe return. There was also the army on the lookout for him so that he could be tortured, dismembered, and hanged. Then there was Cassie. The pain of her image almost doubled him up. It was a violent mixture of longing, fear, disappointment, and joyful excitement that sent his senses quivering and his emotions whipping around in a whirlwind of confusion.

Two choices: the road or the forest. The mountains or the safe path. Home or Cassie and the lake. The risk of capture or the risk of perishing on the journey over the mountains. Cuthbert shuddered as if his whole body had suddenly become unreasonably cold. He turned to look at the blackness of the forest and then made up his mind.

57

When neither Petra nor Ant returned through the gate, Tyrant began to feel uneasy. He couldn't hang around waiting; he was already drawing suspicious looks from some of the guards. Entering the inner city wasn't an attractive prospect. Getting inside would be difficult, but getting out might prove impossible. It was one thing for a tiny woman or a boy to walk through unchallenged, but a big bruiser like him carrying a handy-looking sword was unlikely to be waved through.

When a couple of guards peeled away from their positions and headed towards him, Tyrant's mind was made up. He had to find a place where Petra would know she could find him, but one that also kept him inconspicuous. This difficult combination seemed admirably combined in the inner recesses of the Four King Inn. He even allowed himself a self-congratulatory sigh as he settled down with a drink on the table in front of him. The landlord was still in an accommodating frame of mind and Tyrant felt it churlish to refuse something that helped him blend in even more completely.

The men sitting beside him on the bench seemed friendly enough, though they had reached the point in the evening when all they wanted to do was to drink steadily and stare out into the distance, which in their case was a wall decorated with splatters of the various fluids available in a tavern, including blood. Any opportunity for conversation suddenly disappeared as every occupant at Tyrant's table suddenly grabbed their drinks and left him sitting all alone.

The reason for their flight appeared to be a man wearing a cleaner coat than was the norm around here, who kept his moustache and beard neatly trimmed. Tyrant wondered if they were keeping out of this new arrival's way because they didn't trust themselves not to snigger at the man's peculiar facial hair or whether they knew him as a talkative fellow who they rather avoid in order to concentrate on their staring. Tyrant stayed put, relying on what vestiges of manners and sensitivity he had left to keep him from inadvertently hurting any feelings. Anyway, a good talk never hurt anyone, especially if those soldiers that had followed him came snooping in here.

'You and I need to have a serious talk,' the man said.

'Let me get you a drink,' Tyrant said, waving at the proprietor who had adopted an expression that could be interpreted as either trying to tell Tyrant his credit had run out and that any more drinks would have to be deducted from his payment for licker or sheer terror. Tyrant decided that the arrival of two more tankards in record time meant that whatever the innkeeper was feeling, it wasn't going to bother him.

'I hear you're producing licker and I'm told it's very high quality,' the man said, twisting the end of his beard with one hand while ignoring his drink completely.

'That's right,' Tyrant said, 'but I'm afraid we've sold our entire output. If you want some, you'll have to get it here.'

'You need to know that I'm also in the licker business. In fact, I supply every establishment in Gort. I have what I call a monopoly. That means nobody else gets a look in. Do you understand?'

Tyrant tried his hardest to wrestle with the word monopoly and its underlying concept. He was finding the conversation interesting enough for his mind not to wander into an area where he might be unable to stop himself from bringing up the ridiculous beard and what the man's reasons were for keeping it in that unusual shape. For that, he was thankful, because he was getting the impression that he might be dealing with someone who became easily upset. The way he was being talked at betrayed the directness of a man who took no account of the sensibilities of whoever was being confronted. The conversation at least provided a welcome distraction from worrying about Petra and Ant.

'Not really,' Tyrant said, 'but tell me more about your business. I'm new to all this and could really do with learning the ropes from someone with experience. People call me Tyrant, by the way. Who are you?'

The man's hand strayed to the end of his moustache, which he began to twirl into a point. 'I'm going to be your worst nightmare if you don't listen to what I have to say.'

'I doubt that,' Tyrant said. 'My nightmares are quite special already. All I asked was your name; common courtesy dictates that you give it to me if we are to continue this conversation.'

The man looked behind Tyrant and nodded. Almost immediately, two great big lads sat on either side of Tyrant, squashing him between them and pinning his arms by his side. 'Listen carefully.' The man leaned forward with a smirk on his face. 'I'm the only person who can sell licker. Anyone else I find trying to muscle in on my business gets a blade in their guts. The only reason I'm spending my precious time talking to you now is that your licker seems to be better than ours and I might be interested in taking it on. Now do you understand?'

'I'm getting there,' Tyrant said, trying not to laugh. 'What you want is to buy licker from me. Or do you want our recipe so that you can improve your own?'

The man with the weird beard sat forward in his seat until his face was uncomfortably close to Tyrant's. It was as if he had detected the lack of concern in Tyrant's reaction to the two heavyweights arriving. 'We know how to make it,' he said, 'and we don't need to buy it from you. I'm telling you you're out of business, get that into your thick skull. You can't sell your licker because we control the market.'

'What? Here in Gort?' Tyrant said.

'Everywhere.'

'So, if I decided to take the stuff to Endersky and supply their tavern, you'd object?'

'I've never heard of the place.'

'It's on the edge of the northern wilderness,' Tyrant said. 'I once went there by mistake. I'm only using it as an illustration in order to understand the position you're taking. If there's somewhere you've never heard of it seems churlish for you to be claiming sole access to that market. Why should you care if I sell licker there if you don't?'

'Because,' the man hesitated, 'if they wanted licker they have to get it from us. That's because we have a monopoly.'

'Oh, they want it alright; from my experience, if there's any place in the kingdom that's crying out for licker, it's Endersky. Question is, are you willing to cart your product all that way?'

'No, don't be ridiculous.'

'Then there's no logic in what you're talking about. Your market wouldn't be affected. I think you've got your strategy all wrong. I'm sure there's a way in which we can work together so that your earnings aren't affected by what we sell. There are lots of thirsty men around here and not enough licker to go round.'

Tyrant could feel the bench sagging under the weight it was being subjected to. If the big men spaced themselves out a little better and sat closer to the ends, the situation wouldn't be quite so precarious. These benches had been made to accommodate three normal people, one at each end and one in the middle. Tyrant was heavy enough and the two men attempting to menace him were each at least twice the weight of your standard tavern customer. The bench couldn't be blamed for wanting to collapse, nor could its manufacturers be criticised for such a failure.

Tyrant accelerated the procedure by bouncing down hard on his seat and felt the wood begin to splinter under his buttocks. He stood up quickly to avoid being deposited in a heap on the floor and took the opportunity to use his upward movement to smash his forehead into the bearded man's face.

Years of practice went into the technique employed in the headbutt. Whether it was a naturally bestowed talent or the result of years of being hit on the head, Tyrant's forehead was the consistency of iron. He had a great deal of respect for the oft-neglected benefits of a hard blow to the bridge of the nose and often remarked that it had more instant effect than any damage that might be made with a blade. The man with the beard did his best to confirm this belief, slumping forward on the table and allowing a puddle of blood to soak his fancy facial hair.

The fat guys were struggling to regain their feet. Tyrant interrupted that process by kicking one of them in the head and the other in the balls. Both sat down hard and looked as if they were reconsidering their next move in the absence of instructions from their stricken boss. In order to help their decision-making process, Tyrant grabbed the bearded man by the hair and raised his head enough for a knife to be placed strategically at the side of his throat. Being unconscious, he neither struggled nor protested at this affront. The big men got the message, though, and even when they'd managed to stand upright, made no threatening moves.

'Take him home,' Tyrant said, 'before he gets you all into more trouble than you can handle.'

He could see from their eyes that the fight had been knocked out of them and they didn't rate their chances of successful retaliation. Tyrant could sympathise with them; one second they'd seemed in complete control and part of a well-practised technique designed to frighten him.

Then things had gone pear-shaped in a big way. Sudden shocks like this take a while to recover from and Tyrant wanted them out of there before their minds came to terms with what had taken place.

He stood aside as they dragged the bearded man unceremoniously out of the tavern, then sat down to drink what little ale that was left in his tankard. The bearded man's drink had spilt when he fell onto it, a slight disappointment in an otherwise satisfactory outcome.

The innkeeper came over, face flushed with excitement. 'That was Danby you just hit. He's a nasty piece of work, I'd watch out for him if I were you.'

Tyrant looked at him and wondered who else could possibly have informed mister Danby of their business arrangement if it wasn't him. 'Now's not a good time to be telling me that,' he said. 'I got a little bored with the things he was telling me and even more so by the way he was saying it. What's with that weird beard? He must get into a lot of fights walking around looking as silly as he does.'

'You don't cross Danby if you value your life,' the innkeeper said. 'It wouldn't be wise to insult him.'

'What about our arrangement, then? Are you still willing to buy my licker or are you afraid Danby will come round and cause trouble?'

'It's you he's unhappy with, not me. If you're still able to supply me, I'll take all you can make.'

Tyrant thought over the situation and wondered if he was being given an opportunity to increase the price. After all, there was the extra hazard of Danby to take into account. On the other hand, that probably worked both ways and, anyway, a deal had already been struck. One thing he decided, though, he'd not bother telling Petra about any of this. It might dampen her enthusiasm for the licker business.

Two soldiers with drawn swords came in and began to look around the place. When their eyes locked with Tyrant's, he got the distinct impression they'd found who they were looking for.

58

Lone was reluctant to get rid of her recalcitrant entourage while there remained another desert to cross. She was sorely tempted because Moussa was persistently reminding her that she had promised rich rewards for her safe delivery to the city. Untold riches and a thousand wives were his exact words as he insisted that she had made a solemn promise that had to be fulfilled. She didn't bother to ask him how he could justify the disparity between his lack of trustworthiness and his high expectations of her. As far as she was concerned, any deal had been negated by the attempts on her life. Her efforts to point this out had fallen on deaf ears.

It was wonderful to be here, though. The more she explored the city, the more impressed she became. It was spread out generously along the river banks and protected to the south by a substantial wall, which had a single gate, much in the manner of the inner city at Gort, but on a much larger scale. All the fortifications were to the south; the north of the river was protected only by an earth rampart that looked as it had been built to reduce the inflow of sand from the desert rather than to deter would-be attackers.

The palace here was much more ornamental than the plain functional edifice that loomed over Gort. The tall towers were decorated with gilt and topped by intricately shaped roofs that seemed to have no purpose other than to look impressive.

The reasons why there had been no account taken of any threat from the North concerned her. If this northern desert really was impassable, then travelling home by that route would be out of the question.

Her one comfort was that Malachi had been here and presumably managed the crossing somehow. There was, however, a nagging doubt in her mind that reminded her of her husband's lack of tolerance of hardship, which made his presence here all that more remarkable.

She filled in her days by establishing relationships with merchants on both sides of the river. The northern dwellers fancied themselves as superior to their southern counterparts, an attitude that Lone found both comical and useful. It meant that she could earn a coin or two by negotiating favourable deals involving transfer of goods back and forth across the bridge. It often happened that there was a shortage of some commodities in the north that were plentiful in the south, but the merchants adopted such a supercilious attitude that it became impossible for them to agree terms. Lone had no such difficulties; her powers of persuasion meant that she could buy cheap wherever she needed to and sell for a tidy profit where demand was highest. Eggs were her favourite item. Everyone seemed to keep a few chickens south of the river but northerners believed that was a job for peasants. They still wanted eggs, though, and Lone became engaged in a steady trade, using Moussa's complaining team to transport them across the bridge on a daily basis.

Many of the egg producers were women, another good reason for her to choose this trade, as most of the men she encountered made even Moussa seem trustworthy in comparison. Her favourite chicken farmer was a lady called Mariam, who had a smallholding at the very edge of the desert and beyond the protective city walls. Her remote situation meant that Lone's access to transport and outlets north of the river had brought a great improvement to her income, while enabling Lone to make a good margin herself.

Mariam's face, normally energised and happy, was crestfallen. Lone looked beyond her sad figure and quickly realised what had happened. A paltry few brown hens were picking their way morosely amongst the corpses of their sisters. What was normally a vibrant place full of busy chickens scratching about had been transformed into a charnel house.

'It's happened before, though never quite as bad as this,' Mariam wept as she spoke. 'There must have been a dozen foxes to have committed this amount of slaughter. They kill everything they can catch; it wouldn't be so bad if they just took what they can eat, but they seem to like killing my chickens. By the time my dogs woke me, it was too late. This time, I'll not be continuing. I'm sorry, Lone, but I can't stand to have my heart broken every few weeks. I can get a job as a weaver again; I'll be better off if return to the city and stop trying the impossible here.'

Lone looked at the carnage and felt Mariam's distress. It was disappointing that her best source of supply was pulling out of the business, but there were other places she could get eggs. 'I might be able to help ward off the foxes,' she said.

'Thank you, but I've really had enough. All I need now is to find a buyer for this place; perhaps one of your contacts might be interested in expanding?'

'I'll do better than that,' Lone said, 'I'll buy this place from you myself. I don't have a lot of money at the moment, so I'll offer you a share in the income in addition to what I can raise.'

'You'll need all your money for new chickens and there's no guarantee that they'll last a week before they're slaughtered like mine were.'

Lone realised she would be paying a high price for a patch of bare earth hemmed in on all sides by jungle, but there was something about this place that called to her.

As she left to resume her career as a weaver, Mariam gave Lone one final word of advice. 'Try to prevent chickens going into the jungle. If they do, they very rarely come back out again. There's something in there that even you should be afraid of. The chickens are stupid though, they only think about the insects and the plants in there and you'll lose the lot if you don't keep the fence mended.'

Lone did as she had been advised. She had the fence repaired by her complaining entourage despite their protests. They were adamant that they were expert camel drovers who could not be expected to stoop to manual labour of any kind and that they were being sorely exploited. Lone withheld both food and payment from them until they complied, arguing that she could get cheaper labour if they wanted to starve.

She set traps on the periphery of her hen compound. Over the course of several weeks, her potent bait of dead chicken combined with summoning spells yielded several foxes and a host of smaller predators. There were no more acts of wanton destruction, and her chicken losses were reduced to a handful per week. These simply disappeared without trace, in sharp contrast to the bloody carnage visited by a fox attack.

She resolved to find out what was taking her chickens and spent night after night huddled in a blanket under the stars, surrounded by her sleeping hens. After several nights with no chicken losses at all, she concluded that her presence was acting as a deterrent to the mysterious predator and that some other method had to be found to hunt it down.

Although her nighttime vigils were preventing her sleeping hens from attack, an occasional chicken was disappearing during the day. It seemed that the predator was waiting until her attention was elsewhere, then taking the opportunity to pounce. She was becoming increasingly frustrated by her inability to provide complete protection for her hens.

Her other frustration was the way her chickens seemed desperate to get into the jungle. As Mariam had warned, once they escaped, they were never seen again. Lone wasn't sure that they necessarily met their doom in there. It appeared to her that they liked the shade and the protection of the dense foliage.

Spending time in close proximity to her hens had got them used to her. Where they would once have shied away from her, they now clustered around her whenever she approached. She rewarded them with extra corn, which she fed them individually by hand. Now that they were responding to her so well, she decided to try an experiment. She took three chickens, carried them to the edge of the jungle, and released them. They ran into the undergrowth and began scratching around, pulling worms, and chasing insects. They devoured grasses and plants greedily and appeared much happier than they were in the dried-up sand of the compound. It was as if the jungle was their natural habitat.

The hens disappeared from view, but she could still hear them scuffling around. 'Chickens!' she shouted. All three came running out of the jungle and she rewarded them with a handful of corn. She left them to their own devices until dusk, when she was again able to coax them out, pick them up, and return them to the compound. It was obvious that there was an abundance of free food in the jungle that would reduce her expenditure on corn if it could be exploited. Her problems were the undoubted presence of predators in there and the difficulty of finding eggs laid by unrestrained chickens.

***

The following day was blazing hot and all her chickens were gathered under the makeshift shade she'd arranged by mounting blankets on wooden poles. It was obvious that they were suffering from the heat and she decided to take a chance of losing every one of them by taking down the fence and giving them access to the jungle. As soon as they saw this,

238

they all trooped off together and disappeared into the cooler shade of the trees. Lone wondered if she'd just lost her livelihood.

Towards dusk, she stood at the edge of the forest and called. A handful of sleepy hens wandered out to see what the fuss was about, but the rest were nowhere to be seen. There was nothing else she could do other than to leave them to fend for themselves for the night.

***

After a fitful sleep in which she dreamed that every single chicken had been devoured by a monstrous fox, she went down to the jungle and listened. It was alive with clucking noises and scratching sounds. Some of her chicks ran over to greet her, others continued their pecking around. She watched as two hens engaged in a tug of war over a long worm and she marvelled at the efficiency with which plants were being stripped and devoured. Above her head, she became aware of a long row of hens perched on the low branch of a tree. Contrary to expectations, there had been no widespread slaughter and this seemed to have opened up a massive opportunity for her. The jungle was almost limitless. If she could utilise it for her hens, she could keep an enormous number at very little cost. Her egg business would grow massively and her profits would do likewise, hastening the day when she had enough funds to equip enough camels to stand a chance of making it home.

She walked confidently further into the jungle, enjoying the busy sounds of her hens all around her. It was mercifully cool in here; no wonder the hens were happy. Not only happy, but very much alive.

As she pushed her way through some bushes, her mood changed dramatically as she saw what was gnawing on the carcass of one of her birds.

Its outline was diffused in the dappled light that flickered through the canopy of trees and Lone had to stare hard before she could determine the size and shape of the cat. It was mottled brown and cream, the colour of the desert, and the irregular markings allowed it to blend into the quivering light in the forest. It was a big cat, twice the size of the largest fox that she'd caught, but much more solidly built. It looked up from its meal disdainfully, as if resenting the intrusion but unafraid.

Lone stood still. Her initial anger at seeing one of her hens slaughtered began to dissipate as she took in the magnificence of the beast before her. This was no mangy, flea-ridden fox engaged in wanton destruction. The cat had taken one chicken, but the others seemed unconcerned by its presence, fussing and clucking as they scratched up tasty morsels from the jungle floor. The cat licked at its meal, bit off a small morsel, then swallowed it with a flick of its head. Its attention had gone back to eating as if it had weighed up Lone's capabilities and decided that she posed no threat. She couldn't help but agree with that assessment based on physical attributes. Although the cat was perhaps half her weight, its combination of speed, tooth, and claw made it more than a match for an unarmed human being.

Lone slid the long knife from her belt that she used to despatch the contents of her traps. The cat's attention was drawn immediately, its green eyes darkened as the vertical slits in them widened. A low guttural noise began, deeper than anything she could imagine coming from an animal. It was as if a portal had been opened into a hellish underworld and the wail of angry demons released. The sound was intimidating and she found herself recoiling in fear. Her breath was taken away and she felt an irrational desire to turn and run from the jungle as fast as she could.

With a great effort, she resisted the urge and felt into the cat's energy in search of any weakness or doubt. Her experience with humans had taught her that there was always fear lurking behind even the most aggressive façade and this could be developed and worked on to engineer the downfall of even the strongest.

The cat was clearly irritated by the sight of her knife. Apart from that, she could find no trace of fear. There was a supreme confidence that worried even her. As if conscious of her intrusion, the cat drew back its lips to reveal formidable pointed teeth, then emitted a snarl so vicious that Lone took a step back from the sheer energetic force of it. Now she was really upset; it seemed that she'd encountered an animal possessed by some powerful entity that might be the death of her.

'Cali?'

Yes, Lone.

'This cat seems possessed by a demon, can you tell me its nature and purpose?'

It's a cat, Lone.

'I can see that, but it's more than that, surely?'

Sorry to disappoint you, Lone, but a cat is all it is. What you're finding confusing is the intensity with which this cat embraces its state.

'Can it harm me?'

It can kill you, though it has no wish to do so. It considers you neither a threat nor suitable prey, but it's a little confused as to why you're showing your claws.

'My knife?'

I'd put it away if I were you.

Lone hid her knife in the folds of her belt and watched the hair on the cat's back settle back down. The teeth were no longer bared at her and the noise had stopped. She took several breaths, conscious of the destabilising effect that the cat's actions had on her. It seemed that she had two options, retreat and leave the cat to its meal, or try to kill it and thereby save her chickens.

59

Tyrant watched as the two soldiers moved slowly towards him, hands on the pommels of their swords, and eyes roving the tavern in search of potential trouble. When they reached his table, he remained sitting rather than stand and create an immediate confrontation.

'We've had a complaint,' one of the soldiers said. 'A man answering your description has committed assault, causing actual bodily harm.'

'Then you've got a problem,' Tyrant answered. 'Just about everyone else in this tavern has a very similar style of attire and we all seem to have been avoiding the same barber for a similar length of time. I dare say that most of us have had to defend ourselves from time to time. Are you going to arrest us all, or is there something more specific you can tell me so that I may help you narrow down your search?'

The soldiers exchanged glances. 'Our complainant has a busted nose; he was in here earlier this evening. This is the table he says he was sitting at when the assault took place.'

'And why would a man with a sore nose go crying to the military about it? Haven't you better things to do than pick a fight on behalf of someone whose word might not be trustworthy?' Tyrant asked.

'The man's name is Danby and he's a cousin of the King. We're only following orders to investigate the matter.'

'I'm not sure I can help you in that case. I certainly haven't seen any obvious signs of royalty in here, but I've only recently arrived,' Tyrant said.

'We're sure it was you from the description,' the soldier said. 'I'm going to have to ask you to come with us.'

Tyrant felt a twinge of regret that he'd dealt with Danby so leniently that he was able to retaliate by sending soldiers. A couple of thrusts with a knife would have saved him this trouble. His only excuse was that he had been trying to appear businesslike and reasonable in the eyes of the innkeeper.

'Purely out of interest and I don't want you to take this as any sort of admission, what's the penalty for smacking someone in the face these days?' Tyrant asked.

'That's not up to us,' the soldier said, 'we're just here to take you in. What happens to you after that is none of our business.'

'Fair enough,' Tyrant said, standing up and letting them get sight of his sword. 'But let's assume for the purposes of our discussion that assault on the person of a cousin of the King is a capital offence. After all, everything else seems to warrant hanging these days, so it's not an unreasonable assumption. So, if it were me you're looking for and I'm not saying it is, you understand, I might be thinking that if I come with you, I'll get put in a cell and hanged in the morning. Not a pleasant prospect, I think you'll agree.'

'Like I said,' the soldier took a step back as if appreciating Tyrant's size for the first time, 'that's not our concern.'

'You say that it's not your concern at the moment, but let's assume for argument's sake that I don't fancy being hanged. And let's also consider the possibility that I have a big fuck off sword and the capability of carving you two into tiny chunks if I were minded. This could, therefore, go two ways. Either you end up in pieces on the floor or you decide that the man you've been sent to look for isn't here. You decide, but hurry up and do it. While you're thinking, I'll make my way over to the door and be on my way.'

Tyrant left the soldiers looking at each other. Neither made any sort of belligerent move as he strode past and out into the cool night air. The street was devoid of any reinforcements for the soldiers to call on, for which he felt profoundly grateful.

As he walked quickly away from the Four King Inn, Tyrant decided that Malachi's house was probably a better place for him to wait for the others. He was being bothered by a nagging disquiet about the whole affair, as if he'd neglected something important. Tyrant racked his brains over the significant events of the evening but failed to come up with a good reason for him feeling this way. Then he remembered he'd abandoned a tankard of ale that had been almost half full when he bade goodbye to the soldiers. He sighed with regret for the old days. He was definitely losing his touch.

60

Ant was shivering with emotional turmoil after his encounter with the King. All he wanted to do was to put as much distance between himself and the palace as possible. What had most shocked him was the close relationship between the reviled monarch and Malachi. It was impossible to reconcile this with everything that had gone before. Had Malachi forgotten that the King had ordered his death? More pertinently, why had the King allowed Malachi back into his entourage? Had he forgotten that he'd sentenced the man to death? It was clear that the King trusted Malachi now and Ant wondered where that left him. 'My enemy's enemy is my friend', Malachi had told him often enough. What he'd neglected to explain was whether the old adage worked in reverse. Could it be that any friend of the King was automatically Ant's enemy? If so, how could he continue to do Malachi's bidding?

He hurried through the main gate and headed towards the house he had been brought up in on the outskirts of town under the shadow of the great wall. Heavy boots clattered on the cobbles behind him, but Ant refrained from looking back, preferring to keep his head down and shrink his visibility as much as he could.

Strong hands grabbed his arms and swung him off his feet. There was nothing he could do to resist as he was frog-marched back up the hill to the palace. The soldiers, one on each side and two behind for good measure, said nothing in reply to his protests. If this were some demonstration of Malachi's new-found influence, Ant resolved to have nothing more to do with him. A polite invitation would have been bad enough, but this way memories of his terrible ordeal at the hands of the hangman came flooding back.

Ant was taken through the stone archway of the main gate and deposited in a room within the wall itself. He was left to his own devices in this gloomy but comfortable space, but heard the unmistakeable scraping of a bolt being drawn to ensure he stayed where he was. Fear began to diminish a little, to be replaced by irritation at the way he was being treated. When Malachi turned up, he resolved to make it clear that this was something he wouldn't tolerate.

The solid table in the centre of the room had been laid with bread and meat. There was a flagon of wine and a jug of ale, but all Ant wished for was a drink of clean water, which was not provided. Still, it bode well that he was being catered for, and it looked as if his confinement was going to be brief and bearable.

As time dragged on, Ant imagined Malachi had been detained by the King and unable to get away without invoking his wrath. The original arrangement, to meet at Vargas's house, would have been preferable, giving him time to find Tyrant and Petra and warn them of Malachi's new-found position.

It was this kind of situation where Jeremiah would have been most useful. He could have used this opportunity to range outside the confines of this room, gather information, and prepare for Malachi's eventual appearance. It would have been a comfort to know that Tyrant and Petra had been safely reunited for a start. Then there was the main purpose of their visit to Gort, which was Cuthbert. Perhaps Malachi had word of the young man's whereabouts. Maybe he was going to bring him here? Ant brightened at the thought of sorting out the Cuthbert problem and also that Malachi had made it such a high priority.

A large man with a florid face bearing a stern look crashed through the door and sat down without introduction or ceremony. He waved away the soldiers who accompanied him as if they were flies buzzing around his head. Ant could feel the intense irritation that the man carried with him, so he sat quietly and waited to be spoken to.

The man grabbed a fistful of bread, shoved it into his mouth, and swilled it down with a large swig of wine straight from the jug. His dark eyes fixed on Ant, who got the feeling that all that irritation was about to descend on his head.

'I see you managed to leave a few morsels of my supper,' the man said.

Ant, who had eaten a tiny piece of the bread and taken one small sip of the ale, felt annoyed at this unwarranted accusation. For a start, no one had specified that the food was reserved for this horrible man and anyway, he'd hardly touched it. He took a deep breath, tried to shed the anger he was being infected by, and kept his peace.

'Do you know who I am?' the man asked.

Ant shook his head.

'I am General Conningsby,' he said, 'commander-in-chief of the army. You saw me at the right hand of the King when you were with your master.'

Ant shook his head, more gently this time. His total concentration had been on the odious presence of the King and he'd paid no heed to the men in the entourage. He wondered if Malachi had detailed this overbearing bully to bring him news of Cuthbert, but he doubted it. He tried to feel into the man's thoughts and feelings and what he detected were anger and confusion. Whatever the man had been doing before he came in had obviously upset him greatly and it would take a while for his system to calm down to a more rational level. On the other hand, this might be the man's natural state, in which case the only hope would be to keep the conversation as amicable as possible.

'A boy of your age should be in the army by now. But let's put the prospect of being hanged as a deserter aside for the moment and see if we can't work together to make such an accusation untenable. You're Malachi's assistant, am I right?'

Ant nodded. Conningsby's dark eyes were focussed on him and he could feel the power of that glare adding to the discomfort of the threat.

'Malachi and I have what many might call an accord, a working arrangement, an understanding. Obviously, we both work in the King's best interest as our first priority, but there is still room for misunderstanding between us. That's what I wanted to talk to you privately about. I need to know what Malachi's motives are in all this,' Conningsby said.

Ant could feel the intensity of Conningsby's hatred of Malachi and wondered how they could possibly be working together. 'I'm only an assistant and I've been away for a while. I'm not party to Malachi's thoughts and ambitions,' Ant said.

'Or perhaps you're unwilling to tell me? Loyalty can be a commendable virtue, but is also a dangerous one if misplaced. There are people close at hand who make it their profession to extract even the most closely held secrets from even the most loyal of men. I won't have any hesitation in passing you on to them if I can't get the answers I want from you myself,' Conningsby said.

'I don't think torturing me would be seen as a part of your working arrangement. Malachi would not be impressed if he were aware of this conversation and your threats. With the greatest respect, I would suggest that you let me go in the interests of a continued rapport with my master.'

'That's one possible outcome, but it may disappear rapidly if I get any more insolence from your mouth,' Conningsby said. 'I'll ask the questions and you supply the answers without commentary or making suggestions as to what you might consider my own good. Bear in mind that there's arguably one man more powerful than I am in the whole world and that's the King himself. Others might disagree with that statement and opine privately that mine is the real power behind the throne and that I hold the reins of power myself. So, there's not going to be any intervention from Malachi that might possibly help you. I strongly suggest you abandon any loyalty you might feel towards him for, unless you satisfy me, you have no future. Whatever Malachi might do or think as a consequence does not concern me in the slightest.'

Ant observed the pink-faced man as he spoke. The words were considered and confidently expressed, but Ant detected a shadow of doubt behind them. Conningsby, despite his protestations to the contrary, exhibited nervousness whenever Malachi's name was uttered. There was also an undercurrent that Ant could detect but not at first ascribe to any particular motivation. Feeling into the situation more deeply, a clearer picture began to emerge from the general's thought patterns and behaviour. The underlying emotion wasn't fear of what Malachi might do, it was more like a vague feeling of anxiety about losing out or being left behind.

'Well?' The general pointed his finger at Ant's face as if better to provoke a response.

'I don't see how I can help,' Ant said. 'My master isn't prone to sharing his plans with me, or anyone else for that matter. I've always found him very closed and mysterious. I'm sure he's much more likely to confide in you than he is in me.'

'You can help by answering the question I put to you rather than the one you feel comfortable with. First of all, tell me about your duties. And be frank and honest, for I'm fast losing patience.'

'My duties involve the preparation of the devices known as vedhanas. These can move people from one place to another in an instant. My master uses them to gather information, but I don't accompany him on his travels.'

'I see, so you could make me one of these things, could you?' The general's eyebrows raised slightly.

'Yes, I can make them anywhere, but it's a long and difficult process and doesn't always work the way it's intended to.'

'Like the one in the tower that a damned fool called Ambrose installed against every piece of advice he was given and the whole of Gort was plagued with chaos and bloodshed? I suppose that's an example of one not working properly?'

Ant felt himself getting indignant at the mention of his father's name in such a disparaging way. Ambrose had been instructed by the King to install the device and nobody could have predicted the flood of demonic spirits that were just waiting for the opportunity to create mischief. He opened his mouth to defend his father's good name but closed it again when he thought about the consequences of Conningsby discovering Ambrose's son was sitting at his table. Malachi or no, Ant was certain that such a realisation would seal his fate. 'Yes, I suppose so. But the main difficulty lies in predicting where the end point of the journey might be. It's not always easy to make that choice or get it right.'

'How many of these devices do you know about? And where are they situated?' Conningsby asked.

'I can only tell you about the ones I know; there are undoubtedly many others that I haven't been to.' Ant felt nervous as he surveyed the vedhanas in his mind and tried to anticipate the consequences of revealing each of them to the general. A hollow feeling had developed in his stomach. He had to answer, but whatever he said was likely to reveal secrets that would put the people he cared about in grave danger.

61

Lone sat down on the forest floor, being careful not to make any moves that the cat might interpret as threatening. Then she got to work, moving her energy to feel the cat's life force, probing for a weakness. All she encountered was pure cat.

Every human subject she had ever encountered had weaknesses she could exploit. Self-doubt was the universal substance she could use to manipulate them. Everybody had issues, everyone was constantly comparing themselves to something and falling short. Lone was adept at using this condition to get what she wanted. Once she understood the particular longings that coloured everything, she could make a person do what she wanted by disguising it in familiar self-taught patterns.

The cat was just that, a cat. The cat had no doubts about what it was, nor did it wish even for an instant to be anything else. There were no issues about the kind of cat it was, how it compared to other cats, or any other aspect of its life. It was completely content. There were no goals or ambitions that it longed to bring to fruition, nothing mattered to it beyond the breath it was taking and the moment it was experiencing.

Lone was left grasping at nothing. She couldn't put any doubt or fear in this cat's mind because the cat knew exactly what was going on in its own head. When she tried temptation and reward, she was ignored because the cat already had everything. Once perfection has been reached, there is nothing that can be held up as better. Lone felt frustrated, but at the same time was in awe. This cat was the first being she had ever encountered that was impervious to her wiles. She marvelled at its composure and serenity. Even the monks in that underground monastery hadn't come close to what this cat represented.

Lone withdrew her probing and admitted defeat. The cat's eyes widened slightly as if in recognition of her exit, then it returned to delicately picking at the morsels still left on the chicken carcass. Lone breathed deeply and thought about attacking the cat with her knife, trying to catch it unawares. As the thought passed through her mind, the cat's eyes narrowed to slits and a warning growl shivered her bones. It may have been coincidence, but Lone thought that was unlikely. The alternative, however, was very disturbing. Lone tried to think of warm, comforting things, of friendship and gentleness. The growl stopped. Lone tried very hard not to be alarmed by this turning of the tables.

For a long time, Lone sat and watched the cat, keeping her thoughts as far as possible away from the decision she knew she would have to make. Even when the cat curled up and closed its eyes, Lone knew she had to be careful not to think alarming thoughts. Instead, she visualised a scene where she brought food for the cat and they developed trust and a close friendship. She lay down and relaxed, no longer afraid that the cat might attack her. Cali had summed up the situation; she wasn't prey for the cat and as long as she didn't threaten it, she would be safe. She fell asleep and when she woke, it was dark and the cat had gone.

Lone walked past row after row of her hens perched comically in bushes and on the low branches of trees, all fast asleep. Silent chickens amongst a cacophony of insect noises and the insistent scurrying of smaller animals taking advantage of the darkness.

***

In the morning, Lone returned with a large piece of ox liver to where she'd encountered the cat. For aesthetic or traditional reasons, the citizens of the city eschewed all forms of offal and it could be obtained for next to nothing. Lone was hoping that it might provide a tastier alternative to her precious chickens. The cat was nowhere to be seen, so Lone placed the liver on the ground near the scattered bones of yesterday's chicken.

Sitting very still at a respectful distance, she heard a rustling sound that she thought might herald the approach of the cat. Instead, a huge dog fox came sauntering out of the bushes and made directly for her offering.

As the resentment and alarm shot her bolt upright, prepared to do battle, the cat seemed to materialise out of thin air just above the fox's head. Its weight and downward momentum knocked the fox to the ground and as it struggled to its feet, a paw travelling faster than the eye could see batted it sideways. It lay on its side, panting, blood tricking down its scored flanks. The cat sat down a few feet away and watched.

Slowly, the fox dragged itself away towards the relative safety of the undergrowth, keeping its eyes fixed on its attacker. As it reached touching distance of the bushes, it suddenly regained its vitality and ran away. Lone had been watching the fox's progress and was surprised to see that the cat had disappeared, having not noticed it move. There was a commotion in the vegetation and the cat emerged, carrying the fox in her mouth. She set it down in the clearing with exaggerated gentleness, then backed away to resume her watching pose.

The fox made little movement apart from the heaving of its flanks, which showed it was still alive. The cat watched for a while, then went over to the liver and sniffed it suspiciously. Its fat pink tongue scraped at it a few times then it began to devour it with obvious relish. While it ate, the cat seemed to have lost all interest in the beleaguered fox, who made its painful way out of the amphitheatre and away into the jungle.

Lone sat in awe of the sheer majesty of the cat and what amounted to a severe chastisement of the fox. She wondered how she could ever have even considered for one minute that she might try to kill it. Here was a creature of such power and beauty that even if her hens were in mortal peril from it, she couldn't wish it harm. She also very much liked the style with which it had handled the fox.

***

Lone fed the cat every day and her chickens prospered. She introduced more hens, egg production soared, and there were no more fox attacks. The jungle was providing a rich food supply and her costs were minimal. Finding the eggs was hit and miss at first, but her hens were gregarious and like to return to the same nest to lay. Once she had located the habitual nests, all she had to do was collect the eggs. Occasionally, she stumbled over a nest that she'd overlooked and discovered a mountain of eggs that she was amazed that the hens could manage to sit on top of to lay.

Lone felt more and more at home here. The prospect of another desert crossing hung over her like a dark cloud that she tried but failed to ignore. She knew she had to get back to the north where lay unfinished business and scores to settle. Egg farming was surely just a way of surviving while she gathered strength for the long trek north, though she couldn't help but enjoy the simple pleasures it gave.

Her enquiries revealed that arrivals from the north were limited to a few nomadic camel drovers. It was common knowledge that this city was the most northerly outpost of civilisation and that the desert dwellers in the south were the only ones likely to visit, whether for trade or for war. In the face of this belief, Lone found it impossible to reconcile Malachi's visit with the isolation enjoyed by this city.

How had he managed to make a journey across an inhospitable landscape that must have been even more difficult than she'd endured? Her husband wasn't the hardiest of men, nor was he prone to long periods of deprivation. For him to choose to subject himself to such an ordeal, there had to be a substantial motivation attached. He could, of course, still be searching for her. When she thought about that, it left her cold. Malachi was the kind of man who had more pressing matters to attend to than his absent wife. She couldn't shake off the feeling that she was missing something important.

62

It's all going to go horribly wrong.

Cali tried her best to hide her thought from Lone who was sitting quietly in a shady part of her jungle surrounded by busy chickens. The birds were as crazy as the rest of the inhabitants of this world. They had the most perceptive eyesight of anything she'd ever looked out from, yet insisted on looking away whenever they scratched the ground. It was as if they were intent on giving themselves a surprise each time rather than seriously searching for food. They were also laughable in the way they liked to perch so close to the ground within reach of any predator worth the name. If she didn't know better, she would have thought that these animals liked to live life on the edge.

The Lone part had gone well. At least she could take some credit for getting that difficult woman here and keeping her amused so that she stayed around. The big cat that was lying against her thigh and making such a contented noise was one of the reasons, but Cali could take no credit for that. If anything, the cat worried her slightly because it was unfathomable and impenetrable. Some beings were like that and she was trying to put the cat down to an aberration and ignore it. She had a feeling that this might not be the case, but she couldn't do anything about it apart from being grateful that the damned thing hadn't yet gone for Lone's throat.

Keep an eye on Lone, had been her instructions. Nothing too onerous, and certainly not a job she could refuse when she considered who had requested her to carry it out. As she should have anticipated, this simple command had grown ever more complex. *Bring her to the City on the River.* She'd done that despite the efforts of that unruly band of cutthroats. *Keep her here.* Now she should have been able to claim she'd done her bit and been relieved of any further work. Instead, another imperative had arisen, and she doubted this would be the last.

Jeremiah drifted into the range of her consciousness; she was growing increasingly weary of his bleating and complaining, but he was an integral part of the plan and she couldn't do without him.

I don't hold out much hope for getting all your chickens together in this single basket, Jeremiah said.

Patience, Cali replied, trying not to let her exasperation show. *You've done well so far, I'd say things were looking up.*

Then you should stop looking up yourself because it's all going to go tits up any time now and I'll not be blamed for any of it. Tell your master I did everything you asked and explain to him the human tendency to irrationality.

Your job has been to keep Ant and his father apart; you've done that well, Jeremiah. I particularly admired the way you distracted him with the boy Cuthbert. I can't believe he fell for that, but credit to you for thinking it up and giving it a go.

I suppose it was a bit of a long shot. Jeremiah's energy became a tiny bit more positive. *But I was desperate.*

So, we have Lone here, Malachi will come, and you can bring Ant as soon as he's needed. We've stopped Ambrose and Ant combining their knowledge of the vedhanas, which would have made things extremely awkward. Cali ran through the mental checklist that she'd been set and decided that these small achievements did not form the basis for optimism. A shitstorm of grief was on its way and she couldn't afford to get caught up in it.

Ant's in bad trouble that he might not get out of, Jeremiah said.

Then get your arse back up north and help him.

It's not so simple; he doesn't trust me anymore. He thinks I've been betraying him by informing Malachi of his every move. I'm not sure how he did it, but he also caught sight of me here. It gave me a real shock and I know he felt it.

So you keep saying, Cali struggled to sympathise with Jeremiah's whinging, *but you have to win his trust again. You might even consider telling him the truth. It's not going to hurt at this late stage and if he's as perceptive as you say, it may be the only thing that will do the trick.*

Cali felt a waft of consciousness as Jeremiah pulled away from her. Even if Jeremiah managed to rescue Ant, there were still overwhelming odds stacked against her. She doubted the river god would stick to his agreements when the shit hit the fan, and that one factor could destroy them all. Then there was the mysterious ruler of this fine city. The assumption was that he would remain inactive as he'd done for many years. Jeremiah had been right about human irrationality though, and the most sensible course of action wasn't always the one that happened.

All I can do is set up the scenario as best I can, get the players into the game, and leave matters to take their course, Cali thought. *Even if it does mean they're all going to end up dead.*

63

Cuthbert stood on the road, looking south in the pale light of the half moon. Behind him, the forest loomed dark and dangerous. There was no way he could bring himself to plunge back into the blackness of real and imagined horrors. Being alone was the worst part. Even the company of Grew and the creaking cart had been able to dispel the dangers of the dark and he almost wished he was back in custody.

Ahead lay Gort and potential imprisonment and torture. There was also his home, where his mother would be overjoyed to see him again. Cuthbert wondered if the army would take the trouble of going round to his house to look for him and decided that it was unlikely. Home was probably the last place they'd look for him if they were bothering to search at all.

As he walked, Cuthbert was prone to jump in alarm as he detected movement in the shadows. His heart beat fit to burst at the constant deluge of fear, but he plodded on until the morning sun chased away the demons by illuminating their hiding places. It also revealed him as a bedraggled waif with telltale binding on his hands. Anyone who saw him would know he was a prisoner and, therefore, a criminal of one sort or another. Even if they didn't hand him over to the authorities, he could expect little help from anyone he met unless he found a way to cast off his bonds.

He crawled into the shade of a bush on the opposite side of the road to the glowering forest that, even in the morning light, held the promise of terrible things for him. The rope holding his hands together was old, but thick and strong. Trying to pick it apart with his teeth one fibre at a time wasn't working. Cuthbert reckoned that his teeth would give way before the rope did. He needed a blade or a sharp stone, but his scrabbling around the loose earth beneath the bush yielded nothing but sore fingernails that were blackened by embedded dirt.

When he awoke, the light had almost expired. He'd slept through the whole day and his joy at waking up still alive and free was tempered by a raging thirst and severe hunger. Despite a dream to the contrary, his bonds were still fast around his wrists. Struggling to his feet, he heard the faint trickle of water and, despite his fears, plunged into the forest in search of a means to quench his thirst.

The water sounds grew louder as he made his way cautiously through the trees. He felt disappointed that what he'd heard had turned out to be a lot of water some distance away rather than a little very close by. Nevertheless, he had to slake his desperate thirst and carried on deep into the forest until he fell headlong into a stream. Soaked to the skin, he drank his fill before feeling the chill seeping through his body. Splashing his way out of the water, Cuthbert found it impossible to be sure of the way back to the road because of the darkness and the uneven topography. Animal screams became audible again, there were scuffles in the undergrowth and, when he tried to run away, his progress was hampered by roots tripping him up and brambles clawing at his legs.

'Go away! Leave me alone!' Cuthbert shouted at the top of his voice. The noise he made seemed to deter the scufflers and silence the screamers for a moment or two, but they soon resumed their tormenting cacophony. The sound of his own voice did nothing to reassure him, though. It made him feel weak and vulnerable, as if he'd finally called out a welcome to all the entities that wished him harm. His progress became even more frantic and, as a result, his entanglements became more frequent and even more painful.

As he lay panting and desperately trying to tear away the spiky plants that held his legs, he heard a voice inside his head. *For fuck's sake, Cuthbert, pull yourself together.* It was what he should have been saying to himself for a long time now, but there was something about the thought that made him think that it hadn't been his own.

It's only a forest, for fuck's sake. Trees and plants. Maybe the odd creepy crawly. Nothing to get your pants in turmoil over.

Cuthbert didn't recognise the words as something he might say to himself. The voice in his head was vaguely familiar, though, and a tiny bit reassuring. 'Ant? Is that you?' he said.

Close, but not entirely correct. I'm Ant's helper, my name is Jeremiah.

'Where's Ant? Is he close by? Are you here to help me?'

Ant's in Gort; you should go there and find him.

'But I'm lost in this forest and my hands are tied and my legs are bleeding and I'm tired and hungry and—'

One thing at a time. Stand up. Walk over to that big tree. Good. Now turn to your left and keep walking. Push your way through those bushes. Now you're back on the road. See? That wasn't so difficult, was it?

Cuthbert breathed more easily in the welcome glow from the almost full moon. The shadows seemed to have lost their ability to make him jump. He trusted that Jeremiah would warn him of anything approaching with ill intent. He began to walk south with a lighter step.

Stop. Go to the side of the road. No, the other side. That's right, now a couple of paces to your right. Stop. Look down, search around in the grass.

Cuthbert felt into the damp sward, his bound hands forced to explore in tandem. His right hand encountered something hard and cold; he grabbed it and held it aloft in triumph. 'I've found a knife,' he said.

So you have, well done.

It was a small knife, the kind you might use for chopping carrots rather than something that might be useful in a fight. Nevertheless, it was a knife and its blade was sharp enough to make light work of his bonds. With his hands freed, he adopted a whole new persona. He shed his helpless victim act and replaced it with the more positive frame of mind that might be better associated with a man who had managed to escape from a terrible fate. Now he was unfettered and on his way to meet Ant, who would know exactly what to do.

When you get to Gort, go through the outer gate and take the passage to your left. Ant will be at the house of a man called Vargas; it's a big house with buffalo skulls on the gates.

'But you'll be here to guide me, won't you?' Cuthbert said.

The ensuing silence sucked away the bravura that Cuthbert's fleeting presence had generated, and he began again to start at shadows and wonder what might be lurking there.

64

Lone sensed the unfamiliar presence long before she reached her house. Laden with baskets of eggs, she noticed with irritation the absence of Moussa's camels and cursed him for being late yet again. She resolved to make him suffer for this latest slackness, whatever excuses might pour out of his prevaricating mouth.

She was greeted by the sight of a bulky man seated at her table with his feet resting on her favourite chair. His face had an unhealthy pallor and she could smell the unsavoury sweetness of his breath. When she entered, he remained seated in a way that Lone felt dismissive and rude. Anger began to rise from her depths as she considered the unfriendly nature of the intrusion.

'Take your feet off my chair,' she said, 'and while you're about it, take the rest of you out of my house while you have the use of your faculties.'

'Your house? This whole chicken farm belongs to us. I'm here on behalf of the new owners, so you'd better keep a civil tongue in your head if you want to remain working here. I'll not have some ignorant egg collector telling me what to do.'

Lone was jolted off balance by the conviction in the man's words. With a great deal of difficulty, she resisted the impulse to lash out at him and put him in his place. Show him who he was dealing with. 'Who was it that sold you the business?' she asked, keeping her indignation tightly under control.

'Why, the owners of course.' He looked at her as if she were completely stupid and Lone decided to let that impression stand. 'Moussa and his partners.'

'Why aren't they here to show you around themselves, then?' Lone asked.

'We've been here several times before; we know what we're getting. I'm only here to take over the reins, so to speak, and to collect today's eggs.'

'You must have been here when I was otherwise engaged then.' Lone smiled as she imagined the scurrying about that had been involved to get

259

her off site at the appropriate times. She recalled one occasion when, on Moussa's insistence, she visited a customer in the northern quarter who was supposed to have complained about quality. It turned out that he was perfectly satisfied and she even talked him into increasing his order. At the time, she'd put the incident down to a combination of the customer's reluctance to voice his complaint in person and her own legendary powers of persuasion. Now she realised that Moussa had been carefully setting up this sale for many weeks. 'Where are my previous employers now?' she asked.

'I understand they were traders from the south and were anxious to return to their nomadic life. The transaction was concluded several days ago, so I expect they're on their way home by now.'

Lone couldn't help but laugh out loud. She had noticed that Moussa's constant complaints had slackened off lately, but had put that down to him growing tired of his own moaning and thought nothing more of it. This man was undoubtedly right in assuming that the three men were long gone. They couldn't afford to wait around for her to catch up with them. Now, her journey northwards would have to be done without them. Not only that, but they had taken with them the means to make the journey. All she had left was a burning anger that needed an outlet.

As if in reaction, the man wiped sweat from his brow with an already dripping rag. The calm assurance he had displayed was being replaced by a look of consternation. Lone gripped and twisted at his internal organs. Enough to cause discomfort but, as yet, insufficient to cause permanent damage. His hands went to his throat as he struggled for breath and his eyes darted around the room as if in search of a cause for his affliction or, perhaps, some source of relief.

Lone imagined what she would do when next faced by Moussa's grin and her reaction was nearly the end of the man in her house. He let out a groan and slumped to the ground. She relaxed her grip, withdrew from hurting him, and left him there. Outside, the sun poured its remorseless heat into the scorched earth. She longed for the cool rain of the north, which transformed brown desert into luscious greenery.

'Cali?'

Yes, Lone?

'Why didn't you warn me about Moussa's plans to steal everything from me?'

I can't be everywhere at once, Lone.

'That's not what I asked.'

The intentions of humans isn't something I can advise on. You're the expert, Lone.

'But you must have been aware they had left the city.'

The significance of that fact wasn't necessarily obvious, Lone.

'Are you being purposefully evasive, Cali?'

You seemed to be having fun with your chickens and I don't like to bother you with details.

Lone thought for a moment about the man inside her house and the consequences that might follow his demise. Someone would come looking for him and, even if she dealt with them in the same way, life would become more complex. She would have to go back to watching her back for incipient threats. Cali was right about one thing; she had been enjoying the peace associated with having the chickens and cat for company rather than having to deal with people. Collecting the proceeds of the egg sales was becoming more of a chore because it meant she had to spend time in the city. Something was rooting her into this place.

'Are you feeling unwell?' Lone pressed a cup of water to the man's lips and raised his head gently so that he could drink.

'Thank you,' he replied. 'I don't know what came over me. I couldn't breathe.'

'It's the heat; you've probably been working too hard as well,' Lone said as kindly as she could manage.

He sat up and recovered enough to tell her that his name was Ali and that he worked for an enterprise controlled by the royal household. It seemed that Lone's eggs were considered highly enough at the palace to warrant control of their production. Lone breathed a sigh of relief that she'd stayed her hand. A king wasn't likely to be easily deterred from claiming what he believed to be lawfully his. Killing his representative might have been a very bad move.

'Could you manage something to eat?' she enquired.

Ali shook his head. 'I have to make sure everything is good here and then report back.'

'You can leave everything here to me,' Lone said. 'What you need to organise is transport for the produce, starting with today's collection.'

'I have to look for myself.' Ali stood up and walked shakily towards the door. Lone concentrated on weakening his legs so that he barely reached halfway across the room before he collapsed in a heap.

He looked at her with eyes full of incomprehension. Lone suddenly recognised what had been happening to her and exactly what she had to do about it.

Ali's eyes had taken on a glaze of frightened pleading. They were the only part of him that Lone was permitting to move; she had frozen the nerves in the rest of his body because she didn't want any undue distractions during the long and delicate process that was summoning and binding.

Summoning had been relatively fast, because she knew exactly what spirit she needed to snare. It was the binding spell that needed most of her energy and all of Ali's. She didn't think he was going to survive the process, but his life energy was proving a useful adjunct to her own.

Early on in the process, the cat had appeared and was now curled up next to her. Lone found the animal's presence comforting, even though she could make no practical use of it. The cat purred and preened as if enjoying the swirls of energy that Lone was concentrating into a single strand of power.

The exhausting work went on for hour after hour, day after day, but the cat stayed exactly where it was. Ali's face relaxed into acceptance just before the final wisps of life were pulled from him. Lone's voice rose into a shout as she spat out the final words of the spell.

The little man in the golden turban walked in through the open door and stood next to Ali's corpse. The cat bristled at his appearance, but was quietened by Lone's reassuring touch. 'I must warn you that you are playing with dangerous forces,' he said.

She felt him pulling at the tendrils of energetic binding that she'd so painstakingly conjured. The power he possessed was immense, but Lone knew that the ancient magic would hold a being of even greater force than this one. What she wasn't prepared for was the very essence being pulled from her own body. It was as if she'd carefully crafted the rope, formed the noose, and made the cast, but was physically and energetically unable to prevent herself from being unseated by the reaction of her captive. She'd invested all her energy in the preparation and now she was completely depleted. She was dehydrated, hungry, and tired, which left her without any means to resist the extraction of her own life force from her body. She had no anchor, nothing to hang on to, and no strength with which to do it even had she been better grounded.

Slowly but inexorably, she felt her life ebbing away. The connection between her body and her spirit was being stretched beyond breaking point and she knew that the moment it was severed, she would be completely lost and without form.

It was as if she'd roped a wild stallion but was standing on ice and unable to do anything other than be dragged along wherever the angry beast wanted to take her. She didn't even have the option of letting go; the binding was as secure on her as it was on her captive. The stallion illusion dissolved into a twisting column of spinning sand that swept her off her unsteady feet and threw her over a rocky precipice, where she plummeted helplessly into the cool depths of the river. Great jaws grasped her as they had taken hold of her body before. But now they had her spirit.

She was dragged deeper, beyond any earthly river depth, until the light was all but extinguished. The urge to breathe was still insistent, but this was a false memory, an old habit which was of no importance now. She began to think of all the things she should have done differently. Taken more care. Not bitten off more than she could chew. Showed some respect. Admonitions echoed around her mind and she knew these were not of her doing but the voices of others.

Her mother's face suddenly appeared; at first, sad and afraid, but changing to a grisly caricature as it blackened and burned. Those loving eyes projected a final burst of hopeless anguish before they dribbled from their sockets and were extinguished for ever. *Let that be a lesson,* her father had said. *That's what happens to women who dabble in the black arts.*

Her ten-year-old mind had aged twenty years in the instant her mother had been killed. She had resolved to show the world what a powerful woman really looked like and exact her revenge. She resented the cowardly weakness her father had shown and it had categorised him amongst the feeble men who had been instrumental in her mother's death.

Now it was all over. She had no regrets, though. At least she'd tried. She would take what comfort she could from that fact before oblivion.

Blackness. She was dissolving in the water that pressed down on her. There was a certain peace to be enjoyed now that the struggle was over. Lone waited more patiently than she had ever waited in her life now that she was dead.

The water around her began to vibrate very softly. It was a distracting noise in what had settled into absolute silence. She tried to ignore the hum, but it was insistent and steadily increased in volume despite her efforts. *I'm dead,* she thought, *I don't need a buzzing noise in my consciousness.*

The sound wouldn't go away and she became irritated by it. Her feelings of peaceful resignation evaporated and she determined to track down the source of the disturbance. The more she homed in on the sound, the more intense it became. She could feel a deep resonance inside herself, vibrating in tune with the pulsations.

Suddenly, she was back in her body, sitting in the tiny house, faced by the man in the golden turban whose face now betrayed a mixture of puzzlement and alarm. The cat was pressed against her thigh and was emitting a purr that seemed to saturate the whole area. The very ground she sat on was moving in unison with the vibrating animal.

Lone pulled with her mind on the invisible bonds that held the river god. She watched as he squirmed helplessly; this time his efforts to escape were easily resisted. 'Fetch me food and water,' she said.

'I warn you that nothing good will come of this flagrant breach of the ancient laws,' Zaire said, but as he spoke, a flagon of cool water and a bowl of fruit materialised in front of her.

The cat lay sprawled beside her, paws outstretched with its incisors showing in the approximation of a contented smile. 'Now I have a task for you to perform,' Lone said, revelling in the sweet energy that began coursing through her body.

65

Ant took a long deep breath and watched as Conningsby's face creased with impatience. Then fists crashed down onto the table as the general shouted, 'Answer, boy, or it will be the torturer who asks the next question.'

He means to kill you whether or not he gets the answers he wants.

'Jeremiah?' Ant felt a jolt of recognition. 'I thought you'd abandoned me.'

You have to trust me, Ant. I've no time to explain, I'm here to help.

'Did Malachi send you?'

No, he doesn't know about this situation. You have to get out of this room, and quickly. I'll tell you what to say, just repeat out loud the exact words I tell you, don't deviate and don't add anything. Understand?

'I understand, but I still don't trust you, Jeremiah. You left me when I needed you most.'

'Well?' Conningsby's face was suffused with an almost purple pallor and he was half out of his seat.

'I'm scared of what Malachi will do to me,' Ant said.

'Nothing can be more frightening than the punishment I can mete out,' Conningsby retorted.

'Can you promise to protect me from him if I tell you everything I know?'

'Promises are for you to make and for me to ensure that they're genuine. Speak now, or I'll begin by gouging out your eyes myself as a gentle prelude to the real interrogation.'

'All I can tell you is that Malachi wants something that the King of the southern lands has in his palace. It's inaccessible; he can only get at it if you take your army to the City on the River and defeat the King. Kill him, in fact. Then Malachi will be able to get his hands on the thing he desires above all else.'

'Really? Is this true, Jeremiah?'

'What exactly is this thing that Malachi seeks?' Conningsby's attention was fully engaged now, his face had taken on a less threatening aspect.

'I don't know, some kind of powerful magic I expect. He's been working on this plan for years. Putting everything in place and establishing all the necessary alignments,' Ant continued to faithfully repeat Jeremiah's prompts.

'So, he expects me to do his dirty work for him, does he? Move a whole army down there and fight a battle on his behalf just so he can waltz in when all the danger's past and claim the prize. If what you say is true, I'm grateful to you. However, you must realise that I will have to check your story, don't you?'

Ant relaxed a little. Jeremiah's words seemed to have had the desired effect and calmed Conningsby down to the point where he appeared quite compliant. Jeremiah obviously felt the same as he'd no suggestions as to what to say next, so Ant just nodded and rose off his chair.

Conningsby barked out an order and two soldiers, who had been waiting outside the door for his command, swept in and grabbed hold of Ant before he could resist.

'Obviously I can't trust Malachi himself to corroborate your story,' Conningsby said, 'so I'll have to see how you react under duress. It's quite intriguing how stories change while parts are being sliced off. I've seen men's memories improve remarkably as their private parts have been cut off bit by bit. Take him away.'

The soldiers took an arm each in a steely grip and frog-marched Ant out of the gatehouse and across the courtyard towards the main palace building. 'Jeremiah, what have you done to me?'

I've got you out of the room.

'But they're going to torture me.'

Worse, I'm afraid. Conningsby can't let you live now. He knows that if what we've said is true, then Malachi can't be allowed to find out that he knows about it, otherwise his advantage will be lost.

Ant was half carried, half dragged past the place where he had been hanged. His life appeared to have come full circle.

At the foot of the steps that he knew led up to the prison cells, the soldiers hesitated as if they'd forgotten something or were having second thoughts. 'Wait here,' one said, releasing Ant's right arm, 'I need to go inside and check that everything's ready.'

266

The other soldier began to protest, but he was ignored as his colleague skipped up the stairs and disappeared into the building. As soon as the heavy door closed, the remaining soldier let go of Ant's arm and fell awkwardly to the floor. Ant watched in amazement as his attempts to rise were prevented by a tiny woman sitting on his chest and beating him senseless with a stone.

Petra looked up triumphantly at Ant, then hit the soldier several more times without actually looking at him. 'Come on, we need to get out of here,' she said.

Go inside the palace.

'No, we need to get away, Jeremiah.'

You'll not get through the gate; there are too many soldiers there and by the time you reach it, the alarm will have been given. Go inside, trust me.

'I can't trust you. You left me once before and might have got us all killed. As it is we lost Cuthbert and that's your fault.'

I have Cuthbert, he's safe and heading towards Gort. Now do what I tell you before it's too late.

Ant grabbed Petra's hand and turned her back to face the building. 'We have to go inside, the gate's closed to us.'

She nodded and followed as he led the way through the door and on to the familiar corridor lined by cell doors. The soldier who had just entered was nowhere to be seen.

Third door on the right, slam it and lock it. Quickly, he's on his way out.

Ant ran to the cell and pulled the door closed. As he worked the bolts, he heard a cry of alarm from inside.

Now to the end of the corridor and up the staircase. You know where you're going, Ant.

66

Tyrant watched as Petra was ejected from the vedhana as if she were an unwelcome object found in a mouthful of food. She picked herself up from the floor and looked back at the device, as if expecting something else to happen. Tyrant put down his cup of Malachi's best wine and walked over to greet her.

'I was worried about you,' he said. 'I was thinking of following you into the palace, but I was chased away by some soldiers. I don't think they liked the look of me, or maybe they remembered me from the last time I was here. Where's Ant? He went looking for you.'

Petra continued to stare into the whirling lights. 'He was with me in the vedhana, but now he's gone. I rescued him from some soldiers who were going to lock him up. Poor boy, he looked terrified when I found him.'

'So he should be; a bit of fear never hurt anyone and he's been too ready to put others at risk, I'm thinking. Maybe he'll stop being so driven to make everything conform to his ideas now. I expect he dropped you off here so he could carry on looking for Cuthbert.'

'I don't think so, he told me that Cuthbert was safe and we didn't need to worry about him anymore. It seems his weird ghostly pal is back and lending a hand,' Petra said, taking the proffered cup and consuming the contents in a single gulp. 'Should we be drinking this? What if Malachi finds out we've been here?'

'I doubt he'll miss a flagon or two of wine; anyway, we'll be long gone before he returns. At least I hope we will.' Tyrant felt nervous for the first time since he'd entered the house. Initially, it had seemed a hospitable respite from all the potential trouble he'd been stirring in Gort. There was also the very welcome addition of a few draughts of wine to stave off the onset of what he expected could be a very severe hangover. Now, he felt weariness seeping through his system and this wasn't the place to go to sleep if he didn't want an indignant wizard standing over him when he woke up. 'Back into the vedhana,' he said. 'Let's get home and make some licker. We have a customer who is anxious to pay us well for it and Ant doesn't need us anymore, that's obvious.'

For once, Petra refrained from arguing with him and dutifully stepped back amongst the waving patterns of light. Before he joined her, Tyrant took the precaution of acquiring a couple of full jugs of wine, just in case he needed them for medicinal purposes. He felt the familiar constriction to his breath that prompted him to concentrate on thinking about the vedhana in the forest close to Petra's house. He hoped that she was remembering to think the same thought and grasped her hand just to be on the safe side.

67

Rinpoche sat in his familiar red robes at the side of the path leading into the monastery. Ant tasted the sharpness in the still air of the caverns. There was no weather down here, nor were there any seasons. Every day held the same constant temperature and the moisture content of the air never varied. It was as if time was standing still here, a feeling that was reinforced by the daily routine of the monks. Every day the same, a constant cycle with a gentle rhythm that was both uplifting and reassuring.

'You wanted to speak with me,' Rinpoche said. 'I hope you are enjoying your stay with us as much as Pepper and Col are delighted to see you again.'

Ant sat beside him, feeling the rough earth underneath and the comfort it seemed to offer. 'I wanted to come here to think about things, Rinpoche. I feel as if I'm falling headlong into an abyss. Things are happening that I don't understand and I'm fearful that I won't be able to control the outcome. It's all gone beyond me, I'm afraid. I once thought that I could make a difference, but now I feel pushed and pulled into situations that are not what I intended. I don't know how to explain it better.' Ant looked at the boy who seemed not to have changed at all since they'd last met, whereas Ant himself now stood much taller and broader than before.

Rinpoche sat quietly. Ant felt his eyes resting gently on his face. There was no intrusion in that look, only the attentiveness of someone offering support.

'There's another thing,' Ant said. 'When I met the King, something passed between us that I can't explain but left me deeply disturbed. When I looked into his eyes for a brief moment, I felt as if he were me, that I was looking back out of his eyes at myself. There was a knowing in that look, as if he was aware of everything I thought and all that I'd done. How can that be? How can this King be so different, so powerful?'

'Different?' Rinpoche asked. 'I thought you said that it felt as if you and the King were one and the same. That there was no difference between you.'

'Yes, that's true. But it's only happened with the King. I've looked at lots of people and never felt like that before,' Ant said.

'Then perhaps you haven't been looking properly.'

'Are you saying that the King is no different to anyone else?' Ant said.

'In all the aspects that matter, that is true. But it is also true of everyone else. Separation is the great illusion, Ant. When you see through that veil of deceit, as you have, it can come as a great shock.'

'I don't understand. How can the King be Ant and at the same time still be the King?' Ant said.

'He can't. Neither of you can be other than what you already are, which is the same thing. He is not the King and you are not Ant. These are only constructs that both of you have produced as a result of a misunderstanding of your true nature. We are all one, yet we insist on pretending that each of us is something other than that which we are. What you felt was the truth of it,' Rinpoche said.

'What should I do about it?' Ant asked.

Rinpoche smiled. 'Do?' he asked. 'Why do you have to do anything? If I show you a mountain, do you ask what you should do about the mountain? Move it, perhaps? Or make it smaller?'

'I still can't get my head around it,' Ant said.

'Nor should you try; it's your head that's intent on spinning the illusion. Feel into your body, you'll find the truth there in your heart. Ignore what your mind's trying to persuade you to believe. It's not easy, but it is very simple.'

'Sometimes, I can let my spirit wander outside my body. When I do that, I feel in touch with a great power. Something that has brought me knowledge of far-off places and has allowed me to speak to people who aren't physically present. How does that work, Rinpoche?'

'What you are telling me is that you have become aware of another aspect of our condition. That aspect is a non-physical realm that connects everything and everyone. It can give access to all manner of information because it is infinite. Everything that has happened is there to be viewed, together with everything that will happen. Time has no meaning in the infinite void. Neither is there any form of certainty, for in the infinite everything that hasn't happened, and everything that will never happen, sit equally alongside what might seem real to us. What you find there might not always be either helpful or true. The truth can only be found within you, Ant. That's essentially what we do here. We connect with ourselves, with our true nature, and doing this on a regular basis brings a little more light into the darkness of our misunderstanding.' Rinpoche took a small wooden platter on which exotic fruit was carefully arranged and offered it to Ant.

Ant felt the intense sweetness dissolving in his mouth and coursing through his body. Even his mind seemed to liven up as he ate. 'Where do you get such delicious things?' he asked.

Rinpoche rubbed his hands together. 'We use the vedhana to reach a marketplace that is far away in the south, though distance isn't an issue, as you are all too aware. Would you like to go there and see for yourself? I'm sure that Pepper will be very happy to accompany you.'

Ant thought about the prospect of getting away from all his difficulties and the sense of relief that went through his body was compelling. If listening to his heart was the test, this was something he had to do. He would leave Malachi and the King to their own devices and let Tyrant and Petra go about their business in peace. He could see more clearly now what had persuaded Pepper to abandon his boyhood ambitions and live in this monastery. He didn't understand much of what Rinpoche was saying, but he had a feeling that his mind wasn't meant to take it in, only his heart. Deciphering the mystery of existence was neither possible nor necessary. Sitting, listening, and absorbing were all he needed to do. This monastery would be the best place to do that so that he could let his burden drop off his shoulders and learn to relax. First, though, he needed a trip to warm southern climes where he could put himself out of reach of everything.

68

Moussa felt the comforting slap of the heavy purse on his thigh as his camel plodded across the sand. The city was far behind them now and he had given up casting nervous glances over his shoulder. With three days' start, he reckoned that even an angry witch would find it impossible to catch up to them now.

He thought a lot about the items in his purse, mentally cataloguing his treasures but resisting the impulse to open it up and risk the prying eyes of his comrades. They had all done well out of their sojourn in the city, but Moussa had made sure that he did best of all. The jewels and gold he carried were what he thought of as his bonus for negotiating the sale of the chicken farm. When he returned home to the City of a Thousand Tents, he would be able to purchase a comely wife or two. He let the anticipation of his new life swill around his mind and decided that he would have at least three. A young beauty to impress other men, a strong, experienced wife to do all the work, and a kind, understanding one for companionship. That was it, perfect. Three it was to be, and he had riches aplenty to ensure that they all enjoyed a long and happy life.

Janvir rode up alongside him, his face creased in a frown and his finger pointing ahead. Moussa squinted into the brightness and detected a dark patch on the southern horizon in the direction they were headed. 'What do you make of that?' Janvir asked.

'Looks like a storm to me,' Moussa said and grimaced, 'and directly ahead.'

'We should avoid it if we can; perhaps if we head a little to the east, we may be able to bypass it.'

'No,' Moussa said, 'we must keep on heading south. The sooner we get home, the better. The storm may have blown itself out or moved aside by the time we get that far.'

As if hearing his words, the storm approached at an alarming pace. Before they could take any avoiding action, it was upon them. The whole world was plunged into semi-darkness and Moussa had to cover his head entirely to withstand the sand being blasted into his face. Further progress was impossible, as the camels hunkered down, folded their heads against their bodies and ignored all the entreaties of their riders to stand up and carry them. All Moussa and the others could do was to use what shelter their beasts provided and sit tight under the inadequate protection afforded by their robes and headscarves. Despite his best efforts, stinging sand whipped at Moussa's face, forced its way into his mouth, and filled his nose and ears. He felt close to suffocation and daren't even open his eyes for fear of being blinded.

***

The battering was unremitting. Day turned to night and back into day again. Dark brown into blackness and hope of a bright new dawn was dashed to oblivion. It was all he could manage to take a few sips of water, and even then, more sand than liquid went down his throat. He'd never experienced a storm of such intensity, nor had he known one that lasted so long. It became clear that if he stayed where he was, he would most likely die, but any attempt to move away from the storm depended on his camel's willingness to get up and face the terrible conditions. Several times he cajoled the beast to rise up and carry him towards safety, but to no avail. Moussa had lost sight of Demba and Janvir when the storm struck and he had no means of knowing if they were here or gone, alive or dead.

Moussa awoke from an uneasy sleep to the realisation that his robes weren't slapping him quite as hard and he was having to swallow less sand every time he breathed than he'd got used to. He peered cautiously from his makeshift shelter and saw sunlight for the first time in days. He jumped up, roused his fellows who had almost disappeared under their personal dunes, and bade them ride as fast as possible away from the storm.

The wind whipped their backs, and the sandstorm threatened to overwhelm them again and again, but they managed to run fast enough to keep the worst of it behind them. There was no arguing about the direction they should take; any deviation would envelop them in the deadly blizzard again. In any case, the camels had taken charge now, and they instinctively kept ahead of the storm, changing direction without any need for prompting from their riders.

All he could do was to trust his camel to skirt the edge of the whirlwind and keep him out of the worst of the weather. Occasionally, a stinging blast of sand would hit him from behind with such velocity that he was nearly unseated. Then he'd utter encouraging words to his mount and pull his headdress over his head. He didn't need to expose his eyes to the biting wind that threatened to blind him. Better leave the business of route finding to the camel whose face was more adapted to the adverse conditions.

It was a long, tedious, uncomfortable journey out of the clutches of the sandstorm and it was several days before Moussa could throw back his scarf and accustom his eyes once again to the brightness of the sun. Janvir and Demba had stuck doggedly by his side, but the pack camels had all been lost, and with them, most of their food and water. Moussa looked around him, seeing the dancing brown blur behind that told him the storm was still brewing and a vague smudge on the horizon ahead that suggested they were close to finding shelter and perhaps water in addition.

He urged his fellows onwards, trying to put on a brave face, but knowing in his heart that their chances of survival out here were not good. When the shimmering apparition ahead resolved into the walls of the City on the River, Moussa didn't know whether to laugh with relief at being saved or to break down and cry at the dreadful implications that they foreshadowed.

69

Malachi was weary, the wind was whipping across his face, and his legs were screaming with discomfort. The muscles in his backside hurt so much he doubted that even sitting down would bring him relief. Ambrose had been insistent that he should take the long walk up onto the sides of the valley to view the way that the North Road had been blocked by the avalanche. A description would have been more than sufficient, but Ambrose's invitation had even more than his usual intensity and Malachi had relented. Now, he regretted his compliance and wondered if he was getting too soft in his old age.

Ambrose, in contrast, was picking his way deftly across the broken hillside, hopping from one tuft of grass to the next and avoiding, at least most of the time, the shifting instability that threatened Malachi's balance. A big man with a cloven face plodded heavily behind with an air of someone who had better things to do with his time.

At last Ambrose came to a halt and stood, teetering precariously, above the steep-sided valley that overlooked what had been the North Road. Black earth had flooded the area for as far as Malachi could see. Ambrose took a folded cloth from the sack he was carrying and laid it out carefully onto the ground, smoothing it out as best he could over the uneven surface.

Malachi's creaking legs persuaded him to sit gingerly on a rock whose geometry had appeared flatter and more comfortable than the actual experience confirmed. His backside ached, his breath was coming in gasps, and the sight of Ambrose fiddling about with a bit of cloth did nothing to improve his mood.

'We've all seen the extent of the problem with our own eyes, though I'd have been happy to take your word for it,' Malachi said.

'The problem, yes. But the solution? Wouldn't that be a sight for sore eyes?' Ambrose said.

'I really have no idea what you're talking about. The road is blocked, and the King has gone south with almost the whole of his army. Time is of the essence. I urge you to clear the way as quickly as possible so that you can march on Gort. There's a window of opportunity that we need to make full use of. It may even be better to send your men on foot through the mountains.'

'We're cavalry, not infantry,' the cloven faced man said. 'Our horses can't make the journey over the mountains.'

'Then the road will need to be cleared,' Malachi said.

Ambrose's attempts to smooth out the cloth seemed to be having some success at last. A shimmering light began to play around above the diagram on the sheet, and Ambrose sat back as if in satisfaction. Malachi was impressed with the ingenious way that the vedhana had been transported up the mountain, but was less happy with the size of it. He doubted that any of them could fit into the device so that they might be spared the long trek back to the lake.

Ambrose scooped up a handful of earth and piled it into the centre of the little vedhana. Then he took a small knife from his belt and made an incision in his hand that dripped blood onto the heap of soil. When he withdrew his hand, the whirling lights intensified, the soil disappeared for a few moments, then reappeared. Ambrose took it in his hands and walked to the very edge of the precipitous slope. There, he leaned out and sprinkled out the dirt so that it became caught in the wind.

'What was that all about?' Malachi asked, a little concerned at the ritualistic nature of the act he'd just witnessed and wondering if this was something he ought to have recognised.

'Watch,' Ambrose said, 'and keep quiet, I have to concentrate very hard for this part.'

Malachi felt a pang of indignation; being told to shut up was something he had only previously permitted his King or his wife to get away with without the severest of punishments. Nevertheless, he wasn't in any fit state to cause trouble and sitting quietly and observing the weird things that Ambrose was doing seemed reasonable, even if he felt some resentment at being told to do it. The other man had the look of someone who was fearful about what was about to happen and Malachi caught his growing nervousness. He stood up, legs protesting, and backed away from the edge of the chasm.

Malachi's sense of foreboding grew. He had the feeling that something very bad had already happened and that his body was reacting to the shock even before his mind had registered it. He felt an urgent need to get away from there, not just the edge of the cliff, but the whole area. He desperately needed to return to the safety of his house in Gort, which he was beginning to wish he'd never left. The thought occurred to him that if he was ever fortunate enough to return home, he would stay there indefinitely and leave the cares and ambitions of the world to its own devices. Momentarily, at least, Malachi found himself stripped of all motivation. He only wanted to run away and hide.

With a supreme effort, he stilled his rapidly beating heart and controlled his panting breath. He tried to recognise the irrationality of his thoughts as something he was used to engendering in others.

Still, nothing obvious was taking place, only the terrible fearfulness that seemed to be affecting everyone except Ambrose, who was staring expectantly over the edge as if oblivious to everything, even his own safety.

Then Malachi felt a rumble deep below his feet. The rock on which he was perched was trembling and small rivulets of soil were being shaken from crevices.

'Look,' Ambrose shouted, 'can you see it now?' He began to dance around, dislodging rocks and dirt beneath his feet.

Malachi looked down at the black earth that piled high where the road had once been. Something moved on the surface, and the soil and stones seemed to be turning liquid. This was happening on a massive scale; the entire valley appeared to be on the move. Malachi breathed a sigh of relief. It appeared that Ambrose had succeeded in making a river out of solid matter which, if it flowed in the right way, might reduce the amount of manual clearance that would be needed. It was interesting, impressive even, but he didn't understand why he couldn't just have got on with it in the first place, then told him about it afterwards.

There was something wrong with the flow; it wasn't going in the direction it needed to. Instead, it appeared to be moving in rather than out. The earth was piling itself higher rather than spreading out. Like the sluggish smoke from a damp fire, the blackness rose into a thick column, until its top was almost level with where they were standing. Malachi could see that the apparition was in constant violent motion, as if there were a host of whirlwinds at work to shape it. It was as if the earth itself was boiling.

The column began to twist and change, two distinct branches were being formed at its base as if to steady itself. Legs. With a start, Malachi realised what was going on and his heart grew cold with fear. If he was correct in his anticipation, even the dragon beast in the monastery would have been preferable to the thing he was watching develop.

A crude torso with flailing arms was next to form before a giant head was spun into place. It turned to look at the men gathered on the hillside, its eyes deep whirlpools of blackness. The features etched on its face were constantly changing, but Malachi fancied that he could detect the beginnings of a twisted smile.

Almost overwhelmed by the sheer energy being deployed to do this, he could feel his heart falter with the enormity of what he was witnessing.

The mountain of earth that had formed itself into the caricature of an immense man began to walk south towards Gort.

70

The hardest part of licker making was the way that Petra kept a beady eye on him, Tyrant thought. As if he couldn't be trusted not to consume more of the product than was good for him. The occasional sip for quality control purposes was surely an essential part of the process, but Petra said otherwise and threatened heavy sanctions in the event of any contravention. 'It's the same taters, the same recipe, the same equipment, so it's going to taste the same. Stands to reason. No need for you to intervene at all. Just carry the mash to the still, fill the jars with licker, and carry them down to the vedhana,' she said.

'There might be a faulty batch; wouldn't want to alienate our customers, would you? Surely it's best to be on the safe side?'

'Safest to let the customer decide. If he doesn't like the stuff, then we can discuss the matter further. As things stand, if you decide the licker's unfit for sale, what are you going to do with it?' Petra stared hard at Tyrant as she asked the question. He knew the answer, but didn't think that saying it out loud would do him any good. The look on her face said everything he needed to know. Offering to drink any substandard produce wasn't going to go down at all well.

When the whole batch had been collected in the coruscating melee of light and they were ready to leave, Petra stood next to the device with an obvious reluctance to proceed further.

'What's up?' Tyrant asked.

'I get a bad feeling every time I get into one of these things. I never did like them; I don't trust them to take us where we want to go. Anyway, even if we do get safely to Malachi's house, what if he's there waiting for us? He's not exactly going to be pleased to find we're using his house as a warehouse for licker.'

'Well, we can't go importing licker to Gort through the vedhana in the King's tower, can we?'

'No, we should carry it ourselves like normal people do. Buy a horse and cart and keep them in Gort to ferry product from the North Road to the city.'

'But we would still have to manhandle the jars down through the forest to the road. That's a prodigious amount of work and will take far too long. I promised quick delivery to the innkeeper at the Four Kings. He'll have forgotten all about our arrangement if we don't deliver on time.'

'It'll take a day or so to ferry a few jars down to the road, then a few more to walk to Gort with them. The exercise will do us good and we'll not have to risk our lives in that unnatural device,' Petra said. 'We can deliver enough to keep him happy until we have our cart and can bring the rest.'

Tyrant didn't like the plan at all, especially the bit about the exercise doing him good. Sweating along the road under the weight of licker jars day after day wasn't what he had in mind as a business plan. Sitting comfortably in the Four Kings with a drink in his hand, discussing the price of the next delivery, was more to his liking. 'The road's a dangerous place; we'll be most likely attacked and all our licker stolen before we get in sight of Gort,' he said. 'Even if we do get ourselves a cart, it will only attract the wrong kind of attention. There's plenty of men desperate enough for a drink and a coin or two to make that journey a hazardous one. Why don't we do this first delivery with the help of the device that Ant went to so much trouble to provide us with? Then we'll have money to buy a cart if that's what we decide.'

Petra wrinkled her already well-creased face. She surveyed the rows of jars laid out on the ground outside the house and shook her head. 'I don't want to go to Malachi's house again, though. It wasn't so bad when we were with Ant; after all, he lives there and has every right to come and go through that vedhana thing. On our own, it's as if we're burglars and we risk being treated as such if we're caught. We should go to the device in the cave, take all the licker there.'

'But the entrance is too small for me to use,' Tyrant said.

'That's the beauty of it. We take the licker there, leave it inside where it'll be safe and return here. Then we can walk unencumbered to Gort, get ourselves a cart, and then I can retrieve the licker from the cave.'

Tyrant was still willing to take his chances at Malachi's house, but realised that the licker, or at least some of it, would have to be left there while they obtained a cart. If Malachi returned, it would be pretty obvious what was going on and the prospects of getting his licker back would not be good. Better to use the inaccessible cave, he thought, provided that the vedhana continued to function and enabled him to get out of the place. A shudder went through him as he imagined himself stuck forever inside there because the device had become no longer operational. If that happened, he'd be stuck. Petra would have to ferry food and drink to him while they waited for Ant to come up with a solution to the problem. That was, if they could find Ant again.

The new plan involved a series of long walks, but it was better than anything else he could devise.

71

'You should have consulted me before attempting something like that,' Malachi said. The immense apparition was striding away with confident ease, its movements fluid and well-coordinated.

'I didn't trust you not to interfere and take over the whole process for your own ends,' Ambrose said.

'I still don't trust him,' Garth said. 'I don't see what's changed to invite Malachi here and show him the fruits of all your painstaking research. He'll only steal your ideas and use them against us.'

'What's changed is that the King and his entire army have moved away south and I believe that was Malachi's doing.'

'I'd prefer it if you addressed me directly and didn't talk about me as if I'm not here.' Malachi felt an increasing sense of frustration. These two were talking as if this situation was under their control and had no idea of the enormity of what they had perpetrated. 'Do you know what you've created? Have you any idea of the power it has?'

'All I did was use the vedhana to shift the blockage from the road. I've done it before on a much smaller scale,' Ambrose said.

'No, you haven't, you've made something very dangerous. I've never had experience of one before but I've read enough of the ancient texts to recognise a golem when I see one.'

'A golem?' Garth's face took on a strained look. 'I thought those things were just old tales to frighten children with.'

'Maybe you can call it that,' Ambrose said, 'but the main reason I brought you here was to help me to control it. Use your famous mind control techniques to make the golem do our bidding.'

Malachi shrugged. 'That thing is way beyond any influence I might have. Anyway, we'd have to catch it first, wouldn't we?' Malachi watched as the golem reached the top of a distant hill where it paused, looked back at them, and waved its arm before disappearing from view.

'Where's it going?' Ambrose asked.

'You made it; don't you know?' Garth asked.

'You made it using your own blood,' Malachi said. 'That's what will influence its actions from here on. Think of your own most basic desires and the golem will be imbued with those. What are your motives, Ambrose? What is it that you really want from all this?'

'The same as everyone else, I suppose. To rid us of the King and the threat he poses. To keep us safe from attack. Safety, security, that sort of thing.'

'Then it's to be hoped that the golem finds a way of expressing your desires that doesn't destroy too many innocent lives.' Malachi said. 'You said you'd tried this before. Tell me, what happened to the previous golems that you made? Where are they now?'

Ambrose's face was flushed red in the persistent wind that blew chill across the exposed hillside. 'At my house,' he replied, 'in the garden mostly. I used the blood of mice and cats for those and small handfuls of dirt. The little things just move around like heaps of muck. There's no harm to them at all.'

'But there's also no signs of them becoming inanimate again, are there?' Malachi asked.

'I expected the effect to be short-lasting and that they would quickly run out of energy,' Ambrose said. 'But you're right; the first one was made several months ago, and it's just as active as it was in the beginning.'

'If that's the way of these things, you have been foolhardy in the extreme. Once made, they appear to have a life of their own,' Malachi said. 'You really should have told me about your intentions, perhaps even shown me your handiwork before proceeding to make something on such a vast scale.'

'Like I said, I didn't trust you. I thought you might steal my discovery and use it against us,' Ambrose said, his eyes full of defiance.

Malachi turned to Garth. 'Where were you when all this was being planned? Couldn't you have counselled caution this time?'

Garth shook his head. 'I had no idea of what Ambrose was engaged in. He told me he had a way of using the vedhana to shift the blockage from the road, that's all. He made no mention of creating a golem.'

Malachi turned away and began to walk slowly back towards the lake far below them. He was having difficulty restraining himself from exploding with anger and severely punishing these two stupid and ignorant men. Hadn't it been the same with the first device that Ambrose had installed in the King's tower despite repeated warnings? He'd brought death and destruction down upon the unfortunate citizens of Gort and all because of ignorance and foolhardiness. Now he'd done it all over again, unleashing something he couldn't control on the world without any regard for the consequences. There was no knowing how much damage the golem might inflict. All he could do was to get back to Gort as soon as possible and raise the alarm about what was heading their way. With the King and his army already heading south, there would be little or no protection for the city.

72

The vegetation was becoming ever more sparse, and the sun was uncomfortable in Cuthbert's eyes as he squinted down the long line of soldiers heading south. Behind him were large unwieldy wagons carrying the great and the good and their weighty belongings. The King's retinue consisted of no less than thirty vehicles, together with numerous riders and dozens of smaller carts. In order to make his journey bearable, the King had insisted on bringing two complete sets of everything so that his tent could be sent ahead and ready for him at the end of the day's march.

The King and his retinue travelled a considerable distance to the rear, which Cuthbert was grateful for. His job, as Vargas had described it, was to scout the route ahead, and to do this, he had to ride down the long cavalcade of common soldiery and take the lead. Although he'd done this many times before, this always made him nervous because he couldn't help remembering being roped to the back of a cart after being sentenced to death.

Vargas had made no reference to any potential repercussions regarding his previous army service. He'd welcomed him into his home, told him he was expected, and that he'd accompany him on the long journey south as his assistant. 'If you're good enough to be Malachi's assistant, I'm sure you'll do perfectly well for me,' he'd said.

Cuthbert often wondered who Malachi was, but had been so grateful for the food and clean clothing he'd been given that it seemed too much of a risk to start asking questions. By the time they were on their way, it seemed too late and, anyway, Vargas seemed to be more than happy with him.

Scouting was relatively easy compared to being a pikeman. Riding was much more comfortable than walking along carrying a heavy stick. Not only that, but the soldiers started earlier and finished later than everyone else. They also weren't allowed to stop for lunch as this would lose the whole assembly valuable time.

Until they reached the desert, Cuthbert's job had consisted of trotting to the head of the column and following the road for a while until he judged he could wait for the others to catch up. It was then that he sat and ate a hearty lunch provided for him by Vargas's cooks until the rest of them arrived. Then he'd go on a bit further until the sun started to go down and he had to return to the nice comfortable tent that someone kindly pitched for him every night. Now, he wasn't so sure of the way, but tried to keep his horse heading south by reference to the sun. The rest of them would be following his tracks, so there was a certain weight of responsibility on his shoulders.

His feelings of self-importance evaporated when he recognised the wizened face staring at him from the back of a cart. His first reaction was to notice that Grew had acquired a new cart, one whose wheels seemed to roll along smoothly propelled by a horse with considerably more meat on it than the previous one. Grew's expression suddenly changed; his eyes widened and his legs stopped waving in time to the motion of the cart as they dangled over the edge. He leapt off the back of the vehicle and confronted Cuthbert by standing in front of his horse.

'I never thought I'd set eyes on you again,' he said.

Cuthbert was caught in a momentary dilemma. Should he ignore Grew? Pretend he didn't know him? Ride over him? Act in a dismissive and disdainful manner as might befit his new station in life? 'Hello, Sergeant,' he said, 'how nice to see you. How are you keeping?'

'You are Cuthbert, aren't you?' Grew said.

'The one and the same,' Cuthbert said.

'Then I suppose I should take you prisoner and hand you in.' Grew smiled.

'Did you get into awful trouble because of me?' Cuthbert asked.

'Nothing special, a few grumpy words, but I'm used to them. There were several high-ranking officers asking your whereabouts, but they seemed to lose interest when I told them you'd been rescued by overwhelming forces and taken back to the North.'

'The back of the cart broke, you left me lying in the dark, and I couldn't catch you up again. It was really scary in the forest on my own,' Cuthbert said.

'So how did you arrive here all dressed in fine clothes and riding a good-looking horse?'

'I've been attached to Vargas, the King's explorer. I'm his assistant; my job is to take you all safely across the desert to our destination.'

'Which is what?' Grew asked.

'It's a magnificent city in the middle of the desert where there are great riches and glory to be had.'

'So that's why the King's tagging along, then. To make sure all those riches and all that glory don't fall into the wrong hands.' Grew laughed. 'I have to confess that knowing that we're all in your less than capable hands doesn't improve my estimation of our chances of survival. I don't suppose you've made this journey before and that you know the way?'

'No, I've not,' Cuthbert said.

'But your boss Vargas has?'

'No, he's not either,' Cuthbert said.

'So, it's another case of the blind leading the blind, is it?'

Cuthbert thought about the situation for a moment. Vargas had seemed quite confident that not only did the city they were heading for exist, but that he had a good idea of where it was. How he'd come about this information, he had no idea. Perhaps this man Malachi held the answer. Then a shiver ran down his back. What if Malachi's assistant knew the way and he'd been sent to guide Vargas and the King? In that case, where was this assistant? They all believed that he was that man and therefore he knew the way. But he wasn't and he didn't. He was going to lead them all to certain death, then. Vargas, Grew, and the King were all going to perish because he'd pretended to be someone he wasn't.

Cuthbert swallowed with difficulty; his throat had become very dry and his hands were slippery with sweat, making it difficult for him to grasp the reins. Grew stood aside, waving him past with mock ceremony.

Out in the desert with the first soldier far behind, Cuthbert realised that they were all following his lead and hoped against hope for some miracle that might guide him.

73

'The eggs are waiting to be collected,' Lone said, watching with amusement as Moussa's face struggled to deal with the shock of seeing her again. She could almost see the thought processes churning through his mind. He looked as if he'd been through a rough time, and his companions were an even sorrier sight, clinging on to the bridles of their camels in an effort to stand upright.

Eventually, Moussa swallowed a few times and spoke. 'Eggs?' he said.

'Of course, eggs. What else did you expect? The hens keep on laying even if you three decide to go off on a little jaunt.'

Moussa's face creaked into an expression that combined horror and disbelief. 'But, I thought...'

'I know perfectly well what you thought, Moussa.' Lone was savouring her moment of triumph. Whatever the three thought of her before, they had to be impressed with what she had done to them this time. Or, maybe it was so far beyond their belief, that they'd continue in denial. One thing was sure, if they so much as stepped slightly out of line in the future, she'd get Zaire to feed them to the monsters in the river.

'You thought you'd sell the business and take off with the proceeds. Well, I'm not ready to sell just yet, and I may need you to accompany me during my onward journey. That's if I let you survive that long.'

'But we thought it was for the best. Ali only paid us a small pittance, enough to buy some food for our camels. We expected him to give the full value of the business to you. He promised to treat you very well or we wouldn't have dreamed of making the deal.'

'If any of you think you might get away with trying to cheat me again, you'll be sorry,' Lone said. 'Now, fetch the eggs. There are customers waiting. Tell them I'll be along for payment as usual.'

The bedraggled trio staggered off towards the chicken farm without any further protest. Lone continued her walk across the bridge towards the palace.

That's not a good idea, Lone.

'Ah, Cali, you're back, are you? I thought you'd gone off in a huff.'

Better you keep your head down under the circumstances, don't you think?

'And what circumstances exactly are you referring to?'

There's a man dead, Lone.

'Everyone dies eventually, Cali. I expect his time had come, that's all.'

You killed him, Lone. There will be severe repercussions when it's discovered that Ali died at your hand. He worked for the King, after all.

'He didn't exactly die at my hand; his life was sucked out of him because he got too close to a ritual I was performing. That was his bad luck.'

That might not be the view taken by others, Lone.

'This King, Cali, what can you tell me about him?'

Very little, I'm afraid.

'Very little that you know or very little you're willing to tell me about?'

You know I'd tell you if I knew anything at all.

'I'm not sure I believe you. Why don't you scout ahead for me? Tell me how to get into this palace and set eyes on this mysterious King.'

You'd be wiser to go back to your chickens and hope the whole affair blows over, Lone.

'Is this King more powerful than I am?'

That's one thing I'm sure of. This King wields almost limitless power.

'But I have Zaire in my thrall; he'll protect me and he's the main man in these parts.'

Hardly a man, Lone, he's the representation of a river system. An avatar. Don't confuse the appearance with the reality.

'Whatever he is, he's all mine. I could get him to drown the lot of them or have the city blown to bits by a whirlwind. It's about time I had it out with this King, show him he can't mess with me.'

290

All I can do is to reiterate what I've just told you. This King is very dangerous and best left alone. You would be wise to keep your head down and hope his attention stays elsewhere.

Lone looked up at the walls and towers of the palace. It was an ornate structure that didn't look fortified at all. There were arches all along the perimeter, which allowed free access to the inner courtyards. The intricate carvings and detailed statues showed no signs of any wear and tear. It was as if they'd been newly created a few days ago, their surfaces were smooth as if newly hewn from solid stone. There was a notable absence of anyone availing themselves of the sumptuous lushness of the gardens within the palace walls. Outside, there were throngs of people hurrying about their business with hardly a sideways glance. No guards approached her to ask her business, there were no shouts of alarm at her entrance, and this felt slightly disconcerting.

There was a subtle but very sweet fragrance about the place; she couldn't decide whether it was coming from the gardens themselves or from inside the main building. It wasn't the scent of any flowers she was familiar with, nor was it the heady aroma of the spice stalls in the marketplace. It was an altogether different smell that grew stronger as she progressed.

The main palace building had a ground floor of colonnades, which gave open access to the interior. Above, it stretched high into the air. An imposing massive slab of stone that looked much bigger from close up than it had done on her approach. The air was still and cloying with the heady aroma that intensified as she entered the palace. There was nobody around to halt her passage or to greet her. The place seemed to be completely empty.

The smell began to irritate the membranes in her nostrils and each breath she took created a needle-sharp pain at the bridge of her nose. Lone worried about the atmosphere in this place and whether it might do her irreparable harm. She was finding it hard to breathe and was considering a rapid withdrawal when she heard the voice.

If you're thinking of leaving us, I think you should know that will be impossible now that you've come this far.

The voice in her head was unfamiliar and sounded very sure of itself.

'Cali?'

She isn't allowed in here.

'Who are you, then?'

People call me Jeremiah. Why? I'm not entirely sure. It goes back a long time. I never asked the significance of the name then, and it's too late by far now.

'Well, Jeremiah, I suppose you're the king around here.'

No, not me. My master is that and much more. All I am is a servant to one who has greater power than you can ever imagine.

'Patch? I knew it. It's been him all along. Where is he? I've a few words I need to say to him. He's caused me enough grief to last a lifetime and I'll not be putting up with any more.'

Oh him. Cali has told me about the entity you're referring to. Patch indeed, makes Jeremiah sound regal in comparison, doesn't it? Anyway, he's long gone, won't ever come back if he knows what's good for him. He's a pathetic wimp in comparison to my master.

Lone was beginning to feel sick from the fumes, so she turned back and headed out towards the bright sunlight beyond the palace walls. She longed for a breath of fresh air. Her head was feeling light, and her eyes couldn't focus properly. She was about to step back into the courtyard, but found that she was back in the centre of the building and standing in front of an oblong pool with edges of stone that stood waist high above the polished floor. Here, the odour was almost overpowering in its intensity.

Lone peered into the transparent liquid that filled the bath to its brim. She could make out the prone figure of a large man lying on his back and completely submerged. There was something familiar about his features that made her rifle through her memories to try to come up with a name or the place she'd encountered him before.

The recognition hit her like a lightning bolt, and her whole being reacted as if it had been jolted by a heavy blow. There was no denying it; the likeness was unmistakable. This was a clean-shaven and very much younger version of the man she knew as Tyrant. At the exact moment, the realisation struck her, his eyes opened and looked at her from the depths of the noisome liquid.

74

Cuthbert's eyes were sore. They were also playing tricks on him. He was finding it impossible to focus them properly; everything had become blurred. Ahead of him, the horizon of brown sand was shimmering as if it were molten. Strands of earth seemed to have detached themselves from the ground and were hovering high above where they ought to lie. Weary and afraid, he dismounted and offered his horse the few drops of water that remained in his skin. She sucked them up greedily and her black eyes begged for more.

Vargas had told him in no uncertain terms that he needed to find water today. It was nearing the time when he would normally stop and wait for the rest to catch up with him, but Cuthbert was afraid of what might happen when they did. The water situation was critical and had been exacerbated by the King throwing a hissy fit when he discovered that the water from his twice-daily baths was being given to the horses to drink. According to Vargas, the King was immensely displeased at the thought that animals were ingesting the liquid used to cleanse the royal body.

At first, Cuthbert imagined that the King had been expressing concern about the horses having to drink dirty water, but Vargas had made it clear that this wasn't the case at all. Because the water had touched the King's person, it had to be treated with reverence and ceremonially poured away into the sand. This practice had further depleted the whole water situation and everyone was feeling the strain. Except the King, of course.

Vargas had gone on to describe what might happen if the King became victim to the same kind of deprivation as everyone else. The day his morning ablutions were cut short was the day that retribution would be sought. Vargas made it quite clear that the King knew exactly who was responsible for finding water and that Cuthbert would be first on the list to feel his wrath.

Now his day of grace was nearly over and he'd found no signs of anything except more dry desert. Cuthbert wished he'd taken the opportunity to turn full circle and head back north. He'd rejected this option originally on the grounds that the army was following his tracks and would continue to do so. He also considered the distinct possibility that he'd blunder his way back into their midst and have to explain his dereliction of duty to a thirsty bunch of unfriendlies.

He sat for a while trying to make sense of the wavering patterns of light and wondering what signs might presage the presence of water in this horribly hot wilderness. He presumed he was looking for something green but, apart from the odd patch of scrubby grass clinging desperately to the shifting sand, it was all brown. Light brown, dark brown, and sometimes for a change, a bit of black caused by the shadows in the dunes. Nothing green, though.

The sun was sinking fast. In these climes, he was used to the sudden and dramatic sunsets that transformed hot eye-watering brightness into sudden chilly darkness. He'd run out of water, run out of energy, and run out of options. When the King failed to get his bath in the morning, there would be hell to pay and the scapegoat would be him. It was little comfort to know that Vargas would be the next to suffer, having mistakenly put his faith in an impostor. Cuthbert wondered who this Malachi was and what special powers of water divination his assistant possessed. It had been too easy to accept what appeared to be a definite improvement on his previous situation, but now reality was back in charge. A slight smile drew his lips back from his teeth when he considered the possibility that everyone would die because of his ineptitude. The whole army, generals and all, would perish and so would the King. Maybe this had been somebody's plan all along.

75

The three men sat morosely in Ambrose's house. Malachi's heart was heavy with frustration and dread over what he'd witnessed in the valley of the North Road. He ran through the sparse knowledge he'd acquired regarding the powers and characteristics of golems and felt the anger rising inside at the foolhardiness that might well have sentenced all of them to death.

'You've released a golem, Ambrose. Don't you have any idea of the power of that thing?' Malachi said.

'I didn't know it was a golem, I only wanted a quick and easy way to clear the road. I intended the soil to pick itself up, walk to a convenient place away from the road, and lie back down again. That's all. The first bit worked; all I'm unsure of is where and when the thing will just become a pile of earth again.' Ambrose busied himself with the brewing of tea and cleaning out pots to serve it in.

Malachi caught a quick movement out of the corner of his eye. A mouse had appeared in the far corner of the room; it sat on its hind legs and cleaned its whiskers with its paws as it looked back at him. Malachi's eyes adjusted to the shadows enough to realise that this mouse was indistinct in a very strange way. It had mousy movements and mannerisms, but its shape was vague. Its eyes were just sockets and its body shape shifted and flowed as if it were liquid. Malachi's fearfulness took another step down the road to panic. Everything he'd ever worked for was now in jeopardy, and all because this arrogant man had been dabbling in things he had no right to get involved with.

'That thing up the corner,' Ambrose said and pointed to the mouse-like figure staring fearlessly at them, 'how long has it been active?'

'Oh, not long. A few months, perhaps a year at the most,' Ambrose said. 'It was the result of the first experiment I carried out using mouse blood.'

'And it's still going strong?' Garth asked, waving his hand to refuse the proffered tea.

Ambrose placed the cup in front of him anyway. 'Yes, all this time. I've been wondering where it draws its energy from. There's been no drop off in activity at all since it first became animate. The others have been the same, apart from one that fell to pieces almost as soon as it woke up.'

'How many golems have you made?' Malachi asked.

'Let me see now, that will be seven if you include the one from today. Apart from him, all the others have been small. Too small to be of concern, I can assure you.'

Malachi sighed. 'I don't think you're in any position to make that assurance, Ambrose. Even if today hadn't happened, there would be enough to worry about with six of these things on the loose.'

'That's where you come in, Malachi,' Ambrose said. 'I hoped you might get rid of the little ones for me. They're becoming a bit of a nuisance, if I'm honest. Especially when the cat ones are chasing the mice ones. They're always knocking things over and have ruined several carefully formed experiments because of their clumsiness.'

'Tell me, what happens when a cat golem catches a mouse golem?' Garth asked. 'Surely that's the end of the mouse golem?'

'Not so,' Ambrose said, 'the little beggars are indestructible. They run for their lives like real mice, but when a cat hits them with its paw, they just scatter like dust across the floor. When the cat loses interest, it gathers itself up again and is back to being a mouse. I even tried catching one and putting it in a cage. It just flowed through the tiny openings and ran off. They're like beings made of smoke; they can go anywhere and seem to be indestructible.'

'Yet nothing to worry about?' Garth asked. The question sat heavily on the air for a few moments and nobody seemed to feel like answering it.

'The big golem was made with your blood,' Malachi said. 'What were you trying to achieve?'

'I thought we might be able to give it orders,' Ambrose said.

'By using your own blood you've effectively done that, but in a very dangerous and undirected manner. What exactly will the golem think you want it to do?' Ambrose said.

'To kill the King, I suppose,' Ambrose said. 'I want to protect my friends and family, just like anyone else would. The King is trying to kill us all, so I'm entitled to protect myself, aren't I?'

'We're all entitled to self-defence, but this is something different. Your golem could destroy the whole world and there's nothing anyone can do to stop it. As we sit here talking about it, the city of Gort could be devastated by that thing and thousands of innocent lives lost. Is that the kind of self-defence you feel entitled to claim?'

Malachi stood up, walked warily past the weird mouse, and left his question hanging in the air.

76

Cuthbert sat in the warm, soft sand and watched the sun change from orange to red as it sank. He wondered if this had been the last day of his life and whether he might have spent it more wisely. Sitting in a sweaty saddle, wearing out his eyes in a futile search for signs of water, hadn't been a particularly good experience for his last one. He wished he could have had one more day with Cassie so that he could make her understand how much he loved her and what a tragic waste his life had been without her.

He'd had this feeling before. When he reflected, it seemed to have been with him for a long time now, ever since the terrible avalanche. It had intensified after Grew's announcement that he was to be summarily hanged and persisted ever since. His big regret was that he'd been so scared of the forest that he'd headed south when he should have gone back north to Cassie, or at least died trying.

The shadows were lengthening and he expected the sounds of the cavalcade of thirsty soldiers to be audible at any moment. Then the recriminations would start as it was realised that they would all be dying together in this fiery heat. It was only the order in which they did so that was up for debate. Maybe it would be easier to be the first one to die.

Cuthbert had been paying so little attention to his surroundings that he didn't notice the little man approach and sit down beside him. It was as if he suddenly appeared from nowhere. He was no bigger than a child and wearing a rather unsuitable costume for the desert climate. His turban was bright golden, reflecting the reddish glow of the sunset so that it looked to be emitting flames. Cuthbert sat quietly, trying to quieten his racing heart by telling himself that if this little man meant him harm, he would surely have had confirmation of that by now.

Cuthbert's breath became even enough for him to consider speaking, but he was finding it difficult to think of something to say. Normally, he would have offered some form of hospitality, but the only water he had was long drained from his goatskin and apart from sand, which seemed completely inappropriate, he had nothing to offer. Before he formed an opening pleasantry that felt appropriate, the little man spoke.

'It's a good time of day for feeling alive,' he said.

Cuthbert tried to claw his way past all the worries in his head in order to arrive at the same conclusion. It was hard, but he managed to feel a little of the glory that the setting sun provided. 'I've often wondered how the sun can change colour like that,' Cuthbert said. 'And it gets bigger the lower it gets. How does that work?'

'Perception, like all things in life. It's only a matter of how you see things, not what they really consist of. Take the sun, for instance. When it's high in the sky, there's less atmospheric distortion; the lower it gets, the more its light is refracted by the atmosphere.'

'The atmosphere? What's that?' Cuthbert asked, hoping he wasn't betraying his ignorance of something that everyone else was fully familiar with, but he'd somehow missed.

'The air that you breathe. Don't worry, it's better to enjoy the sights and smells of this world than to explain how they come about. It's all an illusion in one sense, but all too real in another. It's not your place to make that sort of choice. You have to contend with what's put in front of you in the best way you can. That's what I find so interesting in humans. There are as many ways of coping as there are people. Every person seems to react differently to what they experience.'

Cuthbert found this explanation confusing and reassuring at the same time. The little man seemed to be perfectly relaxed and Cuthbert got to wondering if he might know where to find water.

'Excuse me asking,' Cuthbert said, 'but I'm rather desperately looking for water. It's not just for me you understand, there's a horde of people relying on me to find it.'

'Are you Malachi's young assistant, then?'

'Yes,' Cuthbert answered quickly, then regretted the lie as soon as it was out. 'No, I mean. Sorry, it's just that I've been mistaken for him before. That's how I got here. Vargas seemed to be expecting me so I was happy with that. By the time I realised he was really waiting for someone else it was too late to tell the truth as we were already on our way. I don't want you to get the wrong idea. I'm not a cheater. Circumstances have acted against me. I never even met this Malachi, though I've heard Ant mention him a time or two. If there's anyone to blame, it's Ant's spirit guide, Jeremiah. He's the one who told me to go to see Vargas.'

'Oh dear, you should be very careful of anything that Jeremiah tells you to do. I'm afraid he's a very tricky customer that even I'm wary of. I have the impression that it's Jeremiah who's orchestrating all this business while persuading Malachi that he's the one pulling the strings.'

Cuthbert thought about this for a while, dredging through his mind for the things he knew had been influenced by Jeremiah. He came to the conclusion that just about everything Ant had said or done had been under that influence. He felt a hollow feeling inside his chest as he remembered how Ant had known all about the night he spent with Cassie without having to be told. It had probably been Jeremiah making his life difficult all along, including persuading him to go back to the army and eventually ending up here. Cuthbert suddenly felt helpless and alone. There was nothing he could do for himself, it appeared. Everything was being determined for him at the whim of this Jeremiah. 'Who exactly is Jeremiah and what does he want?' Cuthbert asked.

'Jeremiah seems to be a manifestation of the King or at least a form of ally. He's only recently come to my attention. It's the nature of kings that one will seek to have power over the other, or maybe to simplify matters by eliminating a rival altogether,' the little man replied. 'Kings are almost always inhuman, and by that I don't mean cruel, though they are certainly that as well. I've been around a very long time and witnessed the arrival of beings who were jealous of the human experience and wanted to have it for themselves. The problem seems to be that this is forbidden. The laws of the universe prohibit intermingling, and this has given rise to some long and bitter disagreements. Nevertheless, law or no law, it happens. There were once many renegades and outcasts who made their home amongst humans and produced offspring who were neither one thing nor the other.'

Cuthbert didn't understand everything the man was saying, but enough to get a feeling that it was fundamentally important. *Inhuman.* The word kept echoing around his mind, bringing an equal measure of excitement and dread. 'If both Kings are inhuman, won't they want to help each other?'

'Quite the opposite, it seems. They see each other as a threat, perhaps because they're unwilling to share this world or because they both know that they cannot be harmed except by each other. Eliminating that risk may well be the motivation driving both of them on.'

'I don't see how I can influence things either way, do you?' Cuthbert said.

'No, it's not for me to take sides, either. I'm telling you because for once I can speak freely to someone while Jeremiah is occupied elsewhere and can't spy on my actions.'

Cuthbert heard the commotion behind him as sweaty men arrived, dry and breathless. There was a soft thud as a man alighted close by and a voice croaked, 'Where's the water? We have to pitch the King's pavilion and he's expecting it to have a water supply or there'll be trouble.'

Cuthbert jumped to his feet, heart pounding. 'I'm sorry,' was all he could manage.

'Tell them to erect the King's tent on the other side of that dune,' the little man said.

Cuthbert pointed. 'Over the hill,' he said and watched the advance party labour their way up the shifting sand and disappear as they reached the top.

When he sat down wearily, he was disappointed that the little man had disappeared. He wondered if everything he'd been told was just a pack of lies that he'd dreamed up inside his own head and waited for angry men to return boiling with rage over the crest of the dune.

77

Lone's head was swimming; she couldn't control her limbs and her legs inconveniently gave way under her. Lying on the cool smoothness of the stone floor, she could only think that this wasn't a good time to collapse into a helpless heap.

When her head cleared enough for her to realise that the foul stench had gone, she found herself lying on a large bed surrounded by soft cushions. There was a gentle breeze coming through the room, which bore the scent of spices and fragrant produce. Her breath was restored and her heart was beating normally again. She recalled the vision of the man in the pool and wondered whether that had been caused by the fumes she'd been breathing. She certainly hoped so.

Lone rolled to the edge of the bed and off onto the floor. She stood and looked out of the window at the beautiful river that gently curved through the city. She could see the bridge festooned with the throngs of busy people hurrying about their business. Her vantage point allowed her to look beyond the city and towards the area of green jungle that she identified as the place her chickens would be scurrying around in that wonderfully endearing manner.

Someone had carried her all the way up here without her being conscious of what was going on. Apart from the dead man in the bath, she'd seen nobody at all so far, and this made her very nervous. The idea that a corpse had come to life and manhandled her was not a pleasant one. As she shuddered in revulsion, the revived corpse made an appearance.

He looked alive, quite normal, and quite young. Even so, she had a very bad feeling about him that was strengthened as soon as she heard the sound of his voice.

'It is such a fine city, don't you agree?'

Lone looked at him suspiciously. He had lain naked in the bath but, mercifully, was now clothed in plain white. His coal-black hair had been cut short, and his dark eyes betrayed experience beyond his youthful exterior.

'You speak as if it were yours,' she said, keeping the expanse of the bed between them.

'That's because it does belong to me. Its sole purpose is to provide people to worship me.'

Lone formulated a response that incorporated the words pompous and arsehole, but resisted the urge to speak it out loud. Instead, she concentrated on getting her bearings in preparation for escape.

'So, you're the elusive King that everyone talks about but nobody has actually laid eyes on,' she said.

'King, yes. But I'm so much more besides. There aren't any other kings that have been around as long as I have. I'd characterise myself as a god first and a king second.'

'So what does a god like you want from me?' Lone asked. She felt she already had a good idea of the answer she was going to get. The big bed was a worrying indication of the King's intentions.

'Something that my human side seems to never grow tired of. These gonads of mine require emptying at frequent intervals and I have to admit that I find this a great pleasure, the best part of being alive.'

Lone's stomach lurched in response. Surely he could have found himself someone younger and more comely? Someone who might actually like the sort of activities he was looking to engage her in. 'Well, you've chosen the wrong woman. I'm not willing to bear the fruits of your loins, so you'd be better to have another think about the whole situation.'

Her words seemed to cause him great amusement when she'd been hoping for disappointment or, at worst, anger. 'There's little chance of me getting you with child. I've been doing this for thousands of years and, with one single exception, it's never resulted in a child. It seems that gods and humans aren't very compatible when it comes to cross breeding. Which is just as well, because, were I to beget progeny, I would incur the wrath of beings I'd rather keep on the right side of. And even if they failed to notice, there's always the age-old problem of the son eventually growing impatient and usurping the father. I'd rather not have that kind of complication. No, Lone, don't worry about conceiving,' he said.

'I don't understand why you've taken the trouble to take me prisoner just so that you can indulge yourself in an act of copulation. I would have thought you had better and more willing partners to choose from,' Lone said.

303

'Jeremiah thought I might find you interesting,' he said.

'If you want someone to be interested in you, I suggest that you don't open the conversation with a reference to your gonads needing emptying. It makes you sound inexperienced and desperate. Not at all attractive,' Lone said.

'Then what do you suggest that might make our time more enjoyable?'

'You could start by telling me about yourself. Someone who's lived such a long life must have some astounding tales to tell,' she said.

'Very well, I can do that.'

'But not here,' Lone said. 'I don't feel comfortable sitting on a bed with you, waiting for the moment when you lose patience. We need to sit and talk in a more comfortable setting.'

'Follow me,' he said, taking her out of the bedroom and onto a narrow winding staircase. After a long climb, they emerged onto a sunlit platform. Lone's breath was taken away by the height and the vista that spread below. The city looked small from here and its inhabitants seemed tiny. Her view stretched way beyond the outskirts of the city and far into the desert. She liked it here; she felt exhilarated to be so high up.

If things took a turn for the worst, there was always the option of leaping over the edge and denying this boorish King anything he might want from her. She looked at his face, young and smooth, then the cruel eyes fastened on hers and she had to look away. The resemblance to Tyrant that she'd seen when she'd first encountered the King in his chemical pool was still there, but it was only in the cast of his face and not in the way he moved or spoke.

Tyrant was rough and ungainly. Even so, she recognised the honest humanity he had always represented, and it was a stark contrast to the uncaring remoteness that stood in front of her. It may have been the breeze that made her shudder, but the thought of what this horrible King might do to her was almost certainly just as much to blame. Better to end it all with a short downward flight than be subjected to that.

'You can try if you want,' he said, 'but I think you'll find that escaping me isn't so easy.'

Lone sat on the parapet with her back to the world. 'Do you expect me to believe that you've been around for ten thousand years when you behave like you do?'

'I can behave exactly as I wish. There's nothing and no one in this world that can prevent me from having whatever I desire.'

'So why the bath with the smelly water in it? Don't you have better things to do with yourself than that?' she asked.

'Human bodies have a short span of useful life. They decay at an alarming rate and become useless very quickly. The rejuvenation pool is a way of keeping my body exactly how I want it. The alternative is to keep changing from one body to the next. Some prefer that way, but I've grown comfortable in my original guise and would be loath to change after all this time.'

Lone smiled inwardly at the admission. Here was a self-confessed supreme being who had to preserve his body with embalming fluids. It seemed to her that this was a clear indication that he had limitations and this gave her hope. She already knew how to manipulate his arrogance; what she needed now was to turn it into a fatal weakness she could exploit. 'Tell me how you came to be and where the others you refer to are.'

He looked at her as if he was losing interest in the conversation, then he gave a big shrug of his shoulders. 'It's a story that I've not told for such a long time. I suppose there can be no harm in its repetition. It's not as if you'll be telling anyone else, will you?'

'If it's a secret, I promise to respect it,' Lone said.

'It's no secret, but neither is it common knowledge. I've witnessed this world go through many cycles. You might think that this city is magnificent, but it is like a pile of unordered stones in comparison to what has gone before. I've seen humans build monuments of immense beauty and destroy them almost as soon as they're made. Your capacity for destruction is almost too much, even for me to understand. You take great delight in killing and promoting unhappiness. If I were capable of such an emotion, I would be sickened by what I have seen your species do. So don't be quick to judge me, I'm only half-human. It's you that has to take the blame.

'This city has been destroyed and rebuilt a dozen times, but it has been fortunate. There are vast tracts of this world that have been rendered uninhabitable by your penchant for destruction. Some things cannot be reversed even with the passage of time.'

'Half-human?' Lone asked.

'One of the few remaining, I'm glad to say. The mingling of gods and humans was unwise, an aberration that gave rise to much anger and recrimination. The ancient laws forbid it and the unruly ones who disobeyed have been severely punished.'

'I don't understand why a god would risk the wrath of his fellow gods just to make half-human offspring,' Lone said.

'That's because you don't appreciate the unique position you humans are in. You have the middle ground between the ethereal and the mundane. You encompass the real and the imagined. Your heads are in the clouds, yet your feet are entrenched in the earth. You are the lightning conductors through which the most powerful energies flow. Yet so few of you have any inkling of any of that at all. My forebears had the idea that they could combine their own awareness with the human condition and get the best of all possible experiences. That did work to an extent, but it resulted in the human race being decimated in the conflicts that arose between rival demi-gods competing for dominance. You see, Lone, the possession of absolute power is very dangerous without the limitations of responsibility. Eventually, order had to be imposed from the outside and the half-gods were destroyed to prevent them reducing the whole planet to rubble.'

'So how did you survive?' Lone asked.

'I saw what was coming and kept my head down, so to speak. This place is opaque, hard to see inside even by the most perceptive vision. I keep very quiet, make only tiny ripples in the energy of the cosmos and remain unnoticed. At least until now, when your enterprising husband decided it would serve his purposes to intervene.'

'Malachi? What's he doing that is so important to you?' Lone asked.

'He's in the process, or so he thinks, of usurping his own King who I have only recently realised is a similar being to myself. This one has been hiding in plain sight, so to speak. He changes his body at regular intervals and keeps his true power and nature very firmly under wraps. I can't take the risk of being discovered and certainly not by him. He's on his way here as we speak, a journey orchestrated by your husband, who also has no idea what he's getting himself into.'

Lone felt a hollow feeling of dread taking over her body. Now she understood what was being played out, even if she remained unsure who was calling the moves. There was also the cold knowledge that her knowing was something she wasn't going to be able to communicate, particularly with Malachi. 'I understand,' she replied, 'the Northern King is the last remaining demi-god who might threaten your supremacy. I take it that you mean to destroy him.'

'You take it right, Lone. Exciting times, eh? And I'm inviting you to experience it all here by my side. Now, surely that prospect is attractive enough for you to abandon all that posturing and resistance. Think of the power you can help to wield and the excitement of seeing the game unfold.'

'So, all I have to do is give in to your physical demands and you'll let me participate in the battle between you and your rival?'

'Yes, good isn't it?'

'What about the alternative? What if I refuse you?' Lone asked.

'That would be unwise in the extreme. I'd have you thrown off the bridge to Zaire's crocodiles. You have no idea just how unpleasant a death that would be.' His face had taken on an expression of distaste. Lone could feel some of the pomposity was leaking from his posture, as if he had become much less sure of his own importance. Then he resumed his usual supercilious smirk and the moment had passed.

'I'll have to think about it,' Lone said.

'That's not good enough,' he replied. 'Either you're agreeable or you die. I need your binding commitment right now,' he said as the smirk broadened, 'downstairs in the bedchamber. Call it an act of good faith.'

'Then I'd rather throw myself off this balcony,' Lone said. She twisted round so that her feet were dangling over the parapet, then pushed off with her hands. There was a very brief sensation of falling, followed by gently landing on her back on the soft mattress in the bedchamber. His leering face was uncomfortably close.

'I told you it's not so easy to escape me. I'll give you one more chance to abandon your illogical opposition or you'll be delivered into the mouths of those dreadful beasts before you can draw another breath.'

'I'd rather kill myself than listen to another moment of your insane prattling. Either that, or I'll just die of boredom and indifference merely from looking at your ugly face,' Lone said, then spat into his eye for good measure.

Then three men were carrying her, though she could see nothing through the sack she had been placed in. Her hands and feet were tightly bound and a strip of cloth around her face stopped her from crying out. She could hear the murmurings of passers-by and feel the slight incline being negotiated as she was carried to the centre of the bridge. Her head received a painful bump as she was bundled over the parapet. Then she felt the water close in around her.

Two thoughts occupied her mind as she plunged into the river. The first was a positive one. *I've been in this situation before and survived.*

The second was less optimistic. *I neglected to take a deep breath before I hit the water.*

Lone's lungs were already complaining even as her first thoughts were forming. She felt an uncontrollable urge to let the waters flood into her and be done with all this struggling and suffering. The crushing jaws that clamped around her body felt almost welcome as she was swept away with the fast-running currents. It was as if she was travelling faster than she had thought possible underwater, but her shroud gave her no means of gaining any visual reference.

Speed or not, there was no time left for her. The reflex simply took over from her will and the choking fluid swamped her lungs. The pain was sharp and intense for a few moments, then her awareness began to falter. She couldn't breathe, her body stiffened, and her limbs became unresponsive. The pounding in her chest quietened, then stopped altogether. She had a momentary vision of herself wrapped in a sack being propelled by a beast with a monstrous snout, then all she could see was the river, then the city, then the desert filled her view as she rose with breakneck speed, her essence dissipating and evaporating into nothingness.

78

Instead of cries of disappointment and anger, Cuthbert heard rejoicing. A soldier came running headlong back over the dune, stumbled, fell on his face, picked himself up, and confronted Cuthbert wearing a wide grin.

'I don't know what you're doing sitting here in the sand when you could have had that all to yourself until we arrived,' he said.

Cuthbert saw that the man was dripping wet. Slowly, his mind accustomed itself to the idea that he'd actually found water and that he might not be in big trouble after all. On the contrary, if this happy individual was anything to go by, he might actually get some credit at last. Maybe the King would make it clear that all that hanging business was now firmly put behind him.

He got to his feet and followed the damp footmarks over the hill. He was prepared to see a muddy pool for the animals to drink from, but the sight he beheld weakened his legs to the point that he had to sit down. It was a lake surrounded by greenery and it was massive. Soldiers had thrown down their accoutrements, abandoned their clothes, and were cavorting manically in the water. All Cuthbert could manage in the way of celebration was to splash his face and enjoy the sight of his parched horse drinking its fill.

As more and more people joined them, it became more like a huge wild party than a column of soldiers on a mission. It was only when the King arrived to find his pavilion only half-erected that the merriment subsided. A small remote area of waterfront was allocated to the common soldiers for access to drinking water while the rest of the lake was declared out of bounds and for the use of the King and a select few noblemen only.

Vargas congratulated Cuthbert warmly and promised to make sure that the King was made aware of the excellent water divining skills he'd displayed. For the first time since he'd been with Cassie by the lake, Cuthbert enjoyed a long and untroubled sleep.

***

Notwithstanding a groundswell of opinion that a few days' respite would improve everyone's morale and restore the army to its full potential as a fighting force, the King insisted that they push on. Cuthbert was roused before dawn and sent on his pathfinding way. His horse took a lot of persuading to abandon the sanctuary of the lake and head off into the arid heat.

The sun was almost directly overhead when the smudge on the horizon began to resolve itself into a shimmering line of buildings. The nearer he got, the more impressive the city looked. He'd always been in awe of the majesty of Gort, but this place seemed, even from a distance, to be much bigger. The view was so fascinating that he found himself riding through farmland towards a magnificent building whose towers rose many times higher than the palace in Gort.

The thought occurred that he should have waited in the desert for the rest of the army to catch up. This involved the problem of where the desert stopped and the city began. The transition was gradual, first scrubland with the occasional hut, then more fertile land with better-looking houses. There was no outer wall or gate to prevent his passage, so he kept on riding. It would be nice to find some shade and get his horse out of the heat. Preferably somewhere it could do a bit of grazing on proper grass rather than the brown sticks it had been trying to digest recently.

Nobody seemed interested in him as he clopped gently along the streets. Cuthbert wondered what might happen when the whole army turned up. From what he could see, there was nothing to stop them from doing exactly the same as he was. When he reached an enormous stone bridge, he dismounted and led his horse to the edge of the river to let it drink. The fast-flowing waters looked too dangerous for him to bathe in without the risk of being swept away. There was nobody else in the water, presumably for the same reason. It was tempting, though. He'd missed his chance of submersion at the lake in the desert and his flesh was crawling with sand and sweat.

What the hell, Cuthbert thought, *I'll just venture in up to my waist then sit down. There can't be any danger as long as I keep my feet on the ground.*

He waded out into the tepid waters, then lowered himself gingerly, feeling cautiously beneath him for hidden hazards. He'd once heard of a man who had sat on a spiky creature in a lake and died a horrible death. On this occasion, Cuthbert was grateful that his backside encountered nothing more inimical than an uncomfortably large stone. He let the waters lap around his shoulders and began to enjoy the way the sun was making the surface of the river sparkle. Removing his headdress, he threw water over his head, digging his nails into his scalp to scrape away the accumulated grit and dirt. The more he removed, the more there seemed to be to get rid of. His head began to itch and tingle, so he rubbed harder and applied more water.

A sudden feeling of dread made him pause what he was doing and wipe his eyes. Directly in front of him, about a body length away, there were two stationary dark patches on the water. As the wetness cleared from his vision, Cuthbert began to think of these as eyes that were watching him. He froze, unable to bring himself to his feet and flee. Considerably closer were two bumps raised above the general flow of the river. These he considered to be nostrils judging by the sniffing sound that was coming from them. He desperately wanted to get out of the river, but he had the terrible feeling that it was too late and that the moment he moved whatever it was that the eyes and nose belonged to would have him.

A slight swell swept over the nostrils, revealing a long snout that stretched all the way back to the staring eyes. He caught a glimpse of several white teeth, then the waters closed and only the eyes remained visible. Whatever it was, it was looking at him in a most unnerving manner. Cuthbert stared back, his eyes trying to judge the distance that separated him from the jaws and realising with horror that this was slowly diminishing. The thing was coming towards him and with obviously evil intent. Cuthbert remained perfectly still, as if even the tiniest movement would cause the thing to strike. Either that or sheer terror was rooting him to the spot. He decided that whatever the cause of his inaction, it mattered little compared with the prospect that faced him.

The thought came to him that he might be able to scare the thing away by splashing vigorously, perhaps shouting as well for good measure. He thought about this option as the nose slid ever closer and remembered that the eyes had appeared while he was washing his hair, which indicated that the thing may have actually been attracted by his flapping around in the water. He decided to try to back away slowly and carefully by sliding his bottom along the river bed in the direction of the shore. As soon as he made his first small movement, the nostrils rose in the air and he was confronted by an open mouth that looked capable of accommodating his whole body.

A commotion above him on the bridge diverted Cuthbert's attention from being eaten. Something wrapped in sacking was thrown into the river and hit the surface with a splash. The jaws snapped shut, then turned away. The water around him became turbulent and nearly swept him away. He took the opportunity to stand up and drag himself out of the water, anticipating with every hurried step the bite that would sever his legs and condemn him to a watery grave.

By the time he reached the shore, he was blubbering with relief and fear. As he tried to settle his ragged nerves, he wondered who had thrown the sack into the river and what it contained.

79

Pepper led Ant into the bright sunlight where his senses were assailed by intense heat, a cacophony of noise, and the heady scent of spices. It was a stark contrast to the placid underground monastery where the temperature was constantly cool and pleasant whatever the season. Ant drew in a deep breath and savoured the richness of it all.

'Do you like it?' Pepper asked.

'It's amazing,' Ant replied. 'Gort was never like this. It's so,' he sought the right word and found it, 'colourful,' he said.

'It's that alright,' Pepper said. 'The people here are very friendly and will provide you with anything your heart desires. Providing you give them some of this in exchange.' Pepper winked and drew from his pocket a handful of black stones. 'We burn these for cooking, but here they treat coal as a precious stone. They can't get enough of it.'

'I'm hungry,' Ant said. 'Can we buy food with what you've brought?'

'Just these few stones will have us living the high life for as long as we care to stay. We do need to save some though. I did promise Col we'd not return empty-handed.'

Laden with choice produce, Ant walked contentedly through the bustling market and onto the immense bridge that spanned the river. The two boys ate slowly and appreciatively as they gazed into the waters that flowed beneath them.

'Where are we?' Ant asked.

'The other end of the earth,' Pepper said. 'As far south as you can get, I suppose, without falling off the edge of the world.'

'That makes me feel good,' Ant said. 'The further I'm away from Gort, Malachi, and that horrible King of ours, the better. Something has been making me act against my nature. I don't know if it's Malachi's influence or of my own doing, but whatever it is, I've been doing things that make no sense to me now. I stayed away from my father for much too long without any good reason. Even when I saw him and he asked me to stay and help him, I felt compelled to get away from him as quickly as possible. Instead, I contrived some madness about having a boy called

Cuthbert spy against the King on my behalf. To what end, I still can't say. All it caused was a lot of trouble and pain. It may have cost Cuthbert his life. I can't trust that Jeremiah was telling the truth when he reassured me that Cuthbert was safe.'

'Col says that in the end, we can only trust ourselves. Not our pretend self that makes up stories about everything, but our inner self that remains the same whatever happens. Our higher self, Col says, is always right. Look inside, Ant, you will know what you have to do if you just listen to yourself,' Pepper said through a mouthful of dates.

'Listen to you, oh wise one.' Ant laughed. 'Is this the same Pepper whose inner self always wanted to join the army?'

'Yes, it's the same Pepper, but I realised that I wanted to be a monk. Being a soldier was something I knew my father expected from me. It was my way of expressing approval for his way of life. That's why many children like to follow in the footsteps of their parents, and not only in the profession they adopt, but also in the way that they think and behave.'

Ant stopped chewing for a moment and considered his friend's considered words. It was not long ago that any discussion between them would have resulted in a long bout of *yes it is, no it isn't* followed by a scuffle. Now Pepper was holding forth in a very thoughtful manner and saying things that made a lot of sense. Ant thought of Ambrose and how Pepper had always ribbed him about how useless his role as archaeologist had been. Ant had put up a staunch defence, but it was true that until the vedhana had been installed in the King's tower and caused all that trouble, he'd had his own doubts about whether the things his father did were worthwhile. He wondered how his latest project was progressing and whether he ought to go back to the lake and give him what assistance he could. 'We've come a long way since the marketplace in Gort, haven't we?' he said.

'All the way to the ends of the earth.' Pepper smiled.

'I was talking about our characters and how we've changed,' Ant said.

'You're still exactly the same Ant as always,' Pepper said.

'Really?' Ant thought hard about his friend's remark. As far as he was concerned, everything had changed with the hanging. It was at that moment he'd vowed to remove that hideous monarch who killed children in their droves or die trying. He had thought that Malachi was sympathetic to this cause, but now he knew that he was working to a different agenda, one that involved ingratiating himself with the vile ruler just so that he could enjoy power over others. Well, maybe Pepper should be heeded and the old Ant had to return. Maybe that was the true Ant after all and the bitter, vengeful Ant was just a construct that had no real validity.

'Watch this,' Pepper said, taking a bite out of a peach and dropping the rest into the water. There was a plop and a small splash as it entered the water, then the whole river seemed to boil into motion. A dark tail thrashed the water white beneath them, then disappeared as quickly as it had come, leaving the gentle flow undisturbed once more.

Ant reeled back in shock. 'What was that?'

'One good reason not to fall in the river,' Pepper said, his eyes aglow with excitement. 'There's plenty more reasons even bigger and nastier than that one.'

Ant stood a little bit further back, took a breath, then felt his own excitement tingle in his body.

'Look down there,' Pepper said, 'there's one of those monsters about to eat that man sitting in the river.'

Ant watched a man strip off his headdress and splash water on his head, oblivious to the menace. The ominous dark shape just below the waterline was at least twice the size of the man and drifting ever closer to its quarry. There was something familiar about the poor unfortunate, but Ant couldn't recognise him at first. Then a sudden realisation swept through him as if he'd been drenched in cold water himself. 'Cuthbert!' he shouted, then turned to Pepper. 'That's Cuthbert, the one I was telling you all about. He's going to get swallowed up by that thing. We have to warn him. Cuthbert!' Ant shouted as loudly as he could, but there was no response from the man in the river.

Before he could do anything else, Ant received a heavy blow to his head as three men carrying a sack shoved him aside and unceremoniously dumped it into the river. By the time he picked himself up and cleared his head, the men were gone and so was the man in the river. 'Did the crocodile get him?' Ant asked.

'No, he ran out of the water and rode off on his horse as if a demon were on his tail. The croc took the person in the sack instead.'

Ant winced. 'That's not a very nice way to dispose of dead people in my view. Lacks any respect.'

'Who says it was a dead person? Whoever was inside that sack had plenty of life left if the wriggling I saw was anything to go by,' Pepper said.

'Ugh, that's really horrible then. We should have stopped them, Pepper. Rescued the person in the sack, or at least tried.'

'There was no prospect of that, Ant. Those men were too big and strong for us to tackle. Anyway, it all happened so quickly,' Pepper said.

'We need to follow Cuthbert then. See where he's going. Make sure he's alright.'

'He's long gone by now,' Pepper said, 'we'll never catch him up. Are you sure it was your man Cuthbert? It doesn't seem very likely if the last time you saw him, he was in the army to the north of Gort. Maybe you're mistaken; after all, he was a fair way off and we were looking from above. Not only that, but he didn't respond when you called out to him.'

'It was Cuthbert, I know it. How he got here, I have no idea unless the army has marched all the way here with him. I'm going to look for him.'

'You can't go over the bridge; it's not allowed,' Pepper said.

'What do you mean?'

'It's forbidden for us monks to go over the bridge. We're not welcome on the other side of the river, or so I'm told. Anyway, it's a rule and can't be broken.'

'Not even to help someone?' Ant asked.

'This is serious, Ant. Trespassing over there could have repercussions that make life difficult for us. We could be denied our main source of fresh food. I can't take that risk. Anyway, I've sworn a vow to behave properly and it includes obeying instructions from Rinpoche without question.'

'I'm not a monk, though,' Ant said, 'and Cuthbert is my responsibility. I'm going to look for him even if you can't. If you like, you can wait for me here or go back to the monastery. Don't worry about me, I can look after myself. I have to find Cuthbert and take him back to the lake; it's the least I can do after all the trouble I've caused him.'

'Col asked me to take care of you,' Pepper said.

'And you've done as much as you need to. Now I must get going. I'll catch you up at the monastery as soon as I can.' Ant hurried down the slope to the other side of the bridge and onto the road that led past the palace. He looked back to see Pepper's face staring at him with an expression of uncertainty and concern. It was with a great effort that he gave a brief wave, then strode off to follow Cuthbert's tracks.

80

After his narrow escape from the monster in the river, Cuthbert became uneasy. The city that was bright and cheerful now contained only danger and suspicion. The eyes that were looking down at him from the bridge now seemed to hold menace rather than curiosity.

Still dripping from his ill-considered immersion, he dragged himself back into the saddle and pulled hard on the reins to turn his reluctant mount back the way he'd come. Without wanting it to look as if he was running away, he nevertheless urged his horse into what he hoped would look like a stately trot rather than the headlong gallop back to Vargas and the army.

By the time he arrived, the soldiers had been arranged in neat ranks as if readying themselves for attack. Exactly who or what they were going to fight as yet remained unclear. Cuthbert had encountered nothing that might suggest there would be any resistance to them simply marching into the city.

Vargas seemed more anxious than the situation seemed to merit. As soon as he set eyes on Cuthbert, he hurried over to intercept him. 'You're needed at the King's pavilion. He's waiting for your report and growing more irritated by the minute. What took you so long? What have you been doing? Why are you wet?'

Cuthbert opened his mouth to answer, but had difficulty in ordering his reply. Which of the questions should receive priority? It was impossible to decide for certain. 'I was in the river,' he said, taking the last question first and hoping for the best. The prospect of being brought before the King was daunting. He worried that past misdemeanours might be revealed and then he'd be in big trouble. He resolved to be very careful in what he said.

'No time for dry clothes, you'll just have to go in there looking like a drowned rat. And be careful what you say.' Vargas pulled him in the direction of the large tent and thrust him inside.

It was stifling inside the King's pavilion; so hot that Cuthbert imagined he would have boiled away were it not for the cooling effect of the drenching he'd had in the river.

'The man next to the King is General Conningsby,' Vargas whispered, 'and he's not to be argued with. Remember.'

Cuthbert had already decided that he wouldn't say anything, let alone argue with anyone. The King looked up from a small jewelled casket that was laid out on the table in front of him. 'Who's this?' he asked.

'This is Cuthbert, he's been helping me guide you through the desert. He's already been into the city and has taken a look around on our behalf,' Vargas said.

'Cuthbert?' Conningsby stared hard at him, making him feel very uncomfortable. 'Malachi mentioned a Cuthbert but never told me he was a guide. Just asked me not to torture him. Are you the same Cuthbert?'

It was difficult to know for sure what answer would have the least damaging effect so Cuthbert nodded in a way that he hoped could be taken for a denial if the occasion demanded. It was more of a circular motion of his head than a specific gesture of affirmation but even this caused him acute anxiety.

'No time to be reminiscing,' the King said, 'I need this item delivered and I need someone reliable to do it. Can you be trusted to carry out a simple task, Cuthbert?'

'Yes, your majesty,' Cuthbert said, his voice croaky and indistinct to his own ears.

The King opened the casket and prodded at its insides with a pudgy finger. 'There was a time when this sort of thing was second nature,' he said, 'but it's been so long since I last needed to use one of these. There,' the King snapped the lid closed and sat back in his chair, 'that should do it. Now make haste, take it to the palace. You do know how to get there?'

'It's that big building with all the towers,' Cuthbert said.

'Very good, now off with you.'

Cuthbert picked up the casket; it was small enough to fit in the palm of his hand but so heavy he could hardly lift it. Even using two hands, he struggled to carry the beautiful object.

The King was staring at him intently. 'It's a gift for the person who lives in the palace,' he said. 'It's absolutely vital that you make sure it goes inside the building. Take it in yourself. Even if the place is empty, leave it there.'

'But might the wrong person take it?' Cuthbert asked.

'Don't worry, the person it's intended for will get it as long as you deliver it properly. Go into the palace and place the gift inside. Don't let anyone stop you. Understand?'

'Yes,' Cuthbert said, though he didn't. What point was there to a present that the recipient didn't know about? Surely the King needed him to be grateful and acknowledge it? Perhaps receive a gift in return?

'If he's not there, shall I bring it back to you?' Cuthbert asked.

'No!' The King seemed quite adamant on this point. 'Do not bring it back under any circumstances. Now get on with it before we run out of time.'

Cuthbert staggered outside and managed to deposit the casket into a saddlebag, which threatened to slide off his horse until he repositioned it and tightened the girth.

After a slow ride back to the city, Cuthbert dismounted and took the gift into the palace. He walked through the gardens and into the main building without meeting anyone. Inside, the huge place was deserted and there was an unpleasant smell that made his eyes water. The further he progressed inside the palace, the more frightened he became. He was reminded of being in the dark forest, even though this place was brightly lit without any dark corners that might harbour a lurking threat.

Eventually, he came to a small pool bounded by four raised walls of smooth stone. He placed the gift carefully on top of a wall and turned away. He felt a strong compulsion to run away as fast as he could, but tried to remain calm. He took one last look at the casket, checked it was still in place, then gave in to the impulse. He didn't stop running until he'd got back to his horse and, even then, he urged it into a gallop as soon as he was mounted.

When he got back to the army, it was already advancing. Pikemen to the fore, as usual, giving this surge of humanity the look of an untidy hedgehog. Vargas was still with the King and Conningsby, but now they occupied a vantage point high on a dune overlooking the battleground, if it could be called that without any visible opposition.

Cuthbert slid off his horse and prepared to report his successful delivery when a loud bang made the earth shake and sent his horse scurrying away in panic.

81

Tyrant knew he was in the wrong place as soon as he drew breath inside the darkened room. This wasn't the vedhana in the cave near Gort, it was one that he'd never used before, although he suspected he recognised the smell of the place and this troubled him greatly. As he was catapulted out of the device, dragging Petra with him, he felt nauseous and weak. This was the one place on earth he'd vowed never to return to and his instincts screamed at him to leave immediately.

'It's hot,' Petra said, 'too hot for us to be in Gort. It feels as hot as it was in the desert. Let's take a look outside.'

'No,' Tyrant said, 'we have to go back to Gort.' He was finding it difficult to draw breath.

'A quick look can't hurt,' Petra said, 'just so we know where we are.'

'I know where we are and I can't stand to be here. This is the place I was born and where all the sadness began. I've only just remembered what happened here and I can't bear to be reminded.'

'The dream about your mother and brother? Was that here, then?'

'Yes, but it was a long time ago and my memory of it isn't all that clear. It's more of a dreadful haunted feeling and I can't be sure what really happened. My dream was that it was me who stabbed my brother and killed my mother. I know that isn't possible, but I can't get rid of that feeling. Please, Petra, we need to get out of this place right now.'

Tyrant turned to re-enter the vedhana, then stopped as ghostly shapes began to solidify amongst the flickering lights. Soldiers. Unmistakeably soldiers carrying drawn swords and crossbows at the ready. He took a deep breath, grabbed Petra, yanked the door open, and ran outside into the sunshine. The heady smells of the marketplace brought back a longing for his mother that was so powerful he sank to his knees and his eyes poured with tears.

'Come on,' Petra said, 'let's get you out of sight before they come looking for us.'

Half blinded by tears, Tyrant allowed himself to be led through the bustling throng and out to the edge of the city where people were few and far between. The area was mainly farmland with the verdant backdrop of unruly jungle. Petra kept looking behind them nervously and urged him to keep going, even if the threat of being followed seemed to have diminished. 'Let's get all the way into that forest over there where we'll be hidden from view and can wait until the vedhana is safe to return to.'

Tyrant's knees were weak, his legs struggled to support him, and his heavy heart threatened to break completely. He complied wordlessly, managing only the occasional sob as he recalled a moment of joy shared with his mother and brother. The tiny child inside him had emerged now and he needed to grieve at last.

Even when they had settled in the sweaty jungle and were sure that they were safe, Tyrant's body continued to be racked by sobbing. He felt inconsolable, the terrible sadness intensified rather than diminished and there seemed no end to his suffering.

Nightfall came and with it a cacophony of noise to rival Tyrant's own wails. Strange creatures crawled over his legs, pausing briefly in apparent sympathy before continuing on their missions. Tyrant's howls were mimicked by unknown denizens that seemed intent on mocking his agony. The night fell, and Tyrant's uneasy slumber was haunted by his mother's last agonised glance and his brother's gurgling death.

***

The morning light brought welcome respite from the horrors of the night and he felt Petra's reassuring presence against his side as he struggled to regain himself from the lost child he'd become.

Petra's eyes opened. 'Listen to that,' she said.

Tyrant could hear loud screams that this time weren't his own.

82

Ant soon realised the futility of chasing a man galloping away on horseback while on foot. Cuthbert was long gone by the time he drew level with the palace and he paused to admire the building while he drew breath. He knew at once that there was something very unusual about the place, but struggled to pin down the reasoning behind his feeling. Something drew him towards it, though he noticed that the general population seemed to be passing by without even a sideways glance.

As he approached, he observed that the outer stonework of the building was unblemished when every other structure was pock-marked by the ravages of time and the abrasion of the sand blowing in from the desert. A shudder went through his body as he passed through an archway beneath the nearest of the spectacular towers that pierced the sky. He felt a similar constriction as if he'd passed through a vedhana even though there was nothing visible and the sensation was momentary.

He found himself in a gloomy place surrounded by walls of pristine stone. In front of him, on the inside of the tower, was a door constructed of shiny metal. About waist high, set into the wall beside the shiny door, was a circular black indentation that Ant touched carefully with his finger. There was the chime of a distant bell as the door slid open to reveal a tiny room, also made from metal.

Ant poked his head cautiously inside and sniffed the air. There was a faint sweet smell that could have been roses but might easily have been something else. He walked gingerly into the room. Despite there being no windows to let in the sunlight, the room was brightly lit from the ceiling. There was a row of indentations similar to the one he'd touched outside below a small plaque that carried the letters OTIS.

Ant had decided he'd had enough of this claustrophobic space when, without warning, the door closed behind him, leaving him trapped. A sudden feeling of breathlessness threatened to overwhelm him before his mind caught hold of his panic and diverted it into thought. He could feel no presence other than his own; although he'd been trapped in the room, it didn't feel as if there had been any human intent involved. The door obviously worked by magic and if he were to escape, he would have to figure out how he could use it.

Sitting on the floor, he allowed his awareness to flow through the walls of his cage, seeking some means of escape. There were defined energy flows that were unlike anything he'd ever encountered before and resisted all his attempts to access or modify them. He felt them as sharp, hot, and confined into a thin stream that shimmered and flowed through a web of connectedness. Any attempt he made to touch it with his being brought immediate discomfort.

His attention returned to the wall in front of him and he reached out to touch the indentation at the top of the row. The room lurched and his stomach felt queasy, as if he was being tossed about in a small boat. Then a distant chime sounded, and the door opened.

Ant tumbled out into bright sunshine and a dizzying spectacle. He had been transported to the top of the tower by the magical room, and now he could see the soldiers resplendent with their flags and banners that marched steadily into the city. He immediately recognised them as the army of the King of Gort, despite it being impossible for them to have followed him here. For an instant, Ant believed that they had been sent to find him so that he could be returned for torture and hanging. Then he relaxed a little at the absurdity of that thought. They'd certainly not come all this way unless it were for a much more important purpose than capturing him. It then occurred to Ant that they would soon be in control of the city and when they were, his freedom might be in grave danger. He decided to get back to the vedhana as soon as he could and seek sanctuary in the only safe place in this whole world, the monastery.

As he turned to try to work the magic of the metal vedhana, a deafening bang knocked him off his feet, then he heard a crackling noise like green wood being thrown into a hot fire.

83

Something was scraping at her face. Lone reeled in confusion at the idea she possessed a face again. It didn't seem possible. It didn't feel right. She was dead and dead meant no face. No sooner had she recognised the scraping than she was consumed by an agonising pain in every part of her body. She felt her chest jump as her heart started up and the blood began to flow. She'd never experienced pain like it. She felt as if she was being consumed by fire from within.

Her chest heaved, and she expelled river water through her mouth and nostrils in a bout of uncontrollable agonised coughing. Her chest felt as though it might split open as she heaved and dribbled onto the grass.

The cat sat back, keeping itself away from the flow of sputum, as if it had finished its job of revival. All Lone could do with her new-found breath was to use it to scream out her agony. Her blood flowed sluggishly at first, her heart beat erratically, and her body continued to be racked by the most horrendous pain.

Every breath felt as if she was being cut to shreds by tiny knives inside her ribcage. Each heartbeat brought another wave of distress, as if shards of metal were being driven into her limbs. She grew used to the sound of her own screams before the sensations began to diminish from unbearable agony to intense pain. She wished with all her heart that she'd remained dead and vowed revenge on anyone or anything that might have brought her back to this terrible ordeal.

Although her body had recently been full of water, her first non-pain sensation was one of racking thirst. She picked up the cup next to her and sucked at the life-giving water, feeling sharp pins that pricked her fingers from the inside.

She became aware that she was sitting, that the cat was beside her, and that Zaire stood looking completely unconcerned to one side. A welcome silence had fallen.

When she tried to speak, a weird croaking noise was emitted from her mouth at first, but she persevered, repeating her words over and over again until she could recognise them with her own ears. 'I was dead,' she said. 'Why did you let me die?'

Eventually, Zaire replied. 'It was necessary,' he said, 'otherwise he'd have known that you were still alive and come after you. And me as well.'

'You should have rescued me sooner and to hell with him. A being as powerful as you shouldn't be concerned about a half-human King. You could sweep him aside like a leaf in the wind.' Lone was still in pain, but it wasn't so intense that she couldn't feel anger and resentment in addition.

'You underestimate the nature of this King. The only reason that I felt it worth taking the risk to revive you is that he is preoccupied with another matter and is unlikely to ever turn his mind to you again.'

'But you let me die,' Lone said. 'I was gone, finished, my spirit discharged into the great void. It's not possible to bring people back from the dead.'

'Ordinarily, not for me. Not even if I wanted to, and that's highly unlikely. But you and I are bound in spirit by unbreakable bonds. That's the consequence of the spell you placed upon me, Lone. I could have let you go, but that would have made my existence more complicated. There would always be something of your presence for me to contend with. This way, I get to be released and you get another chance at life. It's a fair exchange.'

Lone sighed, noticing that she felt not nearly as bad as she had moments before. Things were returning to normal in her body and this encouraged the thought that the intense pain might not persist for ever. 'Why should I let you go when you're the only protection I have against that horrible man in the palace? Maybe if you kill him for me first, we might have some basis for an agreement.'

'If you knew who you were dealing with, you wouldn't ask that question. Forget about revenge. Neither of us can afford to attract his attention, let alone stand up to him. Be content that you've managed to come out of a very bad situation with your life. The very least you can do to thank me is to remove the spell so that I can be free of you again.'

Lone remembered Malachi's constant pleading when she had Patch under the same control. He'd tried on numerous occasions to get her to release the spirit, but she'd held on until the last without realising what she'd ensnared. That was what had led to all this difficulty. Her stubbornness had cost her a long period in the wilderness, followed by a series of desperate defences of her life. Letting go might be the best option, especially if it prevented Zaire from turning against her. 'How do I know that you won't turn on me as soon as I say the words of release?'

'You don't. Though I can tell you that I would bear no animosity against you. I recognise what you did as an act of survival, something that has a natural place in the world. Keeping me bound under these circumstances does not. I may become so resentful that I cause you great harm.'

The cat was emitting a comforting purr, and the jungle felt warm and familiar. Lone sighed again; the knives in her body had lessened in length and their edge had dulled. If Malachi were here, he would do everything in his power to persuade her to do what Zaire was asking. Lone decided to take the simple way out on this occasion. If it meant sudden obliteration in a sandstorm or a watery death in the mouth of a monster, then she'd just have to take that chance. She was weary and doubted she had the energy to hold him much longer. When she uttered the words that would release Zaire from her thrall, the air around her body crackled with power for a few moments, then she felt the weight drop from her shoulders and a lightness in her stomach.

Zaire stood before her and made a polite bow. 'You've chosen wisely, Lone. I should punish you for your effrontery, but I believe that you don't need any additional suffering above that which you will bring to yourself.'

Lone looked to the side as a man came crashing through the undergrowth and almost ran headlong into her. She stood frozen in recognition for a moment, then gasped his name. 'Tyrant,' she said.

'Lone,' he said, drawing his sword and raising it aloft.

'Oh dear,' Zaire said, just before he disappeared.

84

'Polish it? How the fuck do you polish a stick?'

The sergeant clapped the recalcitrant pikeman on the back of his head with the flat of his hand. 'Orders,' he said, 'orders from the King. Now get polishing or you can go up on that there hill and ask 'im yerself.'

Boris grunted. It was a good grunt, his all-purpose grunt that said everything and signified nothing. A grunt to end conversations politely with the inquisitor satisfied and the recipient content. If he'd been born a bit more noble, his grunt would have propelled him to the top. Ambassador material, that's what his grunt made him. A man who could influence foreign policy with a single sound.

Not that there seemed to be much in the way of foreign policy these days. The King, bless him and glorify his name, didn't tolerate foreigners. They were classed as subjects too ignorant to understand who their rightful king was. The remedy for ignorance was a demonstration of force so overwhelming that everyone learned their place.

Which was why they were here, Boris supposed. They'd trekked for an age through inhospitable desert in order to get to this sun-blasted city and now they were here the King obviously wanted to make a good impression.

It could have been worse; they could have been facing an army of tough weather-beaten southern types with curved swords and bad intentions. Mercifully, it seemed that the Southern King's army either hadn't turned up or he'd been relying on the remoteness of his sand-swept city to keep intruders away.

'How the fuck does he expect me to polish a fucking stick?' Ifer seemed intent on demonstrating his resilience to blows to the head by repeating his original enquiry, this time safely out of the sergeant's earshot.

'Easy.' Boris recognised the voice and winced. Eric was the know-it-all of the group. Self-professed expert on all matters, a close confidant of the King if he were to be believed. 'My uncle was a woodworker. Made wonderful chairs, he did. They was so comfy that you couldn't bring yourself to get out of them once you sat down. Some thought they was witchcraft, they was so good. S'easy to polish our pikes.'

Boris considered the rough piece of tree that he'd been issued. It was a branch recently snapped from its parent and he'd been left with the task of stripping the twigs and leaves from it in order to give it a modicum of military value. It was thick at the base, tapering up to the topmost parts that wobbled when it was moved. Quite how this might be used as a weapon of war was a matter of conjecture. Using it to impress townsfolk, however gullible they might be, seemed a step far beyond the realms of reason.

'Exactly how do you suggest we manage that?' Boris wasn't sure which of the others had spoken, but fervently wished he'd kept his mouth shut. It had to be someone with little experience of Eric the Wise, the all-knowing, the complete arsehole, boring, pedantic bastard.

'Like I said, easy. Just needs a bit of nowse, that's all. First you strip off the bark.'

One or two or the more impressionable pikemen took out their knives and began to hack at their pikes. Boris resisted the urge to join in. They'd been ordered to polish. No mention of stripping off bark. He was convinced that the bark on his pike was holding it together and that there would be very little of it left if it were removed.

'Once the bark's been removed, you need to apply a wood sealing primer then leave this to soak in for at least a day. Once that's dry, you can commence the lacquering process. Mix equal parts turpentine with the same proportion of shellac then...'

'Wait a fucking minute,' Ifer protested, 'did you say shellac?'

'Yes, that's right.' Eric gave them all a look of intense superiority. 'Shellac, a resinous excretion found—'

'Where the fuck do we find shellac in the middle of a fucking desert?' Ifer had been on one before but was well and truly underway now. Boris felt himself grinning as he anticipated the unequal joust between the sweary Ifer and the pompous Eric. It would be a shouting match to warm the heart and a welcome distraction from the sandy wasteland they'd been marooned in.

Despite the attractions of the altercation, Boris couldn't help thinking about the family he'd left behind. In particular, his little sister, who'd relied on him to amuse and inform her three-year-old mind. His heart became heavy when he visualised her inconsolable grief at losing the one person in her world who took an interest. When he left her on her own, she'd become teary and complaining, so he'd taken her everywhere with him. The last memory he had of her little face was her expression of pain and horror as the soldiers had taken him away. She'd tried to follow but one of them had pushed her to the ground and kicked her hard. That's the last he'd seen of little Molly. He'd spent tearful nights weeping for her tiny presence and wondering if she'd ever recovered from the hefty kick.

Ifer and Eric were still at it.

'Go on then, clever clogs, tell me where I can get some. And while you're about it, find me some fucking serpentine.'

'Yeah, and some lacking,' came the chorus.

'Simple,' Eric said, 'any self-respecting wood supplies shop will carry the aforesaid items in stock. There's an excellent merchant I know who will not only supply the varnish you need, but will stain it to any desired hue. You can choose to make your pike appear to be fashioned from any wood at all. Even the humblest bit of birch can be made to resemble the finest oak. Think what a difference that will make to the enemy's morale.'

Boris thought about it and couldn't imagine it making even a tiny bit of difference. The boys who had started the bark stripping process paused and contemplated the damage they'd inflicted on their pikes. Boris was glad he'd stayed his hand. The tatty scrapings looked terrible, and it wasn't the enemy's morale they had to worry about, but the wrath of the sergeant when he caught sight of what they'd done. It was the exact opposite of polishing as far as Boris could see.

'Alright, find a fucking shop with the fucking whatyoumacallit, why don't you,' Ifer challenged.

'I'm sure there will be more than one in the city ahead. All we have to do is find it.'

'Off you go, then. We'll wait for you here. And while you're off shopping, how about you bring me a nice piece of bread smothered in hot chicken fat.'

'And me,' the chorus sang. General laughter announced Eric's defeat and Ifer's victory.

'I'll show you,' Eric protested. 'When we get to the city, I'll get some shellac and put you all to shame.'

'Anyway, I don't see the point of it. I'm not doing it whatever stuff they give us.' Ifer spoke with the authority of a man on a roll.

'It's the order of the King,' someone retorted. Boris looked round to see if the sergeant had returned, but thankfully, he was nowhere to be seen.

'What does that fat old bastard know?' Ifer said, his blasphemy evoking a sharp intake of breath from the gathering.

'Watch what you say.' Eric gathered himself for an attack. 'The King is always right. He can't make a mistake. He's inflammable.'

'I never could get the hang of what we're supposed to do if there's a battle,' Boris joined in the debate. 'I've been made to drag this stick all through the desert for weeks on end and for what? What's the point of it?'

'The point's on the end of your pike,' Eric said, drawing welcome laughter that Boris joined in.

'No, but seriously,' Boris said, 'all we are is a bunch of fourteen- and fifteen-year-olds with no training and a bit of a tree as a weapon. Yet we're right at the front. The first ones to encounter the enemy. Doesn't seem right, that's all. What possible use can we be?'

'We're the vanguard,' Eric said. 'The most important part of the army. What we do is to repel the onrushing hordes, send them packing, prod them into disarray, scare them with our fierceness, and soften them up for the swordsmen to slaughter.'

'We stick the horses, that's what we do,' Ifer joined the discussion in support of Eric. Despite their previous differences, they seemed to hold similar delusions on this subject.

'Take me through the process,' Boris said. 'Along comes a soldier riding a horse. Now what do you do?'

'I stick the horse with my pike. Stop it in its tracks. Kill it dead.' Ifer grinned at the grisly prospect.

'Easier said than done,' Eric added. 'Needs a lot of skill does horse sticking. A steady nerve and an even steadier hand.'

'Also, I suspect, a pike that doesn't wobble at the end and is going to break as soon as anything touches it,' Boris said. 'But let's assume that you've stood firm and so has your pike. Let's say for the sake of the discussion, you've managed to bring down the horse. Then what?'

'Then nothing,' Eric said. 'We've done the job the King pays us to do.'

'We don't get paid,' Ifer pointed out.

'So, the horse is down. What about the rider?' Boris asked.

'Not our concern; like I said, our job, our only job is to stick the horse. We let the swordsmen and the archers deal with the rider,' Eric explained, to a rumble of general approval.

'So, there's this soldier on a horse and you've killed his horse. How do you think he'll be feeling?' Boris asked.

The assembly made several informed guesses.

'Frightened?'

'Upset?'

'Sad?'

'Miserable?'

'How about mightily pissed off?' Boris offered. 'Then there's the general status associated to a soldier on a horse, isn't there?'

'What do you mean?' Ifer asked.

'Well, look around you. There's us, then there's the archers with their bows. Then there's the swordsmen with their swords and shields and chain mail to protect them. Then there's the knights with their broadswords and plate armour. All on foot. Our horsemen are all noblemen, armed to the teeth, and protected with the best armour their enormous wealth can buy.'

'We're not fighting ourselves, you silly man,' Ifer said.

'But all armies will be the same. At least all those with cavalry,' Boris said.

'Maybe they don't have cavalry,' Eric said.

'If they don't, there's no use in having us. Unless you count trying to tire them out a bit having to kill us before they get to the proper troops.' Boris was beginning to feel depressed by his own logic. He'd started the discussion to see if there was anything he'd missed about his station in life. He'd been looking for some rationale for what seemed to him a futile role. He'd only succeeded in fuelling his worst fears to incandescence.

'Imagine just one of our noblemen whose horse has been maimed by a pikeman.'

'An enemy pikeman?' Eric asked.

'If there is such a thing, which I doubt, but yes, let's assume the enemy has pikemen. They are all fifteen years old and armed only with what we are.'

'How many pikemen does the enemy have?' Ifer asked.

'Which of our noble horsemen are we talking about?' Eric asked.

Boris groaned. This was getting stupider by the minute. If they couldn't see his point by now, they would never do. 'A hundred pikemen like us and let's say Lord Carl.'

'Lord Carl, eh?' Ifer said. 'He's got a nasty temper, has Lord Carl.'

'Loves that big chestnut he rides,' Eric said, 'it's his pride and joy. I once saw him chop a servant's head clean off his body just because he forgot to feed his beloved horse. You've made a good choice there, Boris.'

Boris didn't want to make a good choice; all he wanted was to know if there was something in the situation he was missing. Some plan, a fall-back position, perhaps, which would give him a crumb of comfort. 'What do you think, then? Lord Carl versus a hundred of us, or if not exactly us, like us.'

'If one of us killed his horse?' Eric said.

'That's my hypothesis,' Boris said.

'He'd kill the fucking lot of us,' Ifer said with an ominous certainty.

'But we'd fight back, wouldn't we? He'd be outnumbered a hundred to one. Surely one of us would be able to get him before he got all of us?' Boris said.

'Not a chance.' Eric brandished his unpolished pike. 'Not with one of these. Even if you did manage to poke him with one, it wouldn't hurt him and might make him even more annoyed.'

'There you are,' Boris said. 'It's exactly as I thought. We're completely useless. All we can do to assist the King is to allow ourselves to be killed in the hope that this might slow up the enemy and make them easier for the proper army to fight.'

'Ah, but you're wrong,' Eric said. 'Only we have Lord Carl and he's on our side, so it would never happen.'

Boris looked around at the mixture of confusion and uncertainty and took a deep breath. 'Silly me,' he said, 'I really got that wrong, didn't I. We're obviously invincible and our King is inflammable so there's nothing to worry about.'

'Get to your feet, you unruly bunch,' the sergeant's voice came clearly through the hot desert air. 'Get ready to advance. Pikemen, your time for glory has arrived.'

Boris faced the city, expecting the serried ranks of an opposing army to have appeared while they were speculating. His breath let itself out in relief. Still nothing. No opposition. Only an occasional spectator on a distant dune and nothing between them and the city. Far ahead of them and to the left, the imposing bulk of the Southern King's palace with its four tall towers catching the rays of the morning sun. Something twinkled in the far right-hand minaret. A tiny shower of sparks appeared to be heading towards them at incredible speed.

The flying sparkles seemed to pause overhead for a fleeting instant then a deafening sound forced him to prostrate himself on the ground and cover his ears with his hands, but this didn't keep out the screams of the suffering and the stench of burning flesh assaulting his nostrils.

85

The loud noise had come from the direction of the palace. Cuthbert turned and watched as a shower of sparks was flung out of one of the towers. Even in the sunlight, they were bright enough to follow as they streaked through the air towards him. As they came over the heads of the leading pikemen, they suddenly changed trajectory and dropped to the ground.

Gouts of fire burst into the air. Bodies were ripped to shreds by the blast. Burning pieces shot skywards, followed by the screams of those being consumed by the flames. A pall of black smoke hung over the army, and a stench of burnt flesh made Cuthbert's stomach contract.

The King jumped to his feet, screaming expletives that Cuthbert would never have associated with the speech of the nobility. There were words that would have made Grew blush interspersed with cries of frustration and anger.

'What the hell was that?' Conningsby said. 'It's destroyed half my army.'

'Send in the elite pikemen,' the King shouted.

Conningsby shrugged and gave the order, which was relayed to the battlefield by the waving of flags. Cuthbert watched as the ranks of cavalry and foot soldiers parted obligingly to allow the ceremonial troop to walk unsteadily to the edge of the smoking crater that contained the remains of their comrades in arms. As a man, they lifted their shining weapons into the air until they were formed into the spines of a hedgehog, pointing in every direction. The sunlight glinted on the highly polished halberds, and Cuthbert had to admit that it was an impressive sight to behold. He didn't retain much hope for their survival when another crack heralded the arrival of another lethal shower of deadly sparks.

This time, though, the sparks didn't manage to reach the heads of the pikemen. Instead, they seemed to meet an invisible barrier that caused them to glow brightly, then extinguish themselves without causing any harm.

The King disappeared inside his pavilion, still muttering in the foulest language possible. Cuthbert made out the words 'fucking bastard, I'll show him' followed by 'I don't fucking believe it.'

Conningsby was waving frantically for his army to advance under cover of the elite pikes. Reluctantly at first, but driven on by a mixture of threats and promises, the ranks began to move forward. They trod carefully around the charred remains, then hurried gratefully onto more hospitable ground. Swordsmen took the lead, followed by the elite pikemen, and what few crossbowmen that hadn't been incinerated. The cavalry, as yet unscathed, seemed hesitant but reluctant to let the magical protection get too far ahead.

Wave after wave of sparks cascaded ineffectually over the heads of the soldiers as they advanced towards the city.

When the King emerged from his tent, he was clad in strange black garb and carrying a long tubular device that Cuthbert thought looked too blunt to cut and too light to bludgeon with. It appeared the thing was designed for neither purpose as the King raised it to his shoulder. There was a bang and a whooshing noise as something flew towards the palace, trailing a fat flame behind it.

86

Ant watched with horror as the conflagration consumed the soldiers. He caught a whiff that he characterised as burnt pork before he realised what it actually was. His stomach was sickened by the sight and the smell.

Safest place for you up here.

'Jeremiah?'

The one and the same.

'Where's Cuthbert? I thought I saw him by the river.'

Over there, on top of the dune, near the King's tent. He's not been harmed. Yet.

'Yet? So you think he will before long?'

I'm sorry, but it's inevitable. All of them are going to die, including your King. You should be glad, that's what you wanted most of all.

Ant felt devastated by the news. 'Not at any expense. I wanted the King dead to stop him killing others. I have to save Cuthbert; I'm going down there to warn him.'

You can't leave, Ant.

'Why not? Are you going to stop me?'

Not me; it's this place that will prevent you going. It's not really part of the world you live in. How can I explain it? Time and space aren't the same. For example, it's very old here, much older than it is outside.

'That doesn't make any sense to me.'

I'd be surprised if it did.

'Be as it may, I wouldn't care even if I did understand. I need to get out there and help Cuthbert.'

You couldn't do anything, Ant. Events have moved well beyond that. All that has happened is that your King has bitten off more than he can chew. The King that resides in this palace is much too powerful to resist. At least he thinks he is. Oh dear.

Ant looked down at the battlefield to see what had perturbed Jeremiah. A host of shiny pikes had been raised in defiance against the shower of fire that now crackled from the adjoining tower. Instead of more devastation, all that happened was a series of blooms of aerial flame and the soldiers beneath remained mercifully unscathed.

Now that was something I didn't expect and I think it may have come as something of a shock to others as well. There's more to your King than meets the eye, Ant.

'Tell me in plain words what's going on here.'

In simple terms, it's a battle between two kings. There's a historical context in that it appears that both these kings are what you might term gods, or at least demi-gods. It's been rumoured that there are one or two of them left and this little episode has been devised to flush one of them out. Now it seems we've got two of them on our hands.

'So this has been your purpose all along?'

Not so much me as the ones who call the shots, so to speak. I'm just a messenger who whispers suggestions into people's ears. Your friend Malachi is the one who's engineered this little set to. Admittedly with your assistance.

'Why go to all this trouble? If your masters wanted to destroy these demi-gods, couldn't they just come here themselves and do it?'

Yes, that's an option they've tried before. Pretty much the whole world was destroyed in the process, but it's certainly effective. In this case, it's felt that, despite your obvious failings, there's something worthwhile about your species and an attempt to preserve it should be made.

'I'm not sure I believe anything you say anymore, Jeremiah. I think you're just making up stories to stop me from doing something positive.'

Something whooshed past Ant's head, causing him to fling himself to the ground. It felt as if a heavy boot had come down onto his chest and a deafening blast jarred his head. Dust and smoke obscured his vision, but he could feel the whole structure beneath him quiver in shock. When his head stopped banging and his eyes could peer through the fog, he saw that the top of the adjoining tower was missing. The place where the angry sparks that had consumed half the army had emerged was no longer standing upright and had been reduced to an untidy heap of stones.

Oh dear, Jeremiah said, *he's not going to like that one little bit.*

Ant became aware of a lone man striding out from the city to meet the oncoming troop. As he reached the front rank of swordsmen, they raised their shields and began to hack at him. His arm came up, wielding a sword of his own, and the serried ranks collapsed before him; hapless soldiers were strewn dead and dying as he cut them to pieces. Ant could hear the wails of anguish and the screams of the wounded.

As the ranks parted before him, the man strode onwards through a hail of arrows.

87

Malachi was tired of ferrying soldiers through the vedhana five at a time. The twenty or so inside the tiny building were enough to fill it to overflowing, yet he still had as many again to fetch and carry from the tower in Gort. Each journey was a feat of concentration; he had to keep the singular location in his mind or otherwise risk ending up somewhere he didn't want to be. It was hard enough to negotiate a successful transit without the burden of being accompanied by soldiers geared for war with minds full of competing attention.

The excitement of being so close to his objective had long been dispelled by the drudgery of the process. Nevertheless, as he successfully delivered his final batch and ordered them outside into the sunlight, he felt it returning. The sight of the immense palace with its exquisitely slender towers filled him with impatience. He had to get there first; it was imperative that he did. Timing was of the essence. It was essential that the army provided sufficient distraction to enable him to go inside and get the things he desired. He hurried his cohort through the marketplace, ignoring the shouts of alarm from the traders and headed for the bridge.

'Secure the bridge, make sure that any retreating enemy troops are denied passage. We can't have them setting up a stronghold on this side of the river. Defend it at all costs, remember these are the orders of your commander and your King,' Malachi said. 'I'm going to see what I can do to assist the King in his battle for the city. Remember, nobody crosses this river in either direction from now on.'

The heat was stifling and Malachi wished he'd come better attired for the climate. His heavy black cloak was completely unsuitable and made him uncomfortably hot. As he hurried towards the palace, the sweat poured from his brow and had to be constantly wiped from his eyes.

The nearer he got, the more his spirits rose. He could see the army in the distance and even make out the brightly coloured tents that housed the King. There could be no doubt of the army's intent and Malachi was relying on the palace occupants' attention being concentrated on the military threat.

His heart beat faster when he heard the crackle and bangs. He watched as the shower of missiles flew from the tower and his excitement turned to trepidation. Whoever had conjured that response had powerful magic at their disposal. That's what he was after, of course, but something so devastating would be inevitably hard won. Nevertheless, he'd come this far and worked so tirelessly for this opportunity. The fate of the army, or even the King for that matter, was of little consequence as long as he could get his hands on the source of power that he knew was held inside the palace.

As he approached, there was a tremendous bang and one of the towers flew into shards of rubble that showered the ground. Malachi stopped and waited for the dust to clear and the ground to cease shaking. Doubts began to assail him. Thoughts that he had vastly underestimated the protagonists occurred to him. That response had to be from the Gort King's side and he had no inkling of such a possibility despite having attended the King for so long. He thought he knew everything about the King, his ambitions and his shortcomings in particular, but it seemed he was possessed of power beyond Malachi's estimation.

He breathed long and deep. The prospect of the King actually being capable of victory was a new factor for consideration. His assumptions had been based on a tired raggle-taggle army led by a fat incompetent commander and a lazy wilful monarch being destroyed completely. But not before they had engaged with the enemy and provided him with the opportunity he needed to grasp the power he desired.

The palace seemed unguarded, as he had hoped. He'd decided against bringing soldiers along in case he'd had to fight his way in, and it appeared that his judgement had been vindicated. As he prepared to walk unchallenged beneath welcoming arches that led to a fragrant garden, a man strode past him with a purposeful gait without even giving Malachi a single glance.

Malachi stiffened in recognition. The look on the man's face had been one of pure anger, but the face bore an unmistakable similarity to Tyrant.

Inside the palace, Malachi sniffed the acrid stench of embalming fluid and tied a cloth over his mouth in an attempt to reduce the sickly smell to a bearable level. The vast ground floor was featureless apart from the sunken bath in its centre. Standing conspicuously on the raised tiles was a small gold filigree casket that appeared to have been left as an afterthought or parked there and forgotten. It looked so completely out of place that Malachi felt compelled to walk over and examine it despite the worst of the stench.

The lid opened easily enough to reveal a dull metal sphere the size of an apple. His probing fingers detected a thin line running around the ball and when he pushed and twisted, the top popped open, revealing numerals that appeared to be written in red fire.

0:20:44

He was fascinated at this magical display and resolved to take the item and examine the source of its magic at his leisure. It was far heavier than its small size would indicate, so, after picking it up and unsuccessfully trying to place it in his pocket, Malachi decided to put it back and collect it on his way out. He knew exactly what magical items he was looking for and hoped to find them before the King returned.

He closed the lid on the casket and set about his search.

88

Cuthbert watched the King clench his fists in celebration as the huge tower toppled. 'That'll show the bastard we mean business,' he yelled, 'now onwards to victory!'

Conningsby was flailing his arms and shouting at soldiers too far away to hear him, but close enough to get confused. 'You heard his majesty's orders, attack, attack, attack.'

'Look, sire, there's a lone fighter heading our way,' Conningsby said. 'My men will make short work of him.'

Cuthbert winced at the carnage that gave lie to Conningsby's words; the stocky figure just kept on walking through every attack and it was quite evident that he was hell-bent on reaching their position. It appeared that nothing could stand in his way and survive. One man emerged from the crowd of retreating soldiers and placed himself in the assailant's path. He was brandishing a sword and shouting defiance. It was Grew. Cuthbert took in a deep breath as he realised that the seemingly invincible attacker had the look of Tyrant. Cuthbert wished that Grew would stand aside, but he'd spent long enough in his company to know that Grew's ingrained sense of duty and stubborn adherence to army protocol would not allow it.

The man who looked a bit like Tyrant stopped, as if surprised that someone dared to challenge him after all the destruction he'd been dishing out. Grew made a peremptory swipe that failed to connect. The man stepped forward, sword raised, and Grew sidestepped, hacked at the man's arm but missed. Cuthbert saw the King putting the tubular device to his shoulder and aiming it at the fighters. 'No,' he shouted, 'you'll hit Grew.' His words were ignored and the fiery missile sped down the slope, hit Grew in the back, and blew him to tiny shards of burning flesh.

Cuthbert felt sick as he watched Grew's head fly into the air with his hair burning fiercely.

When the smoke and dust and mud shower settled, it appeared that the man had suffered a similar fate to Grew. The King wore a satisfied smile. 'A small price to pay for victory, don't you agree?' he said, presumably in reply to Cuthbert's warning shout. Cuthbert didn't agree.

Grew hadn't exactly been his friend, but he had been a good man, a true and honest soldier who followed the rules even when he knew them to be absurd. Now, his life had been taken by a smug King who knew nothing of rules or fairness. Cuthbert's hand reached down to the small knife he'd acquired when he'd needed to cut himself free on the North Road.

Before he could draw it, he saw the King's triumph turn to concern. The big man had picked himself up from the ground and was walking towards them. Apparently, none the worse for the conflagration that had consumed him.

Cuthbert wanted to run and hide, but there seemed little opportunity to do that here. At worst, the King would have him struck down as soon as he moved. At best, he'd be fleeing through the inhospitable desert. He was also rooted by the drama unfolding before his eyes. The King had regained some of his swagger and was standing in front of his tent as if in greeting to a welcome guest.

'I might have known,' the King addressed the man whose face was wrinkled with fierce intent, 'that the aberration that calls itself Gilgamesh Khan would show up again. I'm correct, aren't I?'

'I am he,' the man said. 'Prepare to die at my hand. You have no idea of the inconvenience you've caused me. Here am I, keeping a low profile, then you turn up and broadcast my whereabouts to the whole universe. I don't know who you think you are, but I'm telling you, you're going to die as suddenly and as painfully as I can manage, given the circumstances.'

'Think about it,' the King said. 'If I know who you are and you've not announced yourself, then what does that make me?'

Cuthbert watched Gilgamesh adopt a more pained expression that suggested he was thinking. This made him look even more like Tyrant than before. 'You could be an interfering scholar, a reader of ancient texts, any manner of things. I don't care, I am Gilgamesh and I am all-powerful. I am a god and you would do well to bow down to me before you die.'

The King folded his arms over his chest then let out a chuckle that sounded a tiny bit forced. Nevertheless, the expression on Gilgamesh's face changed to puzzlement.

'Here's one for you to think about,' the King said. 'First of all, you're not a god, you're a sad half-breed. A bit of a god, maybe, but certainly human and by no means immortal. Unlike a god, you rely on that body of yours. Once it's gone, so are you. Having said that, I'm amazed at how sprightly you're looking after all these years, though judging by your very pale skin, it's obvious you don't get out much. What's your secret? Is there a new face cream I don't know about?' The King laughed heartily at something Cuthbert found indecipherable rather than funny. It was hard to see the comedic value of a big angry man with a sword who was getting more worked up by the minute.

'If you must know, I have my palace protected by a temporal device that keeps everything as it always was. Time is frozen, so I don't have to worry about things deteriorating. It also has the advantage of keeping me hidden from those who might be resentful about my longevity.' Gilgamesh flicked the point of his impossibly thin sword in the King's face. Cuthbert was surprised at the King's lack of reaction to the prospect of being skewered.

'Doesn't work for human bodies, though, does it? Still, you've managed very well so far. All things come to an end, though. Except if you're a god, of course. We go on and on,' the King smiled as he replied. Cuthbert watched in fascination as the sword tip advanced slowly and wondered if he'd be the next to be killed after this Gilgamesh brute had finished with the King. Cuthbert wished he were a bit further away from the action that had encroached within a few paces of where he stood transfixed.

Conningsby jumped in front of the King wielding a heavy sword, moving surprisingly quickly in view of his considerable bulk. 'Allow me to despatch this insolent—'

Cuthbert was left guessing the next word, as it remained unsaid. Nor would he have the opportunity to ask Conningsby what he'd had in mind. *Wretch?* Or maybe something a little stronger? *Bastard?* Not very nice, but probably accurate. *Recalcitrant upstart?* The possibilities were almost endless, but any prospect of observing the effect of Conningsby's sharp tongue was ended by the flickering point of the blade emerging with a surge of blood from the back of his neck. There was a good deal of gurgling involved as he fell to the floor and thrashed around, but nothing to give any clue about how the sentence might have been completed.

Quite quickly, the movements became small spasms, then a last croak heralded Conningsby's final twitch.

As far as Cuthbert could make out, the King was still completely unperturbed, though the blade was back at his throat. Cuthbert fingered his little knife and wondered if he should throw himself into the fray. He looked across at Vargas, whose face was grim but his posture showed no inclination to intervene.

'Well, that's an end to it, I suppose. You'll have to age normally and die quite quickly once your little hideaway has been rendered ineffective,' the King said.

'You're in no position to threaten me in any way; my palace is safe from you and your puny soldiers,' Gilgamesh said.

'On the contrary, the deed is done. Or if it's not been done already, it will be soon. This young man here will confirm that he dropped off a little something inside your palace earlier. Call it a present if you like. After all, it's going to bring everything into the present.' The King laughed. 'Get it? A present that will destroy your precious sanctuary.'

However funny the King was finding this joke, and Cuthbert himself had no idea why it might be thought so amusing, it wasn't shared by Gilgamesh, whose face didn't change at all as he plunged his sword into the King's chest and watched him fall lifeless to the ground. He gave Cuthbert a fierce look that made him brace himself for the same treatment, but Gilgamesh turned and stomped off in the direction of his palace as if he had more pressing matters to attend to.

Vargas bent over the King. 'He's dead,' he reported unnecessarily.

Cuthbert laughed, suddenly seeing the funny side of what had been going on. 'I suppose you're in charge,' he said. 'I suggest you get everyone to pack up and prepare for the long trek home to Gort.' Cuthbert's feelings of amusement were proving hard to stifle. Now that he knew what was going on, he needed to keep his head down completely for a good few years. There was every chance that some serious entities would be despatched to clear up this mess and he didn't want them involving him in their do-gooding. He thought of Cassie and his guts heaved with longing. She would provide him with some compensation while he settled down until things blew over.

Something that Gilgamesh had said before he stomped off to protect his castle was nagging at him, though. Temporal anomaly or something of that nature. Did that mean the device he'd delivered might not function? That would be a pity. Cuthbert watched the fast-receding figure picking his way through the charred remains of the dead and the writhing agonies of the dying. When Gilgamesh reached his palace and finally disappeared from view, Cuthbert gave a shrug of his shoulders, reached down and rummaged through the bloodstained pockets of the dead King. Eventually, he found what he was looking for. At first, he stared hard at the small square tile with an indentation in its centre, then he instinctively extended the thin metal rod that was fixed in one corner before he squeezed hard with his thumb.

He was rewarded with a satisfying cloud of dust expelled from every orifice in the palace, quickly followed by a low, rumbling noise.

89

Tyrant drew his sword and prepared to defend himself. The big cat at Lone's side bristled its defiance and showed its teeth. Lone herself looked tired and careworn. He wondered if the screaming had been hers and decided it must have been. The little man with the turban didn't look the screaming type.

'Put the sword away,' Lone said. 'You know it won't do you any good against me. Otherwise, your little girlfriend will be the first to suffer. I could crush her heart in an instant and you know it. Cat doesn't like swords and I can't be answerable for the consequences if you continue to threaten us.'

There was something compelling, as always, in what Lone was telling him. Tyrant put his sword back and placed a protective arm across Petra.

Lone laughed, a small friendly noise that was at odds with the Lone that Tyrant knew so well. The feeling he got from it was surprisingly reassuring, despite the knowledge that he was almost certainly being manipulated by this devious woman. 'There are those who have perpetrated much worse crimes against me since we last met,' she said. 'Revenge is something I'm determined to take, but not against you. You may have been the one who carried me off and left me in the desert, but you were being compelled by forces beyond your capacity to resist. I have to admit that I once harboured a desire to seek you out and punish you, but that notion was discarded a long time ago. I abandoned you outside Gort, you left me in the desert. I'd say we're even. I have something to give you as a mark of good intention.'

Tyrant felt that if she was hiding her malice, she was doing it well. 'What could you possibly give me to make me trust you?' he asked.

Lone walked off and the cat stretched, eyes still on Tyrant, before trailing her so closely, it was rubbing against the back of her legs. Tyrant took firm hold of Petra's hand and followed them across a fenced area dotted with chicken shit to a rough house made from irregular pieces of timber. Lone indicated for him to look inside. Piled high in one corner of the room were bignuts. 'They're for you. I brought them all the way from the place you left me. Call them a peace offering.'

Tyrant eyed them with some excitement. He'd resigned himself to never having one again and here were, he counted them carefully, sixteen. And all his. They looked as if they were fresh enough to eat, but he had to be sure. One quick swipe of his sword sliced off the top of one of them and he drank the sweet juice within. It was the finest drink he'd ever tasted, and energy flowed through his veins as it cascaded down his throat. Guiltily, and reluctantly, he took the nut and offered it to Petra who finished off what was left in a couple of large gulps. Tyrant then set about cracking the husk on the stone floor and picking off the white flesh, which was just as nourishing and delicious as he remembered.

'Do you recall our first meeting?' he said.

'In the tavern, in Bounty,' Lone replied.

'It was you that hired those two men, wasn't it?'

'Yes, it was.'

'I thought so at the time. You still owe me for that, so I'll take these nuts and call it even.'

Lone smiled at him in a way that made him feel embarrassed. It was as if she needed approval from him and was grateful for anything along those lines. The hard edge she'd shown him before had been blunted; either that or she'd become even more devious than ever. 'The suggestion of the nuts came from the same source that urged me to get you to tag along on my journey to Gort, come to think of it. Maybe we're both being taken for a ride on a faulty cart, Tyrant. It's Patch you have to thank for the nuts. He also made me promise not to harm you as a condition of my release. So now you know.'

'Fair enough,' Tyrant said, 'so we'll be on our way and let bygones be bygones then.'

'First, there's someone that I want you to meet. I'm sure he'll be of interest to you. It can't be coincidence that you're here and so is he. I suspect that Patch has engineered the whole situation anyway, so we're best to go along with it.'

'Who is it?' Tyrant asked.

'You'll know him when you see him,' Lone said. 'Follow me, we need to go over the river and down to the palace.'

'What about my nuts?' Tyrant said.

'You can come back later for them if you want.'

'I might as well leave them next to the portal so I can easily take them with me when I leave. I've got business to do in Gort; there's a batch of licker in the cave just waiting to be delivered and thirsty men ready to drink it.'

'A portal? Here?' Lone gasped.

'Of course, you didn't think we'd walked, did you?'

'So that's how Malachi got here,' she said.

'Malachi? Is he here as well?'

'He was. And I suppose he could be back at any moment. Or I could go to him if you show me how to work the device.'

'We can do better than that,' Petra said. 'We can take you directly to Malachi's house.'

'First things first,' Lone said, 'then we'll see what remains to be done.'

90

Despite the distance, the King's form was unmistakeable and so was the florid bulk of Conningsby. There were two others who confronted the Southern King, one of whom could easily have been Cuthbert. Ant watched in horror as Conningsby attacked but was swiftly despatched. He could hardly believe his eyes when the King received similar treatment in such a brutal fashion. The pale King was heading back towards him and Ant knew he had to get out before he arrived. Trespassers weren't likely to receive anything other than a swift death.

The metal door opened invitingly, but Ant hesitated on the threshold. What if this time the door refused to open again? Could this be some form of trap for the unwary after all? He decided against entering, instead heading off down a long passageway that he felt must connect with the tower on the far side. He ran despite the stifling heat, passing room after room, each one with a door firmly shut until he encountered one that was fully open. He stopped, curiosity demanding that he peek inside.

'Ah, Ant, there you are,' Malachi said, his back still turned. 'Help me get these items into this bag, then roll up those maps over there. We need to take them as well.'

Ant took a deep breath, then looked around the room. It was windowless and lit in a similar manner to the tiny steel room that had transported him to the top of the tower. The walls were lined by row upon row of cupboards, the doors of which had been mostly left wide open. The items inside were mostly unfamiliar to him. 'The King of the Desert is on his way back and he'll be here very soon. Won't he be angry when he finds you engaged in robbing him?'

'Oh dear, I had hoped that our King would delay him much longer than this. Did you see what happened?' Malachi said.

'He stomped through the army, killing everyone before him, then he confronted the King and killed him.'

'Just like that? No big fight? Surely somebody showed some resistance?'

'The King shot some fiery device at him. Oh, and Conningsby had a go, but lasted all of ten seconds,' Ant replied.

'I can't say I'm completely surprised, but I had hoped our King was made of sterner stuff. I suppose we'd better make ourselves scarce. Here, take this bag, but be very gentle with it,' Malachi said.

'What's in it?'

'Treasure beyond price,' Malachi said and smiled. 'Fabled items that will change the world. Instruments that have been referred to in ancient texts but never discovered. With these, we can predict the paths of the stars, navigate with precision, explore the world we live in, and so much more.'

Ant took the bag and peered inside. It contained three items, each of them wrapped carefully in cloth. 'Your father would be astounded by what we've found,' Malachi said, heading for the doorway laden with rolled up charts. As Ant followed, the floor jumped beneath his feet, and he fell to the floor, cradling the bag protectively as he was plunged into darkness.

'Ant, where are you? This way,' Malachi hissed.

Ant rolled himself back upright and felt his way towards where the voice had come from. His hand encountered the edge of Malachi's cloak and he held on to it like a lost child. Malachi began moving steadily along the passageway and Ant began to discern a lighter hue to the darkness up ahead. When they reached the stairwell, enough light was present for them to descend carefully and Ant to let go of his guide.

The stairs seemed to go on and on; Ant worried that they must be entering the bowels of the earth and had missed the opportunity to escape before a welcome blast of sunlight announced their safe arrival at ground level. Ahead of them he could see the gardens and beyond that the fringes of the city. He looked around nervously, expecting to see the angry King confront them at any moment, but there was nobody at all to be seen. That had been a strange feature of the palace, that no one appeared to even visit the place, let alone live here.

Once out in the gardens, his apprehension reduced with the welcome feel of the sun on his head and the fresh scent of the flowers masking the sickly smell of the interior. 'Are we going to show these things to my father, then?' Ant asked.

'That's my intention. There's much to be discovered about their workings, and Ambrose is very well qualified to assist in that provided he can restrain himself from any further foolishness,' Malachi said.

'What foolishness? Are you still harping on about the device in the King's tower? Can't you let that go, even after all this time?'

'I wasn't referring to that particular piece of idiocy, rather to something very recent that might have much more serious consequences. I'll say no more and let Ambrose tell you about his experiments himself,' Malachi said.

Ant wondered what could possibly have a worse outcome than the terrible aftermath of the vedhana in Gort, but could think of nothing. If they could only get back across the bridge and into the vedhana, he could be asking his father in person for an explanation very soon. Malachi had reached the archway leading out of the garden, but instead of hurrying to put as much distance between themselves and the palace, was standing still, staring towards the city as if he'd seen a ghost.

91

'We can just step back into the device and be back in Gort,' Petra said. 'What's keeping you here, Tyrant?'

Tyrant couldn't bring himself to leave, to take the simple way out. This place had him captivated now, and he knew that there was unfinished business he had to attend to. Even if, as he fully expected, that business would end up finishing him. He was certain that Lone was leading him into danger, but he had the feeling that he could either face it now or be forever running from it. There was only one person that Lone could be referring to.

They were stopped at the bridge by soldiers who sought to prevent their passage. Lone stepped forward and spoke to them. 'On whose orders are you stopping us?'

'The King of Gort,' a soldier responded.

'Him personally? His august majesty walked all the way here and told you what to do?' she asked.

'Well, no, not exactly. The instructions were actually given by Malachi, the King's highest-ranking advisor. So, they might just as well come directly from the King himself.'

'Malachi? Is he here?' Lone asked.

'Yes, he's gone ahead to inspect the damage on the Southern King's palace and see how the battle is progressing.'

'I have to speak with him,' Lone said. 'If he enters that palace, he will be in grave danger.'

'Nobody is to cross, no exceptions.'

'Not even his wife?'

'He said nothing about his wife being expected.'

'Let's say it's a nice surprise, especially if it turns out to be one that saves his life. Now let us through and follow us to the palace. Your job here is no longer the priority,' Lone said.

Tyrant could see the doubt in the man's face gradually clear. Lone was obviously plying her legendary powers of persuasion, and they were having the desired effect. Tyrant found himself becoming impatient with the officer for even hesitating as long as he did. Her argument was totally convincing. Before Tyrant could begin to remonstrate with the man, he relented, called his comrades to follow, and led the way over the bridge and down the road leading to the palace.

A sudden shock made the ground heave and Tyrant's chest was thumped hard by an unseen force. The already smoking palace was consumed by dust and debris, which hung in the still air, forming a haze that was slow to clear.

92

'Stop.'

The voice froze Ant in his tracks. His stomach constricted as he turned around to see the Southern King emerge from the ruins of the palace. He looked remarkably unconcerned for someone whose hair was on fire.

Ant was fascinated by the tendrils of sooty smoke that were rising from his head. An occasional crackle of flame erupted amongst the blackness. The King's face was smeared with black and his white tunic was ragged and torn. Nevertheless, he was walking casually from the debris as if this were an everyday occurrence of little import.

Ant clutched the bag to his chest. He felt transparent and naked. The King's gaze felt as if it were penetrating to the deepest core of his being. It was as if everything he'd ever done was being displayed, including the pilfering that he'd been engaged in when the palace collapsed into ruin. Now he was compelled to offer the contraband to its rightful owner and kneel before him to await his fate. Mercy wasn't something he expected. All he could hope for was a quick death with as little pain as possible.

He took half a step towards the smouldering King, ready to confess his misdemeanours and return the stolen property.

The King absently patted the crown of his head to extinguish a blaze that had flared up and was threatening to spread more widely. 'Malachi,' he said, 'are you trying to avoid me?'

'Yes, of course I am,' Malachi replied. 'I would rather not confront you under these trying circumstances for fear of what you might do to me.'

'Admitting the truth for once in your life may just have saved you,' the King said and laughed. 'This is all very inconvenient, as you might imagine. I'll have aged considerably before I can restore the place to its normal function and you know I don't like to age. Keeping this body the way it is has been something of a chore, preventing me from making anything other than a few local forays from time to time. Now I'm going to be exposed to the glare of that merciless sun for a while and all because of your King and his cunning device.'

'Had I been aware of the tricks at his command, I might have been able to warn you, sire. Sadly, I had no idea of his capabilities, sire. Our arrangement was simply that I bring him here for you to confront, knowing your reluctance to make the trip in the opposite direction and the vedhana not being an option,' Malachi said.

Ant found the tone of his voice reassuringly confident in the face of this powerful man whose palace was in ruins, apparently because of something that Malachi had contrived. There was also the consideration of the treasures that had been looted and how their desire for a smart getaway was prompted in no small measure by anxiety not to get caught.

'Had you known, Malachi, I would have expected you to keep quiet for fear of spoiling the surprise. It was much more fun this way, though how your King managed to explode the device after I had already killed him is a question I have to admit that I'm struggling with.'

'I expect it was some contraption with a time measuring machine,' Malachi said.

'Then the timing was impeccably calculated,' the King said, 'so that I had arrived back at the palace at the exact moment it exploded. Look at me, I'm a complete mess. It'll take more than a bath to get rid of some of these marks. I might even be scarred for life. Still, a bit of excitement is good from time to time and I've not had a fight worthy of the name for such a long while. It does make me wonder about your King, though. There may be more to him than either of us guessed.'

'Your majesty is wise beyond measure; if you say he's dead, then I have no doubt that he is. From a personal point of view, I find that reassuring, as I wouldn't want him to turn up in Gort again looking for revenge against me,' Malachi said. 'Which is where I need to be getting back to as soon as possible. The desert air doesn't suit me, I'm afraid. I've also just seen my wife approaching and I would very much like to have the opportunity to find out where she's been all this time.'

'Your wife? Are you sure?' the King said.

'Believe me, there's nobody else alive who's even remotely like her. I'd know her anywhere, though she's developed a darker complexion and let her hair grow to an unusual length. Here she comes now; I'll introduce you to her if you wish.'

Ant watched as the King's face creased and his eyes narrowed. 'I don't think that any introductions will be necessary,' he said.

93

It had been a slow day for eggs. Moussa wiped his brow and gestured to Janvir and Demba. It was a sign of resignation, a signal that the day was done. He knew they would take the lead from him and expect to be protected from Lone's wrath when they came back, still bearing most of the eggs they'd left with. Maybe she'd still be absent when they returned; he certainly hoped so. She'd gone missing a couple of days ago, but even in his most optimistic moments, Moussa couldn't bring himself to believe that they'd seen the last of that woman.

He, even more than the others, was feeling sick and tired of making the short trip over the river day after day. The same labourers in the same fields giving him the same wave. The merchants in the bazaar giving him the same disdainful look. The women, busying themselves amongst the stalls, hardly giving him a second glance.

This wasn't what he did. The same journey every day was punishing his soul in a way that she couldn't possibly understand. He longed for the vast uncharted reaches of the desert where his special skills of camel handling, combined with unerring navigational ability, made him a prince amongst drovers. Here, he was unappreciated and demeaned by the nature of the work she compelled him to perform.

If she were waiting for them, he would tell her to try selling eggs in the face of an invading army, in the teeth of a major conflict, and with death all around. He'd done his best; they all had. At least they'd safeguarded her eggs and brought them back to her. She'd no doubt come up with her own version of matters, point out all the things they should have done but failed to think of. *Why didn't you sell them to the army?* He had an answer to that inevitable question which went along the lines of *they seemed more intent on screaming with agony than purchasing eggs.* Their regular customers had been mostly absent, having wisely put as much distance as they could between themselves and the conflict taking place on the outskirts of the city. Those that had stayed put, either out of prurient interest or idleness, said that eggs were something they knew for certain would be better left to another time.

Moussa felt exposed sitting high up on his camel; he'd seen some fiery projectiles whizzing through the air towards the palace and he was now getting very close to the tower that they had brought crumbling to the ground. As if in response to his worrying thoughts, the palace seemed to dissolve into a cascade of flying stones that almost swept him from his perch. His camel signalled that she'd had enough by bending her knees and inviting him to alight, which he did in the interests of shielding himself behind her considerable bulk in case more debris was flung in his direction.

The fog cleared slowly, revealing a deep rent in the side of the building that offered easy access to the interior where none had been previously. Moussa thought for a moment, then waved to the others to follow him inside. Something catastrophic had happened to this palace, which meant that nobody was likely to object if he took a look around. Palaces were the very places where items of great interest might be found. Some of these would be easily portable and made of gold. Moussa still had the proceeds of the sale in his purse, but these would be meagre in comparison to the rich pickings he might find in a recently destroyed palace.

Janvir and Demba looked around nervously when they joined him inside the broken building. 'There's nobody here except us,' Moussa said, speaking loudly to try to dispel the creeping and whispering the others had adopted, 'but we need to look sharp before everyone gets the same idea. Let's grab what we can carry and be off.'

Moussa led the way along a corridor strewn with rubble until he came to a large room with a broken door. Inside, he found shelf after shelf of books, but no signs of anything valuable. Moussa had never seen the point of writing things down; there were so few in his acquaintance able to read the squiggly marks that passed for writing. This place was testament to the folly of collecting useless items when the same shelves could have accommodated real treasure.

The next room he managed to access seemed more promising. There were items stacked against the walls, which he could not identify. Most of these were metal tubes, some with wooden attachments, and none of them looked to be made from anything precious. He decided that these were purely utilitarian objects, though their purpose was completely beyond him. He had already decided to abandon this chamber and seek elsewhere when Demba staggered over to him bearing a wooden crate painted an unusual shade of green and with black splodges, making it look most peculiar. Using his knife, Demba prised the box open to reveal a dozen or so dark grey eggs with strange handles attached.

Moussa picked one out and weighed it in his hand. It was heavy enough to suggest there might be gold inside, but scraping at the outside did nothing to confirm or deny the supposition. He handed the thing back to Demba, who began tugging at a ring attached to the handle. When the ring had been worked free, the whole handle flew off across the room. Demba shrugged, placed the metal egg back into the box with the others, then, staggering under the weight, carried it out of the room. 'They're not gold, you fool,' Moussa shouted as he disappeared from view.

As if in reply, the walls disintegrated, the ceiling collapsed, and Moussa was flung bodily into a corner where a cascade of stones battered him into oblivion.

94

'I might have known that you'd turn up in the midst of all this destruction.' Lone looked into her husband's eyes and detected an uncharacteristic nervousness.

'I thought you were dead,' he replied.

'She was dead,' Gilgamesh said. 'I'd be interested to hear an explanation for her reappearance in such fine fettle after I had her fed to the crocodiles.'

'We've been apart for a long time,' Malachi said and turned towards Gilgamesh. 'I'd appreciate it if we could get on our way without further delay. As we agreed, my part in this is done and I need to take my wife back to Gort, where we have a lot of catching up to do.'

'I wonder if she has other priorities,' Gilgamesh said. 'From the looks of her, she thinks her business with me is far from finished. She's even brought some help along, presumably in an attempt to teach me some manners.'

Lone couldn't help but smile at the notion, especially coming from someone who had obviously been on fire until very recently. She wondered if his latest travails had weakened his powers and whether this might provide an opportunity for her to exact revenge. For it was revenge that she was committed to exacting, even if there was only a small chance of success. She had to try, despite the probability that it would get them all killed.

The soldiers were confronting the King now, brandishing swords and aiming crossbows. 'Kill him,' she ordered, 'he's an enemy of your King.'

'Not just any old enemy.' Gilgamesh smiled. 'The one who actually managed to kill the fat idiot. Your King is dead; if you fancy your chances where your whole army failed, then be my guest. Make my day, bring it on, let's get ready to rumble, do your worst, come on if you think you're hard enough.'

Lone decided that Gilgamesh had succumbed to madness, probably derived from too many blows to the head and being set on fire. He was ranting, screaming meaningless phrases that were obviously designed to provoke an attack. Before she could offer any words of advice to the soldiers, they did attack. It was inevitable given the circumstances, she realised. They were soldiers; he was a braggart who claimed the death of their King and they must have felt they had no option.

The first crossbow fired. A bolt embedded itself almost up to the feathers in Gilgamesh's neck. 'Ouch,' he said, his face twisting into a grimace, 'that hurt. Oh dear, I think you've done for me now.' His legs wobbled comically as he rolled his eyes. For an instant, Lone thought that he'd been critically wounded, but his eyes burnt as brightly as ever and she quickly realised he was enjoying the situation. A long thin sword appeared in his right hand, then darted towards the nearest soldier. It was a strike as swift as a startled snake. One thrust that left the hapless soldier with a glazed expression as he slowly sank to his knees. He clutched at his chest as if in disbelief at what was happening to him, then lay down on the ground and expired. His comrades released three more bolts and then attacked with swords, only to meet the same fate. Gilgamesh's sword tip flashed and danced in the setting sun that coloured it the same as the blood that gushed from the soldiers' wounds.

'Stop,' Malachi shouted, but by the time he'd uttered the word, the attack had been carried out and repulsed with deadly effect.

Lone stepped forward until she was within a sword's length of Gilgamesh, who was engaged in plucking the bolts that protruded from his body. She summoned up all the strength she could muster and squeezed at his heart. It felt solid. Immovable. He showed no signs of discomfort as he dragged a crossbow bolt out of his shoulder together with a small spurt of blood, which soon stopped flowing.

Lone squeezed until her energy gave out, then stood panting with exertion, ready for the inevitable sword thrust that would end her life.

'There's no need for any of this,' Malachi said. 'There's been some degree of misunderstanding, but nothing that can't be resolved in a friendly manner.'

Lone found the effect of Malachi's calm words to be exactly the opposite he intended, at least as far as she was concerned. Despite her tiredness, she was sorely tempted to turn her attention his way and try to shut his big mouth once and for all. The smirk on Gilgamesh's face wasn't helping her mood either. 'Misunderstanding?' she said. 'This bastard tried to have his way with me and when I refused, had me thrown into the river. Call that a misunderstanding?'

'Exactly.' Malachi's voice was as unctuous as ever. Lone wondered why she had ever believed anything he'd said to her. 'It can all be put down to cultural differences. They do things differently here in the south. You have to make allowances.'

Lone watched the effect of her husband's words on Gilgamesh. He seemed to be enjoying himself and his sword point had dropped from level with her throat and was now pointing at her feet. 'Take her away, Malachi,' he said, 'before I finish the job those crocodiles failed to do.'

Lone took a deep breath. Her initial plan had been to get the soldiers to kill him, with help from Tyrant if necessary. Now she'd seen what he could do, there was no prospect of success. She remembered very well the effect of a single bolt hitting Tyrant in the shoulder when they were escaping from Gort. Then, he'd been completely incapacitated and would have perished without the intervention of her unruly demon.

There was no doubt in her mind that there must be a significant connection between Gilgamesh and Tyrant, but from what she'd witnessed, there was no comparison when it came to capability. Using Tyrant for her revenge now seemed to be foolish in the extreme.

Annoying though he might be, Malachi did have a point and she would have to swallow her pride in the face of unassailable odds. She began to regret her impulse to bring Tyrant along to face his lookalike and expected that he would take a similar view and join her in making a strategic withdrawal while they still had the opportunity.

95

Tyrant watched as the soldiers were despatched with consummate ease. He saw the lack of effect from the crossbow bolts and remembered the debilitating pain he'd had to endure when he'd been struck by one himself in Gort. It had almost killed him. He'd spent a long time recovering and even now, years later, the wound still bothered him at times.

It wasn't the man's powers of recovery that worried him, though. It was the smell of fish that was suddenly clogging his nostrils and a deep dread that was making him weak at the knees and threatened to overwhelm him. This was without any shadow of doubt the man who had killed his mother and his brother with one thrust of that wicked rapier. Tyrant breathed a deep sigh, then staggered forward stiff-legged to confront him.

Malachi's syrupy voice was coating proceedings in sweet intent, despite the display of dead men strewn about at their feet. He knew he was being urged to give it up, to walk away. If there was really an opportunity to do just that, it might be the wise thing to do. The way the soldiers had been slain and the disdain with which the hits from the crossbows had been treated meant that he would have very little prospect of prevailing against this prodigious warrior. Nevertheless, he felt he had to try. Not out of anger, though. His mother's murder was the source of such deep cold sorrow that hot anger could form no part of it.

Tyrant was convinced that he had to face up to this man or continue to be haunted by the spectre of his mother's killing and spend the rest of his life running away from it. It might be impossible for him to prevail, but he had to take what chance he had of ridding himself of the foul influence.

There was one positive aspect to the prospective fight, and that was the weapon his opponent had chosen. If anyone cared to listen, Tyrant's opinion on the rapier as a weapon was long and scathing. He rated it even lower than the pike, which was often worse than useless. The problem with a rapier was that it wasn't even a proper sword. It was a toy devised by eccentrics to demonstrate their ability to overcome its many shortcomings. If you ever managed to defend yourself with a rapier, you could indeed claim to be a special fighter. Until he'd seen this man in action, Tyrant had only ever seen or heard of rapiers being used successfully against men wielding similar blades. Anyone with a proper sword or even a half-decent knife was almost bound to defeat someone foolish enough to insist on using a rapier.

For one thing, a rapier was usually too flimsy to withstand a decent parry. Even if it was met by an arm, it would easily bend out of shape and be rendered next to useless. Another drawback was the one-dimensional attack. A rapier could only hurt you if it poked a hole in you. This involved a stabbing action, which was as limited as it was predictable. A real sword could poke, prod, slash, cut, bash, and generally come at you from any direction. A rapier had to be moved in a straight line. Admittedly, it could be moved very quickly, but this was small recompense for the lack of freedom of manoeuvre. Rapiers, in Tyrant's estimation, were useful only in duels and then only against people stupid enough to be using one themselves. He had the feeling that they were so popular for settling differences because they rarely managed to inflict significant harm. In common with the much-derided pike, once a rapier was pushed aside, it became useless.

'You killed my mother,' Tyrant said.

The King's eyes had been darting from Lone to Malachi but gave him their full attention now. 'And who are you?' he said.

'They call me Tyrant.'

'Never heard of you, nor do I recall killing your mother. Don't get me wrong, I'm not denying I may have done what you say I have. I've killed many people and lots of them were women. I take it your mother was a woman, or are we talking some kind of large hairy ape? Now that might be something I'd have a better chance of remembering.'

'It doesn't matter. I remember. I saw you do it.'

'Better to have taken it up with me at the time, then. At least we'd know what we were arguing about. Or didn't you have the guts? I see by your ample girth that you've been successful in developing that part of your body, but I can tell you that it's only an expression. Being fat doesn't make you brave, whatever they say,' the King said.

Tyrant drew his sword and held it carefully across his chest so that he could sweep aside any rapier thrust with a single movement. That's if he could move quickly enough.

'Hold on,' the King said, 'your friends have all perished before your eyes. What makes you think you can avoid a similar fate?'

'Look at me,' Tyrant said. 'Don't you see the resemblance?'

'Resemblance to what? All I see before me is a man who looks as if he's had a hard life living in a midden. Are you trying to tell me you and I look alike?'

'Similar enough to be father and son,' Tyrant said, 'or at least that was the inference I made when I set eyes on you.'

'Then you must have special eyesight or an addled mind. I'm Gilgamesh, I don't have any offspring. I've made it a rule. Having a son would be too much of an inconvenience, even if it were possible. I've been bedding women for a very long time and procreation hasn't occurred except on very rare occasions. And then I've sorted out the matter in the most expeditious manner possible. Are you saying that you were somehow overlooked?'

'We were twins. You killed my brother when you murdered my mother. Now it's your turn to find out what it's like to be slain,' Tyrant said. He watched as Gilgamesh narrowed his eyes for just an instant. It could have been fear or, at least, the beginnings of doubt. Tyrant wondered if his reluctance to allow himself any children was because he feared that his prodigious powers would be passed on and this would leave him vulnerable. It hadn't happened. Even if he was the son of Gilgamesh, he didn't possess his remarkable resilience. However, Gilgamesh didn't know that.

Tyrant watched Gilgamesh's eyes as the tip of his rapier was raised to point at his heart. He knew that by the time he registered any movement from the blade, it would be too late. He had to rely on an early warning if he was to survive the first thrust.

'That's enough,' Petra screamed at him. 'Leave him to the ruins of his palace. Come home now, Tyrant, there's people that need you and licker to be peddled. He isn't worth killing. Look at him, all shiny and white, as if he's not been outdoors in years. Let him go back into his cave and stay there.'

368

Tyrant forced himself to ignore the distraction and kept focussed on trying to anticipate the inevitable thrust. Gilgamesh's pupils contracted a fraction and Tyrant whipped his sword across his body as soon as he saw it. Even then, it was almost too late; he managed to deflect the rapier from his heart, but only into the fleshy part of his shoulder. It withdrew as quickly as it had struck, leaving a stream of blood and excruciating pain. Tyrant used up every fibre of his will to remain stoic in the face of the awful wound. He stared hard at Gilgamesh, then said, 'Ouch, that hurt. Oh dear, I think you've done for me now.' He allowed his legs to perform a wobble in what he hoped was an exact mimicry of when Gilgamesh had been shot. He was rewarded by a tightening of cheek muscles and a marginal furrowing of Gilgamesh's brow. Even considering the pain and the prospects of bleeding to death, Tyrant felt that the fight was going much better than he could have hoped.

'Even if you do display a bit of resistance, you should know that there is no weapon ever made that can harm me. No blade is capable of cutting my flesh. Nothing you do with that sword of yours can damage me,' Gilgamesh said.

'Don't be too sure,' Ant called out. 'That sword has Ishtar's image on it.'

Gilgamesh's discomfort was even more noticeable as he stared at the sword in Tyrant's hand. A start of recognition passed over his features before the look of disdain re-established itself. 'Where did you get that?'

'It was a gift from the gods,' Tyrant said. 'I expect they wanted me to let you have it back. Do you want it?'

'Haha, very funny. I say yes and you stab me. I wasn't born yesterday.' Gilgamesh tipped his head to one side. Tyrant noticed that the rapier tip had lowered a fraction and was quivering very slightly. *Maybe he really is worried.* If that were the case, there would never be a better time to attack.

96

Cali felt a burst of excited energy that heralded Jeremiah's arrival.

'It's all kicked off down there. Big time. You should make yourself scarce, Cali. I'm not sticking around to see what unwelcome attention is attracted by this inappropriate anachronistic display. They've been firing missiles at each other. You hear me? Fucking missiles. I can't believe anyone would be so foolish.'

'You've lost me, Jeremiah. What's so bad about missiles?'

'Tek, that's what missiles are. Forbidden things that should have been long forgotten and have no place in these times. It's shocking enough to find out things like missiles still exist without having their destructive power demonstrated by two entities who should know better. Something like this can't go unnoticed and this place is likely to become a battleground for some serious players. There are plenty out there who can't resist a good fight.'

'You still haven't explained what you mean by a missile. Did someone throw a rock or two?' Cali said.

'I'm talking about missiles that were developed long ago in the Dark Ages. Metal things full of explosives that fly through the air.'

Cali wondered if the strain of all his machinations had sent Jeremiah mad. He'd been rushing around trying to get all the participants in the same place and now they were having a battle. If that's not what he wanted, then he should have done things differently. Anyway, she guessed that he was merely obeying his instructions, just as she was. Stick around and watch, Patch had said. So, she was going to do exactly that, whatever Jeremiah might have to say. 'Explosives?' she asked.

'Things that make a bang. Oh, I can't talk you through the history of military hardware and the various capabilities of weapons. Let's just say that Gilgamesh has a palace full of things he shouldn't have and that the King from the North has arrived with his own inappropriate arsenal. Things are supposed to be settled with bows and swords around here. Keeps the casualties down to a reasonable proportion of the population. Otherwise, everyone gets killed and the whole process of civilisation has to begin yet again. I'm not sure that this planet can withstand another major conflict without becoming totally uninhabitable. It's all very unsatisfactory.'

Cali couldn't see the problem. Humans were interesting at best and deeply irritating at worst, but she couldn't understand why their survival might be important. She thought of asking Jeremiah that question, but something told her that his answer would be long and complex. She wasn't in the mood for Jeremiah and his rants, and she wished she'd not bothered him about the missiles. If he was nervous, then that was his affair. He had his own set of priorities that she didn't share. He liked to go around influencing people and manipulating their actions. She couldn't even communicate with most humans, let alone tell them what to do. It made life simpler and she was glad of it. Whereas Jeremiah might be called to account for what he'd caused, she remained an innocent bystander. The entities that he was so scared of upsetting wouldn't even notice her.

97

Tyrant believed that his talent for sniffing the right time to force home an advantage was one of his primary survival methods. Gilgamesh's confidence had momentarily been rendered less than absolute. If the time wasn't right now, then it was never.

Yet Tyrant hesitated.

Petra's words had stuck in his mind. Maybe she was right. Now that he'd seen him in the flesh, he needn't be worried about the fear creeping in on him in the night. He knew what he was running away from, and that might be enough. There were more important things than settling grievances, though this was the mother of them all. A bit more life might be preferable to a futile gesture that would almost certainly end up killing him.

There was the licker business, after all. He'd never had a trade of any kind and the satisfaction he'd felt when he'd done the deal with the tavern owner was a far better feeling than he'd ever experienced after a successful conflict. All fighting ever brought him was a vague sense of relief and a haunting regret about its unnecessary nature.

There was Petra. She had grown very attached to him, so much so that he knew she'd get very sorrowful over his death. The poor woman was used to a hard life and didn't deserve it to be made any harder by him.

Life had gotten better since he'd met Petra. Not easier, it was too full of things that had to be done and there was less of the leave it until tomorrow lifestyle that he'd enjoyed when he was wandering around on his own.

Recently, he'd spent more time in a proper bed with a roof over it than at any time he could remember. It was both comfortable and comforting, and he'd grown used to it. A damp patch of bracken had often been his best option in the past, but that seemed so unattractive now he wondered how he'd been so insensitive.

On the balance of things, it was obvious what he had to do. Give Gilgamesh his sword back. Walk away. Go back to Gort through the vedhana taking those luscious bignuts with him. Resume the licker business and forget about the past. Live for the present.

Tyrant relaxed his shoulders and breathed deeply. He swung his sword gently and stared into Gilgamesh's eyes. The King was waiting for him to make the first move, which could be backwards and away or forwards and fight. The man was invulnerable. He'd defeated an entire army and killed the King of Gort. He'd despatched half a dozen of the most proficient fighters in the land without breaking a sweat. Tyrant knew he had no chance of winning if he did battle.

It was the look on Gilgamesh's face that triggered him into action. The same sardonic expression that had been embossed on his memory and then hidden away under a curtain of grief. Tyrant felt an overwhelming urge to wipe that grin off his face, even if only temporarily. He brought his sword across his body, anticipating the rapier thrust, which came as an immediate reflex response. The rapier was swept aside, Tyrant advanced, grabbed Gilgamesh's neck with his free hand, and smashed his head into the bridge of the King's nose. A thousand tiny lights burst into his vision just before the crushing pain hit. It was like head butting a piece of stone and just as foolish. Tyrant's legs felt wobbly, and he realised that he'd probably knocked all the fight out of himself and saved Gilgamesh a job.

Tyrant took a couple of steps backwards and was astonished to see Gilgamesh do the same. The King's hand was raised to his face, and he wore a look of real distress. Maybe it hadn't been a waste of energy after all, Tyrant thought, his head still swimming with pinpricks of light.

Gilgamesh almost had his back against the looming wall of the palace now and wasn't bothering to hide the fact that he'd been hurt. 'Now that's what I call interesting,' he said. 'Nobody's ever tried that move on me before; I'll have to watch out for it in future. Well done. I applaud your bravery, but don't let that fool you into thinking that I'm going to let you get away with your life after striking me like that. When I've done for you, I'll make sure your little woman is taken care of as well, you can be sure of that. Does she like swimming with crocodiles? Or would you suggest I just poke her one with my rapier? The metal one, of course, she's really not my type for anything else.'

373

'You have to contend with me first,' Tyrant said, but his words lacked conviction, even to his own ears. Nevertheless, he hoisted up his sword and waited for the attack that would certainly finish him off.

Tyrant noticed how Gilgamesh had been keeping in the shade of the palace walls and seemed reluctant to expose himself to the full glare of the sun. He took several steps backwards with the intention of drawing him out of the shadow and, as he did, felt a dull thud that brought a trickle of fine dust out of the gaps between the stones in the fabric of the palace.

A series of louder bangs shook the air and Tyrant watched as a large hole formed high on the palace. Enormous slabs of stone hurtled towards him. In the instant before he turned and ran, it seemed as if the whole palace was collapsing. As large stones began to crash to the ground around him, a heavy blow to the back of his neck pitched him face down onto the ground. More blows followed to his legs.

He tried to move, but his body wasn't working. His arms and legs were pinned, his body crushed, and he could do nothing else but close his eyes and wait to be completely buried.

98

Lone couldn't stop herself grinning when Tyrant head butted Gilgamesh and sent him sprawling against his palace wall. She quickly realised that this demonstration of effrontery would almost certainly result in her own demise and, most probably, that of anyone who had witnessed the attack. It was going to be impossible for him to maintain a reputation of invulnerability if there were witnesses that could testify otherwise. And, as Tyrant had once told her, reputation is everything.

There was nothing she could do except watch the interplay between the two protagonists, which threatened to come to a rapid conclusion at any moment. Tyrant was backing away when the walls of the palace blew out. She thought she caught a glimpse of Moussa's face through a hole high up in the wall, but dismissed this as fanciful. She backtracked rapidly, then quickly realised that Tyrant was going to be buried in the rubble.

Without hesitation, she ran to assist him, finding Petra's tiny hands already tugging in vain at the prone figure. The whole side of the palace was slowly toppling towards them: if she remained where she was, she would be killed for certain. She grabbed Tyrant's shoulder and heaved. The body moved a fraction, but stuck again. It was hopeless; she'd done what she could, but it hadn't been enough.

Still, she forced herself to persist, even if it meant her own death. She'd left him for dead once before, but that had been a different Lone. A Lone who could live without regret.

A stone bounced off the side of her head and unbalanced her. She gave one final heave and felt Tyrant begin to move. Cat had grabbed him by his neck and was dragging him out of the debris. It was so powerful that Lone felt herself being carried along with it rather than assisting with the rescue. The cat didn't stop until they were clear of the palace gardens, then it disappeared as quickly as it had arrived.

Lone sat panting next to Petra and watched as the rest of the palace came down. Then she realised with a prickle of delight that Gilgamesh was under all that stone and must have been killed.

Malachi helped her regain her feet, then began sweeping dust from her hair and shoulders. She pushed his hand aside. 'If that's all you can contribute, then I'd rather do without your help,' she said.

'How was I to know you'd turn up here hell-bent on revenge against the most powerful being in the world?' Malachi said. 'I was only trying to defuse the situation so that we could make our escape. It's good to see you, by the way. I've been looking long and hard for you, but feared that you were lost.'

'You can't have looked seriously for me. I've been here long enough, and it seems you're a regular visitor.'

'I was looking for you everywhere, including here, but you were nowhere to be found. In fact, as far as I could tell, you weren't anywhere. Even the most thorough of searches failed to detect you,' Malachi said.

'So you decided to use your time more profitably by assisting this despot?'

'There was an opportunity, so I grasped it. This palace is full of the most amazing treasures and I decided to try to get my hands on what I could. To the benefit of everyone in the world, not just me. These items that Ant has safely in that sack represent knowledge without price. With them, we can navigate the world, position ourselves in the heavens, predict celestial events, all manner of things. It's the dawn of a new civilisation,' Malachi said.

'So you've done all this for everyone else's benefit, have you?'

Malachi gave her the enigmatic smile that she knew so well. 'Not entirely, but there will be benefits for all. Eventually.'

'There's a whole palace for you to loot, then. You'd better get to it before everyone else gets the same idea. Be careful nothing drops on your head while you're in there.'

Malachi's face clouded over. 'That's a problem,' he said. 'We have to guard this place to make sure that none of the treasures in there fall into the wrong hands.'

Lone couldn't help but laugh. 'So now Gilgamesh is dead, you want to take over yourself. I might have known.'

'That's not what I'm talking about. I'm perfectly satisfied with the items in Ant's sack. Unfortunately, there are other things in there that would spell disaster to us all if they fell into the wrong hands. Weapons of such immense power, the whole world could be destroyed.'

'Oh, Malachi, you are so melodramatic. I doubt that could happen. From the looks of the palace, whatever was in there that was destructive seems to have done its worst. You're being greedy, as usual.'

'Believe me, Lone, there are items in there that must not be allowed to see the light of day.'

'Well, I don't see what we can do about that apart from getting back to Gort as quickly as possible and leave all this far behind us. You should have thought of this before you hatched your plan.'

'My plan, I'll have you know, was sound. If our Northern King prevailed, he would have ensured that none of the secrets ever emerged from Gilgamesh's palace. Obviously, Gilgamesh did triumph, so that wasn't even an issue until you turned up with that big aggressive lump in tow. Even I couldn't anticipate that.'

'Help me move Tyrant,' Petra said, 'I don't like the look of that storm that's approaching. We need to get him back to the vedhana and home where he can safely recuperate.'

Lone looked up at the storm clouds that had suddenly gathered. They were like nothing she had seen before, huge black whirling things roughly in the shape of a colossal human figure. What looked like massive legs were stomping their way towards them in a very disturbing manner.

'That's no storm,' Malachi said. 'That's a golem. A huge pile of earth that's been animated.'

'Then all the more reason to get out of its way,' Ant said. 'Petra and I aren't strong enough to carry Tyrant; we need your help.'

'Have you seen how quickly it's approaching?' Malachi said. 'We're not going to outrun that thing, I'm afraid.'

'Then we'll have to hope that it passes by and leaves us alone,' Ant said.

'I think it may be looking for you, Ant,' Malachi said. 'Your father created it as a means to clear the North Road. In the same way that he started all the mayhem in Gort with his vedhana in the tower, he had very little idea of what he was doing. He created something so powerful it's beyond anyone's control. Now it's followed us all the way from Gort because of some vague notion implanted by your father when it was created.'

'Here,' Ant said and passed the bag of precious items to Malachi, 'if it's my father's work, then I should accept responsibility for it. Help Petra with Tyrant. You too, Lone. Get away if you can; I'll wait here for it. If it's looking for me, then I might be able to delay it long enough for you all to reach the vedhana on the other side of the river.'

99

The huge stomping beast bore down on him. The others had dragged the prone Tyrant out of the palace garden and towards the river. If he'd expected any protest against what he was attempting, then he'd have been disappointed. Petra was intent on saving Tyrant; of course she was. Lone seemed uncharacteristically concerned about the big man and had surprised him with her perilous rescue from the collapsing masonry. Malachi had his bag of treasure and was acting true to form by making that his main priority. In fairness, he'd made it very clear that he couldn't influence the golem. Nobody could.

Even so, the massive caricature of whirling stones and earth seemed to be acting with purpose. It slowed as it approached, its head casting about from side to side as if it were searching for something. Or someone. Its eye sockets housed conical maelstroms that appeared to be revolving at an even faster rate than the rest of it. The whole thing had the look of hundreds of vedhanas that were keeping prodigious amounts of earth in constant motion. He wished he'd been more attentive to his father's request now. If he'd been there to help, this monster might never have been spawned. Instead, he'd been intent on thwarting the king with his own poorly thought-out plans.

The sound of stones clattering to the ground drew his attention away from the golem. Tyrant's sword lay discarded by the pile of rubble that had consumed Gilgamesh. As he stooped to pick it up, the ground began to tremble. He recoiled in horror as the tip of a thin sword emerged from the side of the heap. Larger stones were displaced and bounced their way to the ground. The sword protruded further, far enough for him to recognise it as Gilgamesh's special weapon. He gripped Tyrant's weapon tightly as he strove to control the panic caused by the sight of Gilgamesh's fist punching free from beneath the massive slabs. The whole pile shook as the rest of his body began to emerge.

The legs of the golem were firmly planted either side of the palace and its torso loomed high above Ant, blotting out the sun. He tried to communicate with the thing, projecting his mind outwards and attempting to see through the whirlpool eyes. All he could detect was total blankness.

If there was any recognition, it was too deeply hidden in a great swathe of nothingness for him to engage with.

Gilgamesh's head suddenly thrust out of the debris, and the look on his face was that of someone who was very upset. With great difficulty, Ant tore his gaze away from the angry demi-god and returned his attention to the golem that was slowly enveloping him. Stones began to hammer against his head and body. Stinging gusts of earth whipped his face. Breathing became difficult as he was sucking up muck into his nose and mouth. There was a tightness across his chest and as he made one final attempt to wrestle with the phenomenon, the world closed around him and everything went black.

It made no difference whether his eyes were open or tightly shut, the darkness was complete. If he was careful, breathing was possible provided that he drew in air gently enough to avoid his nostrils being clogged with earth. There was nothing he could do but try to survive as long as possible. Grappling with the golem was impossible, there was nothing substantial for him to get hold of. Its mind was as equally diffuse as its form and just as inaccessible.

Ant found himself thinking of his father. If what Malachi had told him was true, Ambrose had sent this monster to find him. But to what purpose? It had found him alright and he wished it hadn't.

His body was being carried aloft by the whirlwind of dirt. Having lost contact with the ground, Ant's capacity to centre himself and produce coherent thoughts was diminished. All he could do was to hold on to the intention behind the golem's creation. *You've found me. Well done. You've achieved everything you were created for. Rest now.*

Ant's head emerged from the whirlwind of earth and he found himself looking over the city from a dizzying height. Even the single remaining palace tower from which he'd watched the battle unfold was far beneath him. A gasp of horror flushed out his fear of falling and replaced it with a dark dread. The tiny figure of Gilgamesh was clearly visible, standing proud of the devastation. Tyrant's brave efforts, even assisted by the sudden collapse of the palace, had been in vain. The awful man was indestructible.

Stop Gilgamesh. Bury him.

Ant had never wanted anything as much in his life. The intensity of his desire surged through his whole being. If it had been within his power to drop from the sky in the hope of dealing at least some damage to the Southern King, he would have gladly sacrificed himself for that small victory.

As if his wishes were being heeded, he felt himself falling. The whole monstrous pile of earth was subsiding beneath him.

As he landed, the air was painfully jolted from him so that he lay breathless in the soft soil. Wiping the dirt from his eyes and mouth, Ant sat up and felt into his body. Everything was intact despite his heavy fall.

He was sitting at the highest point of a mountain of bare earth that now dominated the landscape of the city. Beneath him, on the lower slopes, he could just about make out the pointed top of the palace tower. Gilgamesh must be buried directly below him. Deep enough, he hoped, that not even he would survive.

The golem was gone. Its energy had dissipated, leaving only this huge pile of northern soil to mark its existence.

100

Tyrant was feeling very relaxed. So relaxed that he was in danger of sliding off the bench and under the table. This would be unfortunate on two counts. First, it would interrupt the flow of drinks he was receiving from well-wishers and second, it would diminish his reputation.

He was sitting at his usual table in the Four King Inn. The landlord brought over another tankard and pointed to a man sitting in the far corner of the tavern. Tyrant acknowledged receipt of the beer with a cursory nod and the glow of satisfaction and pride engendered in his benefactor shone back at him. The man's companions clapped him on the back as if he'd managed some heroic feat and did their own share of grinning.

If he were honest, Tyrant didn't want any more beer. Refusing, however, was not polite, and now he was left with the delicate balance between helpless inebriation and good manners. He decided to drink this one much more slowly and hope the initial burst of enthusiasm had left the packed clientele.

Licker sales were going very well. The army had returned, what was left of it, and now there were the coronation celebrations to contend with. If they could have made ten times as much, this place could have sold it. The Four Kings had also gained popularity because of Tyrant's more than occasional presence. Tales of his exploits in the south had somehow reached Gort even before he did and been magnified in the process of telling. Now it seemed that his fracas with Gilgamesh had been translated into a series of heroic deeds performed by a man who was now considered to have god-like attributes.

Falling into a drunken stupor might not fit in with the high regard with which he was being held. Tyrant took a long deep breath and a tiny sip of the beer which had begun to taste more like urine.

There was a commotion by the entrance as several men pushed themselves into what had been previously declared a full establishment. These were men who were big enough to brook no argument, even from the colossal doorman. There were five of them and Tyrant gradually realised that he recognised three of them. Two were the large men he'd once had to deposit on the floor after they had sat next to him. The other was their leader with the unmistakeable moustache, Danby. His nose was bent to one side and had a more crooked appearance than the first time they'd met.

The other two were big men, even in comparison with the original pair of heavies. One of them, however, stood head and shoulders above the rest and was carrying a crude club fashioned from the trunk of a sizeable tree with a rusty metal spike protruding from the thick end.

Danby stood in front of Tyrant's table, but kept far enough away to avoid being head butted again. 'I warned you the last time I saw you; now you're going to regret you ever tried to peddle your inferior licker in these parts,' Danby said.

Tyrant remained seated. In his present state, there was very little else he could do. Standing up would have been a real tour de force. Anything further would have been impossible. His feeling of relaxation was quickly evaporating, though.

He weighed up his options as he listened to Danby's threats, which were being accentuated by him waving his sword in Tyrant's face. The most effective belligerent move would entail picking up the table and depositing it on Danby's head before using it as a makeshift shield against the two crossbows that were being pointed at him. The main problem with this lay in the sheer weight of the table. It had been crudely fashioned from far too much wood. He doubted he could drag the thing very far, let alone pick it up. Even tipping it on its side might involve a request for assistance and that would do his reputation no good at all.

The second idea involved falling over backwards and pretending to be dead. If Danby had only come here to shout at him a little, this might work. The size and quality of his henchmen indicated a more physical intent, though. Danby could have turned up alone and screamed abuse from the doorway without going to the not inconsiderable expense of hiring those bodyguards. Sadly, Tyrant concluded that Danby meant him very serious harm and that if he pretended to be dead, it might not be long before he wouldn't need to pretend.

The atmosphere in the inn had changed. The raucous laughter and strident voices had stilled and an air of quiet expectation had descended. A collective breath of anticipation was released, which contained a fair amount of nervous laughter.

The giant thug looked threateningly at a man sitting close to where he stood, who had let out a blurt of merriment. Tyrant watched as the man mouthed the words *that's Tyrant.*

The giant shook his head. All five men sitting at that table nodded vigorously while wearing grins from ear to ear.

The giant stood and stared at Tyrant, who held his gaze with as little concern as he could muster under the dire circumstances. His eyes broke contact and lowered to look at the giant's formidable club that Tyrant doubted he would be able to lift, let alone swing about with one hand as the giant was doing without any obvious effort.

There was a look of distaste on the giant's face as he lay the weapon gently on the floor, propping it up against the nearest table as if it were made of delicate porcelain rather than likely to make a hole in the ground if he dropped it. His comrades watched him lay down his weapon with looks of surprise, which deepened when they were informed in a loud whisper of the reason he'd done so. The two crossbows were lowered and their bolts carefully removed and returned to their quivers. The man with the sword sheathed it so slowly and gently it was as if he didn't want to disturb the slumber of a tiny sleeping animal that had lodged in his tunic. The three men then turned around and headed for the exit, accompanied by yells of derision from the audience.

Danby turned to see what the commotion was about. Tyrant knew that this was probably his one and only chance to hit Danby where it hurt, but the combined effects of the beer and the still troublesome wounds in his neck meant that he could only sit and wait as the giant approached, arm outstretched.

'Tyrant?' the giant asked.

'Yes.'

'My son is your biggest admirer. He's built an entire City by the River out of mud, and fashioned some figures of you and Gilgamesh from wood and rags. He plays for hours pretending to be you. He's head butted several of his little chums already and he's only four. He'd be really proud of his dad if he knew I'd shaken the hand of the real Tyrant and thanked him personally for saving the lives of us all.' The big hand was extended further so that Tyrant could reach it to give it a perfunctory squeeze. 'If there's ever anything I can do for you, please ask,' the giant said.

Tyrant took a deep breath. The look on Danby's face had changed from derision to surprise and now was bordering on panic. His sword tip was no longer dancing in front of Tyrant's face. 'I might be able to use a big lad like yourself in my business,' Tyrant said. 'That's if you don't mind hard work carrying licker pots and dragging a handcart.'

'It would be an honour; when can I start?'

Tyrant gave him directions to Malachi's house and told him to be there tomorrow to meet Petra when she came through with the next consignment.

'In the meantime, is there anything else you want me to do?' the giant said, throwing a meaningful glance in Danby's direction.

'I'm sorry, I didn't realise, please forgive my impertinence,' Danby muttered as he beat a hasty retreat amid a welter of catcalls and whistles.

Tyrant picked up his tankard and took a large swig. This time, the beer tasted sweet and satisfying. *Now that's the value of a reputation,* he thought.

A man dressed in a dark cloak sat down opposite. 'What was that all about?' he asked.

Tyrant smiled across at Ant. 'Interviewing for a job carrying licker about,' he said.

'They seemed to be well armed for that kind of thing,' Ant said.

'You can't be too careful when you're moving licker. It's well sought after. Lots of unscrupulous bandits would like to get their hands on our licker, so it needs a special sort of employee.'

'Are you ready for the coronation festivities?' Ant asked.

'Can't make licker fast enough to keep this place supplied if that's what you mean.' Tyrant laughed.

'I had once thought that you might have been the new king. At least that was my wish.'

'I'm really not the kingly type, Ant. The new King will be far better suited to the job. I'm a bit surprised he agreed to it, but I suppose he's changed a fair bit since we first dug him out of the hillside.'

'He's changed a lot,' Ant said. 'But I can understand why. He's survived some terrible experiences. Everyone was impressed by the way he led the army back across the desert, then had the confidence to claim Cassie's hand in marriage. She's really excited about being Queen and

Bea is equally delighted to be a princess. I think he's the obvious choice; a young man of humble origins who has transcended all his tribulations and come through so much stronger.'

'Agreed,' Tyrant said. 'There's not a better man for the job in the world.' He raised his tankard. 'Here's to King Cuthbert, may his reign be long and prosperous.'

THE END

Printed in Great Britain
by Amazon

75251387R00224